LOOP'S END

A Novel

Loop's End

A Novel

Chuck Rosenthal

 Hollyridge Press
Venice, California

© 2007 Chuck Rosenthal

All rights reserved under International and Pan-American Copyright
Conventions. Published in the United States by Hollyridge Press.

Hollyridge Press
P.O. Box 2872
Venice, California 90294

Cover and Book Design by Rio Symth
Cover and Author Photos by Gary Goldstein
Manufactured in the United States of America by Lightning Source

Publisher's Cataloging-in-Publication

Rosenthal, Chuck, 1951-

Loop's End : a novel / Chuck Rosenthal. -- Venice, Calif. :
Hollyridge Press, 2007.

p. ; cm.

Reprint. Originally published: Layton, Utah : Gibbs-
Smith, 1992
ISBN: 978-0-9772298-9-5

I. Title.

PS3568.O8368 L65 2007   92008625
813'.54

14 13 12 11 10 09 08 07   10 9 8 7 6 5 4 3 2 1

For my mother, Eleanor Rosenthal
(1921-1978)

and my father, Red Rosenthal
(1921-2003)

My hat is old.
My teeth are gold.

I have a bird
I like to hold.

My shoe is off.
My foot is cold.

I have a bird
I like to hold.

My hat is old.
My teeth are gold.

And now
my story
all is told.

—Dr. Seuss

Loop's End

≈≈≈≈≈First Plums of Summer

KARL KEPT ONE CANNON on the front porch, one on the back. He kept that cannon on the back porch tilted in the air because he believed the air to be the new enemy. There were no more good things coming from the sky, the underside of dark wings. That was as much as he wanted to explain about it, so he pointed a cannon at it. My mother, Helen, called it a densely packed logic. She understood Karl because a seed of understanding had been planted behind her ear. He was nuts so she understood him.

Helen was convinced that someday Karl was coming over to our place with his guns, not that he'd have to walk far, living next door, and blow us all away. Stuff like that was happening every night on the TV news which Helen slept in front of because she was too tired after work and supper to watch it. But somehow she knew about that stuff, just like she knew that someday Karl was coming over with his guns, even though he'd been our neighbor for years and never went over anywhere and blew away anybody. Helen knew too much to be bothered with the facts.

For the longest time Karl kept his front porch cannon pointed across the street at the new batch of Puerto Ricans renting upstairs from Dean Danger. Dean Danger wouldn't rent to anybody else but Puerto Ricans and every new batch came in with foam dice and parrots and Puerto Rican flags and horn music and every time Karl pointed that cannon at them till they got wise and put out an American flag, usually on the Fourth of July. If you wanted to communicate with anybody around there the last thing you did was talk to them.

So it was the Fourth of July and Angela and Rafael Corona put out their American flag and Karl shifted that little howitzer on his front porch so it pointed up in the air just like the circus cannon in the back. Then he got Karl Jr. who looked a lot like a walking red bristled paint brush and the two of them rolled the circus cannon off the back porch and onto a wooden cart, just a plank on two wheels. Karl Jr. stood there like an empty toothpaste tube, not quite as bright eyed, while Karl went in and put on his buckskins, came out with his daughters Beema and Maggie and an American flag on a pole, gave that flag to Karl Jr. and headed for the street, Karl Jr. leading the way with that flag, Beema on one side and Maggie, with that limp she had from birth because she didn't have a complete hip so it was really impossible for her to walk at all, Maggie on the other, and Karl pulling that cannon on behind. That's the way they went up and down the street, with Karl Jr. waving that flag and Karl waving his hands and Beema and Maggie doing shuffles and kicks and pushing out the palms of their little hands saying, "Shoot! Shoot!"

It was the Fourth of July. A mug blue rag day. We'd all eaten our hot dogs under the dull blade sky and then sat on our porches waiting for it to rain, clouds so low you thought you could touch them if you stood on a stool.

Angela and Raphael Corona put on horn music and released their parrots who flapped around the parade like tarot cards. Our neighbor on the other side, Big Dick Jinx, hands on his hips and bleary-eyed, stood with his son, Stinky, the most famous and effeminate athlete in Erie, Pennsylvania, if not the world, Stinky in his pink chenille robe; across the street the Funsters peered from behind the sand bags on their porch roof, Jimbo behind his telescope, Funly in his silver space suit, Grandpa Funster standing over them like a cross of dead wood; and across from Karl's, Dean and Tina Danger stood like dark foghorns, the Dialecticians, other than Willie and myself, spread on the steps below, lazily experimenting; down the street toward Celebration Avenue the Magicians blew opium from their top porch and next to them the Appalachians threw beer cans, the first excuse they had to get rid of any trash in weeks.

I was on our porch with my younger sister Neda who put out a Pall Mall and strolled over to the railing blowing smoke. My mother, Helen, was in the house behind some shade or another with my brothers Joseph and Andrew, those reluctant angels, on either side of her. I guess she figured she could duck if she saw something coming. She'd given up me and Neda to the phenomenal realms, like spiritual fatted calves.

My father, Red, was in the living room by himself, sitting next to the Zenith which was on but he couldn't see. For years he sat there and watched Helen watch TV from the couch, though now that Helen didn't watch TV anymore, she just turned it on and slept, he watched her do that. In fact the older Red got he was doing a lot more watching and a lot more waiting. He was, in Helen's words, becoming a passive force. He hadn't knocked out all the doors in the house for a couple of years. He hadn't destroyed one single brand new appliance that he'd bought for Helen after she got her job and started making more money than he did and so could buy anything she wanted. Helen didn't want anything to do with that stuff anymore. What she wanted was a new coat or a new dress or some nice diamond re-engagement ring, from Red of course, she wasn't going to buy herself any of that stuff, and of course Red inscrutably never did any of that, and of course she never asked him, no, those two had settled into a period of quiet vendetta. We were in the eye of the hurricane and what Red was doing in there was watching. And whether or not he was learning anything you couldn't tell because Red liked to learn stuff and not let anybody know he did; that was his big secret on the world and he was so good at keeping that secret you might think he'd never learned a goddamn thing.

Karl and Beema and Maggie and Karl Jr. marched up the street and down the street and up the street and down the street and after that they did it one more time, then they dragged that cannon back to their house. "Come on," Karl said to me and Neda, "I'm going to put one in the Bay." He and Karl Jr. pulled the cannon to the back of the house and pointed it out the back of the yard, north, exactly in the direction of the Erie Bay, except that there was some two miles of city neighborhood in between.

So I went inside and found Red sitting next to the Zenith not watching it and looking at the paper not reading it. He thought Karl was nuts but Karl was his neighbor.

"Well, you want to know?" I said to him.

"Don't tell me," said Red. "He's going to shoot the fuckin thing."

"In the Bay."

"Somebody ought to call the goddamn cops."

Well that meant Red wasn't going to do anything. If he was going to do anything he'd get his bowling ball, though before he got the bowling ball he'd say something about getting a ball bat. Anytime Red couldn't think of a response to a situation he said he'd get a ball bat, and if you pursued the matter he got his bowling ball, which, in his hands, produced miraculous destruction.

"Your mother's in the goddamn basement," said Red.

Helen was in the corner of the potato cellar, though I'd never seen a potato in it; everything that broke, Red stuck it down there, and with Red around there was a lot of broken stuff: refrigerators, stoves, lamps, chairs, picnic tables, swing sets, toasters, toys, doors, there were a whole lot of broken doors down there, but not one potato, if we ever found a potato down there we'd probably have to change the name of the place; and of course one of Red's favorite ways to get mad was to go down there and look at all that worthless junk filling up his potato cellar, why somebody didn't go down there and clean that place up was a mystery to him. But Helen made a rat path through all that junk and lately, and the more lately it got the more often it happened, she'd think everybody was crazy and go down there and hide out. Helen never walked the line between sanity and insanity, you had to give her that, she had her feet firmly planted in both.

So that's where Helen was, down there underneath all that junk with Joseph and Andrew, one on one side and one on the other, a couple of sacred mysteries if you ever saw two, and she hugged one to each breast even though they were now both bigger than her. In between was her statue of the Infant of Prague. She was telling him something, but I couldn't make it out. When I got down there Joseph and Andrew split, so it was just me and Helen and the Infant who'd been in a bit of a slump since he got Kennedy elected and stopped World War III. Helen knew it and he did, too.

"We should have moved years ago," said Helen.

I stooped down and touched her knee. "Red's not moving, and he's the mayor around here."

Helen held up the Infant. It was summer and he had on his white robes and white booties and had white satin in his crown. Of course he still held the world in his palm. "I promised him Red would convert." Helen wasn't simple, but she knew the world turned on small things.

"It's not even pointed this way," I told her. "It's pointed at the Bay."

"You think that matters." Helen held the Infant upside down and shook him. "See that?" she said. "See?"

Well that was a little too apocalyptic for my taste. "I'll go talk to Karl," I told her.

Karl and me had been through a lot together but you couldn't really say we had any influence on each other. We liked each other well enough, got each other in trouble a few times with booze and guns, made each other some money with a couple of burglaries, and in a kind of existential response to all that, we tended to drift apart. Then I got married and left the neighborhood for a while.

Karl's Tibetan wolf dog, Einstein, and Honky, Red's white shepherd were going at each other through the wire fence and underneath that you could hear some kind of marching band music coming out of a radio and over that Beema and Maggie screaming and giggling when Karl Jr. grabbed them by the hair and bonked their heads together, something they'd all been doing ever since I knew them which I'm sure said something about their endurance and intelligence if you wanted to bother analyzing something like that. Karl was cleaning his circus cannon and he looked happy as a pancake.

I grabbed Honky by the collar and he bit my wrist and held it. That dummy was as big as the moon but not much smarter, if you shot him he'd take it as a form of attention, which meant the only person who had a chance of controlling him was Red, but letting him bite my wrist at least made him shut up. Karl chased Einstein back into the weeds in the corner of his yard.

"The Bay," I said.

"Yup," said Karl. He went over and grabbed Karl Jr. by the top of that paintbrush of a head of his and Karl Jr. started swinging at him like a pinwheel, didn't look like his head was quite attached, which was something you might have guessed just by trying to talk to him.

"Settle down," said Karl.

"I'll kill you," said Karl Jr.

"Kid's going to be okay," said Karl, scratching his own red head with his hand that only had a couple of partial fingers on it.

"Think you could miss?" I said to him.

"It's a pretty big bay," said Karl.

Well I knew those cannons as well as anybody, other than Karl, and there were times they didn't exactly perform as they were supposed to; they didn't break down the Funsters' bomb shelter door during the Cuban Missile Crisis, Red had to do that with his bowling ball, and there was that Christmas that one of those cannonballs landed right in Grandma Emma and Grandpa Whitey Loop's backyard, among other errant shots, so I knew as well as anybody that the damn ball might or might not actually make it to the Bay, and there was plenty of city in between if it didn't, but Karl knew all that too.

Karl let go of Karl Jr. and let him spin off into the Milky Way, then he got one of his cannonballs from the basement and started to prepare the cannon. You had to think he'd just been too good for too long and sat through too much. He'd watched Red rub out any number of appliances, cars, and trees with his fists or with his bowling ball.

Then there was that racket Funly made when he hijacked Neda's rocket. During the Cuban Missile Crisis Karl failed to knock out Funster's bomb shelter door with this same circus cannon; no doubt about it, that was a failure. And even though he and I'd had plenty of exploits on Lake Erie, including *The End of the World*, well for that we should have ended up wanted for conspiracy, piracy, robbery, assault with deadly weapons, as well as driving a boat without a license, but facts were that we got away with it and nobody wanted us at all; we were wanted men unbeknownst to the world and, living as one does in the minds of others, it was obviously getting on Karl's nerves.

So it had been a long, long time since the two of us had talked.

Karl put powder in that cannon, packed it, then powdered and packed it again. Off to the side, Beema and Maggie were now in full swing. They kicked their legs and pushed out their little palms and said, "We're going to SHOOT the cannon! We're going to SHOOT the cannon!" pushing out their little palms every time they said "SHOOT." Karl chuckled to himself as he set the fuse. That's when I realized that only a block away, in that same direction, my very own son, Visitor Loop, was visiting with my friend, the great Dialectician, Willie, in his attic.

"Karl," I said.

"What about that little wife of yours?" said Karl.

"What about her?"

Karl held up that partial hand of his, one of his universal answers.

"Gone," I said. "You know that."

"She was probably unfaithful," said Karl. He lit the fuse. "Too bad, I kind of liked her."

The cannon went off.

Downtown, the combination Fourth of July—We Love Erie Day Parade wended its way from the Public Dock toward Perry Square. There, on the grandstand, the mayor and city council and local war heroes and various dignitaries and rich people and some recognized especially smart people like the presidents of colleges sat to salute the high school bands and fire engines and Scottish bagpipers and Girl Scouts and clowns and Shriners and car dealers and antique car collectors and myriad Fourth of July—We Love Erie Day queens who sat gownful and waving from the tops of backseats of convertibles.

At the center of that grandstand, next to the mayor, with his family standing around him like a bunch of proud fish, sat Erie's biggest hero, the enfeebled Bobby Hansen, who, along with the Pennsylvania Coast Guard Reserve, repelled the Cuban invasion of the United States on Lake Erie not so many Fourth of July—We Love Erie days ago. Bobby Hansen. Once one of the best all-around athletes in the city, he was struck down one Christmas night when a madman slipped into the Hansens' home. Bobby wrestled with the killer, saved his family, and almost managed to hold the burglar there until the police arrived. In the fight he suffered a blow to the head that paralyzed him from the neck down. But he fought back, and in a few short years cured himself completely when many thought he would never walk again.

The primary target of the Cuban first wave was the Lake Erie cruise ship, the *North American*, a luxury liner that hit all the major tourist ports on the Lake: Ashtabula, Sandusky, London-Ontario; and packed with Pennsylvania dignitaries, the governor, state senators, and some of the richest and best families in the state, including the Hansens. She was headed back to her maiden port in Erie to celebrate the combination Fourth of July—We Love Erie Day celebration at the Public Dock.

In mid-afternoon a Cuban destroyer broadsided and boarded the *North American*, pirating her cargo, robbing her passengers and taking them hostage. Only Bobby Hansen's tremendous stealth diverted them. Though he'd only recently made his miraculous recovery from quadriplegia, he snuck aboard the Cuban flagship and sabotaged the Cuban Central Command, holding them off with only a .22 pistol until being overcome, bashed on the skull with a rum bottle, just as the Coast Guard Reserve appeared on the scene. In the confusion, the *North American* got away, and then the Pennsylvania Coast Guard Reserve surrounded and sunk the Cuban fleet, causing a major fish kill. Pieces of that Cuban fleet were still washing ashore and the Puerto Ricans in town had to carry I.D. cards to prove they weren't Cuban.

Of course there was only one person in the whole city who questioned any of that, and that was Funly Funster who was up in space at the time in the space capsule he'd hijacked from Neda; though he happened to land it in Lake Erie on the same day as the invasion. Lucky for Funly, me and Karl were out on the Lake in Karl's boat, the *Armada*, out there waiting for the *North American* like everybody else in town who owned something that floated. We plucked Funly out of the water, which saved him from a lot of harassment from various government sources. I know this sounds fantastic, but it's true.

Ironically, Funly doubted there ever was a Cuban invasion on Lake Erie. He didn't think those Cubans could transport that fleet down the Saint Lawrence Seaway piece by piece in submarines, and he didn't think they could build it in secret. There was something fishy going on, that's what Funly thought. He was a hard-headed realist and six months in space in a garbage can hadn't changed that.

"Listen, Funly," I told him. "Don't bother us with the facts."

Facts were, it was the Fourth of July in Erie, Pennsylvania in the United States of America, 1965, and it was the Fourth of July down on 24th Street between Celebration and German avenues where Karl Marxman wheeled out his circus cannon and launched a fist of poverty and patriotism at the sky, his new enemy. That cannonball rose over 23rd Street and the attic where my only son Visitor Loop communed with Willie, the great Dialectician, made an elbow in the blue and headed west like fate, looping toward the downtown and Perry Square where the huge parade of high school marching bands and Boy Scouts and police on horses and Veterans of Foreign Wars and Campfire Girls and fire engines and clowns and drum and bugle corps paraded by the grandstand where the mayor and city council and local dignitaries and especially Bobby Hansen and his family sat to review them. At the end of the parade came the Erie contingent of the Pennsylvania National Guard, and the Pennsylvania Air Guard which consisted of one broken

Korean War jet that they kept on the Ohio border though occasionally rolled into town on a trailer for special big deals, and the famous Erie, Pennsylvania Coast Guard Reserve which annihilated the Cuban naval invasion of the United States on Lake Erie and which now stood at a salute in front of the grandstand in front of that hero Bobby Hansen.

Over the brawl and drum of lousy marching bands and the distant pops of mean teenagers' firecrackers, a dull *baarroom* rumbled the air, almost unnoticeably, and then a simple whistle of prescience before that dull rodent of light, Karl's cannonball, appeared in the sky above the grandstand, above the parade, above the Erie, Pennsylvania Coast Guard Reserve which stood saluting Bobby Hansen and the mayor. But almost nobody noticed; there was too much excitement. Nobody's eyes but the hero eyes of Bobby Hansen caught a glimpse of that dying piece of lead. But Bobby Hansen, once again incapacitated, couldn't even warn them. That cannonball came down, filling Bobby Hansen's eyes with a vivid recollection, a meeting of minds. It took a great effort on his part, but Bobby Hansen, who hadn't spoken a word since the day he sacrificed himself during the invasion, summoned every ounce of soul and flesh, and like a great dying vacuum cleaner, screamed. Bobby Hansen screamed.

The music stopped. The Coast Guard kept their hands dumbly in salute. The mayor turned. Everyone on the grandstand and at the parade turned to look at Bobby Hansen, now faint and exhausted, his eyes like round dark bowls of lead, while the cannonball passed overhead, sailing northwest toward the Bay.

It was two days later when a police car rolled up in front of Karl's, took everybody by surprise because a lot of us had never seen a police car in that neighborhood, we hardly ever saw a garbage truck either, they must have figured we ate our garbage, but there it was, a police car, as black and white as Saturday afternoon, and Karl, of course, didn't even wait for them to get out of the car, he came out his door and stood at the top of his steps, and by the time those cops got out and got their doors closed, Red was out there and I was out there, and

Big Dick Jinx and Dean Danger were out, even Rafael Corona was out on his porch above Dean Danger's, though he pretended to be watering his plants and feeding his parrots. From Funster's rooftop a point of light sparkled from his telescope, the helmeted silhouettes of Jimbo, Funly, and Grandpa Funster peering over the sandbags. No doubt about it, the men knew who they were in that neighborhood.

Those cops came around to the front of their car and put their hands on their hips and looked all around, they looked at Karl who had his arms crossed, then they looked all around again. One of them, the younger one, was kind of pudgy and gray, looked a little bit like a liverwurst with a belt on, the other looked pretty much like a keg of beer with a head and arms and legs, like in one of those Falstaff commercials, of course none of us drank Falstaff around there.

"Okay," said Falstaff. "Everybody go back in your houses."

"Why," said Karl. "These are our porches and our houses." He was grinning that grin of his where all you could see was his bicuspids because that's all he had left up front.

"We don't want any trouble, just go back in your houses," said Falstaff.

"We were in our houses before you got here," said Red.

"Well go back in them," said Falstaff. Obviously he missed the densely packed perlocutionary logic of Red's phrase.

"Who the hell are you to come down here and tell us to go back in our houses," said Red.

"We're the goddamn police and we're telling you to get back in your goddamn houses!" yelled Falstaff.

"We ain't seen a cop here in twenty years," said Big Dick.

"It's a real peaceful neighborhood," said Karl.

Faintly, from the top of Funsters' porch, you could hear Grandpa Funster adding, "Cheese soft nights, soft and wanely! Milkbone heaven!" Everyone in that neighborhood knew that Grandpa Funster had really died years ago, and the longer he was dead, the more poetic he got, even if a bit obscure.

Dean Danger usually didn't say too much and he didn't say anything right then, just kind of stood there like a dark box car.

But it seemed pretty clear to me that those cops didn't come to 24th and Celebration for the first time in twenty years just so they could tell us to get back in our houses, no, like everything else around there, the conflict escalated way before the issues ever got out, and that's the way things went for at least an hour, old Falstaff yelling at us that he didn't give a shit what we thought, they were the police and they could tell us to get back in our houses if they wanted to, and us pretty much saying back that we didn't give a shit who the hell they were, these were our houses and we'd get in and out of them as we felt like it, until we heard squawking inside the patrol car and old Falstaff turned to go answer it and Karl said to him, "Don't get back in that car."

"What," said Falstaff.

"I said don't get back in that car," said Karl. "That's all we need is more goddamn cops down here."

"It's my damn car and I'll get in and out of it as I want to," said Falstaff.

He stepped toward his squad car and Karl took a step down from his porch and that's when that silent Liverwurst pulled out his gun.

It didn't take more than a second, I don't even know where all that armament came from, there were just a lot of snaps and clicks and then there was Red with his bowling ball, Karl with one of his M-16's, Dean Danger with his shotgun, and three blue-gray barrels pointed over those sandbags on the Funsters' roof. Big Dick Jinx ducked behind his railing, but back at Karl's, Karl Jr. had slipped out onto their porch roof with his .22 rifle. Falstaff stopped cold with his back to the police car but Liverwurst grinned like to tell us he had us just where he wanted. Things got quiet for a little bit, so it looked like we weren't going to talk about who had to or couldn't get in what anymore, though I couldn't help thinking that these unsteady balances of power, of which I'd had some experience, usually didn't end up so good for somebody, and they usually went awry because of some unforeseen or unknowable variable, like that volatile paintbrush, Karl Jr., on top of Karl's porch roof.

Falstaff was a bit older than Liverwurst and it looked like he was one of those kinds of cops who liked to throw his authority around, but when things got tight it made him calmer. He gazed around the neighborhood at the spread of weaponry, then he looked at Liverwurst who was getting tighter and grinnier by the minute, and then he looked around the neighborhood again. "Okay," he said. "Now put your guns and bowling ball away."

"You put yours away," said Red.

"We don't have to put our guns away," said Falstaff.

"Everything here's registered and legal," said Karl.

"That's fine," said Falstaff. "Just put them away."

"Who the hell he think he is," said Red, pointing his bowling ball at Liverwurst, "coming down here and pulling out a gun."

"Did you pull your gun out?" Falstaff asked Liverwurst.

Liverwurst shook his head, no.

"Yes he did," said Big Dick from behind his railing.

"What rough beast, its hour come round?" yelled Grandpa Funster from the Funsters' roof. People around there always said that being dead all those years didn't have much affect on Grandpa Funster, but it had become clear to me, with what little education I had, that death was turning him into a visionary and plagiarist.

"Listen," I said to Falstaff, "maybe you should tell us why you're down here."

"We don't have to tell you why we're down here," said Falstaff.

"Maybe it would help."

"Help who?"

"Help everybody."

"We're not here to help anybody."

"You sure aren't," said Red.

"Listen Mr. Bowling Ball, I want you to keep out of this," said Falstaff.

"I don't have to keep out of this," said Red.

"Why are you down here?" I said.

"Keep out of this," Red said to me.

"We're investigating something," said Falstaff.

Eventually we did find out why the hell they were down there, though it took a few hours, as you can imagine, the way that conversation was going, and of course why they were down there was exactly why we knew they were down there in the first place. That cannonball that Karl fired on the Fourth of July traveled northwest quite aways, might have made the Bay had it gone straight, and landed right in the backyard of the picnicking Archibald Strong and his lovely wife, Helen's niece, Audrey-Mary Pell-Strong, right down there behind his mansion overlooking the Bay on the West Side where Archibald had just bought out giant stretches of blighted bayfront and coterminously become interested in a big urban renewal project, right down there where Helen's Father, Stanley Pell, used to own apartments but lost them, among other things, when he got rubbed out during the Depression, in this case because he stopped collecting rent. You couldn't imagine an economic frailty in that town without those Strongs sweeping in to strengthen it, they were an altruistic bunch. But very recently they'd been having some kind of picnic or social occasion in the backyard of their new mansion and somebody ended up with a big metal ball in their soup.

I suppose those Strongs saw that as somehow uncalled for, and recalling Archie Strong's great legal victory only a few years ago over a Korean faucet company when he stumbled into his bathroom for a drink of water that night not so long ago and injured his hand on a faucet handle, almost lost the use of all his fingers, but through the miracle of his own tenacity and the help of doing card tricks, card tricks, card tricks, recovered the use of his fingers and sued the Korean faucet company for millions, winning the suit, of course, well, recalling that, Audrey-Mary Pell-Strong told that story now every time Helen's relatives got together for Christmas, it did a lot for Archie and Audrey-Mary's self esteem, so, well, recalling that, Archie and Audrey-Mary Pell-Strong hired a private ballistics expert and commandeered a major police investigation and evidence was beginning to point obscurely toward our neighborhood and Karl Marxman who coincidentally enough had a cannon on his front porch, though anybody could see that you couldn't fit a cannonball in that howitzer, and if he was lucky, his wife Sophie was already on the back porch sitting on that circus cannon.

The other bad part of all this was that there was a broken soup bowl and some bent silverware and a smashed Hermes picnic table, all of which had to be replaced; also you weren't allowed to have workable cannons in the city, you could have antiques if you kept them indoors in a museum-like situation, but you couldn't have cannons that fired sitting around on your front porch; also, that idiot Archie Strong ran over and tried to grab that cannonball right after it landed and burnt the tip of one of his fingers on his good hand.

Well somebody had to step in and mediate this and why not a Dialectician, so amidst all that ballistics I brought my dialectical skills to bear before anybody could tell me to shut up; I told Falstaff that we were obviously a peaceful neighborhood, why else hadn't they had to send any police down here for twenty years, and we didn't know anything about this cannonball stuff, anybody could see that you couldn't put a cannonball in Karl's howitzer, but we didn't want any trouble, and obviously, with all these guns out, trouble was certainly a possibility; so Karl would promise to put his cannon indoors and take out any of its firing devices, and we, as a neighborhood, would take a collection right then and there to pay for Archibald Strong's broken soup plate and bent silverware and Hermes picnic table, not that we felt liable, but that we all firmly believed in a stable social system and hated to see what would happen if the rich started getting poorer, further, I happened to be closely related to Audrey-Mary Pell-Strong, as improbable as it might seem, so I'd personally go over there and check into Archie's finger, buy him a bottle of scotch and allow him to perform card tricks in front of me until every bit of his feelings of disgruntlement and social injustice dissipated; I knew that deep down in he really wasn't a bad guy, he probably just got his feelings hurt having his picnic mo mentarily busted up; he was sensitive and probably took it personally, but a good drunk would cure all that.

I could see this Falstaff might have enjoyed bossing people around but he was no dumbbell; we'd been standing around with guns pointed at each other for so long that it was status quo. He may have thought I was full of bullshit but I was offering him a way out of there without turning tail; he could take the apology, have that cannon put away, and go back with the money for Archie Strong, also write up a nice report where he came off as quelling a potentially riotous situation, the un-mentioned alternative being a showdown of arms where he'd undoubtedly be shot to shit. If that wasn't enough for them down at the police station, they could send somebody else back out to clear things up, maybe the army.

"Okay," said Falstaff, "but I don't want that retarded kid pointing a gun at me." He pointed to Karl's roof where Karl Jr. was glistening like a Coke bottle, a little less intelligently; actually he was a good match for Liverwurst and anybody with a Popsicle of prescience would have seen that right up there on Karl's porch roof was the future of the Erie police force.

It was simply a concession, that's how you had to see it, you had to start little by little. So after a lot of coaxing and threatening we final-ly got Karl Jr. off the roof. Karl took his gun away and promised he'd take him out to the woods the next day and let him kill anything he wanted and Karl Jr. wanted to kill a moose or a killer whale, obviously he had a preference for killing things difficult and threatening or lumpy. Then Karl sent him around the neighborhood to collect the money to pay back Archie Strong. Meanwhile Karl dismantled his howitzer, it was no skin off his back, he could have it back out there the next day and for another twenty years before anybody ever noticed, then showed Falstaff the parts, lining them out on the step, and rolled the howitzer into the house.

But that old Falstaff was nobody's fool, he wanted those cannon parts, and it looked like we were going to be right back where we start-ed until Karl Jr. got back from his rounds with the money and we barely had enough to pay for that soup bowl, which turned out to be worth about six million dollars, let alone the silverware and Hermes picnic table. That's when I had to promise to go over to Archie and Audrey-Mary's and repair the picnic table and unbend the silverware, and Karl had to give up his cannon parts, he had more in his basement anyway, it was just the principle of the thing; all of which made me realize, rather ironically, that I was the only one of all those dingbats capable of exercising this compromise because I was the one who didn't have any principles, consequently my level of personal involvement was growing by the minute, proving, to my mind, that contrary to the commonly held belief that people without principles were unscrupulous, in fact people with principles ran roughshod over people without them. Falstaff was probably just going to pocket most of that money anyway.

By that time the sun was going down and the shadows of houses were stretching into the street like oil spills and it was pretty much implicitly settled that none of us were going back in our houses if we didn't want to, so all we had to settle was this gun issue, minus Karl Jr., though his adult twin, that gun-toting Liverwurst, wasn't exactly a syllogism of predictability; he'd been holding his gun out in front of him in both hands with that silly grin of his for over six hours and the only thing that changed was the color of his armpits, kind of a funny pea color, looked like he was trying to sprout some seeds down there; that character had hero written all over him, at least Falstaff waved his gun around when he talked.

It took a while, but we finally got it all settled that Red and Falstaff would count to three simultaneously and when they got to three everybody would put their guns, and in Red's case his bowling ball, down at the same time; the cops would put their guns in their holsters and get back in their car and everything would be settled, at least for a little while. Behind us, the sun set into the Lake like a cold, fresh plum, reflecting into the windows of the homes, while there on the porches and street of 24th Street everybody agreed to put their guns away, finally, everybody promised they'd do it. Red and Falstaff said, okay, and then they started to count: one, two, three; and on three, everybody put everything away.

Except that ridiculous Liverwurst. As soon as everything got settled down he whipped out his gun again and pointed it right at Red. "All right," said Liverwurst, grinning like a hot tin roof, "you're all under arrest."

That's when the shot rang out.

Liverwurst spread his arms like Jesus. He went to his knees. Then the rest of him hit the cement with a little thud.

"Forgive me," yelled Grandpa Funster from the Funsters' sandbagged porch roof. "They were delicious, so sweet, and so cold."

ᨊ ᨊ ᨊ ᨊ The Emperor of Ice Cream

WELL YOU DON'T SHOOT a cop and get away with it, that's probably written on a rock somewhere in the Cradle of Civilization, but you also never know how people are going to act in a crisis, which if it proves anything, only proves you just have to keep your generalizations vague enough and you'll more or less be correct most of the time. Of course any number of things could have happened.

One of them was a whole flood of cop cars rolling into that neighborhood like eight-balls. Those cops barricaded the corners and made an alley of cars down the center of the street, sandwiching them-selves in between, guns popping over those patrol cars like fish heads. I crouched behind the porch railing with my little .22 and thought about Helen holding her Infant of Prague upside down, all his skirts up over his head and his little crown fallen into her lap. Karl already had his circus cannon pointed out his front door. Red stood behind one of the pillars that went up from the railing and held up the roof, his nose breathing like it held a tiny Marine Corps, his head tilted toward the street, his bowling ball a sweating black sponge in his hands. In the fading light I heard Stinky softly ooo-hooing, a waning cradled moon, and from across the street, Grandpa Funster like an echo calling, "April, cruel, April and cruel."

Behind me I saw Neda's head peeping out from the front window. Lately, in her turn toward beauty over genius, she'd become more exotic, her eyes like great black wings. "The scary part of life," Neda said to me through the screen, "is vocabulary."

Well Neda'd saved the day before with more oblique references than that.

She engineered *The End of the World*. She got Jimbo's giant stuffed fish out of his station wagon.

"Help us, Neda," I said.

"Pray," said Neda, "I'm getting the hell out of here."

Minutes later I heard the shots out toward the back, on 23rd Street, where Neda was dropped. That's how we knew the whole block was surrounded. Karl unleashed with his cannon and blew away two police cars, Red let loose with his bowling ball and took out two more with a combination shot, though when the ball rolled back to the front steps he got winged retrieving it. "Goddamnit," said Red. It was a good thing he didn't know Neda was dead or he would have been out there with his bare hands; even if he didn't really like her that much, Red got pretty sentimental about family in a crisis.

"Next time you go get it," Red said to me, looking at his bloody arm like he had a sliver.

"Right, Red," I said. I think that was the first time I ever called him Red to his face, a bad sign.

From across the street a volley boomed from Funster's and Danger's. The police returned fire and Karl Jr. was smitherated from Karl's porch roof, something Karl couldn't see because he was down below with the cannon.

We responded from all sides, and after that there was only one cop car left that was right side up and had any tires. There was silence down there in the middle of the street, then a white flag came up.

Well I don't know what your supposed to do when the cops surrender, it's not like you can just put them in the basement and keep them well fed. That was probably something we should have thought about before we entered that little foray in the first place, but there was old Falstaff with a white hankie on a rifle barrel waving away behind a patrol car that looked like some kind of predigested food stuff. But somebody had to say something, it wasn't like we could just put our homes on a boat and float out of there. "Okay," I yelled. "What?"

"You surrender?" said Falstaff.

"I don't think so," I told him.

"You're probably in big trouble," said Falstaff, "There's probably a lot of laws getting broke here."

"I don't think us surrendering is the answer to this," I said.

"Every minute there's probably more and more laws getting broke," said Falstaff.

"You got any dead people over there?" I asked him.

"That's none of your business," said Falstaff, "That's police business."

"Well we don't surrender yet," I said, which seemed like a good enough answer for the time being because at the moment it was hard to visualize how things could escalate.

"Well okay," said Falstaff, "but just remember you're probably breaking lots and lots of rules for this."

After a while we all just pretty much sat there watching each other again, back to that, except every once in a while Falstaff would put up that flag and tell us about all the rules we were probably breaking, then soften his demands. First he just wanted us to give up the culprit, that being Grandpa Funster, then he just wanted us to promise to give up the culprit at a future date, and that went on and on until finally he was asking us to just let the police leave; if we let them out of the neighborhood they'd just leave us alone and everybody'd forget about the whole thing. That sounded like a pretty good deal except that it was absurd. But it was a starting point. Maybe if we got them out of there we'd have a couple hours to pack up the neighborhood and move it to North Dakota.

That got us all yelling back and forth across the street and from porch to porch, discussing what we should do, though we finally really did all decide that no matter what, it was probably better to have those guys the hell out of the neighborhood, if only for a little while, instead of sitting there armed smack dab in the middle of it. So we eventually accepted that. We said they could have safe passage out of there, though of course they had to leave their guns, kind of a moot point considering all the guns everybody had already. We had to talk about that for a long time.

Of course at the time none of us knew that Neda was already an historical subject, and Karl didn't know that right up on Karl's roof Karl Jr. was much deader, though probably no dumber, than he'd ever been in his life. No doubt about it, locally speaking we were experiencing a major event, probably something newsworthy. On top of it all, amidst all this gun toting and deaf dealing there were lots of people, probably all the smartest and most innocent people in the neighborhood, like Helen and Joseph and Andrew, and the Dialecticians, one of whom, somewhere, had my son and legacy, the one and only Visitor Loop, sequestered into some niche, safely away from this conflict of dualisms. Not that it was a time for clear thinking, but in the last half-decade or so I'd got pretty used to these little confrontations, if not with authority than with somebody else. There was always a fatal calm that overcame you in a situation like this; when the only alternative is deaf the possibilities seem endless. In fact as Karl and Falstaff reached an end to the whole gun negotiating business, I started thinking maybe we could live on as an armed neighborhood, set a up a few barriers, issue some pass cards, get some I.D.'s. The mind is a tool, that's what I was thinking as the police filed out of there row by row, gunless as a parade of juiceless prunes, and ideas are little robots.

Things degenerated as soon as Karl yelled to Karl Jr. to go out and collect all the guns; Karl Jr. being in a little less responsive state than usual, his spirit was willing but his flesh was dead. Then we noticed Neda was missing. It was time for a cool head; I was thinking it was time for me to send my robots into the chaos. But we were all still knocking around in the middle of the street like a bunch of skinless wieners when the army showed up.

It would have reminded me of the Russian invasion of Hungary had I been there, which I hadn't; piles and piles of big green trucks and jeeps and artillery stacked up on each corner, you'd have thought they were looking for somebody dangerous. Karl took one look at that fleet of green pods and jumped in his truck; I guess he decided this was one waiting game we weren't going to be able to wait our way out of. He didn't get as far as the corner of Celebration Avenue before, unlike on all the movies and TV shows, they shot his tires out. He took so much lead in that cab you could see the blood oozing out the bullet holes in the doors.

Now the Funsters' house went up under a barrage of mortars. Big Dick Jinx lay motionless at the base of his porch, where poor Stinky soon left him, hooting out of the neighborhood at the speed of sound, a ball of fire. From behind a junk pile of police cars, Red jumped up and flattened a jeep. His ball returned and he picked it up, spun, and took out a sand bagged machine gun in front of where Funsters used to be. Across the street a patrol had moved up Dean and Tina Danger's front steps and into their front door, firing into the vestibule.

Things looked pretty bad. In fact, it looked like there wasn't going to be anybody left but Red. I thought he'd never die, but I was with him on the street when he took his last one and he didn't say a fucking thing to me, he just handed me that bowling ball. When his last breath went out the earth shook, and I looked back to see our house in flames, and beyond the neighborhood blocks and blocks in a sea of flames, and somewhere in that flaming house, somewhere in there, Helen and Joseph and Andrew and the Infant, and somewhere beyond, Willie, the Dialecticians, and my own son, Visitor Loop.

But none of that happened.

I suppose, being the last one left, I could have just died and kicked this whole thing up to another plain, but that smacks of a kind of dualistic thinking which I try to avoid. No, the fact is, all that was one of any number of things that could have happened in any number of given moments, because everything that happens or doesn't happen has its own life. Stories are just things inside other stories, like multiplying the world by itself over and over until you get satisfied with an explanation. Some of us never get satisfied.

So old Falstaff must not have been too keen on his partner because after Liverwurst hit the cement Falstaff pretty calmly went to his patrol car and called in an ambulance and another car. There was a lot of blinking lights but not too much commotion, and they very quietly plopped Liverwurst into the ambulance and then went over to the Funsters' where Grandpa Funster was waiting for them. They read him his rights.

"Tootings at the wedding of the soul," said Grandpa Funster as they put him in the back of the patrol car. "Bluish clouds above the empty houses."

"Tell it to the judge," said Falstaff.

"Immaculate syllables," said Grandpa.

We all watched in the street as they cavalcaded Grandpa Funster on out of there.

Of course I'm not sure any of that happened either. The only thing I'm sure of is how I thought it all happened the first time, Karl shot that cannon off and the ball disappeared into the clouds and never came down. Some things just end up in the air, that's a metaphor I've learned to live with.

Archibald Strong, for whatever reasons, possibly because he was telling the truth, said he'd had a perfectly ordinary afternoon luncheon on the Fourth of July down on the Bayfront in the back yard behind his mansion, and nothing came out of the sky and he didn't have an Hermes picnic table, Hermes didn't even make picnic tables and nobody'd believe them if they did. Maybe Falstaff just made that whole story up. Or maybe we just misunderstood him. Yet once you started dealing with that older generation of Funsters, things just went haywire. For certain, Grandpa Funster was a mysterious and poetic man, and I guess it just took an odd event like this to make me realize it, and it would have taken even more to make him realize it, he didn't even know he was dead, though neither did Grandma Funster, know she was dead, that is, but at least they got her in the grave, bodily, if nothing else.

Before any of this happened, and after I lost Kara Ruzci, sometimes I'd drive Funly Funster and Stinky Jinx and Grandpa Funster out to the protestant cemetery near the Peninsula and we'd walk through the graves like the Four Horsemen on foot. Autumn was usually the best time because they had a great tree collection in there, maples, oaks, chestnuts, elms, hickories and sycamores, huge magnolia trees and dogwoods; those dogwoods burned redder than the maples when they changed, and I remember that every time when Helen dragged the family out to the Catholic cemetery to see her dead dad, Grandpa Stanley, who died during the Great Depression, Helen made Red tell us the story about how Jesus was crucified on dogwood, and that's why dogwoods were all short and twisted now and turned blood red in the autumn; that was one of my favorite stories and I was sorry I hadn't thought of it on my own, because even back then I knew that an explanation had to get in pretty deep before it made any sense. Of course right there next to Grandpa Stanley's name, Stanley Pell, with his birth and death dates, was Bush's name, only it said Esther Pelkowski, not Pell, that was one of the few victories Bush garnered for having lived so long, if she'd have died first she'd have died Pell, and now, as it was, Stanley was lucky he didn't get re-Pelkowski'd; and right there under Bush's name was her birth date and her death date with 19__ right after it and of course every time Helen saw it you knew what she was thinking, she was thinking that the coming holidays might hc Bush's very last, in fact coming up in December we might be having Bush's last Last Christmas, because she sure was old, Bush was around before machines or condoms or anything.

Now in the spring the cemetery always had that odd simple contradiction, flowers popping up, trees budding, rows of bloomed tulips and magnolia bushes blombed with pink flowers, while underneath, cement boxes full of dead people. It never turned the trick for me. But getting in Kara Ruzci's Ford Falcon and driving through the autumn with Stinky and Funly and Grandpa Funster, everything moving toward death like some slouching beast, made me feel a bit like a ghost in a cold steam bath. There were some times, of course, when I'd just go there myself with the Visitor and our pooch, Polly Doggerel, and sit, watching the two of them dart from the shade of graves, and think of the long road of sorrow across Pennsylvania to the grave of Kara Ruzci, next to her brother's, below the hill where we were married. On those days, even in late October cold, I'd drive out to the Peninsula, to the lake, like I used to with Kara, strip naked on the deserted beach and swim.

Red was getting old enough now to think about death, though he never really talked about it, it was Helen who talked about it because she wasn't that concerned with the grave, she was concerned with the transition, that's what she had in common with Willie, but death meant the grave for Red because when he took the family to see Grandpa Stanley he always started walking around to the other double graves and looking at the stones; who was dead, who was left alone and for how long, who was still waiting; and there was Kara Ruzci, my wife, buried next to her brother in New Jersey, no grave of mine next to hers.

But when I went out to the protestant cemetery with Grandpa Funster, we'd make our way through the dead leaves to the Funsters' plot where Stinky cleaned up around the grave and put gladiolas in the urns on either side, and Funly dropped to his knees, took his hands out of his trench coat, folded them, and bowed that flat-topped head of his, while Grandpa Funster stood in front of the wide low stone with Grandma Funster's name and dates on one side, and his on the other. According to that stone, and anybody else you'd want to ask, he'd died some ten years before she did. And Grandpa Funster said, "These wrinkles are nothing. These gray hairs are nothing. I am the same boy my mother used to kiss," or something like that, as the wind rose and blew through the dry trees. Funly raised and tilted his head, twisting an eyebrow. He swore Grandma Funster'd been up there in that space capsule with him, and of course it would have been hard to disprove. Stinky hooted softly to himself like a tiny, far away train, his lavender silk scarf slilling in the wind. Clouds rose from over the lake and it grew dark, as Grandpa Funster's spread arms slowly closed and wrapped around himself. "Love," mumbled Grandpa Funster. That's what I thought he said. "Love." Though it could have been something else. Then in the quiet underneath the wind you'd swear you heard something, a voice underneath that chorus of voices in the back of your ears. Then things quieted down. The sun came out.

"I am driven by innocence," said Grandpa Funster, "My passion for milk is uncontrollable still."

You'd just never have guessed those Funsters to be such a mystical bunch.

Nonetheless, for whatever reasons you might want to imagine, Grandpa Funster, passion for milk and all, was now in jail, and his bail was over a million dollars so he was stuck there and never getting out if it was up to anyone in authority. That Liverwurst was dead meat shot dead, even if he'd been a notorious bigamist from Winnemucca, Nevada, which later came out in the investigation of the case. The state prosecutor claimed he had Grandpa Funster's oblique confession and wanted to put him in the chair. The state said Grandpa Funster was a man of violent intentions and poetic excuses and neither of those would ever be unleashed upon the public again.

Sometimes on weekends, instead of going to the cemetery, I went down to the jail with Funly and Stinky. The guards brought out Grandpa Funster and sat him down in a chair behind the thick Plexiglas panels. He looked like a piece of old bark.

"How you doing, Grandpa?" said Funly.

"Are they treating you okay?" said Stinky.

"Don't worry, Grandpa," said Funly, "we'll get you out of here, even if we have to bust you out." The guards had already frisked Funly at the door, got every one of his guns, not that it mattered because he had all that stuff registered, in fact by that time Funly probably had more authority than they did, you figured he'd made some hook-up with the CIA simply because he'd stopped talking about it.

Of course I didn't say anything.

"A dire bird dangled down in fire," said Grandpa Funster. You had to give him one thing, among others, over the dead years he'd picked up a sense of syntax.

"Don't worry, Grandpa," said Funly.

Grandpa Funster did not look worried.

〰 〰 〰 〰 〰Pere du Nom

TIME PASSES, things change a little hit. The older I got, I started seeing things in older, simpler ways. There were lives of time,
streets of time, days of time. I got a job collecting garbage.

The only hard part about the job was the work. We started
around 2:30 A.M., just after the bars closed, and went and got coffee,
then hit the streets making as much noise as we could. You carried
your own can into somebody's back yard, dodged the clotheslines,
kicked the dog, found the garbage and stuffed about four cans of what
somebody thought was well packed garbage into your own, that was
after you got the cat or rat or possum or whatever mammal you found
in the cans out of the can and onto the lawn. Then you put the can on
your shoulder and squatted under the clotheslines and kicked the dog
and yelled back at whoever's yard you were in and was now awake
bitching at you for making so much noise while you were back there
discovering their fucking garbage. Then you threw the garbage up into
the dump truck, though of course by the time you were halfway
through with your first route there was a lot more garbage than there
was truck so somebody, usually the newest person on the crew, I, myself, had to go up onto the garbage pile and stamp it all down so you
could throw more garbage up there without having to drive all the way
back to the incinerator and then come back and complete the route.

After each route we went hack to the incinerator where most everybody went down to the garbagemen's lounge which had a snack and

coffee machines as well as a table in it and said things like, "cunt! ass! boobs!" It was such stimulating stuff I started spending my time watching the trucks come in and pour their garbage into the incinerator. A million tons of waste on fire, a hundred thousand things from a hundred thousand lives burning at my feet.

That job gave me a tremendous amount of free time as long as I didn't sleep. After work we went back to the bar we'd closed and opened it up again, then I drove to Willie's, where the Visitor spent most his time, and dropped in on the late morning experiments.

"Dad!" said the Viz. I don't know where he got his looks, he didn't look like me and he didn't look like Kara Ruzci; he didn't look like Red or Helen, and I didn't think he looked like Barbie or Louie Ruzci either. Any time I thought about it and tried to put it in words I always ended up thinking he looked like some kind of sandwich, which only made sense intuitively; he didn't really look much like a sandwich, his life was just sandwiched.

I gave the Visitor a big hug, then I put him down and he ran to Willie.

"Dad!" said the Viz.

"When he start that?" I said to Willie.

"It is some new big fing wif him," said Willie.

"Dad!" said the Visitor to a nearby beach ball. He gave Polly Doggerel a pat on the head. "Dad! Good Dad!" said my only son Visitor Loop.

"That's not your dad," I said.

"I, myself, fink he is advanced for his age," said Willie.

By this time the rest of the Dialecticians, Raymon, Revis and Revco had rummaged in to Willie's attic, looking for their places on the pillows.

"Dads!" said the Visitor to the Dialecticians.

"He is some kind of radical monist nominalist," said Raymon. I grabbed the Visitor by the hand and took him back over to Polly Doggerel.

"This is not your dad," I said to him. "This is Polly Doggerel. Dog," I said.

"Dad!" said the Viz.

"Hot dog," said Polly Doggerel. It was muffled underneath that dog yawn of hers, but it was discernible.

Revco reached in his black leather Dialecticians jacket and pulled out a hot dog and gave it to Polly Doggerel.

"It would seem to me you have lost touch with your family," said Revis.

"This isn't an issue of familiarity," I said to Revis.

"I, myself, would see it as precisely an issue of familiarity," said Willie.

"It is an issue of semantics," said Raymon.

"Dad!" said the Viz to a nearby pillow.

"Myself," said Willie to the Viz, "I would prefer not to be called fis dad.

Well I suppose I wasn't spending nearly as much time with the Visitor as I should have, and I guess he got kind of used to having me around every second back when Kara Ruzci was alive and had the job and all me and the Viz did was hang upside down all day at home and look at photography books, but now I had to work, and Red worked and Helen worked, and Joseph and Andrew and Neda went to school, not that Neda would have been good for the Viz anyway, the wax in his brain was too soft to deal with an omniscient and precarious intellect like Neda, as conventional and beautiful as she'd now become, no, there just wasn't any way around it, besides, this whole dad thing was just a temporary malady and getting worried about it would just get me started thinking that something that happened first was somehow going to explain what happened later, and once that kind of thing started there was no return. If the Viz wanted to call everything and everyone dad it was okay with me, I'd just wait him out.

Sometime in the afternoon, when all the experimenting was done, I got the Visitor and Polly Doggerel and went over to Red and Helen's where sometimes we stayed in the front bedroom with Joseph and Andrew. Of course Neda had her own room, being female and dangerous, and Red and Helen had their own room at the back of the house so on Sunday mornings Red could lay with his head at the bottom of the bed near the back window and listen to the choir of the Baptist Church right behind our backyard.

That front bedroom went to me and the Visitor and Andrew and Joseph and Polly Doggerel, all of us boys in our own right except for Polly who was a dog. That room was just a pile of mattresses and clothes, in theory the clean clothes in one pile and the dirty in another, which was easy enough because by now me and Joseph and Andrew were all nearly the same size and the Visitor wasn't, so it was easy to sort his out. Polly Doggerel didn't wear any clothes and the rest of us put on anything else we wanted and fought about it later. Of course nobody around that place could smell anymore, except for Red, all our olfactory capacities somehow disappearing some time between when Pope Pius XII opened that letter from Our Lady of Fatima and the death of that little chubby rascal John XXIII, so sometimes we got that clean pile and dirty pile mixed up, which was mostly a semantic distinction anyways.

Now that Helen was Executive General Secretary of Marycrest College the only clothes she cleaned was hers and sometimes Red's; it was something she'd been dying to abandon for years and now she had a vocational inspiration; came up to that animal pit of ours on the second floor one afternoon when we were all there and said, "I don't know if you've noticed, but you've been wearing clean clothes all these years," and of course that was a revelation to us, not that we were unthinking people but I guess we figured they were spontaneously regenerating in our drawers. Though she hadn't completed her sentence, if we'd been astute we'd have concluded that the visit wasn't meaningless and that Helen had offered us a suggestion, albeit unfinished. But we let her leave the room and never thought another thing about it until somebody, I think Joseph, noticed that all our clean clothes had disappeared.

Well it was a reasonless universe but it had been good to us in terms of clean clothes for a long time. Nonetheless, the crisis forced some organization upon us and that's how we developed the Pile System.

Though if you thought you had to go somewhere where you had to worry about stinking, and wanted to wear something that was in what you thought was the dirty pile, it was always a good idea to get it out of there and hang it up on a door or something so it could aerate over night.

I'd been raised in chaos, this I understood, and there are any number of degrees of order and chaos that can arise from chaos and one of them was going on when me and the Viz got to Red and Helen's that afternoon. Lately Helen had been realizing things and one of the things she realized was that she was a big shot; she made more money than Red, she had a hotshit title, she got dressed up for work every day and ran a whole college for various degrees of intellectuals and nuns, yet she did not control, not even one-half control, her own house. I don't know who the hell she thought did, but I guess she thought Red did, and I guess he thought he did too, which was absolutely wrong but widely enough believed to be a point of contention. At present, the focus of this misapprehension seemed to have rested itself on space issues. Helen said she didn't control anything but the holy room, which she had to give up on holidays anyway, and the kitchen which she didn't want; Red controlled the rest of the house; he controlled the living room and the front room, the stairway, the bathroom and the whole rest of the upstairs, he controlled the basement which was full of every broken machine in the history of the universe, the attic which he never let anybody else go in and who knew what was up there, the porch, the front yard, the back yard, and even the bedroom which they were supposed to share but didn't mostly because he was a giant who spread his arms when he slept and sweated and so made her just have to huddle in one little corner of the bed like a forlorn mouse.

"A forlorn mouse," said Red. His glanced toward the closet where he kept that bowling ball. He'd lived with Helen all those years and still didn't know that she never started an argument that she hadn't won before she opened her mouth. For Red to even enter this one he'd have to admit he didn't control everything, in fact he'd have to go right down the list and show he didn't control *anything*, which was absolutely true. Occasionally he arose from the chaos and threatened complete destruction, even carried it out, and that got our attention for a little while, but even so, you live through only so much total annihilation before you grow slightly impervious. On top of that, Helen didn't even want control of the goddamn house, even I figured that out after about an hour and a half. Subterfuging down underneath all this household imperialism was the manifest destiny of the Infant of Prague.

It was years ago, almost beyond memory, even before *The Year of Two Hundred Books*, that Helen started her holy object proliferation and Red, who at that time was the only money maker in the house, banished all those Sacred Burning Hearts of Jesus and statues of Our Lady of Fatima and Our Lady of Lourdes and Our Lady of Guadalupe and St. Theresa and St. Francis Assisi and St. Joseph and St. Peter & Paul and the Our Lady of the Immaculate Conception crushing that snake Satan under her heel atop the world, and all the crucifixes and angels, to the holy room where Helen held holy hegemony. But now that place was stuffed and stuff was sneaking out.

At first you'd wake up in the morning and couldn't cross the holy room and get into the kitchen because all those statues would be lined up at the doorway, leaning their little heads into the living room. You'd have to pardon yourself and wade your way through to get some breakfast. You might think you heard grumbling but of course that was absurd. Later on, they started appearing places. You'd be watching the Browns on the Zenith, get up for a snack, and when you got back St. Christopher had your place. Wake up from a nap and there in your nose was the baby Jesus holding the world in his little hand. Turn away from your dinner plate and the next thing you knew St. Philomena was sharing your pot roast. Those characters didn't move much while you watched them, but when you turned away they were fast as light. Less sane people than us might have been alarmed.

"I'm not in control," said Helen. "I'm just in charge."

Nonetheless, it was a human universe so somebody had to be responsible, and Helen, being Catholic, knew that better and before anybody, so she went on the attack. She was pulling her weight and now she wanted her space.

"Goddamnit," said Red. "I'll get a goddamn ball bat." Which would have been enough to keep me in the holy room if it wasn't enough to get those statues back in there. Red wasn't getting any better at sophisticated argumentation but he was getting faster at knowing he was licked. Though now he'd unwittingly gone right for the internecine throat; if you destroyed those statues you were supposed to get them re-blessed and incinerated and buried in holy oil, not smash them to little bits with ball bats.

"Dad!" said the Visitor, spreading his arms toward Red.

"I'm not your goddamn dad," said Red.

"He's just a child, Red," said Helen.

"Dad!" said the Visitor to Helen.

"I guess he's picked up a bad habit," I said.

"Where the hell you been," said Red, "He's been doin' this for months. It's not a habit its a goddamn law."

Well that was a stopper, but the rule around there was that if Red said anything smart you just ignored it, usually, unless you wanted trouble.

"A law?" said Helen.

"A behavioral law for chrissake," said Red.

"Dad!" said the Viz, I think he said it to me.

"That's right," I said, "I'm your dad."

"You been reading again, Red?" said Helen. She reached down and picked up the Viz, which was unusual too, because she was normally pretty cool with him; it was Red who liked to play with the Viz; he'd wear waste baskets and do head stands and any number of ridiculous things to make him laugh, any of which if you mentioned he'd kill you for. Helen had raised her kids, but as much as she loved us, she didn't really like any of us, not that I blame her. Of course deep down, underneath that stoic exterior, she still didn't like us.

"This is just a stage," said Helen. "He'll grow out of it. Right Viz?"

"Right, Dad," said the Visitor.

"Ah shit," said Red. He went to the vestibule, opened the first door, stepped through and opened the second, clenching his fist at the screen door. He paused, then opened it and went out, remarkable restraint, I don't know if he was just getting old or his door salesman job had increased his respect for doors.

"Things are a lot better around here than they used to he," I said to Helen.

"Well," said Helen, "wait till he finds out I'm pregnant."

Red went over to Jimbo Funster's. For years, after he'd fight with Helen he'd go over and see Jimbo, only in the old days Red would knock out every door in the house first, then go over and let Jimbo show him his fishing rods and homemade bullets and guns. Jimbo'd show Red his guns and in not too long he'd be telling Red he should have a gun, and of course Red always said he didn't need a gun, he could do anything he needed to with his fists or a ball bat, which wasn't true, he did his most lethal destruction with his bowling ball, but it was true enough, and before it was all over Red was feeling like deep down in he really was kind of a gentle guy, and then he took home some deer steaks or catfish and thought about putting all his doors back on.

But those two were a little older now and been through a lot and a lot of things had changed. When Funster went to his sandbagged porch top now, it wasn't to monitor the invasion of blacks, nope, now the blacks were everywhere and he went up there to see if he could find anybody white. In fact Funster didn't even call them blacks anymore, he called them blacks, he even thought some of them were okay. There were good and bad blacks just like there were good and bad whites, except that there were probably more bad blacks because they had so much to overcome. You could talk to Funster now and he'd tell you right out, most blacks were okay, they just spent too much time on the streets, especially the women, and spent too much of their money on their cars instead of their homes, and they drank too much and spent too much of their money on drugs, and the men didn't stay home enough, they were always out running around and fucking everything in sight and getting too many women who weren't their wives pregnant, especially white women, they should stay away from the white women, in fact they should probably have fewer babies in general, and they didn't mow their lawns, blacks were bad about lawns, it was hard to deny it, and they tended to be lazy and you couldn't trust them, but other than that they were okay and certainly better than the Puerto Ricans.

So Funster had changed, and Red had changed too; why there he was, after a fight with Helen and over at Funster's and he hadn't even knocked out a single door. And Funster didn't show him guns anymore when he came over. Funster took him in the house and they had coffee with Betty Funster in the kitchen or had a beer on the porch and listened to the Funster's little daughter, Mosha, practice her tuba; and then Funster took Red into his living room and showed Red his stuffed animals. He had a ceiling covered with antlers and walls of hanging animal heads, deer heads, fox heads, wild cat heads, raccoon heads, wolverine heads, squirrel heads, bear heads, elk heads, and a moose head; stuffed pigeons and stuffed doves, stuffed turkeys, stuffed pheasants, stuffed quail, stuffed geese, stuffed hawks, stuffed ducks; he had those ducks hanging from the ceiling by wires so they'd be flying in the shape of a V; he had a diorama in one corner of a little deer family with grass and trees and a little pond, a poppa deer with a great big rack and a pretty brown momma deer with big dark eyes and a little tiny baby deer with the cute white spots still on its coat; he had a glass cage display with rocks and a painted-in ocean and a bunch of penguins looking at the ocean while two California seals beneath them were frozen forever in the act of sexual intercourse, tape recording of the ocean going on behind; near the ceiling, up on top a paper mache mountain, was an American puma surveying a flock of chubby sheep; and in the center of the room, right on top a coffee table, a Pennsylvania black bear, trailing behind him a whole squadron of dead stuffed hunting dogs.

But that wasn't all. That room had a glass floor and if you flipped a switch it turned on a light underneath where there was a whole room of aquatic stuffed stuff. He had schools of stuffed bass, stuffed perch, stuffed walleye, blue gills, catfish, garfish, sunnies, carp and sturgeon, coho salmon and rainbow trout; beaver dams chock full of stuffed beavers and in the walls weasel dens, possum dens, muskrat dens, families of playful stuffed otters swimming on their backs and sliding down mud slides; near the bottom of the room, slipping around near rocks, stuffed crawfish, stuffed newts, spotted as well as Texas, stuffed salamanders, stuffed mud puppies, and on the floor, two teams of stuffed bull frogs playing baseball with toads for umpires, tree frogs and leopard frogs piled into the grandstand, huge greenies in the aisles selling hot stuffed freshwater mussels and clams, bags of fresh popped flies and guppies and water bugs; and in the very very back of the underground room, breaking water over a giant replica of the state of Florida, the great blue stuffed marlin that Funster caught on his vacation to Florida during the Cuban Missile Crisis.

But Funster didn't stop there. Funster had teddy bears sitting amidst the elk horns, panda bears mixing it up with the penguins, a whole family of Winnie the Poohs sitting around the deer pond having a picnic; he had stuffed monkeys playing around the cougar paws, kangaroos hopping in front of the bear; he had green tigers with red stripes next to the squirrel heads and baby blue elephants flying with the ducks; there was a rain forest of multi-colored gorillas and chimpanzees, pythons and boa constrictors, panthers, cheetahs, ocelots and margays; and down underneath, in the Gulf of Mexico, a pod of Flippers, some of them wearing football helmets with turquoise dolphins on them, and several families of whales, all ducking and diving under an air corps of stuffed flying fish.

Not that Funster stopped there either, there was even more of that stuff, but there's a point where the truth will challenge the imagination.

Deep underneath all that Jimbo Funster naturalia, in the basement where Jimbo once hooked up his short-wave to talk to Funly when Funly's orbit crossed the path of the Great Lakes and in particular Erie, Pennsylvania, Funly Funster himself, flat-topped, now a thin dark mustache like a pencil line above his lip, stood in a pit of maps and charts of the Great Lakes, though his special attention went to Lake Erie, Lake Ontario, and the Saint Lawrence Seaway, all of which he had diagramed and coordinated on a giant lighted table; every niche and island marked, every lock dissected. He had his pencil out and his thinking hat on. If the Cubans could sneak a fleet down the Seaway to Erie, the Russians could do it, he knew that, though he just couldn't figure out how, which meant it must be impossible, and then what, what? something, something, that's what, that's what he kept thinking to himself, there's something, something, something, and it had to be thought about very hard.

There wasn't much left of that Funster household now, just Jimbo and Funly left to do the great things. Grandma Funster, much like Crow, hadn't been heard from since Funly got back, which made you think maybe that's why Grandpa Funster finally went off the deep end, turned that poetic vision of his into existential reality and ended up in jail; Betty Funster'd gone back to canning things, and she was good at it; Funly's little sister Mosha was quiet and chubby and played the tuba.

It's hard to say what Red got out of going over there, maybe it showed him what happened to people when their insides got out, probably it showed him that what this country needed was another Depression. Red was thinking maybe he'd grow a garden next year, build a silo for Honky and let him bounce up and down until he launched himself, then turn the rest of the yard into a beautiful garden; corn, tomatoes, pole beans, giant purple egg plants like winter clouds; he'd replant the prune tree that got him so mad one day he beat it to shreds, and the big wild cherry tree that a storm blew down one day and Red couldn't get damages from the insurance company because they said it was an act of God, put insurance men on Red's shit list forever, and he'd go across the street and plant new elm trees where all the old ones used to be before the Dutch Elm Disease rubbed them all out, he'd plant huge trees there and cover up all those run down houses. Whatever it was, before Red was done with the Funsters he was thinking about rebuilding, replanting, redoing.

"What ya think," said Red to Funster. "We could turn it around."

"Turn wh-wh-what?" said Funster.

"Everything," said Red.

"Then it would all be b-b-backwards," said Funster. Since Grandpa Funster went to jail, Jimbo'd started to see things differently, he was becoming more abstract and more concrete at the same time.

Meanwhile, downstairs, underneath the lighted table filled with graphs and charts of Lake Erie, Lake Ontario, and the Saint Lawrence Seaway, Funly descended through his trap door and followed the tunnel to the bomb shelter where, in the back of the supply room, under a dim light, he examined his detailed blueprint of the Erie Jail. In the kitchen, Betty Funster lifted a wrack of Mason jars filled with tomatoes from a pot of boiling water, while far off, in her back room, Mosha Funster played, *ooompa-pa, ooompa-pa, oompa-pa, oompa-pa.*

Myself, I went over to see Karl. It'd been a long time. Maybe it had something to do with Helen's pregnancy, something in me thinking about empty graves got me back down in Karl's basement. Karl looked up from the corner of his work area where he had his guns on racks along the walls and just gave me a bit of a nod. Across the basement, in the opposite corner, his pig stood and snorted.

"Been thinking about roasting him for Halloween," said Karl without looking up from his work table. "Maybe Christmas."

"Pig's last Christmas," I said.

"Could be," said Karl. He scratched his red and white beard.

"Ornk," said the pig.

"He's not the conversationalist Crow was," I said to Karl, I went over and patted that pig on the head and he rolled over to let me rub his belly.

"Nope," said Karl. "Never was. Probably not going to change now."

Well some things change and some things don't. I stood there with my hands in my pockets and watched Karl fiddling over that work bench. Since that cannon ball incident, not only did he have those cannons back out, but also had mounting devices for all his automatic weapons in his windows.

"How you like garbage collecting?" said Karl.

I took that rhetorically. "You miss Crow?" I said.

Karl pointed to his lunch bucket. He was back to work at Bucyrus Erie which seemed to have recovered from the recession as well as the negative the political reaction they got for selling cranes and bulldozers and graters to the Eisenhower administration who gave them to Castro before he turned Commie. "You pack one of those?" he said. "You start packing one of those, you know you're in a rut."

Well I'd thought about packing a lunch bucket. I went to work in my work khakis and brown garbage stompers and a blue work shirt and big brimmed soft hat to keep the garbage that leaked out of my can from seeping down my neck, and I thought a nice silver lunch pail would look good with the outfit, give it a touch of professionalism. I even consulted Stinky and he agreed, silver was the right color. Though there was something a little incompatible about packing lunch and collecting garbage, I didn't plan on filling that little tomb, just carrying it.

"It represents our participation in cycle and repetition," I told Karl.

"I don't own a cycle," said Karl.

"A rut is a circle," I said. "A hole is by definition unfilled."

"Come over here," said Karl. I guess he realized that if he allowed me to keep going I might have had a thought, and who needed one. "See this?" he said, and he showed me some new kind of cannon with a longer, narrower barrel than the one we used on our boat, the *Armada*; it had a base that pivoted 360 degrees and a swivel that let you point it straight up or down if you wanted; it was a lot lighter too.

"For the roof?" I said.

"I'll need a lot bigger one for the roof."

Well if he wasn't going to fortify the house that only meant one thing, though you had to figure he wasn't planning on going back to robbing houses, you didn't need a cannon to burglarize houses, and since the Cuban invasion you had to figure the lake was no longer safe or intelligent territory. There was only one train that went through Erie anymore, going from Chicago to New York, but that went through at around 2 A.M. and nobody was on it. I suppose there were a lot of people on the freeway; we could mount the thing on his truck and head for the I-90, but roads were very confining things. On top of all that, I felt good about being, for lack of a better description, dead to the world. I'd always admired Grandpa Funster, in an ineffable sort of way, and now I thought I had, by luck, joined his ranks in my youth. I figured I'd seen everything and now I was happy being a grunt. It transcended fatalism.

"I'll need help," said Karl.

"No thanks," I said.

"How long you been collecting garbage?"

"Forever."

"Well," said Karl. "I'll see you when you're ready."

～～～～～And of the Son

Big Dick Jinx Experiments with Deaf

THE COLLEGES AFTER STINKY JINX were like frogs on a dark night. No doubt about it, Stinky was the greatest athlete in the history of Erie, PA if not the world. He was so good at everything that South High signed him up for every sport and never scheduled a simultaneous event. They took him out of the water polo matches and taxied him to the basketball game, pulled him in the fourth quarter and sent him over to the ice rink for hockey. Stinky thought hockey was some kind of puck ballet; he could have played the game in his underwear, though he didn't, he wore a beautiful sun gold uniform with rose ribbons on his shoulder pads that spun like a skirt when he did his triple 360's before slipping the puck into the net like a soft-shoed gazelle. He spent the winter under a sun lamp so he could play the game with a tan. He looked like Troy Donahue, Fred Astaire, and Bobby Orr.

In the fall Stinky swam, played football, wrestled, ran cross country. In the spring he dominated track, tennis, golf, and especially baseball where he alternated between pitching, short stop, and his favorite, center field, where he received standing ovations for his beautiful pirouettes, his graceful somersaults, his lightening, sky stopping *grande jetté sur l'air*, all of which helped pass the time between the balls and strikes and occasional hits. Defensively, Stinky rubbed out the bloop single as well as the home run. With Stinky out there, there simply was no opposite field. And with the bat he was a magician of ontology, his bat always hit being, his ball always found Void. Though he loved base running too much to hit home runs, his most favorite thing of all being to get caught in a run-down; watching Stinky caught between the bases was like watching a hawk caught in the sky; space was Stinky's element.

But the bottom line was that Stinky really didn't like sports. He liked the arena, he liked waving to the fans, but I don't think he understood a game he played, because I was the one who taught him everything he knew which was a little less than what I knew which wasn't much. Stinky'd have me over for tea and we'd read *Cosmo* or *Glamour* or the *National Enquirer* and after a while he'd say, "Jarvis, they want me to play a new game. Not one of those get there first games, I think it's one of those put the ball somewhere games," and then I'd tell him where to put the ball and that was that. Stinky put a ball anywhere he had to and did it faster and more gracefully than anyone in the human race.

No, Stinky didn't like sports all that much. He liked the camaraderie. He liked hugging and jumping and he took a tremendous pleasure in avoiding blocks and tags and tackles. He loved designing new uniforms, in fact did beautiful things with scarves and ribbons and flower decals, an idea he got one New Years while trying to find the parades and accidentally ran into the Rose Bowl and saw all those football uniforms with roses on the sleeves, you never know where you'll find a fashion idea, and now Stinky could design a whole team's uniform with each single one uniquely embroidered with honeysuckle or tulips or gladiolas or gardenias; Stinky believed that everyone on a team was an individual, besides, not even the most rude, uncultured person could strike out, without conscience, against a flower.

But that really wasn't why Stinky played sports. Stinky would never have kept on if it wasn't for Big Dick. Now that high school was over and just when Stinky thought he was done, sixty-seven million colleges descended upon him and he got drafted by the Boston Celtics, the Houston Astros, the Denver Broncos, the Montreal Canadians, the

Detroit Lions, the World Champion of Roller Derby Bay City Bombers, and the Winnipeg Jets.

"Oh boy!" said Big Dick, and every second he wasn't in that Buckhorn potato chip truck of his, delivering pretzels and pork rinds and cheese puffs and potato chips, he was on the phone negotiating with every sports institution in the world.

We were on Stinky's living room floor watching *General Hospital* while he flipped through a pile of college brochures. Stinky wore a beautiful flowing mauve silk shirt and his eye shadow matched it. He looked pretty good.

"Philadelphia Textile sounds nice," said Stinky.

"Too small," said Big Dick from the phone.

"They're not nifty dressers?" said Stinky

"Not in Philadelphia," said Big Dick.

"Maybe I should go pro," Stinky said to me.

"Pro what," I said.

"The Broncos aren't going to let you redesign their uniforms," said Big Dick.

"Doesn't anybody want me in LA?" said Stink.

"Go to college in LA," said Big Dick, "then win the Olympics and then go pro."

"Texas Abeline," said Stinky to me. "Isn't that a fish dish?"

"It's a cemetery," I told him.

"Texas Arlington is a cemetery," said Big Dick.

"I probably couldn't get on a soap coming out of cemetery school," said Stinky. "Aren't there any schools named after flowers?"

Big Dick put down the phone and held his chest. "Ug," he said, "heartburn." Too many barbecued pork rinds, and you knew Big Dick was too conscientious to eat fresh ones; he probably filled up on the ones he got back unsold from the stores. He burped a few more times and went in the bathroom.

"Mom was right," Stinky said to me. "You can't please him." He showed me his new nail color. "I'm trying to think of a sports uniform this would go with," he said. "Some hand game."

"Pinochle," I said.

"Are there pinochle teams?"

"In theory," I said.

"Maybe billiards," said Stinky. "I think you need balls to have uniforms if you're not running or jumping."

"This sports business has its limits," I said. "You might be the greatest athlete in the history of the world, but you're not going to change everything."

"Hoo-hoo!" said Stinky, "Right! *It* will change *me*!"

"Guuuh!" said Big Dick from somewhere in the trophy room.

"Oh-oh," said Stinky.

"Guuh," said Big Dick.

"I lent Funly that big trophy," whispered Stinky. "Filled it with flowers to brighten up that dreadful basement."

"You want me to go get it?"

"Oh hoo," said Stinky. "He melted it down. Some higher cause."

Well the only thing to do was to go face Big Dick in the trophy room, which really was quite a place, filled with great gold and silver cups on wood bases with any various number of golden athletic forms atop many of them, frozen into myriads of stretching and running and leaping poses and multifarious activities involving sticks or balls or both, and amidst all that, of course, flowers of every imaginable kind and hue, and of course all the walls were mirrored and each trophy had its own individual spotlight popping up to highlight it, except right at the very middle where once stood the great silver bowl that the mayor of Erie gave to Stinky Jinx on TV to acknowledge Stinky's unsurpassable gifts to the worlds of sports and fashion there was now a big lit up nothing with a mirror reflecting nothing.

"Why Dad," said Stinky when we came into the trophy room, "you're on the floor."

"Guuh," said Big Dick. He was pointing vaguely into the air, but you had to figure he was pointing at that blank spot.

"I suppose I should have rearranged," said Stinky.

"Glaaaalg!" said Big Dick. Now he was clutching his chest and he looked kind of too red and too pale both at the same time.

"I don't think this is a pork rind problem," I said to Stinky. I'd seen too many experiments in my day, not to recognize one when I saw it.

But by this time all the commotion had brought Big Dick's wife and Stinky's mother, Pat Jinx, into the trophy room from out in the living room where she'd already got off the phone to the hospital.

"I told him," said Pat Jinx.

Big Dick's eyes started to bulge.

"This happened to his father when Big Dick married me instead of becoming an Eagle Scout," said Pat Jinx.

Big Dick began to shudder; his tongue came out but it didn't look like itself, it looked more like a burned omelet.

"Now stop it!" said Pat Jinx.

Well somehow that seemed to do it; something burst inside Big Dick and then most of the red drained out of his skin. His tongue went three quarters of the way back in and he said, "phlrrrlt." If I can recall, not that I'm very successful at recollection, when Neda did this she was a lot more poetic and it added something; I'd have to remember that when I conducted my own experiments, not that I had any more poetic instincts than Big Dick, maybe I'd have to save some of that garbage money and hire an epitathologist.

"Now Dad," said Stinky. "You can't just spaz out every time one of these silly trophies goes missing."

"Get it back," whispered Big Dick.

"The paramedics will be here in a minute," said Pat.

"You can't enjoy what's here if you're dead," said Stinky.

"I don't care if I'm dead," said Big Dick. "Get it back."

"Funly melted it down," I told him. It might have been like hitting ants with hot dogs but I'd come to believe that information was the soul of every situation, and the closer to the truth, the more irrelevant.

"Get another one," said Big Dick, his breath fading. "Win the Olympics."

"*Some*body is going to have to drive that potato chip truck!" said Stinky.

"Pat can drive the truck," choked Big Dick.

"Oh you think so," said Pat.

That's when the paramedics came in and wrapped Big Dick in a big white sheet with just his head sticking out, which I suppose was a good sign, that they left his head out.

"Go to LA," said Big Dick as they wheeled him out to the ambulance. "Win the Olympics."

"Not while my own Dad is flat on his back," said Stinky. "There's a family to support here."

Big Dick yelled out of the ambulance, "I'll call the Lakers. They'll trade a draft pick for you!"

"Have you seen their uniforms?" said Pat Jinx.

"Hooo! Right!" said Stinky. "Purple and gold! That went out with the Empire!"

Pat Jinx left with the ambulance and I went back in the house with Stinky and helped him throw away all the brochures.

"I think the Olympics are in Mexico next time," I said to Stinky.

"Well *ole!* to that," said Stinky Jinx.

∿∿∿∿ And of the Holy Ghosts

Autumn Refrain

ONE GOOD THING about being awake all the time was that I was never asleep, not that I had any fear of being unconscious, I would have been happy to be unconscious, but any time you went to sleep you always woke up somewhere, then you spent the night knocking yourself in and out of any number of places until you got back to someplace you recognized, not that you were happy to be there, it was just familiar and you settled for it; so then you were back where you started. Not that I found stasis disquieting or unsatisfying, after all, I was a garbage man, I didn't see any reason to put up a fight to stay where I was; being stuck in your ways is as much a struggle as anything else.

This is what I told Willie.

"You have always wanted to end up somewhere," said Willie. He had a scant beard now and his hair looked like a very intimate sponge family. He'd also taken to wearing wire rim glasses and a white lab coat with black nylon knee socks, though he still wore high tops, one black and one white. You might think it was eccentric and you might not.

"Somewhere else," I said.

"Maybe it has somefin to do wif your melanin."

"I'm just thinking because I'm human," I told him. "So I've got to think about something."

"Maybe it is the opposite or neither," said Willie. "To be or not to be. It is not about you, it is about the verb."

Lately talking to Willie was like talking to the inside of a boxing glove, it was crazy, but it was better than talking to the outside.

"Finkin is fear, wifout the *is*," said Willie. He went to the tool box and dropped some pellets in the hookah. "One does not live in the life or in the dream, but in the metaphor. But is metaphor illusion? What is the illusion, finity or infinity?"

"Affinity," I said.

"You see," said Willie, "you are better already."

Well I knew there was a razor somewhere amidst those fine hairs of tautology and simplicity, and it could probably cut you to shreds and explode you into little bits, probably would have been the best thing for me, too, that's why I just shut up and took the hookah stem.

"One of these days," I said to Willie, "I am going to go to sleep."

"Fis is almost inevitable," said Willie.

So I spent the day there in Willie's attic before heading down to Razio's bar on the West Side where I met the rest of my garbage crew; I was with a regular crew now, in the first few weeks they always stuck you with some crew that was a week behind in some tough area of town and saw how long you'd handle twelve hours a night of hauling slop on raw shoulders before quitting for a more intelligent occupation like Welfare. If you made it through that you started substituting on regular crews, which wasn't a whole lot better because people didn't get sick on easy nights. After that, if you still didn't quit, you got to substitute for guys who went on vacation and that's when you realized that some garbage routes were cleaner and shorter than others, particularly if you were working an Italian truck.

When it came right down to it there were two kinds of trucks and two kinds of crews working garbage in Erie, Pennsylvania, but it broke down to only one kind of difference; there were Polish trucks and Italian trucks and you couldn't get a goddamn job collecting garbage in that town unless you were one or the other; I had to put right on my application that I was Polish, because it was obvious I wasn't a wop, though you wouldn't believe how many different races of people went into the Mayor's office for those jobs, because that's where you had to apply for them, right to the Mayor, and said they were Italian or Polish, because if you weren't one of those you might as well have been a grape or a foghorn; even given that, I had to pull every one of Helen's connections to verify that Bush really did ship over to America on a boat and scrub floors in the rectory of Holy Rosary, the Polish Cathedral of Erie, Pennsylvania just to get an interview, and the dago that interviewed me was no slouch either, you had to know your *kieshka* from your fucking *guamki* or you weren't going to convince her. That's how I got hired on a trial basis, because there was a lot of suspicion about my name being Loop and Red being German and most of all not Catholic, they just didn't have much luck with protestants in the garbage corps, it wasn't a matter of prejudice, it was a matter of induction from past experience. The darker races didn't like collecting garbage either and by not giving them the job you saved them that repetitive process of self discovery.

But I was lucky. There was a shortage of dagos and Polacks that summer. I applied, and there was a pocket of Italian Lutherans in town, so they took a risk on me.

So when I finally got crewed, which was a big step, getting crewed was a lot like going tenure track from what I can gather from what Helen said about Marycrest, I got crewed on a Polish truck, which meant, unlike the Italians, we got a dump truck instead of one of the new compactors that you just loaded at hip level at the back and it crushed up all the garbage for you, which had particular bearing for me because stomping the garbage on the top of the dump truck was my job and it was good to know there was a machine out there doing the thing you hated. The Italian trucks also started at ten at night and were done before we showed up for work at 2:30 in the morning because they got short routes in middle class neighborhoods, which were the good kinds, the two bad kinds being the poor ones and the rich ones because poor people had cans full of fish and corn and watermelon rinds which were sloppy and heavy, besides their cans usually being in lousy shape, and the rich had too much garbage, they shouldn't have even used garbage cans they should have used garages, but I guess the garages were already full. Of course you know what trucks got those two kinds of neighborhoods.

My opinion about all that being, who gives a shit. We still spent most our time between routes, riding in the truck or watching the garbage burn in the incinerator or drinking coffee with cream and sugar, and once I got crewed the Head of Garbage gave me a brand new garbage can because like all the novices I smashed my first one to shit on the first night and within a week it drooled garbage all over me; it's important to be delicate with your garbage can; and now that I had a regular truck I could memorize the route and know which houses to go to and if the garbage collectee wasn't some kind of nut who hid his garbage every week I knew where the clotheslines would be and what hole the dog was coming out of and whether or not to expect exotic mammals in the garbage cans and approximately how much of what kind of garbage would be waiting for me when I got there; there was something to be said for it, it was non-dualistic.

So around 2 A.M. I drove the Falcon down to Razio's to catch last call and pick up the rest of the crew who'd been drinking there all night, which consisted of the driver and captain, Fatty Schlosky, who only *only* drove the truck and told everybody what to do and never ever touched any garbage and looked like he'd spent a few too many weeks on the island of the mushroom people, and Zippy Freeburg who had a dead Polish mother and who as far as I could gather was the only non-Catholic collecting garbage in Erie, Pennsylvania, not counting myself who permitted my implicit affiliation with the *One True Church* so I could get the job. Both those guys were in their late fifties and had been collecting garbage all their lives.

"This is a lousy job," said Zippy. He looked a lot like a bald eagle without the feathers. "You like this job, Loop? I bet you don't like this job."

"You find any dead babies tonight, don't tell me," said Fatty Schlosky. "If some chick comes out and wants to fuck, you tell me, but don't tell me about any dead babies."

"This job's okay," I told Zippy.

"You only say that because you do most the work," said Zippy.

"That's right, try sitting on your ass all night," said Fatty.

One thing about those two guys, they said true stuff and meant the opposite.

"You get old," said Zippy, "and you have to avoid work. Avoiding work is hard."

"Yeah," said Fatty, "don't get into the habit of avoiding work, because it's too hard."

In general they were an honest and subtle pair, particularly at rest. When you got them in motion they had their other conversation, which started that night, as it did most nights, somewhere into the middle of the first load when I had to get in the back of the truck and start stomping down the garbage.

"You do that real good," said Zippy. When I stomped garbage everybody else got to take a break from avoiding work because you couldn't drive the truck with me up there precariously balanced on fish heads, that would be unsafe, and you couldn't expect Zippy to be hauling garbage out of back yards while I wasn't, that would be unfair; dialectically speaking, I was the fulcrum of modicum up there.

"Yeah," said Fatty. "You do that so pretty I could fuck you."

"You couldn't fuck anything," said Zippy.

"Nothing will fuck me," said Fatty.

"This is shit work," said Zippy. "We got to go on strike."

"The Italians will never strike," said Fatty.

"They're avoiding more work than we are," said Zippy. "They'll strike."

"They run everything already," said Fatty.

"You just have to make them think it's their idea," said Zippy.

"They get laid on their garbage routes," said Fatty. "They'll never do it."

"I'd do it," said Zippy. "In the thirties I was a Socialist."

"In the thirties I got laid all the time," said Fatty.

"You going to strike with us, Loop?" said Zippy.

"When's the last time you got laid?" said Fatty.

"I'm on strike from getting laid," I said.

"You're just a nutty kid," said Fatty.

"Wait till you get old," said Zippy.

"I *have* to wait," I said.

"I hate this fuckin job," said Zippy.

"Why don't you work at the foundry," said Fatty, "I hear those guys get laid all the time at the foundry."

"I'm old and I got to work a fuckin job like this," said Zippy.

"Cunt and piss," said Fatty.

And that's the way it went, we had that conversation about sixty-seven thousand times a night, it had a vacuous and despicable comfort to it, like watching an empty train yard.

Well that was the night we worked two slum routes before moving up to Glenwood where, just like the contours of that ritzy place, we started on the outside where the garbage was plentiful but at least sensible, and spiraled our way into the pit of ritziness where planets worth of garbage were stored at the backs of yards filled with tennis courts and patios and swimming pools and glass bubble domed outdoor whirl pool baths; the only thing you didn't find stuck in their garbage was Egyptian slaves. But the stroll to the garbage in those places could be scenic and relaxing; it stirred in me the kind of vicarious sensuality of an empty amusement park and reminded me of my days up in Glenwood when my intentions weren't so virtuous and banal. People of this type tended to keep their yards well lit and usually kept their dogs in the house, in fact it was so alienating to think about the absence of the dogs it almost ruined the absence of the dogs. Of course once you got to the garbage pile you could spend sixteen hours getting all the garbage out to the curb.

And as fate would have it, one of the places I got to collect garbage, about halfway into that spiral up in Glenwood, was Bobby Hansen's. Somehow or another our lives were mysteriously intertwined. I noticed those Hansens hadn't built any ramps or anything on the outside of their house, and when I peeked inside, as I often did, feeling as though I were on intimate terms with the place, I noticed they didn't have any electrical chair lifts or any other such kind of Bobby Hansen support equipment either. No, Bobby Hansen had returned from the vegetable world once and he could do it again. Off to the side of the kitchen those Hansens had turned a little side room into Bobby Hansen's bedroom, and on my way back to the garbage I liked to peer in there where Bobby Hansen lay in his dawn bed, eyes wide, living the life of the mind. I'd tap on his window to get his attention and share a few moments with him. I'd tell him, through that window, about his neighbors' yards and his neighbors' garbage, because one thing for certain, neither before nor between nor after his fatal accidents, Bobby Hansen had never worked a day in his life.

Bobby Hansen, you are a metaphor for one kind of life, and I am a metaphor for another. That's what I told him. Together we were a mixed metaphor of tricks, a sad bag.

Bobby Hansen's eyes shifted and he watched me through the window like I was some kind of ring worm. "I am your garbage man, Bobby Hansen," I told him. "I am your garbage man."

After Bobby Hansen's it was all down hill. We worked our way to the center of the spiral where Zippy and Fatty left me off at a castle that along with its tennis courts and swimming pools had a driveway filled with multiples of vehicles with foreign names and a garage about the size of a small motel. In back of that was the garbage, packed in several dozen eight foot high plastic cans, that was the latest modernity up there in Glenwood garbage, plastic cans, quieter and harder to break. Of course nobody up there knew how to pack a garbage can so I could pack several of those polyurethanoliths into my metal can simply by pouring them in a little at a time and then getting on top and stepping on it. Then I'd transfer the rest into one or two of their big cans that I already emptied and haul all that out to the curb. Using that method at most places I could fit about several tons of garbage into two cans and haul everything out in one trip, one can on each shoulder, but these people had too much garbage and their garbage cans were too big. It took several trips to get all their shit out of there and sometimes that could take a half an hour or an hour depending, not that it mattered anyway because that was my last stop and while I was back there Fatty and Zippy went off and finished up the rest of the route which usually took a peculiarly long amount of time, sometimes as much as a couple hours, I guess it was their private time together. Sometimes I spent up to an hour and a half just waiting there on the curb outside that house, sitting in the center of Sodom with the garbage, because I knew, I had plenty of time to look through that trash and what wasn't empty booze bottles was the kind of waste material that would move lesser Dialecticians to envy; besides, you can't squash a booze bottle and weren't allowed to break them, so I had to separate them into their own a plastic can, which took time and perusal.

That's what I was doing back there when I got interrupted.

"Mr. Garbageman," somebody said.

And I said, "Yes?" but I did not look up, it is senseless to look up when one is perusing garbage.

"Could you help me with something?"

"I doubt I could help you with something or anything," I said. I was studying a California cabernet that was best served after two to eight years of storage and at the time it struck me as an interesting concept Neda used to store Mars Bars; I *was* wondering about storing things and eating them later and its implications for waste.

"Listen," she said, because inside that plastic garbage can I could still recognize that the voice was female, "I think this pertains to garbage."

"It has to do directly with garbage, "I said, "Pertinence isn't strong enough. Contrary to what some people might think," I said getting out of the can, "garbage is a deductive field."

I suppose I was supposed to be stunned by what I saw because that's the kind of look she had on her face; she was tall and kind of slender and muscly at the same time; she had on some kind of long pink silky thing, television bed clothes, not the kind of thing you'd see at Sears, her hair red wavy brown and she had some freckles; in fact she was young, younger than me, her eyes were very blue and she had very full lips, and it was those lips that were pushed out just slightly in a way that made me think I was supposed to be stunned, in the set of those lips were many and varied scenarios and I, myself, was not much one for the scenarios.

"You got more garbage somewhere?" I said.

"In the house," she said.

"We don't go in the houses and choose garbage," I told her. "It requires too much discrimination."

"Just help me move some things out," she said.

"Someday," I told her, "people are going to have to take their garbage to the curbs themselves. We won't have to go back in the yards and search for the garbage. And there will be great trucks driven by remote control, with robot arms that pick up the garbage and put it inside and crush it into jet fuel."

Well she didn't seem to have too much to say about that, so I told her something else.

"Garbage collectors won't have to work," I said. "Garbage collectors will only think the words of collection and transformation. Garbage collectors will think the words to fuel rocket ships." I don't why, maybe I was stunned by my own realizations, a victim of my own words, but all that almost brought a tear to my eye. I barely choked out that last little bit about the rocket ships, and I could see she was touched.

"Listen," she said, "I have a dolly in the basement. Help me move this stuff out and then you can keep the dolly back here for the garbage cans."

"I would prefer a forklift," I told her

But she just turned toward the house and I followed her, because there was something about her that was conducive to following, in fact she probably could have just walked out there and tapped me on the shoulder and I'd have followed her in there; fate is character, that's what I told myself.

"I'll separate out the booze bottles from now on," she said.

"Don't fuck with the garbage," I said to her. "I like the garbage the way it is."

So I went in there and helped her cart stuff out of that labyrinth; coffee tables, easy chairs, stuffed animals, tennis rackets, record albums, couches, put all that stuff out on the curb with the rest of the garbage that I went back and got with the dolly. When I got done my wealthy friend gave me a thermos of martinis.

"My husband's a professional soccer player on tour," she said. "I'm going to remodel."

"My wife is a professional dead person," I said, and waited for Fatty and Zippy in an easy chair with my thermos of martinis.

"Help me put these statues away," said Helen.

That place was havoc. It was hard to conjecture, because the facts were too blatant, but it looked like those holy artifacts had broken into Helen's Mogen-David. There were a lot of open bottles around and a lot of statues flat on their noses. That holy room table was stripped of its pads and its extensions were out, there was a net across the middle and Ping Pong paddles and balls all over the holy room; up by the Infant there was a tiny line score card and it looked like St. Christopher had rubbed out Our Lady of Guadalupe in three sets. Usually when I came by in the morning while Helen was getting ready for work and before Red and everybody else got up, I had to put a few statues back in the holy room and pick up a few Buckhorn potato chip bags from in front of the Zenith, but this was the first time I'd walked in on a debacle.

"Helen," I said, gathering up several versions of the Blessed Virgin, "this isn't normal behavior."

"On the part of whom," said Helen. "Certainly not on my part."

More often than not you had to realize that Helen was piloting a different kind of vehicle and all she had with the rest of us was radio contact.

"It's been a long time since Red blew up last," I said.

"He's big," said Helen, filling a plastic bag with empty Mogen-David bottles, "but there are a lot of these little guys. And Red's not as young as he used to be." She gave me the trash bag.

But I gave it back. "I'm off duty," I said.

So Helen took those bottles out herself, waited at the back door for Honky, that furry land shark, to hit the house a few times, let him open his maw once or twice, which pretty much covered the whole back door, then stepped out and calmed him down. That Honky dog was a giant, and when those jaws of his opened up at the back window you thought you were living in a mouth, but around Helen he was just a cup of warm milk. You'd think if she could handle a monster like that and run a college she could handle a few thousand inanimate statues, but not all parts of all circles intersect, that's simple enough to understand.

That house-ramming must have woke people up because I could hear Red thundering around upstairs and in a few minutes the Visitor came flumbling into the holy room wearing too many very large clothes.

"You got to learn that pile system," I told the Viz. "You got the little pile with the little clothes, it's pretty simple."

"Dad!" said the Viz.

"That's right," I said, "I'm your dad."

"You thought that pile system was intuitive," said Helen as she came back in, "but it's not."

"Just keep the statues out of our room," I said.

Honky's huge maw opened against the holy room back window and for a minute it got dark in there.

"Dad!" said the Viz.

"That's not your dad," I said. "I'm your dad."

"He knows who you are," said Helen.

"Dad!" said the Viz to Helen.

"You're living in a semantic Dad plenum," I told the Viz.

"He'll straighten out eventually," said Helen "Or he won't."

"He's genetically intransitive," said Neda, coming into the holy room. She looked like the last beautiful thing on earth. She had a build like a DNA molecule, hair the color of the sky just after sunset, skin like lit neon. Her eyes drove through a room like a Ferrari with blue head-lights. "If I recall, Kara Ruzci had a fascination with duplicating and then altering visual imagery. Though you don't offer an ostensible pretext of artistic mediation, you nurture an almost Parminedean tenacity for denial. In your quiet way you are constantly holding forth, a Bartleby the Scrivener of the inner eye. Don't you think the dog should be fed?"

"Dad!" said the Viz to Neda.

"That's right," said Neda. "I'm your dad."

Well the trick around there was knowing when your bell got rung, which you couldn't always hear over the din.

That's when those two ding-dong brothers, Joseph and Andrew, came in.

"You're wearing my shirt," Joseph said to me.

"No, I'm not," I said.

"He's wearing my shirt," said Andrew.

"Who is?"

"All I know is, somebody's wearing my shirt," said Joseph.

"Dads!" said the Viz.

"Those are my pants," said Andrew to the Viz.

"Looks like there's a little identity problem up in that pit," said Helen.

"Dad!" said the Viz to his pants.

That's when Red barged into that holy room with a baseball bat.

"The next time one of these god-damn things move," said Red, "I'm gonna blast it."

I think he was talking about the statues.

"I feel sick," said Helen.

"You can't be sick," said Red.

"I think I'm too ill to work," said Helen.

"You can't be sick," said Red.

"At this point," said Neda, "your statements are simply illocutionary and speculative. Let's defer escalation and feed the dog."

Red raised the bat a little and gave Neda a good long snarl. I don't know what happened while he was thundering around in his sleep, but it looked like he woke up in the old days.

"Your father thrives on immediate escalation," said Helen.

"It's all I got," said Red. "I use it."

Well you had to hand it to Red, he'd spent a lot of time thinking in the past few years so he could stay the same.

"Dad!" said the Viz to Red.

"I'm not your goddamn dad," said Red, though he said it to me not the Viz.

Andrew was taking my pants off and Joseph was taking off my shirt.

"You better teach your kid the pile system," said Andrew, "or we're going to spend a lot of time like this."

"Dads!" said the Viz in our direction.

"He's zeroing in," said Joseph.

"He gets me right every time," I said.

"Call into school for me Neda and tell them I'm sick," said Helen.

"Don't get sick," Red said to Helen very calmly. "You've used up all your sick."

"I'm sick for a very special reason," said Helen.

"You throw up easy," said Red.

By that time Joseph and Andrew had all my clothes off and were out of there. Neda was on the phone.

Red peered cautiously around the room. He looked real close at every one of those statues. His nose quivered. "This place smells like decay," said Red.

"I don't smell anything," I said.

"You ought to get that fixed," said Red. "Somebody could fix that."

"Who?" said Helen. "A doctor?"

Red rested the ball bat on the floor, handle down, and looked slowly around the room again, then he went out, got his tie from the closet where he kept it on a hook, tied it very precisely, then put on his suit jacket. Then he reached in there and got his door catalogue and bowling ball and went out to the Studebaker Rainbow.

Helen held her stomach. "I'm going to have to tell him tonight," she said to me.

"Tell him after I go to work."

"No," said Helen, "I want everybody here. The more bodies he has to maneuver his way around the better."

        ॐ   ॐ   ॐ

Well who knew what Neda'd been up to since she finished high school. Unlike her days when she was a fat genius hated by everyone yet managed to fix every class election and every award so she became class president and *May Queen* and *Catholic Girl of the Year* just to spite everybody; she graduated having won every award in the world history of high school and turned them all down; the only one she probably might have taken was the science fair award she would have got for that rocket and space capsule that launched Funly, but Funly ruined that when he hijacked it. Neda didn't apply to any colleges, though one day Helen came home from Marycrest and got it in her head that Neda should apply for a scholarship to the Cleveland School of Art and Design and spent the night filling out the forms and signing papers right and left, and even writing clear, concise affirmative essays that Neda herself would never have penned saying how bad Neda wanted to go there, though the problem was that you had to send in some sample art work and that was the one thing Helen couldn't do, Neda had to do that.

Of course Neda never did any art and didn't want to go to the Cleveland School of Art and Design so she spent the week painting and sculpting and inventing multifarious contradictions of space in clay and on canvas and then taking slides of it all and giving it to Helen to accompany the application. This was the mind of Neda, when that scholarship came she was going to take it.

That was a big campaign for Helen. Way back before World War II Red turned down a scholarship to the Cleveland School of Art and Design so he could go to work at the Forge and pay for Grandpa Whitey and Grandma Emma Loop's house, which they no longer owned, they gave it to Uncle Bif and Aunt Jelly who never paid a cent for it and now Whitey and Emma lived in a little room at the back, and Helen turned down her scholarship to Villa Maria College so she could marry Red, so I think Helen saw this as some big important kind of destiny and eventual righting of imbalances, Helen still being very big on the way the world evened itself out.

And insensitive as I was to psychological subtleties, I nonetheless noticed that Helen hadn't bothered to pass that torch to her oldest son, not that I hadn't supplied reason enough, but you had to hand it to Helen, unlike a lot of mothers, she used the reasons. Between Red trying to kill me half my life and Helen ignoring me most of it, I might have got the impression I was unloved if I hadn't known better, based, of course, on reasonless assumptions and no evidence; a lot of religions had done more with less. But the facts were that I loved Helen but Helen loved Neda who didn't love her back, which is the stuff of great stories if not, on occasion, real life.

So the Infant had been on a bad streak and Helen was turning down the screws. Since he got Kennedy elected and stopped World War III, things had turned. Kennedy was a corpse now and that little chubby loving Pope John XXIII was dead too, not to mention Kara Ruzci. Somewhere buried underneath all this was Helen's original and mysterious pact with the Lord which resonated tremendously for her in that interstice between the phenomenal and less phenomenal, though the only result we saw, other than Helen's claimed influence on world events, was that Helen never ate candy. And on the bottom of that buried stuff, there was Red who the Infant was supposed to have converted to Catholicism years ago, running around more Lutheran than Luther, a blithe heathen blithe in his stasis. The only good thing about that trench war was it kept Helen too occupied to notice her kids were godless. So the Infant's ass was on the line. He hadn't done dick in a decade, or at least a half-decade, and if he didn't come through Helen was going to melt him down. She launched into three consecutive triptychs of novenas, the last of the nine ending on the twenty-seventh night which was the eve of the day that she and Neda were to hear from the Cleveland School of Art and Design.

Helen lit the holy room up like a stadium. She was so busy in front of the Infant she barely had any time to spend buried under all the junk in the basement. She pulled out all her relics and holy items and made all the other statues stand or kneel facing the Infant of Prague up there on top his box on the ugly dish cabinet arabesque at the back of the holy room. Helen got out her medals, her rosaries, her scapulars, she brought in blessed candles, she ate holy sausage. She got on the hotline to the

Infant's mother. It was a campaign of tremendous proportions, so tremendous that on one occasion even Neda noticed.

"I think he really wants me out of the house," said Neda.

Well it was either that or love.

The night before Neda's scholarship notification was due, because we all knew Neda should get a scholarship and not just get admitted, Helen stayed up all night in front of the Infant, completing the last prayers of the last rosary of the last novena which would all end as the sun came up over Celebration Avenue. Then Helen would get everybody up and get ready for work and when she came home Neda'd be standing there like Dorothy in Kansas with her scholarship from the Cleveland School of Art and Design. But that's not what happened. Helen fell asleep in front of the Infant and I guess some of those myriads of candles or maybe one of them must have overflowed its wax and the fire followed it down and pretty soon the holy room was on fire, Helen sleeping underneath the flames like St. Theresa and the Infant presiding over the inferno like Vincent Price. We'd all be dead if Red hadn't smelled the smoke and come down stairs and put the whole business away with the garden hose and wet blankets. Then the next day Neda got rejected from the Cleveland School of Art and Design.

You'd think a catastrophe like that would have caused some changes, but it didn't. Red never said a word about any of it ever. What he did that night was heroic and if he did something heroic then automatically he couldn't talk about it, it was part of Red's heroic code, so the whole thing slipped through a crack in the world, gone as dawn. And Neda, being a genius, knew that being a genius was exactly what kept her from getting into the Cleveland School of Art and Design, otherwise she wouldn't have gone along with any it of this in the first place. And of course Helen knew all that too, that's why she took it to the Infant. No doubt about it, Helen didn't waste her prayers on petty concerns, she wanted a miracle. She took off every little bit of the Infant's garments, right down to his little ceramic bare butt, and made him stand in the corner. Come to think of it, that's when the discipline in there among those other holy replicas started to break down.

Now me and Neda were both out of high school and living at home, though I'd at least made an attempt to get out of there and I did have a job. Right at the moment we had time to kill while Helen waited for Red to come home from work so she could *tell* him what she had to tell him, in her mysterious way waiting for the precise day that Red, after years of relative composure, woke up with a ball bat in his fist. Still, you could spend a lot of time in that house talking to everybody and go years without having talked to anybody, people just kind of threw their conversation into the morass and waited for the monsters to show up. I hadn't really talked to Neda since she took me out to the Old Maid's Field and told me where to stick the *Armada*, though at the time she told me it was the last thing she was ever going to do for me, as if that was doing something; but her being so omniscient and me being so capricious, I believed her; what did I care about talking to Neda anyways, it was like the obtuse massaging the oblique. But Helen was upstairs puking and we were waiting for Red to come home and blow up the house and it felt like old times.

"Come with me," said Neda.

And we went across the street to Dean and Tina Danger's, but we didn't go in the Danger's door which was on the left, we went in the door on the right and up the narrow hallway of stairs to Angela and Rafael Corona's where Neda knocked and a woman's voice yelled back and we went in.

If there was one thing you could say about that neighborhood, you could say it had a contagion of interiority. That apartment looked like you folded up Brazil and put it in a parrot's cage.

That place was full of snake plants and pineapple plants and creeping vines and palm trees, there were coleuses and philodendrons, orchids and geraniums, spider plants and flowering sicalilia, along the walls, silvery creeping gangloim; floating down from the ceiling as if suspended in air, huge Jupiter tertenalia; you'd have thought you were in a giant terrarium if it wasn't for the animals.

Underneath all that foliage things were moving around. There were lots of chameleons and several Iguana, huge unclassifiable rodents, cats the size of snowshoes. Occasionally, packs of furry little dogs woofled through the underbrush and skirted your feet. In the air and on lamps and perches and hanging upside down from chandeliers, a million birds of a million colors; canaries and wrens, doves and cockatoos, parakeets, makaws, storks, cranes and, of course, parrots.

In the center of that room was a woman who you had to infer was Angela Corona, because the only Corona you ever saw outside was Rafael when he left for work or went out on that second story porch to feed the two or three parrots they let out there at a time. Angela Corona looked like a Puerto Rican Grandma Emma Loop, her skin a little darker, her eyes a little browner, her face e little flatter at the chin. She had hands like fat starfish dressed to kill. She looked pretty relaxed there playing with her cards at a card table, but already I could see that she liked to sigh a lot and every time she did she relaxed a little more, looked like any minute now she was going to disappear underneath her own pile of clothes. Around her she kept various accouterments of what I guess was fortune telling, lots of card decks, animal bones, palm charts, sky charts, zodiac charts, and a big globe with an electric cord coming out of it, had a little on-off switch on the cord and right now it was off. Me and Neda went and sat down on the other side of the coffee table from Angela Corona.

"You got a lot of nice animals and plants here," I said.

"In the future," said Angela, "I will be here taking care of it."

Neda lit a Pall Mall. "Rafael's a microbiologist," she said.

"A Ph.D.," said Angela, laying down a card. "In the future I will remain married to him."

Well I could see that Angela Corona had a real grip on the future. I looked over at Neda and she blew smoke and looked back at me, and then I looked at Angela Corona and she looked up and looked back at me.

"Neda likes to come here and smoke cigarettes," said Angela.

Neda puffed, exhaled, then paused. "That's true," she said.

"In the future, if you would like to come, it will be okay with me," Angela said.

Angela Corona kept playing cards and Neda looked off into space. I looked all around at the vegetation and the hanging parrots. I looked at those two. You'd think, seeing as I was there, there'd be a reason for me being there, especially since, after all, Neda brought me.

Angela Corona inspected the cards in front of her. "I will make a dinner tonight," said Angela Corona. "Later, I will bathe. During dinner," she put down another card and looked up at me, "I will kiss Rafael."

Neda took her flask from her purse and poured herself a double shot, then poured one for me. Angela was drinking port wine. Neda lit a cigarette.

"She knows everything about you," said Neda. "She knows your wife is dead. She knows you're a garbageman who never sleeps. She knows your only son calls everything 'Dad'."

"And how does she know this stuff?" I said.

"I told her," said Neda.

"A bird corroborated," said Angela Corona.

"A bird," I said.

"Yes," said Angela.

"Knowledge proceeds from geometrical points which have no form, no substance, no extension. They are intercise," said Neda.

Angela Corona put down an ace of hearts.

"Of lines. Of the histories of the histories of lives, objects, events," Neda said. "Reality emerging from substanceless, timeless points."

"Look," said Angela Corona, "a two of spades. So in the near future, I will probably like you."

"It's a system of spontaneous co-origination," said Neda. "Leaving traces of nonoriginary originals. We don't recover, we create."

"Birds can see the points," Angela Corona said.

"Birds eat them," I said.

"Maybe," said Angela Corona. "Who cares?"

"Action is a form of speech without language," said Neda.

"Illusion," said Angela Corona. "Who cares?"

"Maybe the Buddhists," I said.

"That's a good one," said Neda. "The points explode."

"The birds eat the points like corn curls," I said.

"You're not as dumb as you look," said Neda.

So that's when we went into the next room which pretty much looked like the last room except there was about a third of it curtained off. In that curtained off section, that's where Crow was. He had a waterfall bird bath in there, a stash of corn curls, his very own cushioned divan. He took a good look at me with one eye, then turned his head and gave me a good look with the other. Then he looked at Neda. "Gotta cigarette?" he said.

Neda gave him one and lit it.

"You're not going to say hello to me?" I said to Crow.

"Talk's cheap," said Crow.

"Why don't you go back to Karl?" I said to him. "He misses you."

"Why don't you go back to Karl?" said Crow. "He misses you."

Crow could say the same thing you said with a different meaning or no meaning at all.

"Deaf," said Crow. He took a long drag on the cigarette and blew out his beak holes.

"It's dangerous work and shitty pay," said Neda. "He's got it good here."

Angela Corona put out her hand and Crow rubbed his face on it like a cat. "He is a smart bird," said Angela. "But he is a bird."

"God I bless ya," said Crow. He pulled a box of chocolates from underneath the divan and gave one to Neda and one to Angela Corona. "Sweets for sweets," said Crow.

"The only sentience on the block who knows how to treat a woman," said Neda.

So Crow survived *The End of the World*, as did me and Karl, as well as Funly, and it looked like the only ones who didn't was that Cuban invasion fleet. You might have thought a bird would have more loyalty, but I guess Crow'd just grown too old for guns; he never got along with Karl that well anyways. Now he was collecting nonoriginary space-time intercise for Angela Corona so she could foretell in her cards what she was going to do later that day. But he could have been friendlier, I stuck up for him when birds weren't so popular in that neighborhood.

We left Crow and went back into the other jungle.

"You tell anybody anything other than about yourself?" I said to Angela Corona.

"You're making a specious distinction," said Neda.

"Here," said Angela Corona, "hold this globe up to your face."

She handed me the globe and I held it.

"Closer," she said.

"How close?"

"Up to your face."

Well I did, I put that thing right up to my nose but all it looked like was an unlit, opaque plastic bubble, until she turned the thing on. It was a globe of the earth.

"What do you see?" said Angela Corona.

I saw Cuba. "Cuba," I said.

"Let me see," said Angela Corona, and she took the lit globe and held it up to her nose in the same position I did. "I, too, see Cuba."

Down in Funly's basement, Funly and Stinky were melting down Stinky's trophies to make an outer shell for Funly's submarine. They had some kind of double boiler hooked up on top the Funster furnace and a chute that led down from there into a mold. Stinky, the fastest being in Erie, Pennsylvania, if not the world, made lightning trips from Funly's basement to his trophy room and back again, a ribbon of gold, trophied light. "Hoo-hoo!" said Stinky's voice from somewhere on that light path. And somewhere else, upstairs, Mosha Funster sat blasting in her tuba, *oompa, oompa, oompa, oompa.* Funly barely looked up from his melting or smelting or whatever he was doing, he just jerked his head towards his wall chart of Lake Erie, Lake Ontario, and the St. Lawrence Seaway.

"If I don't try it myself I'll never know," said Funly.

"He can't go wrong with *this* one," said Stinky, appearing at the basement door with an armful of track trophies. "He has to succeed to fail, and if he fails he proves his point!" Stinky was as devoted as ever to Funly and who the hell knew why. He was as cynical about Funly as anybody could be, but he'd do anything to spend time with him, including melting down all his trophies so Funly could submarine out the St. Lawrence Seaway.

"What's Big Dick going to say when he gets out of the hospital?" I asked them.

"Oh, " said Stinky, "we'll simply replace them with *plastic!*"

"That's it," said Funly. "Plastic." Those months in space really didn't do much for him, he was skinnier than ever and it looked like his flat-top, which was a little long and disheveled, was going gray; he looked like a fuzzy dumpling on a broom stick.

By now I was over in the other part of the basement booking at the cockpit of that submarine. I could see where the radio system was just a copy of what Funly already had down there before his space flight, but the rest of that instrumentation looked pretty complex, and as far as I knew, nobody ever did go back and retrieve that space capsule out of the lake.

"Isn't technology wonderful?" Stinky whispered to me.

"Yeah," I said. "Who built this for you?" I said to Funly.

"Why Neda, who else?" said Stinky.

"Neda?"

"Who else?" said Neda.

"You didn't learn from last time?"

"I learned plenty," said Neda.

"This time I got control," said Funly. "I could park this in Brezhnev's garage."

"I hope you do," said Neda. You had to hand it to Neda, she'd become a more tactful being, and no less omniscient; helping Funly build that submarine was like God letting you miss Mass on Sunday. It got a little quiet in that basement for a minute while Funly grunted at his smelting factory and Stinky went off hooting for more trophies. Upstairs, you could hear Mosha Funster marching around on her little chubby tromping Funster feet, her tuba going, *oompa-pa, oompa-pa*.

Stinky was back with a stack of golden football figurines.

"Hoo-hoo!" said Stinky to Neda. "Meet me at the rink?"

"Eight o'clock," said Neda.

"I want nuclear capability in this tin can," said Funly.

"I'll think about it," said Neda.

"Nuclear capability or ice skating?" I said.

"I want nuclear capability in the potato chip truck!" said Stinky. "Can you imagine?"

"Figure skating?" I said to Neda.

Neda lit a Pall Mall and broke out her flask. "It calms me," said Neda. "Want to join us? Or do you need a drink?"

Well if somewhere out there in space, like on the moon, there was a way to take pictures of the earth, then sometimes you'd have to drink all day to keep your continent in front of the camera. I had a drink with Neda and then Funly dragged everybody over to his map of Lake Erie, Lake Ontario, and the St. Lawrence Seaway.

"I just got to time the locks," said Funly. "I'll slip through underneath a ship."

"Notice," I said, pointing at the Niagara River. "See anything there?"

"A nice place to honeymoon!" said Stinky.

"If a Cuban can get down it, I can get up it," said Funly.

"He can bore through," said Neda, "or go around. If the French can portage, Cubans can portage."

"They put canvas over the subs, dressed like gypsies, put back in on the other side of Buffalo," said Funly.

"A submarine and a freighter can't share one of those locks," I said.

Funly handed me an encyclopedia article that said a young inventor named Lodner Phillips from Marine City, Indiana had launched a home-made submarine in Lake Erie, to search for hidden treasure, in 1853.

"It sunk, Funly."

"What the hell do you know," said Funly. That was the maddest I'd seem him since that afternoon before Jimbo shot me. He reached inside his coat, and fingered the handle of his .38. I guess he felt a lot of pressure, with Granpa Funster in jail and Jimbo going soft, to do something important and brave, anti-communist, patriotic and idiotic. He started to sweat. He looked like a worn out toothbrush. But I guess I was just in a bad mood.

"Listen Funly," I said. "The Cubans didn't come down the St. Lawrence Seaway in submarines. They didn't come down in anything. They didn't come down at all. There weren't any goddamn Cubans in the lake ever and there wasn't any invasion. I know that and Neda knows that, anybody knows that."

"Oh yeah?" said Funly.

"Yeah," I said.

"The whole city and the whole Coast Guard's lying," said Funly.

"That's right," I said.

Funly looked at Neda. It got pretty quiet but for that *oompa-pa, oompa-pa* of Moshe Funster upstairs and then Stinky, gazing slightly skyward and softly whispering, "hoo-hoo-hooo!"

Neda looked at me with eyes narrowed, eyelids half-closed, that old look she used to get about twelve minutes after her last Mars Bar. "Stinky," said Neda, "go get Mosha and bring her down here with her tuba."

Well it was hard to know who was arguing for what, must have been the state of the art, you just got your weapons out and fuck the issues. Mosha Funster was down there in the basement now with her chubby little feet and head, and lips that reminded you of the Appalachian Mountains in motion, because she wasn't too happy about her tuba getting absconded to prove that Funly could or couldn't drive his submarine through the Niagara Falls and up the canals and out the St. Lawrence Seaway. I don't even know why Funly wanted to do it, because he had to know it was impossible, so why bother and why fail, or why succeed. So why tell him he couldn't do it? But Neda, that unmoved mover, had Funly pretty much convinced that submarining out the St. Lawrence Seaway would be as easy as crawling through Mosha Funster's tuba.

"Hoo-hooo!" said Stinky Jinx. "You can't crawl through a tuba!"

"That's right," said Funly to Neda. "You can't crawl through a tuba."

"You can," said Neda. "There are biblical precedents."

Mosha Funster sat down and folded her hands on her belly, she looked a little gray, like you'd imagine a brand new baby elephant.

"Please," said Mosha Funster, "don't stick Funly in my tuba."

Well anywhere else in the world that discussion would have ended sometime before the allusion to biblical precedents, that is camels crawling through the eyes of needles, but we all knew there were rich people in heaven, in fact they probably owned it.

Stinky placed a hand on Funly's shoulder. "Funly, I really don't think you can crawl through a tuba!"

Funly sneered.

"What we perceive as phenomena," said Neda, "is a network of coterminous points in concentric sheaths from which our perceptions themselves are inseparable, so to us, within the cone, perception enunciates itself as a mere icon or intelligibility, subsequently we create patterns and destiny, or closer, patterns create us and we sense destiny. It's a matter of alignment," Neda said to Funly. "You can understand that, can't you?"

"Yeah," said Funly. "Sure." He looked real hard at that tuba like he felt some kind of kindred yearning, that long flat-top of his looking like it wanted to paint the ceiling. "So?"

"So if you want to do something," said Neda. "Do it."

"Hoo-hooo!" said Stinky Jinx. "I just really don't think you can crawl through a tuba!" You had to hand it to Stinky, he really had a bead on this one.

Funly put that tuba on its side and looked in. He looked pretty skinny, but that tuba had lots of curves, especially near the end where the mouthpiece was, and there at the tip it was a pretty tight fit. Looking at it you might think it was impossible. But Neda'd built Funly that rocket, and she built that space capsule, kept Funly alive up in space for months, in fact if he wasn't such a coward he could have come down whenever he wanted, but even as it was, even though he'd hijacked the damn thing, took a ride that was supposed to be for a different kind of rodent, she brought him down in Lake Erie and even had me and Karl right there to pick him up. And even if you couldn't ride that submarine out the St. Lawrence Seaway, still, she'd built it, and you knew if Neda built it, it was going to work, in fact, even though the Cubans didn't come down the St. Lawrence Seaway, that Funly probably would get out it only made sense. Neda was a genius and it was plain as day that Funly was going to crawl through that tuba.

"Please don't stick Funly in my tuba," said Mosha Funster.

Well that's all it took. Funly was in that tuba like a bat out of hell. His head went in, then his shoulders disappeared. That looked about as far as anyone could fit, but Funly kept heading in and in no time he was in as deep as his waist. He gave a little flutter kick and went in another half foot. He pushed off with his toes and went in up to his knees. He had to start wriggling now, because you had to figure it was getting to be a pretty tight fit, but soon enough he was up to his ankles and in a minute or two only his feet were left. Then there was a little grunt from inside that horn and Funly was gone.

You had to figure Funly'd already traversed the impossible and it was just a matter of time before he slithered out the other end, but it got pretty quiet in that horn. We waited a little while and then Stinky went up and gave it a little knock.

"Funly!" said Stinky.

"Just a minute," said Funly.

There was another grunt and then you could see one of Funly's fingers, then a few of those Funly flat-top paint brush hairs sticking out. There was a tremendous groan. That tuba shook. Then those fingers and hairs disappeared. It got quiet again.

"I'm stuck," said Funly from somewhere in that horn.

"What Funly?" said Stinky.

"I'm stuck."

And Neda nowhere to be found.

છ   છ   છ

I thought maybe I'd pick up the Viz and head over to Willie's, but Karl caught me in front of the house.

"Come on," he said, "Help me run the dogs."

"You don't run your dogs." Maybe he just needed a reminder. He kept wolf-dog Einstein in the back amidst the weeds, place was so overgrown that all you saw back there was that giant dog head moving around like a brown moon on the horizon, though our side wasn't much better, you couldn't mow with Honky back there, in fact you'd have thought there was just a peculiar wind wending through that yard if he didn't occasionally launch himself skyward like a white rocket; that dog was the most concentrated amount of reasonless behavior ever accumulated on the earth. Anyway, you couldn't pry those two out of those yards with a crow bar, you'd have a better chance of getting the yard than the dog. The rest of what Karl had that you could identify as dogs didn't take walks, they lived on the porch roof, in fact by this time there had to be generations of them up there, some of them so untouched by human intent they were close to noumenal.

"Well then let's go for a ride," said Karl.

"Okay," I said, "just a minute," and went in and checked out the Viz who sat in the bathroom where Helen squatted in front of the toilet, her eyes hollow like dark ancient bongos.

"Dad," said the Viz.

"That's right," I said. "I'm your dad."

"He can stay with me," said Helen.

Seeing Helen there on the bathroom floor must have flushed the toilet of my unconscious. A low fluteful voice rose inside me as I thought about Helen looking like death and talking about being pregnant. There were enough graves and wombs, enough for all the world, more than the whole world could hold.

I went into the pit and got Polly Doggerel who was sleeping on what I figured to be the clean pile of clothes. She was wearing a T-shirt and a pair of the Viz's jeans.

"You got to learn this pile system," I said to Polly Doggerel, stripping off those clothes. Then we went out and got in Karl's truck.

This time we headed out toward the West side, a pretty quiet ride down through the downtown and out the West side industrial district past all those factories with the names of people who lived up in Glenwood like Halden and Sydney and Lovell and Grant and of course Strong, and even out past the Erie Forge where Red got his first adult job, and out past the Bucyrus Erie where Karl worked when one of his hands or arms wasn't smashed to shit from some industrial accident, and down past the American Sterilizer and Carson Lumber and then down past the sewage plant to the Erie Bay where we drove by all the bayfront mansions with their giant towers built on top the third stories so their owners could look out off the cliffs and over the bay and Peninsula to the lake and beyond to Canada; I imagine if you got your binoculars out you could watch the deer feed on Presque Isle, or see somebody picking somebody's pocket in London, Canada. We went by driveways full of Ferraris and Porches and motor boats and catamarans. I might have thought it a pretty circuitous route if I thought we were going anywhere. All this time Karl said nothing and I said nothing; the only sound in that truck other than the motor being an occasional yawn from Polly Doggerel underneath which you could distinctly hear the enunciation of "want a hot dog." It was one of Karl's idea trips. He'd drive me around until I got the idea.

Karl headed south again until we hit the Erie International Airport, international because they had a charter flight once a month to Toronto, and we parked behind a fence somewhere off the main runway and drank Jim Beam with Koehler Beer and watched the private planes come in, little Cessnas and Piper Cubs, some twin engine jobs, an occasional propjet. Those things came in and out of private garages and then men in three piece suits and every once in a while a woman with a scarf or a hat got on or off, sipping champagne or cocktails and pressing themselves merrily against the wind.

Then we drove down toward the lake again, through some deserted farms and finally off the road completely and through a patch of woods and into a field that ended abruptly on a cliff that overlooked the lake, looked like somebody used to try to grow grapes up there because there was lots of grapevine wreckage, old pieces of grape trestle and wire; Polly Doggerel got out of the truck and went for a swim. She didn't float much anymore but she was still an agile little creature and managed to just kind of run down the cliff without coming off, hit that little beach at the bottom at about a forty-five degree angle and bounded into the lake. I wouldn't have minded a swim myself but I couldn't negotiate the cliff. It was a good early fall day I noticed, the sun and sky both warm and pale.

Me and Karl shared a drink and then he said, "Come over here," and I followed him into a stand of trees where there was a small cave; Karl went in there and came out a few seconds later tugging something on the end of a rope, looked something like a badly-constructed balsa wood cow. Then he unfolded it, first the tail section, then the wings, looked like he was setting up a tent, but in a few minutes there it was, an airplane. It was kind of blotchy thing, silver and blue in different places depending from where you looked.

"Camouflage," said Karl.

"It flies?"

"If it has to."

I ran my hand on the body. The skin of that plane felt like a dry fish.

"Neda?" I said.

"Who else?" said Karl. "She helped a little. He walked over and patted the nose of the plane just behind the propeller.

"Cannon goes here," he said. "Lots of people taking junkets to New York, Toronto, Detroit." He came over to me rubbing that mutilated right hand of his. He had a scar on his forearm that looked like a ladder. "Bought yourself that lunch bucket yet?"

Well I told Karl I wasn't interested. Garbage had been very good to me. Though the issue wasn't really economic, nor even moral. I was convinced by then that I didn't even think my own thoughts. They thought me. And where they came from who knew? So morality was irrelevant. The issue of choice was a dualism I'd split long ago. I'd just come to realize, while I was gazing at that airplane, that my life was operating amidst some kind of presence, or maybe even presences, it was hard to determine because I didn't want to think about it, and every time I turned around it felt like I was walking on a stage, some ambiance imbued with prescience, like I was somebody else's process of discovery, like somebody was trying to make me conscious against my will. Not that I took it personal, that's what I told Willie.

"If you become Existential," said Willie, "fis will be a long haul."

"A long hall with no doors," said Revis.

"Don't no exit me," I said. "There are too many doors and everybody's inviting me in."

"They are inviting you out," said Raymon. "Through the doors which are not there."

Revco looked at me and stuck out his bottom lip.

"The Dialecticians are contemplating the draft," said Willie. Unlike Willie, himself, who hadn't been to school for years, and me who got escorted out, those other Dialecticians had, with great stealth, managed to flunk their way into high school. But I guess somebody finally noticed they'd been in there for almost a decade and decided to graduate them on out of there whether they wanted to or not. Unfortunately it was a very bad time to get nudged out of high school if you weren't a classifiable invalid like Willie, himself, or irresponsible for a family, like me.

"It is the big door and the big draft," said Revis.

"And the Dialecticians are not interested in divesting the Asians from their selfhoods," said Raymon.

Well you had to hand it to those Dialecticians, they could brood with the best of them. It got me thinking about everybody else in that neighborhood. You probably couldn't draft somebody who was stuck inside a tuba, but now that Stinky wasn't going to college, they might try to draft him. Then Joseph and Andrew would be getting out of high school.

"Maybe Helen can pull some strings and get everybody in college," I told those Dialecticians.

Revco raised an eyebrow.

Willie closed his tool box and put it under his pillow. I noticed he didn't keep his hammer next to him anymore, though when I tried to think when was the last time I saw it, I couldn't remember, it could have been years.

"We are changing the nature of fis experiment," Willie said. "I fink maybe it is time to hold the frog to the fire."

I wasn't in the best of moods when I got back to the house. Those other Dialecticians had the time to let their fowl get cold, time to experiment, but I had to go to work, and not before seeing Helen through the greatest crisis since she went out and got a job. I'd been through several of these changes in experiments and trusted Willie completely, I just didn't always listen to him, in fact the more I thought about it, I hardly ever listened to anybody, and most the trouble I got into had to do with something I could have avoided if I listened; maybe I was a born follower who refused to follow; maybe I had to open up my senses and listen more; maybe when Angela Corona said "Cuba" she meant "tuba" but there wasn't just a tuba on that globe; a consonant here or a vowel there could mean everything.

But I had to work for a living and deaf was the only thing close to sleep I got, so maybe I'd just string out my stash till the experiment got changed back again. Up there in the pile system each of us had our more or less one and only untouchable pile and at the moment that was a very important pile to me.

Before I went in I gave Polly Doggerel a dollar for hamburgers, no sense having a young dog witness carnage. Inside, Helen was out of the bathroom and gathering up statues in a laundry basket to take back into the holy room.

"You should just get them little ball bats and let them fend for themselves," I told her.

"They're not the saints themselves," said Helen. "They're just effigies. They wouldn't have a chance."

"Maybe we should just take them to the zoo and turn them loose."

"They're too little for the zoo," said Helen, I noticed she had all the shades down and I followed her around the house as she snuck up to every one and then lifted it just a little at the edge so she could peek outside.

"He's probably going to come through the front door like he always does," I said.

Helen glanced at me sidelong. We were in the kitchen and she was keeping an eye on the Jinxes' house across the driveway. "You're father is no dummy."

That might have been true and might not, but God bless Red for his intellect because you had to look at him and look at Helen and find your own incisive wit in the admixture, a good argument for emergent characteristics if you asked Neda, but Red's intellect was not usually what you had to deal with, except that maybe you didn't want to give that intelligence of his the impression you were outsmarting it, in that sense you had to deal with it, because if Red thought you were being smarter than him then he might exercise his right to destroy you; you had to hand it to Red, he could hold that card and he could play it.

"It's not safe here," said Helen. She circled the holy room, peering out the edges of shades, bracing herself for the house battering we got when Honky caught her peeking out the back. "It's not safe."

"It's never been safe."

"I'm thinking of the baby," said Helen.

"Don't worry, Helen," I told her. "There's no past, there's no future, the individual is dead."

"There's only one way to live," Helen answered me, "whether you're an atheist, the devil, or Christ, and that's like you could be dead tomorrow." Helen went into the kitchen and to the kitchen window, peeked out. "You're going to have a baby sister. And they're going to try to kill us."

"They?" I said. "Who's they?"

In the front room my other sister, Neda, the already born, was with my only son.

"Who am I?" said Neda to the Viz.

"My Dad!" said the Viz.

"That's right," said Neda. "I'm your dad."

"Go upstairs and get your brothers," Helen said to me, going to the front window. "When your father gets home I want bodies."

I was on my way up there anyway, where Joseph sat in the center of the Pile System like the Buddha in shutdown, one hand over his good ear, the other holding a pair of Jockey shorts that Andrew tugged on.

"You're needed downstairs," I said.

"You're wearing my shirt!" said Andrew.

"No, you're wearing my shirt," said Joseph.

"You're wearing my pants!" said Andrew.

"No, you're wearing my pants," said Joseph.

"How can he hear you?" I said.

"He's been in everybody's piles," said Andrew. "He has no regard for order."

"The Pile System is dead," said Joseph. "Gone. The Pile System is detonated."

"Who's been in my special pile?" I said. My special pile over in the corner beside the mattress that I never used had been tampered with, in fact it wasn't even a pile anymore; my deaf wasn't there, my camera wasn't there, my gun wasn't there.

"Neda," said Joseph.

"Neda?" I said.

Andrew hit the wall with his fist and took out a pretty good chunk; he packed a pretty good wallop for a blue kid with a receding hairline. "Neda wasn't in your pile, he was in your pile. He's gone nuts. He doesn't care about anything anymore."

"The Pile System was a myth," said Joseph. "A fabrication. It never existed."

"It was a functioning myth!" screamed Andrew. "It brought reason and order to chaos!"

"It wasn't very orderly," I reminded him.

"The Pile System was not a system," said Joseph. "It was a *nada* system."

"Its existence is verified by our noticing its absence," said Andrew, going about the room and putting clothes back in piles. "Without the pile system there's no material cross referencing for this room's intersubjectivity. We might as well be dogs or babies or little statues."

I guess all those years of talking to the dead had an effect on Andrew after all, if nothing else, keeping what little those two brothers of mine had in common, in common. But ever since that big Franky Gorky let down some Bush's Last Christmases ago, Andrew'd pretty much given up on the dead as a preadolescent fascination; in general they were as boring as anybody else only deader, and it was pretty obvious that as little as you might have done when you were alive, you had even less to do after you died. Of course he was bonded in some way to Helen, we all knew that because Helen always told us, though that didn't mean they always got along; ever since Andrew cured Bobby Hansen Helen expected more and more from him, and I guess Andrew learned that you don't get people off your back by doing things for them and he hadn't done anything for Helen since. Of course Andrew wouldn't be alive, and probably certainly not blue, if it wasn't for Helen, and Helen would be dead if Andrew hadn't come along to let her discover how the doctor almost killed her when she had Joseph. You just can't unwrap that kind of stuff and expect it to dance. Joseph was beautiful and spent a lot of his time ignoring people admire him, but Andrew was blue, and I guess he redirected the rigor of his mysticism into the Pile System; unbeknownst to us, Andrew had been the architect of an evolutionary anarchy so subtle we'd have thought it didn't exist had we bothered to notice the misimpression of its absence.

All that aside, they were still tugging on those Jockey shorts.

"These are mine!" said Andrew.

"I'm sorry to have to tell you this," said Joseph, "but these are mine."

It was a pity to see that once mystical union come to this, though I had to admit, that Pile System, whether it existed or not, had made me realize that the fewer clothes, the fewer piles, and the fewer piles the less discernment, thus I'd stopped wearing underwear and good thing, otherwise I'd probably been in there tugging with the two of them.

Joseph let go of those jockey shorts and Andrew went out the open front window on the wings of the momentum.

"The Pile System is defenestrated," said Joseph.

By the time Andrew got back in, Joseph was transferring what was left of the Pile System out the front window and into the street.

Andrew picked up a pair of corduroys I'd never seen on anybody.

"Are these yours?" said Andrew.

"Why yes," said Joseph, "I believe they are."

Andrew threw them out the window. And that's the way it went for the next ten minutes, those two politely asking each other what was whose and each claiming it and the other defenestrating it, like Chip and Dale. It might have gone on for weeks until that whole place was cleaned out except that those clothes started coming back up. We went out on the porch roof and there was Red, about knee deep in the ex-Pile System.

Red didn't say anything, but that pile system got rapidly refenestrated; it was a good thing it was a soft system because Red didn't hold back long or much pitching it back on the porch roof, in fact just looking at a T-shirt you wouldn't think somebody could knock you down with it from twenty feet away, which just goes to show the worthlessness of both facts and common sense. When Red got done he picked up his brief case and bowling ball and door catalogue and came in.

Downstairs Helen was already on the couch under that afghan she'd been knitting for Bush's Last Christmas since World War II. Red was roving, bowling ball bouncing on fingertips like a beach ball. Red was looking for statues but those statues weren't coming out, looked like they had a little more sense than half the people they were statues of who'd ended up martyrs. By the time Red got back to the front room we were all in there, Joseph and Andrew on the couch next to Helen, where she liked them, Neda on the radiator, and me standing in the archway to the next room. Red sat down in his chair next to the Zenith and popped that bowling ball, caught it on his index finger, spun it, spun it across each of his other fingers, then popped it again. The place was pretty quiet but for the thudding of Honky against the back of the house, something you probably wouldn't have noticed unless it stopped. The house went, wonk, wonk. Helen looked at Red and Red looked at Helen; it felt a lot like sitting inside a nuclear warhead.

"The Studebaker is getting pretty old," said Helen.

Red flipped the bowling ball to his left hand on the other side of the chair without even flicking his wrist. "It was new when I bought it," he said. Which was 1951, before they stopped making them.

Helen snuggled a little deeper into her afghan. She said, "The house needs painted."

A little ripple passed through Red's muscles and he let the bowling ball slip into his palm. His shoulders rose, then went down again. "We going to eat tonight?" he said.

"Do you know what I'd really like?" said Helen, "I'd like to learn to play the piano. It a would be nice to have a piano in here. I'd like to take piano lessons. The house needs music. I'd like to fill this house with music," said Helen.

"Piano music," said Red.

"Yes," said Helen.

Red squinted. He looked around the room. He looked at Joseph and Andrew, he looked at Neda, he looked at me. He looked back over his shoulder at the picture of St. Joseph with his hand on the boy Jesus who stood on St. Joseph's carpentry table. They both had halos. Then he looked across the room above the couch at the two angel baby pictures; each angel baby facing the other with hands folded and tiny white wings sprouting out their pale blue night gowns. Inside that Red head of his that was now thinning a little at the crown and graying slightly at the sides, he was trying to crack the *prima facie*, but that wasn't the kind of stuff Red cracked; Red cracked trees and houses and refrigerators, and if he had to, men. Red was a volcanic planet and it would be years before he'd be able to support any of the more subtle organisms. He lowered his gaze and looked at Helen.

"I'm going to have a baby," said Helen.

Red's jaw clenched and the bowling ball trembled under his grip. "A baby," said Red.

"Yes," said Helen. "I'm pregnant."

Red stood. He transferred the bowling ball to his right hand, his chest expanding like a sun. His skin turned a shade darker and the freckles on his forearms grew together. He looked around the room, pumping the bowling ball.

He turned and walked out, took a long look inside the holy room, then picked up the phone in his left hand and ordered two large pepperoni pizzas. He put down the phone. "I'm going to need some help with those pizzas," he said to me.

I hadn't been alone in an automobile with Red since I was a little kid sometime before Helen bought the Infant of Prague and manifested her religiosity in long knock-down drag-outs designed to save Red from hell. Back then I thought Helen held all the cards and Red was a goner, went so far as to make a pact with the Lord that the devil could have my soul instead of Red's so Red could go to heaven, told Red about it one Saturday morning on the way downtown to buy me a special pair of wide shoes because I had a high instep and triple-E width, like Red, and my toes had decided to reinvent my foot by lining up vertically, I told Red about trading my soul for his and Red looked at me like I was some kind of aberrant cupcake filling; I guess, unbeknownst to me, I'd pretty much admitted that I thought he was hell bound. He said something to me like, well, maybe we'll be lucky and both end up there, which wasn't really in my plans, my plan was to get Red off the hook and then get let off myself for being so self-sacrificing, though even then I knew that God, being all-knowing and all-present, knew I figured that, and seeing as I knew he knew, even a deathbed repentance was precluded unless I didn't plan one, but I already had. By that point I was looking over at Red and thinking I'd made a big mistake. He probably did belong in hell and we'd both end up there. By that point I was starting to think that hell might not be so bad if I didn't have to deal with Red eternally trying to kill me, though Red must have thought it through too because he never let me in that car alone with him again. Red and I'd had maybe three conversations in our whole lives.

Number four was on deck.

We got in the Studebaker Rainbow and took a right on German, into the darker parts of the ghetto, took another right onto 21st Street which was now half burned down lots and half two story shacks, and came out on Celebration Avenue where there was an old Italian bar named Barfoni's run by the family of South High's basketball coach, big fat Barry Barfoni, except no Italians went there anymore, everybody in there eating pizza and meatball sandwiches and spaghetti was drinking Schlitz Malt Liquor and Old English 800; there weren't many Chianti drinkers in that crowd. But we weren't in there yet. Red parked outside the place and we just sat there. "That pizza won't be ready yet," said Red. He put his right wrist over the top of the steering wheel and leaned his left elbow on the door. He rubbed his chin.

Now I'd pretty much given up talking to Red, convinced by the last three times, but at least I wasn't afraid of him so much anymore. After I got married he stopped trying to kill me, and after Kara Ruzci died Red's violence took a pretty big plunge in general, a good example being me sitting outside Barfoni's with him waiting for pizza instead of running for cover back at the house while he threw the kitchen stove through the back wall. Though as I thought of it there, I didn't know what the hell we were supposed to be afraid of anyway; I suppose Red reacted poorly to any change whatsoever, and Helen was always a good barometer of that, but why would Red care if Helen was pregnant, it would put Helen back in the house where he thought she belonged, though it would cut her salary for a while, but that would make Red the breadwinner again, add another kid, and he liked kids, it was Helen who didn't really like kids. I guess there was enough ambivalence in all that to make Red crazy, but it didn't.

"You like collecting garbage?" said Red.

"It's okay."

"You like it?"

"It's okay."

"You going to collect garbage all your life?"

"I don't know."

Red looked at me. "You ought to get educated. You could do it. You're not stupid. You could do something."

"I'm doing something."

Red looked out the front window again. "You could learn something," he said.

"I know plenty."

"You think you know," said Red. "You always think you know and then you find out you don't."

"We're having a big talk," I told him.

"That's right," said Red. He looked at me again. "Your kid calls everything 'Dad.'"

"I know that," I said.

"You know how to fix that?" said Red. "You just smack him till he gets it right."

"I don't care if he calls everything 'Dad,'" I said.

"Sometimes you have to hit people," said Red, "It's a sad thing but it works."

"I don't care," I said.

"Right," said Red. "You don't care." He was staring out that front windshield again, out and down into the depths Celebration Avenue where some part of his life used to be.

"You don't sleep," said Red.

"That's true," I said. "Let's get that pizza."

"It ain't ready yet," said Red. For a moment he put the side of his head against the driver's window, then he lifted it again. "I get thinking done here."

"And you're thinking about having another kid."

"Your mother can't have another kid. What you think that operation was about. She ain't a woman anymore."

Red sure had a delicate way of stating things. I guess I forgot about that operation Helen had after Andrew was born and before *The Year of Two Hundred Books*. And she did stop having babies after that, as well as change her behavior some; she started building that holy room and eventually got a job, though you could hardly say she wasn't a woman anymore. But those two were in each other so deep you couldn't get one out of the other without killing them both.

"That operation ruined her," said Red. "Let's get that pizza."

We picked up some Pepsi and went home where we saw Helen peeking out from the side of the front shade, she dropped it when she saw us, and we went in and ate pizza and drank Pepsi and turned on the TV which nobody watched, especially Red who sat next to it as usual. Neda showed the Viz his pizza and asked him what it was and he said, "That's my dad!" and Neda said, "That's right, the pizza is your dad," and then Red took the Viz and threw him in the air and caught him a thousand times and then put lampshades on the both of them and then held him upside down with one hand and tickled him with the other. Then Red got out his guitar. He put the Viz on his lap between his stomach and the guitar. He played "Rudolph the Red Nosed Reindeer" and "Taking Mary Home"; he played "When Jimmy Rogers Said Good-bye," "There's a Star Spangled Banner Flying Some-where," and some song that sounded like "*El Rancho Grande*," as far as anybody including Red could figure because nobody spoke Spanish but Neda and Red wasn't speaking it.

The Viz laughed and clapped and banged on the top of the guitar and even grabbed the strings, but that didn't bother Red, he had more strength in a finger than the Viz had in his whole self and just played right through him. Every once in a while Red looked over at me like he was the only father who ever existed in the whole world. Then Red played "The Yellow Rose of Texas" and looked at Helen. He squinted as he sang and I swear I saw moisture at the corners of his eyes. He played "You Are My Sunshine" and Helen put her hand on her belly like the day I told her I was going to marry Kara Ruzci; Helen put her hand on her belly and said, "It's a good thing he loves kids so much." She said it softly to the air, you wouldn't have heard it if you weren't watching her close like I was, and I don't even know who it was to, God I guess, good old God; Helen put both hands on her stomach and looked to heaven. That was the first time I ever thought there might be something wrong with Helen.

That night, before work, I went out and got myself a lunch buck-et, a nice silver lunch bucket that went with the blue of my work clothes, a pretty silver lunch bucket with a bottom like a casket and a top like a belly.

It was a week later and Fatty and Zippy were talking about getting laid and going on strike; I was in the back of the truck stomping garbage.

"You do that pretty good, Loop," said Zippy.

"Thank you."

"You do that so good I could fuck you," said Fatty.

"You like doin that, Loop?" Zippy said to me. "You like stomping garbage?"

"I like it okay," I said.

"I couldn't do it, I'm too old, I couldn't stomp that shit like you do," said Zippy.

"Then it's a good thing I do it," I said to him.

"Yeah," said Fatty, "it's a fuckin good thing. But if you didn't, you know what?"

"You'd find somebody else."

"That's right," said Fatty.

"Nobody should have to work like this," said Zippy, sitting down on the curb. "It's hard and inhuman."

"In the future," I said to him, "great machines will come out of the sky like golden ash trays. They'll dissolve the garbage with particle beams and absorb it into themselves. Garbage men will be at the controls, thinking the words of dissolution and absorption. Garbagemen will be the poets of the disposable society. Garbage will fuel intergalactic travel. Garbagemen will feed the stars."

"We should get laid more," said Fatty. "If you work like this you should get laid."

"We got to strike," said Zippy. "Where would this town be without garbagemen?"

"Corporations would gain control of the garbage," I said. "They'd build their own ships. We'd be on the outs."

"They'd find somebody else to do it," said Fatty.

"Nobody else'd do this," said Zippy.

"That's tautological," I told him.

"We could demand what we wanted. We'd get some time off," said Zippy.

"We could get laid," said Fatty.

"We don't have a Union," I told them. "It's against the law."

"Fuck the law," said Zippy.

"I could fuck my sister-in-law," said Fatty.

"It could come down to guns," said Zippy. "We'd be on the news."

"You ever been in a gun fight, Zippy?" I asked him.

"We ain't going to get in a gun fight," said Zippy.

"We can't even get laid," said Fatty. "How we going to get in a gun fight?"

I finished stomping the garbage and we went back to work until the back of the truck got full and we had to have that conversation again. Then we finished the first route and went and had some cream and sugar with some coffee in it at a place across from the stadium that gave us free donuts if we illegally took their trash and garbage, that meant more stomping and more conversation, before we dumped the load at the incinerator where I got to sit over the pit with my empty lunch bucket and watch all that potential rocket fuel burn in the pit of hell. I sat there trying to remember the last time I slept and thinking that everything was certainly a metaphor for everything else. Then it was back to work. We ran the next slum route, had that conversation a few more dozen times, had cream and sugar with a little coffee and free donuts at a place where we picked up trash illegally, then dumped that load and headed for Glenwood.

Where I got to have my weekly visit with Bobby Hansen who, it seemed, had taken a turn for the worse. He didn't even have his eyes open when I got there and he was hooked up to machines and bottles. He looked a long way from another comeback, I even had to knock on the window to get his eyelids to flutter, though when he did open those eyes he looked like he was holding oceans in there instead of brains, if there was any life in there you had to imagine it or wait for it to break water. It was intimidating, because there were ways in which I felt responsible for Bobby Hansen; he made me think crazy; he roosted anachronistic ontologies in my coop. One minute, long ago, Bobby Hansen was going to wring my neck, and the next minute he was a vegetable. The world had worked its machinations around me a million times and there I was, looking in his window, collecting his garbage, a pantheon of ghosts waiting for me to fall asleep. But I wasn't in jail. I didn't even feel like I should be in jail.

After that I got left off by Fatty and Zippy at the castle where there was a dolly waiting for me back by the garbage and everything was already sorted out into separate cans; wine bottles in one can, booze in another, paper in a third, soft garbage in a fourth; there was a fifth can filled with various paraphernalia, exotic bottles, waterpipe stems, hypos, tubes, spray guns, capsules, nitro tanks, whip cream cans, seltzer modules, ether rags; it was the best of the cans. Of course having everything already separated ruined the rationale of perusal, but I had a lot of time and perusal doesn't always need a rationale. I dallied in the booze can, trying to keep track of all the different kinds of scotches and how long they were aged, because this aging thing had sparked something in me. I noticed over in the soft garbage that they aged cheese and some smoked meats too, seemed to be a European habit, and wondered whether I should try to memorize the bourbons or move on to the wines; wines looked like they could really occupy you. I was saving the drug can for last, thinking maybe I'd take a few specimens to show Willie, when I got interrupted.

"You don't have to work with the empties," she said. She was wearing something similar to the week before, rather sparse and silky, though this time it only came down to above her knees and was baby blue.

I, myself, was sitting amidst all that garbage, which I'd emptied onto the lawn, feet folded underneath my butt, empty scotch bottles lined up on the right side, a line of bourbons starting on the left.

"I do have to work with the empties," I said.

"Not exclusively."

I sat there examining a bottle of Jack Daniels, stuff had been aged seven years, in oak.

"I don't put out the garbage for you to study it," she said. "And I separated it so you wouldn't have to."

Well she studied me, too, and that wasn't why I was there either.

I looked up at her from underneath the brim of my denim garbage hat. I had to tilt my head pretty far back. "I bought myself a lunch bucket," I told her, "and I keep it empty. Emptiness is empty too." I don't know what it was about her, but it looked like she had the power to pour me. I tried to remind myself just then that she was a woman and that my tendency to regard everyone as simply human often blurred certain essential distinctions.

"Nihilist, huh?"

"That's empty too," I said.

"Well come inside and help me move some stuff."

This woman was no dipshit, that's the only reason I went in there, where it was warm as a lamb. I hadn't really noticed that it was a cool night until I got in that house. In the living room, or one of them anyway, out of which I'd moved most of the stuff I moved for her last week, a fire crackled in the fireplace, and in the center of the room, built into the floor, sat a big square bubbling tub. Fast work.

"Couldn't have been done without you," said my friend who, even though it was a lot warmer in there than it was in the yard, had put on a robe. "You want a drink?" she said.

I yawned. I couldn't remember the last time I'd yawned.

"Sit down," she said. "We'll have a drink, then you can help me."

So I sat down near the tub in a cushioned chair that looked like a horseshoe and in a few minutes she brought out a couple of orange drinks in glasses that looked like bubbles. You had to stick your whole head in the glass to get a sip, and when I did, that stuff was so warm and beautifully pungent I almost smelled it. We sat there real quiet, staring over the steam of that hot tub and into the fire; I crossed my legs and put my drink on my knee like my uncles did at Christmas; I rubbed my chin with my other hand; I looked over at that young woman, who I was starting to notice happened to be beautiful, but she wasn't looking at me, she was looking at the fire. I was wondering how the other people who serviced this place got treated. I was thinking everybody should treat their service people this good, there'd be less resentment.

"So how's soccer season?" I asked her.

"What soccer season?"

"Your husband's soccer season."

"I don't know anything about soccer," she said. "Besides, he doesn't play soccer. He's a surfer. I get the two mixed up."

Well I could understand that, they both started with "s" and had their consonants and vowels in the same places. They both required too much footwork.

"He's Chilean," she said, "He's the Chilean National Champion. He surfs wherever it's surf season."

"It's never surf season here," I said.

"No," she said, "It never is."

She got up pretty quickly, but then just stared into the fire, palm up, drink on her fingertips. Then she walked over to me. It's hard to say, but there was a suggestion in the way her thighs touched, though I couldn't even see them, there was just something in the air that filled me with the way her inner thighs met like angels when she walked.

"What do you want moved?" I said.

She looked down at me, her eyebrows barely furrowing. "I'm re-placing all the couches and refrigerators."

Took me over an hour to get all those couches and refrigerators out of there; some were upstairs, some were down, some were in the basement, though she had an elevator in there so the only tough part was getting them down to the curb. All those refrigerators had auto-matic ice makers. Some were so big you a could camp out in them. If we could've got them on the truck we might've made some money, but I guess she had somebody else picking that stuff up, like the Salvation Army, besides, that stuff was too big and heavy to steal for a profit, it wasn't worth it. When I got done I went back in the back yard and put all the garbage back in the cans and took it out to the curb. Fatty and Stinky weren't back yet so I went up to the front of the house to look for a name on the door or near the door or maybe some old mail, but I couldn't find anything. Of course I had this habit of peering through windows and the next thing I knew I was watching that young woman in her hot tub, not that I planned to catch her in there, you couldn't see anything but bubbles anyway. Then she noticed me.

Usually my cultivated single unmindedness kept me steps ahead of manipulation, but in this case I was dumb. She took a hot tub naked with her window curtains open and I looked. I couldn't stand there waving at her, so the only thing left to do was go back inside.

"You want another drink?" she asked me.

"I got to wait for my truck."

"You have time," she said. When she breathed her breasts emerged from that bubbling water like the undersides of rose petals. She pointed to a cabinet near the fireplace where I found bourbon, Wild Turkey 101, aged eight years, and a small refrigerator for ice.

"I missed one," I said.

She said, "Take it with you when you leave."

I sat back down in that padded horse shoe, watching the aqua bubbles of the tub slide around her, then watching the fire.

"You want to get in?" she said.

"No."

"You want to know who I am."

"I think that sweet drink you gave me was too rich for my stomach," I told her.

"If I gave everything away," she said, turning toward me, "would there be anything left to give?"

Well logic-smogic, I was a Dialectician. "In the future," I told her, "waste will be eternal, immutable. Waste will tick off our mortality in half-lives, the only permanent thing we leave."

"Garbagemen," she said.

"We'll control it. The thoughts of garbagemen will govern the eternal. The thoughts of garbagemen will be the poetry of eternity."

She looked away and worked her lips a little bit, like she was about to receive a kiss. You had to hand it to her, she was smart and rich and beautiful, but sometimes all you get in life is the power to deny and other than that you ain't got shit. I was feeling dangerous things in deep places.

"I got to go," I said.

She nodded slightly at the air. "Put some logs on the fire for me. Please."

I did. It was a nice fire, a deep red orange, old with heat, the kind of fire you could watch for a long time, the kind where you could see peoples lives burning.

"Take the rest of the bottle," she said to me, "and the refrigerator."

So I did, I corked the bottle and unplugged the refrigerator, put it under my arm; I picked up the bottle in my other hand. "My name is Jarvis," I told her.

"Jarvis."

"Loop."

"Okay." She smiled at me. "Okay, Jarvis Loop."

I rested the weight of the little refrigerator on my hip. I said, "So who are you?"

"Do you believe in the devil?" I asked Willie.

"I believe in the metaphor of the devil."

I don't know how his experiments were going since the Dialecticians had once again stopped experimenting with deaf, but his skin had taken on a rather gray hue, in fact if the rest of him weren't there to disconfirm it, you might say he looked an awful lot like a corpse. I, myself, was still nursing my stockpile which Neda found for me underneath the new, though debatably existent, Pile System, so I still maintained a healthy glow. But every once in a while Willie launched a reform movement and halted all the experiments. They were only a raft, and you didn't carry them around with you after you crossed the river. He lay back on his huge pillows, sipping water.

"But what metaphor of the devil for what thing?"

Willie's his eyes shone like dull hub caps. "Nofing. Fings are fings until one finks about them, then they are metaphors. Fis is how one becomes a murderer of angels."

"Why I never sleep."

"Or shoots ghosts on winter nights."

Or become a garbageman, or hear the choir of the dead inside you, like the voice of a dead lover, whispering.

Sometimes Willie was just too ineffable. I preferred to think that stuff just ran in the family.

That Saturday me and Stinky and Funly decided to make one of our visits to the County Jail to see Grandpa Funster, only Funly, of course, was still stuck in that tuba which Stinky wheeled around on top Mosha Funster's little red wagon. He kept that wagon in Big Dick's Buckhorn potato chip truck where Funly now spent most his days helping Stinky keep Big Dick's business operational while Big Dick relaxed in the hospital, the doctors trying to decide how to clean at all that pork rind residue out of his arteries. Stinky was a big hit in all the stores with his talking tuba and a lot of the big stores wanted him to come by on weekends to hand out free cokes and wieners and perform amazing feats like jumping over the Buckhorn potato chip truck while juggling several large cans of Buckhorn popcorn, potato chips, and pretzels while meanwhile his tuba, sitting on a little red wagon yelled hilarious stuff like, "Where's Neda? More soup!" and "Get me outta here!" Big Dick's potato chip business was booming, and good thing because Funly could consume a lot of soup. Funly got to eat a lot of hot Jell-O too, which he didn't like, but Stinky thought it was good for his blood and Funly didn't have a whole lot of choice. Stinky just crammed a tube into the mouthpiece of the tuba, put a funnel on it, and poured. Funly must have done something with it because it never came out the other end, except of course when Stinky had to put that tuba over a bed pan. That was as close as Funly Funster ever came to being a regular guy.

Stinky brought Funly over and set him down in the living room while me and Stinky tried to decide whether to take the Falcon or the potato chip truck down to the jail. In the holy room, Bush and Jon had dropped by for a visit and the two of them were in there with Helen and Red playing pinochle, a new and developing ritual which, like most group activity that happenstanced around there, occurred because of the dipolarity of the ambivalences involved.

Uncle Jon never liked to go anywhere anymore, but he always listened to Bush because she was his mother and besides it ran in that family to think that any moment, let alone Christmas, could be Bush's last moment, and he didn't a want to send her off to a madhouse like ours to cavort with a dangerous killer like Red and then never see her again; he'd never live that down; he'd probably end up in hell for that, besides, during World War II Uncle Jon and his invisible navy became pretty endeared to pinochle and now that he and the men had less to do, being pretty glazed on Thorazine, they needed competition, besides, it just wasn't a three-handed game. Uncle Jon's hands didn't float anymore but he could play pinochle without ever looking up from his cards. His men went around the table and came back and told him what was out and what was in everybody's else's hand. He knew when to bid and when to hold. He knew who had meld and who had dick. He knew everything without ever looking up.

That's why he had Helen for a partner. He wouldn't play with Red because Red had tried to kill him too many times and he couldn't play with Bush because Bush was the best cheater in Erie, Pennsylvania, if not the world; Bush and Jon together would win every bid and every hand; but Helen loved the game out of some love of purity and mathematics and chance and so wouldn't cheat, which offset Jon's omniscience.

Red played because he got to keep an eye on Jon who by himself might do something so dangerous and insane that Red would have to kill him, and of course Red played pinochle like a bull played hopscotch, with a lot of intensity but too many feet, which offset Bush's cheating. I know Neda would have been glad to jump in that bunch, but that would have been like putting three VW's in a phone booth.

Now Bush, she just liked to play pinochle.

And Bush didn't mind Red. Though he was protestant and German and gigantic, he was really the only person in the world who Bush could turn to in a pinch; her sons were worthless, though they did well for themselves, Stanley a head chemist at GE and David with land in California that he bought with the money he got from selling the farm that he bought with the money that Red and Helen lent him and he never paid back; her other daughter, Frances, lived in Detroit and only visited once a year, usually during one of Bush's Last Christmases; she had her cousin Edju in Cleveland but Edju was worse than worthless because be used Bush's money to emigrate to America and set himself up and now he was a rich civil engineer and never gave Bush a penny, not even the money he owed her, besides, he spoke seventeen languages all at once and all poorly, and finally and frankly Bush and Helen weren't all that close. Bush always resented Helen from way back when she was the baby of the family and Grandpa Stanley, Helen's father whose soul was in hell, made Helen his favorite and let her out of chores and gave her puffs of his cigar and sips of his beer and whiskey and sent her to the drug store to play numbers for him and when she came back let her keep the change which Bush had to pry out of Helen so she could get food on the table and give money to the Church. She thought that made Helen spoiled, impractical, and goofy, which Helen proved by going out and marrying a heathen protestant who didn't even go to a college. Bush never got a penny out of any of those kids, not even Helen, and they hardly ever came to visit her and when she needed them they weren't around, except for Jon who was destroyed by World War II and was now nuts; Jon might be there, Jon might always be there, but he was never really around. Things were around Jon.

But Red, well, if Bush needed a ride to the grocery or the doctor she could call him and he'd come and get her, and if she needed and extra buck now and then for sausage or duck's blood, Red had it and gave it, even if he didn't have much, and she could always count on

100 ≈

Red to share whiskey and chocolate with her, she could always count on Red to *bring* whiskey and chocolate when the rest of her no good family who were hardly ever around and never brought her anything scolded her that it was no good for her health which, she had to admit, had deteriorated rapidly over the last sixty years or so. No, Red was the only decent one in the bunch; it was just too bad he was going to hell.

"Where's Neda?" said Funly when we brought him into the living room.

"Hoo!" said Stinky. "Where's Edju? I'd like to play some chess!"

"Let's take the Falcon," I said. "We can put Funly in between us on the front seat."

"Get me outta here!" said Funly Funster.

"Do you want some soup, Funly?" said Stinky.

"There's a message for Funly," Helen said from the holy room. "It's by the phone."

"Knock, knock, Funly," said Stinky.

"Who's there?" said Funly.

"Neda says, 'You'll never steal one of my space ships again.'"

"I promise to never steal another space ship," said Funly.

"Not from inside a tuba you won't!" said Stinky.

"Tell her to fix the submarine controls so I can run it from inside the tuba," said Funly. "I'll need some radar in here. A short wave. Some soup."

"And a can opener?" said Stinky.

"One of those little ones," said Funly.

"Sounds like you got a talking tuba in there," said Bush, making bid with her meld.

"In a manner of speaking," I said.

"There was a time," said Jon, "when that kind of thing wouldn't go unnoticed."

"We've all noticed it, Jon," said Helen. She took the opening trick with an ace of hearts.

"Then it's time again," said Jon.

"Time for more whisky," said Bush.

Helen led a nine and got up. "We're out of whisky," she said.

She went to the window and peeked out, by lifting the side of the shade.

"Red," said Bush.

Red got up and went into the kitchen, coming back with a new bottle of Guckenheimer. "What are you checking?" he said to Helen.

"The neighbors," said Helen.

"The neighbors don't need checking," said Red. "You just checked them a minute ago."

"Everything needs checking," said Jon. "We're human beings and that is why God put us here, to check up on things."

"Red, why don't you check and see if there's more chocolate," said Bush. "God would like it and I would like it." She led a king.

Red got up again, but not without taking a slow hard look around the holy room. He had that ball bat underneath his chair.

"You just checked the statues," said Bush. "They're not going anywhere."

"They don't have to go anywhere," said Jon, "They are closer to God than Red will ever be."

Red pointed a finger at Jon. "I'll put you close to God," said Red.

"Helen," said Jon, not looking up, "sit down and play your other ace."

"I don't have another ace," said Helen.

She sat down. Red came back with a box of chocolates for Bush. Helen played her ace and took the trick.

Just then Andrew came down the stairs with the Viz and Polly Doggerel. Andrew had one of my work shirts on, Polly Doggerel wore the Viz's shirt, pants, socks and shoes, and the Viz had fur all over him.

"He'd tried to put on Polly Doggerel, this morning," said Andrew, "This is what happens when people abandon the last vestiges of order."

"Dad!" said that furry Viz to Stinky Jinx.

"I'm not your dad!" said Stinky.

"Dad!" said the Viz to the tuba.

"That's right," said the tuba. "I'm your dad."

I pulled that ball bat from underneath Red's chair and gave Funly a good ***BONG!***

"Ouch," said that tuba, Funly.

"Dad!" said the Viz, extending his furry palms to me.

"You're one for three," I said to him, picking him up. "Does he have anything on underneath that fur?" I said to Andrew.

"This is what happens," said Andrew, "when essential facades are abandoned for inessential truths, when powerful myth systems are dismembered by fact; this is how the world ends, a heap of broken images."

"Heap of broken images," mumbled Red.

"You never know what's underneath something," said Funly from inside that tuba.

"He's had a lot of time to think in there," said Stinky. "Funly, maybe it's time to read a book!"

"I'd need a little flashlight," said Funly.

"I wouldn't trust him in there with any machines," I told Stinky.

"There's always something under something else," said Bush.

"And we must check up on all of it," said Jon, brooding over his last few cards. "Because we have no faith, we have to get to the bottom of everything."

"Shall I peel an onion for us?" said Helen, getting up to check out the back window. "Or do you want to continue playing pinochle?"

Honky must have caught her looking because the house shook slightly.

"Don't peel an onion," said Red to Helen. "It will make you cry."

"So you're that jumper with the talking tuba," Bush said to Stinky. "In those big supermarket parking lots, you're just another circus act."

"Yes," said Stinky, "but I only do it for the glamour and the notoriety!"

We took the Falcon down to the jail, Funly in the front seat between me and Stinky and the Viz and Polly Doggerel in the back. Then of course we had our problems getting through security at the jail.

"What you got in that tuba," said the guard.

"Nothing," said the tuba.

"It's related to Grandpa Funster," I told him.

"That killer knows this tuba?"

"It belongs to his granddaughter," I said. You'd have to think he'd believe me, after all, I had a tuba on a wagon, two indiscernible furries, and Liberace with me; he had to believe somebody in that bunch.

"Believe me," said Funly from inside that tuba. "There's nothing in here."

"We'll decide that," said the guard, and they took Funly away.

Fifteen minutes later they were back. "Okay," said the guard, "the tuba's okay but you have to leave the dog." He pointed at the Viz.

"That's not a dog," I said. "That's my son. That's the dog," I said, pointing to Polly Doggerel.

"Well you'll have to leave them both," said the guard.

"Neither of them are dogs," I said, remembering how Kara Ruzci would have handled this. "They're both my sons."

"Dad!" said the Viz to the guard.

"Hot dog," said Polly Doggerel.

"Okay," said the guard, "but they're both very furry."

"Their mother's dead," I said.

"I bet," said the guard. He was clearly one of those people you couldn't bother with the facts. He frisked me and Stinky and then let us in.

"You certainly know how to handle authority, Jarvis," said Stinky.

"Only other peoples'," I said.

"And Funly certainly can hide in a tuba!" said Stinky.

"Like the back of my hand," said Funly.

They brought Grandpa Funster out to his Plexiglas booth and sat him down. He had on a gray jump suit and black high-top sneakers. His fingernails were clean and his skin funeral pink.

"How you doing, Grandpa?" said that tuba, Funly.

"I am a mechanic without machines," said Grandpa Funster. "A rush of forms. The end and the beginning in each other's arms, dragging my life behind me in a sack."

"We'll get you a good lawyer," said Funly. "If that doesn't work we'll bust you out."

"A rat's alley," Grandpa Funster whispered. "A dog far hence. Earth with forgetful snow, feeding a little life with dried tubas."

"He's stopped making sense," said Funly.

"He mentioned tubas, Funly," said Stinky.

"Dad!" said the Viz to Grandpa Funster.

"That's not your dad," I said to him.

But Grandpa Funster's dead eyes shifted. A piece of his upper lip grinned. "I cried in my youth, too," he said to the Viz. "My blood, unfurled, with the unused evil in my bones. The Moon, the Moon, is at the door!"

Well they took Grandpa Funster away after that. They didn't like him getting too excited; they didn't want to lose him before his trial and not get the chance to kill him themselves.

"I am calling from a place beyond!" yelled Grandpa Funster. "Beyond love, where nothing, everything, waits to be born!"

So we went to the cemetery where the leaves had already turned and died, dusting the ground like the old breath of trees, brown and noisy under our feet and in the bare limbs. We put Funly down in front of Grandma and Grandpa Funster's grave, then made piles of leaves for the Viz and Polly Doggerel to play in. Stinky wandered off into the sycamores. The Viz and Polly Doggerel raced through the piles. In front of the grave a low groan of *ooompa* swept through the tuba. And I thought of that grave far away on a hillside in New Jersey where Kara Ruzci who touched me and slept with me and sang to me lay, a corpse in the ground, in another field of death.

Her son, the Visitor, raced from a pile of leaves with the dog behind him. He rubbed his new furry palms at me. Spread his arms.

"Dad!" he said.

"That's right," I said to him, picking him up. "You got it that time."

∿ ∿ ∿ ∿ ∿Thanksgiving

HELEN SPENT THANKSGIVING in the potato cellar, hiding under all those broken machines. Holidays tended toward disaster around there and I guess it only took Helen a couple decades to jump to the conclusion that she may as well start out where she thought she'd end up. She got out of bed early, had some coffee, and took the Infant down to her Red shelter. Of course without the Infant in the holy room that place went nuts. By the time Red woke up those statues were coming up the stairs like the musical notes at the beginning of the Mickey Mouse Club, two by two and humming.

Red must have gone to bed remembering the next day was a holiday because he woke up with a ball bat. By the time he came out of the bathroom the toilet was still vibrating, Honky was pounding on the back of the house, and those statues were humming to a crescendo. Red met them at the top of the stairs. It was slaughter. But they'd asked for it.

When I got back from collecting garbage that morning that place looked like a church blew up. There were arms and legs and heads and torsos ankle deep on the floor, crosses and swords and wings battered into the walls. A film of plaster dust, still holy in its ambiance, floated in the air. Red sat next to the Zenith listening to the Thanksgiving parades, the ball bat still shaking in his right hand, his bowling ball trippling across the fingers of his left. I noticed he didn't rub out anything extraneous. The pictures of the angel babies still faced each other on the opposite wall, St. Joseph was still holding the boy Jesus on top of his carpentry table above the Zenith, though he held him a little closer, the plaques of the Sacred Burning Hearts of Mary and Jesus were unscathed.

"Don't let me miss the balloons and Santee Claus," said Red.

I went looking for Helen and found her underneath a pyramid of white appliances. When she saw me crawling toward her she held up the Infant.

"Who are you?" she said.

"Jarvis."

"My son, Jarvis?"

"Yes."

"I thought so," said Helen.

"What about the turkey?" I said to Helen.

"It's in the sink," said Helen, bringing the Infant down to her chest. "It didn't move, did it?"

"Red says the statues came after him," I told her.

"So your friends are all rubbed out," Helen said to the Infant. He appeared unfazed. "Your Uncle Jon is right about your father," she said to me. "He's not stable." You could see what she was thinking; you just couldn't leave a protestant alone with a bunch of statues.

"You always cook the turkey," I told her.

"I'm not cooking the turkey."

"I thought you and Red were getting along a lot better."

"It's Thanksgiving," she said.

"You hardly cook anymore," I said, "I thought you liked cooking the turkey."

"Every argument you muster will end up with me cooking the turkey," said Helen.

Well maybe there was a nutty strain on Helen's side of the family, but they were incisive. I crawled back out of that subterranean junk yard, got myself and Red a beer, then worked my way through that statue rubble and joined him in the front room for the Thanksgiving parades. The end of those Thanksgiving parades in New York and Philadelphia and Detroit were the only things Red ever crawled out of his chair next to the Zenith to watch; he always got a big kick out of seeing Santee Claus in New York and then Philadelphia and then Detroit, bing, bang, boom; it gave him a sense of balance and mysterious synchronicity, that Santee Claus could be in three different places at almost the same time, and he could see it on TV; it was better than the leaves changing, better than the first snow; it was regular and amazing.

But not this year. Not so far. Red was sitting in his chair next to the Zenith with his weapons of meditation. Sometimes he stuck out his bottom lip.

"No balloons yet," I told him.

Next to the Santee Clauss he liked those giant balloons of Popeye and Donald Duck and Woody Woodpecker. Red said once he was in New York on Thanksgiving for business and he saw the big Thanksgiving Day Parade and was right underneath those giant balloons of Popeye and Mickey Mouse and Felix the Cat. Boy, that was something, said Red.

"When were you in New York?" I asked him.

"Once," said Red, "a long time ago."

"Who's Felix the Cat?" said Neda, who'd come down the stairs and into the front room. She brushed some rubble off the couch and took a seat.

Red didn't tell Neda who Felix the Cat was; Neda was a genius and already knew.

"Look at this," said Joseph to Andrew as they entered the room. "Some kind of detonated pile system."

"You laugh," said Andrew, "but this is what happens when you destroy a system: fractionalization, dismemberment. Without system there is no context for individual insights."

"Without organization, no analysis; without wholes, no parts," yawned Neda.

"Form is like the Emperor's new clothes," said Joseph. "Rubble is the substratum. Rubble is life!"

"This rubble is the statues," I told them.

"This is the dust of consciousness," insisted Andrew. "That's the difference between statues and rubble!"

"Baloney," said Joseph.

"You're in front of the TV," said Neda.

"Red," I said, "the balloons are on."

Red got up and stood in front of the Zenith. This year it was Rocky and Bullwinkle and Underdog.

"I don't know these," said Red, "All the goddamn cartoons are changing."

"Your ass is in the way, Red," said Neda.

Red sat down on the couch. He rested the ball bat against his thigh. He held the bowling ball at his belly. "You should get your kid," he said to me. "He'd love this."

Well every year Red made us watch these parades and we all hated it.

"I don't know where he is," I said.

"He disappeared under the Pile System," said Andrew.

"What Pile System?" said Joseph.

"This is really something," said Red. "This is really special." But he didn't seem too excited, in fact I saw his shoulders sigh. "Everything's changing," said Red.

"It's still balloons," I told him.

"Hey Red," said Neda, "there's a Santee Claus."

It was around this time that Red always got up and started tickling everybody and poking them in the ribs and saying, Look! Look! There's Santee Claus! There's Santee Claus! Red really loved Santee Claus. But Red just sat there.

Neda poked him in the ribs. "Look Red," she said. "There's Santee Claus."

"Yeah," said Red.

"Hey Red," said Joseph, "there's Santee Claus."

"Your kid ought to see this," Red said to me.

"Okay," I said. I was willing to do anything to get Red hopping around again, that house felt like the last days of the expanding universe. I went up to the Pile System and rooted around underneath, it was kind of just one big pile now, until I got hold of something furry. I held it up, but it didn't say "Dad" so I figured it was Polly Doggerel. In a little bit I found a sleepy Viz, put some of his own clothes on him, and carted him down, to the front room.

"It's too late," said Red, "They're already in Detroit."

"He'll still see Santee Claus."

"Only one," said Red.

"Come on, Red," said Neda.

I put the Viz on his lap, next to the bowling ball. "Look," Red uttered to the Viz, pointing at the TV, "Look. There's Santee Claus."

"Dad!" said the Viz to Santee Claus.

Red put the Viz down and got up. He went to the front door.

"Where you going?" I said.

"Funster's."

"You can't go to Funster's," I said. "It's Thanksgiving."

"I can do what I want," said Red, "I'm grown up."

"You're going to miss the Detroit Lions," I told him. "You're going to miss Texas-Texas A&M."

"Detroit always wins on Thanksgiving," said Red. "Texas always clobbers Texas A&M."

"Santa Claus always shows up, too."

"He's supposed to show up."

We looked at each other for a while.

"And your Mother's supposed to cook a turkey," he finally said.

"Maybe she'll come back upstairs," I said.

Red put down the ball bat. He handed me his bowling ball. "Here," he said. "Don't bust anything."

ℨ   ℨ   ℨ

Thanksgiving was in a shambles in that neighborhood, even at the Funsters'. Red went over there and a caught them right at the turkey table with its two empty seats on the far side, one for Grandpa Funster who, despite his death, was now in jail, and one for Grandma Funster who, despite all her liveliness, somehow ended up in the grave. At the head of the table Jimbo Funster sat like a leg of lamb, while Mosha Funster, to his right, stared forlornly at her once musical tuba now filled with Funly. Betty Funster held a carving knife limply in the air above the unstuffed turkey carcass. There was just too much other stuff stuffed around there.

"Have a seat," said Betty Funster.

"You got a tuba at the table," said Red.

"It's F-F-Funly," said Jimbo.

"I forgot," said Red. "How come you want to be a tuba?" Red said to that tuba, Funly.

"Get me outta here!" said Funly.

"You ought to call the fire department," said Red.

"They won't t-touch it," said Jimbo. "They'd have to use a b-b-blow torch."

"They're afraid Funly would burn up like a rocket," said Betty.

"That's very cheap, Mother," said Funly.

"You w-weren't d-down here worrying," said Jimbo to the tuba.

"That's right," said Betty Funster, tapping the tuba with a wooden spoon. "Cavorting with sputniks."

"Ouch," said Funly.

"I want my tuba back," said Mosha.

"Make N-N-Neda get him out," said Jimbo.

"I can't make anybody do anything," said Red.

"That's not true," said Betty Funster. "You're the mayor of the neighborhood." She gave Red some turkey and Red thought, what the hell, turkey's turkey. "Without you," said Betty Funster, "this neighborhood would be a slum."

Meanwhile, back at the house, I pulled that turkey out of the sink, washed him and patted him dry. I tore up loaves of bread and mixed it with sage and pepper, boiled the turkey neck and giblets and chopped up celery and onions, fried them in a bunch of butter and added it to the broth and bread. Then I mushed all that shit together, opened the back end of the bird and stuffed that son of a bitch. Put him in the oven at 350.

Red came home a little later, after Detroit had upset Green Bay and about halfway through the third quarter of Texas drubbing Texas A&M. I already had the flour in the turkey grease, the yams baked, the potatoes in the bowl waiting to be mashed, the pumpkin pies in the oven; I had the Ocean Spray Cranberry Sauce out of its can, the kind with the lumpy whole cranberries in it like Red liked and the smooth jellied kind that Helen liked; they sat on the table, cylindrical and pristine, the lumps from the cans shining deep maroon in the afternoon light, the serial numbers of the cans glistening at the tops. I mashed the potatoes, popped the pies, stirred the gravy, set the table. I told everybody in the front room to come and eat and when they got in the holy room I gave a knife to Red. "Carve," I said. Then I went back in the basement to get Helen.

"Are you coming with dignity?" I said to her.

"Is there a choice?" said Helen.

"You tell me," I said.

She gave me the Infant and followed me out of there. When we got to the holy room I put him back on top of the dish cabinet to watch over us while we ate and survey his rubbled empire.

It was a quiet meal but it wasn't such a bad one. I made whipped cream for the pie, served coffee, poured everybody a little Mogen-David cordial. As we finished, a ray of autumn sun slipped through the windows and shown gold and hopeful across the holy room table. I stood up. "Okay," I said. "Let's go to the zoo."

"The zoo ain't open," said Red.

"It's open," I said.

It was a barren, leafless, Thanksgiving Day and I made everybody put on their winter coats and then dragged them out to the Falcon where I put Red and Helen in the front and Neda, Joseph, Andrew, the Viz, and Polly Doggerel in the back. I drove straight over to State Street and then out south of town until we hit the zoo where the front gates were open and unattended. We walked over to the kiddy section which was closed, nothing in it but a few stray pigeons who tried to hit us up for garbage. Then we went up the hill to the new area where they kept various bears and some tigers in open environments surrounded by deep pits, the kind of thing that Louie Ruzci, Kara's dad, made his fortune in, probably came up here and built these Erie animal environments with his son-in-law Arnold right after they finished the ones they did in Youngstown; they looked like pieces of the moon made out of paper mache, not really the kind of place you'd picture a bear or a lion or a tiger spending much time. We went up to see the sun bears but they were sleeping in their cave, so we went over to see the black bears but they were sleeping in their cave; the brown bears and grizzly bears and Kodiak bears were sleeping in their caves, and the Siberian tigers were sleeping in their cave too, though the polar bears were out, sleeping next to their pool. It made Red sleepy. He yawned.

Then we went over to the smaller animal cages and watched some sleeping foxes and sleeping wolves, some sleeping porcupines, weasels, raccoons, owls and, ironically, a sleeping turkey. In the section for grazing animals things were a little livelier. The camels and giraffes weren't out, but there was a buffalo and some goats and several deer standing around. I gathered up some dead grass and gave it to the Viz, then held him up so he could stick it through the fence. Sure enough, one of those moppy old deers came over and bit him. The Viz pulled his hand back in and looked at it, then he showed it to me. There was something in his head that wasn't saying "Dad" but he managed to suppress it.

"There are a lot of things out there that aren't your dad," I said to the Viz.

"Not me," said Neda, taking him from me.

"No," said Andrew, "I'm his dad."

"Don't listen to him," Joseph said to the Viz. You know who your dad is." He poked himself in the chest.

Helen took the Viz from Neda.

"Goddamn kid," said Red.

"Poor thing," said Helen.

"Dad!" whimpered the Viz to Helen.

We followed Polly Doggerel down to the indoor zoo where they kept the monkeys and lions, but there was nothing going on in there, just a lot of sleeping and masturbating. Sparrows, perched on the rafters, skittered into the monkey cages and stole food. The monkeys threw shit at them. Polly Doggerel arfed at a few sleeping lions. A guy who looked like a janitor came out and said we couldn't have animals in the zoo and we'd have to leave, besides, the zoo was closed anyways.

"I told you," said Red when we got home.

"But we had a good time," I said to him. "Didn't we? Didn't we?"

I didn't work that night, so spent the evening at Willie's. The Dialecticians on bourbon and cigarettes now, gathered around a card table, playing poker and raising smoke.

"Where is the little radical monist nominalist?" said Raymon.

"With a dad," I said.

"That could be anywhere," said Revis. As he got older his voice became more and more of a croak. "You should take care of him. The Dialecticians like him."

I took a look at the bourbon they were drinking. Old Lucky Times. "This bourbon isn't very aged," I said.

That got me some raised eyebrows.

"Forty months," I said. "Forty months is nothing for bourbon."

Silent Revco rubbed his square chin and examined the bottle.

"And it's made in Pennsylvania," I said. "Real bourbon is made in Kentucky, though there's some decent sour mash in Tennessee."

Revis polished off his shot of Old Lucky Times and opened a Swisher Sweet. "He spends a little time with the other people's garbage cans and then presumes to pontificate to the Dialecticians about their bourbon."

"In the future," I told Revis, "garbagemen will move waste from planet to planet. The control of intra-galactic waste will permit garbagemen to meld the archaeologies of galactic cultures. They will decide who shares in the lasting forms. Garbagemen will be poet-kings."

"It is a malady of his melanin to acquire good taste," said Raymon.

Revco poured me a shot and grinned.

"You want in?" said Raymon.

I looked over at Willie but he was concentrating on his cards, his bad hand stroking his chin.

"No thank you," I told Raymon. "I have too much pinochle in my genes, it could prove dangerous. Besides, I work for a living and need my money to feed and clothe my family and save for the future."

"So you will have a house when the world ends," croaked Revis.

"Do not worry," said Revco slowly, offering one of his occasional utterances.

"Yes," said Raymon. "We are not playing for the money, we are playing for the Fate."

"They have decided," said Willie, "to settle fis draft fing among themselves."

"We are deciding who will be the soldier, who will be the inmate, and who will be the Canadian," said Raymon.

"You deciding tonight?" I said.

"It is a tournament," said Revis. "It could take days."

"Or years," said Revco. "Because Willie, himself, always wins," said Raymon.

Willie took the hand, reshuffled and dealt, dealing me in. Revco poured me more cheap bourbon. I took a Swisher Sweet from Revis.

"Not this time," I said, I'd drawn three queens and two kings.

"We are playing low ball," said Raymon.

"You got to call that before the deal," I said.

"Fis is not the case here," said Willie.

Which is how those Dialecticians played it. They decided what to play after they all had their cards and got the second deal and completed their hands. It made the game more dialectical and produced myriad ridiculous discussions. We argued about that hand for an hour or so before we eventually played it and Willie won.

"Fis is fun," said Willie, collecting all the cards and match sticks.

We played that way till dawn, though by then all us other Dialecticians, other than Willie, himself, were just sitting there discussing how to beat Willie who didn't even participate in the discussion; he just put his cards down and waited for us to get done, then picked them up and beat us. Those Dialecticians might have been playing with the Fate, but the Fate wasn't playing with them.

"What shall we do?" said Revis.

"Let us play another hand," said Raymon.

Revco poured drinks and broke out the cigars.

"Willie," I said, "I got to talk."

"Talking is a fine fing," said Willie.

"I'm getting scared, Willie," I said to him, which was certainly an interesting thing to say because I hadn't felt scared at all, though I have to admit, now that I said it, I did feel scared; made me wonder whether I could have avoided the whole thing by just keeping my mouth shut.

"Because," said Willie, "you have bought yourself the empty lunch bucket."

"It seemed like a good idea at the time," I said, glancing toward those other Dialecticians.

"Do not worry about the Dialecticians," said Willie, "They are filling their own buckets."

Sure enough, those other Dialecticians were talking like we weren't even there, as if Willie had taken him and me to another space-time coordinate, one of those dots only the birds could see but they ate them.

"You fought because you learned deaf was a real fing that you hadn't made it up," said Willie. "You fought experimenting was the tool, but it is not the tool. Fis is the first and last fing, but it is not the only fing; not the very first or the very last. Fis is why I, myself, am not already a part of deaf, but deaf is part of I, myself."

"You're saying I can't stay awake forever."

"Among other fings," said Willie.

"I'm starting to feel like I'm somehow responsible for what's happening around me," I said to Willie. "That Kara Ruzci is dead because of me. That her brother is dead because of me. That I made Bobby Hansen a vegetable, and Stinky a star, and put Funly in that tuba. That I made Red a violent man and Helen a nut. That I killed Tony Blanion. That there is a line of death reaching back from me to the beginning of the world, and forward to the end."

"No," said Willie. "You are nofing, even to your own foughts."

"My thoughts don't need me," I said.

"They do not mind you," said Willie.

"I mind them?"

"I hope not," Willie said. "Underneaf everfing, you harbor a grudge against simplicity."

"Simplicity."

"Fis is true. And complexity. What is the experiment?" Willie said.

Well Willie'd just about dialecticized me to shreds when Revco grinned through that time warp.

"How many?" said Revco, I needed a ten for a straight and didn't get it.

"What game?" said Raymon.

Willie rubbed his chin with his bad hand. He wasn't even looking at his cards.

⩥ ⩥ ⩥ ⩥ ⩥ Bush's Last Christmas

I T WAS ANOTHER Bush's last Christmas because you had to figure one of these days Helen was going to be right. On the garbage
route, all through the holidays, people left out various gifts for
their garbagemen: boxes of candy and cheap bottles of whisky and
champagne; they left notes on their garbage cans to look in the milk
box or come to their door, then, because Zippy and Fatty thought it
was the fairest way to do it, we brought that stuff back to the truck to
divide up and amidst all that sophisticated divvying based on seniority,
rank, and other intangibles, I ended up not getting shit. The only time
I really got anything was if somebody left cash, but that wasn't too often because Fatty and Zippy knew just who those people were; that
was the only time I ever saw Fatty get out of the truck.

One place that left cash that year was the Hansens. I had my usual
chat with Bobby at the back of the house and noticed he looked a little
worse for his Thanksgiving turkey. He had tubes in his nose and tubes in
his arms and tubes down his throat; he had bottles and bags of liquid
going in and going out. His head looked like a little pale rock. I don't
know why I lingered there so long, except that I guess I had the time; this
Christmas route, with everybody getting and calculating and stashing their
Christmas gifts, went long and slow. I looked around a little bit.

Those Hansens had improved their lock system over the years,
you could see that just by walking by the windows and looking for
how you might want to break in, but the Christmas lights were the

same as the night I played with them years ago when I tried to make my entrance less illuminated; each window framed in red or blue, alternating red, white and blue lights along the gutter under the roof, little white stars of lights in clusters against the dark frame. That new room, where Bobby Hansen stayed now, was an extension and had a wheel chair access ramp built onto its door. The windows had the same high locks, bolted at the top, but the door was simple, just a key lock in the knob and a sliding bolt. After I unhooked the storm door I had those locks taken apart in about two minutes with my work knife; put them right back together, too.

I don't know what got into me, I don't know why I wanted to be in there with Bobby Hansen after all these years, face to vegetable with my old nemesis and archego Bobby Hansen who in his own unspeakable ways had run my life silly, but there was something calling me in there to tap him on the forehead; maybe I wanted to give him some love and maybe I just wanted to offer him a final ignominious intrusion. I got those doors shut quietly and turned toward him. Then, suddenly, I felt like somebody poured hot lead in my head; it got cold in my stomach and I got dizzy.

That's when I felt a gun barrel in my ear.

"Belly up, turtle head, even little sharks eat fish," said Tony Blanion.

"You can't shoot me," I said to Blanion in a gravelly whisper. "You're immaterial."

"Tell that to that angel you smoked not so many Xmases ago, hotel teeth."

"Listen, my friend," I said to Tony Blanion, because in many ways we were intimate. I delicately lifted two fingers and removed his gun from my ear. "I got news for you. You're dead."

"Don't bother me with the facts, astral ass," said my old friend, Mr. Tony Blanion.

I tried to get a look at him but he kept stepping behind me.

"Don't worry about it, I haven't aged a day."

"If you're not going to shoot me," I said, "leave me alone."

"I'm just here to remind you, carp collector," said Blanion, "that you're in my territory and you're not getting out. Everywhere you go, I peed there already. On you I got the cosmic contract."

I had to hand it to Tony Blanion, he always kept me well informed, but quick or dead or both he was difficult to talk to, he just mixed too many metaphors to take seriously, in fact I'd barely thought about him since that night I woke up with his corpse on the eve of *The End of the World* and he tried to rhyme threat with beret.

"So how's things on the other side?" I said to him, "Still working on your French?"

My friend Mr. Tony Blanion jammed that gun hard into my ribs. "Okay maggot lover, think about this. I fuck your wife in the Afterlife." Then he wrapped me hard on the back of the head.

Well it was hard to tell if what I'd been doing was sleeping, but if the last few moments were the fruit of my unconsciousness, I'd been right to stay awake the last few years. Though I sure couldn't keep on breaking into people's houses and then falling asleep, that kind of behavior could be disastrous. I looked over at Bobby Hansen whose skin looked an awful lot like one of those plastic bags people used to line their kitty litters. I went over to him, watched the scarce movement of his thick chest, watched the moisture form and evaporate on his cheeks and forehead from pores like little volcanoes. Bobby Hansen, Bobby Hansen, I thought. I had the urge to think something significant, something to breach the havoc I'd wreaked on his life, but all I had in my head was his name. "Bobby Hansen," I said outloud. "Bobby Hansen, Bobby Hansen." But Bobby Hansen didn't move. I bent down and kissed his forehead. It felt like a cold pond.

In the back, by the Hansens' garbage, there was a note that apologized for not leaving the usual bottle of Cutty Sark, but said there was an envelope in the milk box, which I went to even before transferring their garbage into my can and found thirty bucks inside a holy Christmas card that had three tall white angels singing over a manger with the baby Jesus in it, gold halo over his head, arms spread with olive branches in one hand and a globe of the world with a cross on top in the other; it said "Hail Christ, the King." I went back and got the garbage, threw it on top the truck, and gave the card to Fatty and Zippy.

"Where's the fuckin Cutty Sark," said Fatty.

"They didn't have time this year," I told him, "Their kid's too sick."

"That Bobby Hansen kid," said Zippy Freeburg. "That's a real tragedy."

"It sure is," I said.

"What's it take to get a fuckin bottle of Cutty Sark for your garbage-man?" said Fatty.

"They probably left money," said Zippy.

"No," I said, "just the card."

"Goddamn kid," said Fatty. "We taught you everything you know."

"That's right," I said. I climbed the back of the dump truck and waded my way to the cab where I began to stomp the garbage.

"He just got lucky," said Zippy. "That's all." He sat down on the curb and wiped his forehead. "That poor Bobby Hansen," said Zippy.

"His parents are fuckin loaded," said Fatty. "Kid probably got laid more than I ever got laid."

"I went to high school with him," I said. "He got laid all the time. He was notorious."

"He's a human being," said Zippy.

"Some fuckin Socialist you are," said Fatty.

"It's Christmas," said Zippy. "Socialists are human beings."

"Hanukkah," said Fatty. "You're a Jew."

"Jews are human beings," said Zippy.

Well it sounded like Zippy was on to something that had to do vaguely with humanity.

"How about if we help Loop with the castle this week," Zippy said to Fatty, "then take him with us."

"I don't want to know where you go and I don't want to go with you," I said.

"He's getting laid at that castle," said Fatty.

"He ain't getting laid," said Zippy.

"I am," I said.

"No you ain't," said Zippy.

"How come every week you're moving refrigerators or stoves or dishwashers or something out of that place?" said Fatty.

"Okay, where do you guys go?" I said.

"We can't tell you," said Zippy. "You got to come."

"We're unionizing," said Fatty.

"Don't tell him," said Zippy.

"What does he care, he's getting laid every week in that castle," said Fatty.

"He ain't," said Zippy.

"City employees can't unionize, it's against the law," I told them.

"He wants to work like this all his life," Zippy said to Fatty.

"You know we could have a compactor," Zippy yelled up to me. "You wouldn't have to throw this shit ten feet up in the air. You wouldn't have to stomp it down. These people could put their garbage out on the curb for us so we wouldn't have to kill ourselves on their dogs and clotheslines."

"Then they'd fire two-thirds of us and Fatty'd have to get out of the truck and throw the garbage in the back."

"That's why we got to unionize," said Fatty. "We should have clean places to go when we get done, to get laid."

"I'm already getting laid," I said.

"You ain't getting laid," said Zippy.

"Right now we just transfer material from one owner to another." I finished stomping at the back of the truck and hopped down. "What we need is a place of our own to keep this stuff. In the future, if we can control the waste, the only lasting element of the universe, we'll control the eternal verities. The waste of stars becoming conscious. Garbage-men will write the language of galactic history."

"He's nuts," said Fatty.

"I'll be dead," said Zippy.

"We're not taking you with us," said Fatty. "You go to the castle and get laid."

Well if you made too much sense people refused to believe you, it's the plight of revolutionary thinking; so I figured I'd just have to listen to Fatty Schlosky for a change; Zippy didn't know how close he was to being wrong, that's what I was thinking, in fact right there, riding on the bumper of that garbage truck and holding onto the outside mirror, because there wasn't room inside unless I wanted to sit between Fatty and Zippy on the transmission, I was re-evaluating my status as a sexual being. Willie was right, I wasn't like Grandpa Funster who, somehow, through his long and odd love with Grandma Funster, broached some ontic crack; Grandma Funster did her bit; she played ghost, she came back now and then; she was in the annals; pulled a few tricks when nobody was around, appeared in some dreams, spoke, on occasion, to select individuals notorious for their receptivity; she was the mirror image of the other side of Grandpa Funster's coin; her body was dead and her soul was a nuisance. Grandpa Funster, dead as he was, simply refused to admit it; he refused to participate in the conventions of death; I don't even remember, myself, when he died, but from what I hear he was buried one day and back the next. Probably couldn't have got away with that in any other neighborhood in the city. But Kara Ruzci didn't do either one. I'd seen my old friend Mr. Tony Blanion, but I hadn't seen Kara since the day she died.

Well there's nothing like Christmas Eve on the bumper of a garbage truck to get you thinking about the big things. I was counting the legions of the dead. I took off my denim hat in the air of Christmas light and felt the cold astral wind.

Willie always said there were two kinds of experiments, experiments with Deaf and experiments with the Other. Those were the big metaphors, the big dualism splitters, and I'd been avoiding them both. But suddenly I felt it was time to take them on. I was thinking about a warm fireplace and hot whirlpool bath and sweet liqueur. It was Christmas, 1965, and I wasn't dead yet. I had to face it, I wasn't dead.

When Fatty and Zippy left me off at the castle I didn't even go back to the garbage, I went right to the front door. I didn't even knock or ring, I knew she kept an eye out for me and all I had to do was wait there, besides, I felt like I should be exuding confidence, for one thing, and for another, though that door was about ten feet tall and eight feet thick, I could see right through it. I saw my mysterious friend approaching, coming down the stairs in her pink silk robe, her breasts hinting at the *V* where it opened on her chest. Her hair was brushed back and she was thinking about replacing all the hassocks. She flew across her living room and foyer softer and quieter than moonlight on a patch of warm night, then stopped at the door. I waited for her. I waited quite a long time before I noticed the piece of paper sticking out under the doormat.

She was having Christmas in Tahiti with that Paraguayan surf champion husband of hers. She'd be gone till sometime in January. We'd have a little celebration when she got back.

Something just told me the surf really wasn't that great in Tahiti. That's what I was thinking as I headed back for that garbage. In fact I was in a pretty dour mood. It was clear to me that I was a rusty Dialectician; got the experiment mixed up with the tool; before I even knew the experiment I'd tried to put my future where my mouth was. I stopped in the driveway and watched the cold air come in and out of my nose for a while. There were a lot of empty bottles in that back yard, in those garbage cans: wine bottles, bourbon bottles, scotch bottles, uninvestigated liqueurs and aperitifs, cheese and meat wrappers from Europe, things that only a week ago had made me perfectly happy. They were worthwhile things to contemplate, as valuable as anything.

But when I got back there, all those big cans were already dumped out and separated, the wines and bourbons and scotches lined up by age, the cheese and meat wrappers divided by nation, the drug paraphernalia piled into discrete bunches demarcated by the drugs applicable to their use. In front of every section was Rolodex that indicated what was what and cross referenced everything according to quality, region of origin of the individual ingredients, and the nation-source of the final product, refined to state or county or village as well as importer and place of distribution, if known. Sitting in the middle of all that organization was a kid that looked about five years old. He had brown floppy hair, a short sleeved shirt with horizontal stripes, little bib overalls, and Buster Brown wingtip shoes.

Somehow, seeing all that stuff pre-organized took the interest out of it for me. The only thing left for me to do was put it back in the cans and cart it out.

"Did you do all this?" I asked the kid.

"In a manner of speaking," he said.

"Mind if I put it back in the cans and cart it out of here?"

"No," he said, "you can do what you want with it. It's not my stuff."

I started putting that garbage back in the cans, going out of my way to mix it all back up. All of a sudden I realized that there was a natural state for garbage; I felt a momentary meld of scatology and eschatology, that at the bottom my actions were meditative, a contemplation of frayed, syntactic pathways which crossed themselves like DNA strands in the soup of my real. Putting that garbage back in those cans made me feel like I was putting my life back together.

"Well," I said, throwing some hypos on top some empty cartons of Jarlsberg Beer and Stilton cheese. "You're right, this isn't your stuff. Once it gets in these cans it's my stuff. Garbagemen don't just collect garbage, they control garbage. Someday, someone's going to come along and reinvent the language of waste. Then the language of waste will be ours, the technology of waste will be ours, the waste will be ours. Do you know what I'm saying?"

"Garbagemen will rule the world," said that little kid.

"That's right," I said. "You're a smart little kid."

"Not really," he said. "I just know your thoughts."

Well maybe he wasn't five. Maybe he was seven or eight. Maybe he just watched too much TV. Kids'll say the darndest things; look at the Viz.

I had everything pretty much put back in those cans when I happened to notice this kid didn't have a coat on.

"Where's your parents?" I said to him. "You live around here?"

"Getting ready for my Christmas."

"Don't you believe in Santee Claus?"

"I did," he said. "Years ago. But a lot's happened."

Well how many years could that be? "Maybe you'll grow up to be the garbageman who turns all this around," I said to him. I tried to pat him on his cold head but he backed away.

"I won't," he said. "It's too late. It's too late to grow up. It's too late for everything."

"You're a weird kid and you should put a coat on," I said to him, going back to the cans. I pulled the dolly over and got the first one ready to take out to the curb. "You know what I'd do if I found my kid running around in the middle of the night without any clothes on?" I said.

"You'd kill him," he said.

"That's right," I said. "I might have to kill him."

I turned to look at him, but he wasn't where he'd been, in fact I don't know where the hell he went. But I could hear him from wherever he was. He said, "I don't have to. I can do anything I want and I don't have to do anything."

Well it'd been a long and troublesome night for me and I had better things to do than argue with a smart aleck disappearing act.

"Go home," I said, wheeling that garbage out to the curb.

"I don't have to," he said. I don't know where he was but it sounded like it came from everywhere. That little "I don't have to" voice shook the whole world.

(The Story of Franky Gorky)

Franky Gorky would have been my neighbor, but he died before I was born. He was the nicest kid in the whole universe but he lived in his own little world. In the morning, when the birds sang, he thought they'd waited up all night just for him so they could sing outside his bedroom window. When he went to the zoo and fed the bunnies and the pigeons and the lambs in the little children's petting zoo, he thought wild animals were eating right out of his hand. He shared his toys with other kids mostly because he hardly thought about his toys; they usually had too many little mechanical parts to figure out, or came unassembled, and his dad, Gary Gorky, never bothered to put them together for him. Franky Gorky was the nicest kid in the whole world because he never thought about where the hell he was. Franky Gorky was playing around with big ideas before his time.

For one thing, Franky Gorky couldn't separate his will from the world. When he woke up, after the birds sang for him at his window, he got hungry and there was breakfast waiting for him every day. When he wanted to go outside after eating, the outside was there waiting for him, right outside the inside every time. In the summer it was warm, just like he was told it would be, and in the winter it was cold with plenty of snow, and he never had to wear his bathing suit in the snow. In the summer, he got his little round inflatable swimming pool that his mother, Greta Gorky, blew up for him and filled with water from the hose, and it was never too deep. Christmas always came at Christmas, lunch always came at lunch. It got so that Franky Gorky couldn't decide whether things were there because he wanted them or whether he wanted them because they were there, appearing from out of nowhere and making him think them and then want them, or worse, making him want them before they even appeared.

This is why, for the longest time, Franky Gorky was the nicest kid in the universe. He was thoughtful the way most other people were thoughtless, without thinking about it. He couldn't separate a wish from a fish. It was all up to him and it always came out okay. Always getting everything he wanted destroyed his desire. Franky Gorky was just too abstract, the victim of a powerful intellect and a vapid imagination. He just couldn't come up with anything he didn't want. Everything was just fine, but he thought about it too much.

Franky Gorky might have been a keen observer had he ever noticed anything, and one thing he never noticed was the sky. Though one night, in fact the night of the anniversary of the bombing of Pearl Harbor and the eve of the Blessed Virgin Mary's Immaculate Conception, his father, Gary Gorky, pointed up to the sky at a weird crescent shaped light that looked like something a flying Arab might have left up there and said, "Hey Franky, look at that."

"What's that?" said Franky Gorky.

And Gary Gorky said, "It's the moon."

Names never really turned things around much for Franky Gorky. Things were always pretty much called what they were called, though if you changed the name it didn't change the thing, so it was all pretty much the same anyways. So having *the moon* in his vocabulary didn't help him much with this at all.

"What's the moon?" said Franky Gorky.

And Gary Gorky told him, as good as he could, because after all, Gary Gorky really didn't know that much about the moon either and, besides, he was talking to a little kid.

Gary Gorky told Franky Gorky that the moon was like the sun, only the sun only came out in the day time, but if you watched for the moon you'd notice it came out pretty much whenever it wanted; sometimes it came out at night and sometimes it came out during the day, also the moon got big and little and changed colors and shapes. The moon did whatever it wanted. The moon didn't have any responsibilities. The sun had to dry up rain water and make things grow. The sun had to show up every day. But not the moon. Even the stars had to come out at night. And the stars had to stay little. The moon was always on vacation. Sometimes it even left town and didn't show up day or night. It just split. Went to California or Tahiti and shone down there.

Franky Gorky's Dad, Gary Gorky, had a real working class understanding of the moon. But Franky Gorky was too young to understand that his father's Weltanschauung was alienated. Gary Gorky himself didn't know that and anyway it was just a theory.

But the point was clear. The moon could do anything it wanted, just like Franky Gorky.

Well finally Franky Gorky found something specific to think about and soon he was obsessed with the moon. Something speechless in him told him you couldn't have two all-powerful wills running around roughshod in the same area and it was up to Franky Gorky to find out who really was in control here, him or the moon, so right off Franky Gorky wished that the moon would get bigger.

Well the moon was going to get bigger anyways, it happened to be a waxing crescent that Gary Gorky pointed out to Franky Gorky in that dark rich Pearl Harbor Immaculate Conception sky, so sure enough, it did. In fact one night it got so big and white and cold that it woke Franky Gorky up from his sleep with its light, and when he went to the window it swooped down to cover his face and suck out his bones. That's when Franky Gorky figured out the moon was made out of white bones. The moon was made from the bones of all the children of the earth who woke up at night. Then, just before they called to their parents, it sucked their bones out. In the morning their parents found their little puddles of flesh and eyeballs staring out plaintively. But those children weren't like Franky Gorky. They were naïve and believed that calling for their mom or dad in the middle of the night could protect them. Nothing could protect them from something like the moon.

Franky Gorky turned his head. He covered his eyes from the light. He wished for the moon to get smaller. And sure enough the next night, it did.

Either Franky Gorky was in charge of the moon or the moon was outguessing him. So Franky Gorky watched the future like a wet rag. Furtively, he kept his glance to the sky as the moon diminished and Christmas grew near. He knew he should be thinking about the birth of the Baby Jesus who came to save the world, and the Wise Men bearing gifts, but he was preoccupied with the moon. Every night the moon grew smaller and smaller until Franky Gorky worried that the moon would disappear. That's when he remembered that the moon might go to California or Tahiti. Franky Gorky wondered whether the moon might go to California or Tahiti for good. Then when all the children of California and Tahiti had all their bones sucked out, he would be responsible. Where would he send the moon then? Cleveland or Ashtabula. Maybe Buffalo.

And that's when he remembered his grandmother, Grandma Gorky, who lived in Buffalo, and every year she came to see the Gorkys for Christmas. Grandma Gorky was old. She could tell him things his Dad, Gary Gorky, might not know. And Grandma Gorky would know when the moon was in Buffalo.

Franky Gorky might have been a strange kid. He might have been abstract and unimaginative. Maybe, sometimes, he got his will mixed up with the world. But this time, he was right. Three nights before Christmas the moon disappeared on schedule, but this time it did not come back. It was the famous Christmas Without the Moon. Not too many people in Erie, Pennsylvania back then bothered to watch the moon, most of them were too busy working and besides it was Christmas, there were other concerns, and usually in Erie in the winter time there were so many thick clouds hanging in the sky you were lucky to see the sun, in fact the sun shone through the cloud layer so faintly that people might mistake the sun for the moon if they didn't know better, though people who did know better, those who knew where the moon was supposed to be, could usually find it, even in the winter, some time or another, even if it was just a little winter sliver in the cloud blanket, they could find it slipping through with a little shine. But not that winter, not that Christmas. That Christmas nobody could find the moon anywhere.

Well maybe there was a waxing crescent moon, a silver sliver somewhere in that Erie winter sky. Maybe it was just too cloudy. But on Christmas Eve day the sky cleared after a morning snow, and all day long in a sky the color of a Chevy Impala, the sun burned like its automatic cigarette lighter. Though in the evening, before the sun hit the lake, a storm rolled in and covered the town before anybody could spot the moon.

Somebody needed to make a phone call! That's what Franky Gorky thought. Somebody had to find out where the hell the moon was!

though Franky Gorky himself would not say hell. But it was dark. It was Christmas Eve. And Franky Gorky didn't even know how to use the phone. He knew it involved numbers and dialing and speaking, but he couldn't quite put it all together. He needed to hear from California or Tahiti or Buffalo! Somebody had to make a phone call!

Just then the Gorkys got a phone call. It was Grandma Gorky who always came to visit the Gorkys every Christmas, who in fact had come to visit the Gorky' for Christmas for ages beyond memory, even before Franky Gorky existed.

"Ask her about the moon!" yelled Franky Gorky to his mother, Greta Gorky, as she hung up the phone.

"The moon?" said Greta Gorky. "I'm afraid Grandma Gorky may not make it for Christmas tomorrow," said Greta to Gary Gorky. "She's very sick."

"That's too bad," said Gary Gorky.

Franky Gorky tore at his hair.

"What's the matter?" asked his dad, Gary Gorky.

"Gaaahg!" said Franky Gorky.

And his parents put him to bed because they knew how attached he was to his Grandmother.

Franky Gorky never spent a worse night. Instead of thinking about how Baby Jesus had come to save the world, and even instead of thinking about all the presents he was going to get Christmas Day, he thought about his wanton and capricious wishing which had sent the moon to eat the bones of the children of Tahiti or worse made the moon disappear altogether, and how he'd wasted himself with all his wishing and thinking about the moon to the point where now even all the normal things he used to barely have to wish for at all, like his Grandma Gorky coming for Christmas, became impossible. What's more, he realized he didn't know how to use the telephone. He wished he knew, but that didn't happen either. Franky Gorky cried himself to sleep that Christmas Eve night wishing everything would just go back to normal, that he'd wake up and it would be winter and Christmas and the moon would be back to do whatever it did whenever it wanted, and that Grandma Gorky would come to visit, and that in time, at some normal, right time for children to learn to use the phone, somebody would teach him how to use the telephone. But he'd frivolously wasted a lot of wishes. It might be too late.

That next morning Greta Gorky woke up at dawn and went to Franky Gorky's room where Franky was already up like a dart and barely listening to the birds who were singing at his window. Greta took Franky over to the big black telephone and showed him how to dial his Grandma who answered on the other end and said that she felt a lot better and would be driving to Erie so they could expect her in about two hours. Franky Gorky checked with his parents to make sure it was Christmas and then went right to the big front window and looked outside where a light snow had fallen, the limbs of the trees like the inside of ice cream bars, the lawns like white carpets laid between the glistening black sidewalks and streets. He didn't even want to open his presents, not yet, he wanted to wait for Grandma Gorky to get there and when she did he would ask her about the moon and she would tell him everything was fine, then everyone would go inside and open presents from each other and Santa Claus with the best part being that everybody gave Franky Gorky something but he never had to give anybody anything back because he was the little kid and he was special.

Franky Gorky's presents sat under the tree like great colorful square balloons filled with future. Gary Gorky sat nearby in his favorite chair, reading the paper. Greta Gorky sat in the kitchen with a cup of coffee. Franky Gorky sat at the big front window waiting for his Grandma Gorky to come and complete the whole business about everything getting back to normal. And Grandma Gorky sat behind the wheel of her car driving Route 20 from Buffalo, New York to Erie, Pennsylvania. All the Gorkys were sitting and waiting for different things but only one thing was coming.

Everybody on 24th Street between German and Celebration Avenues got a lot of early Christmas visitors that Christmas so when Grandma Gorky arrived she couldn't find parking on the Gorkys' side of the street and so had to park on the other side in front of the Funsters'. But before she could even budge from her car Franky Gorky did the most unexpected thing, in fact he even surprised himself. He jumped up from the window and without even putting on a hat or a coat, which would have been the normal thing to do in the winter, he ran outside yelling, "The moon is at the door!" He darted between two parked cars and headed out onto the black glistening street where he slipped on a patch of ice and got rubbed out by a drunk driver.

Grandpa Funster happened to be watching it all from the Funsters' front porch where he'd come out to open the door and let in the very first Christmas air, and from that day on he felt a lot older.

Franky Gorky's parents, Gary and Greta Gorky, took Franky Gorky's Christmas presents, and after the funeral left them at his grave. They kept his room exactly the way it was the day he died. Years later, when Gary Gorky was at work and Greta Gorky at the grocery store or outside hanging the wash, I'd sneak in there with Franky's younger brother, Georgie Gorky, who later ended up in juvenile court for helping Stubie Stucka change peanut butter jar lids and mustard jar lids on grocery store shelves and stealing candelabras from Greek Orthodox churches, we'd sneak in there and smell Franky's pillow and touch his rosary and check out the ancient bird excrement on Franky Gorky's window. On every Christmas after that fateful day, the Gorkys took presents to Franky Gorky's grave and left them under the stone that said, "Franky Gorky, Our Little Stinker," then returned home and lit a candle in the middle of 24th street, right where Franky Gorky got wiped out, and there they waited until another driver came along and whizzed over that candle and it got wiped out too.

Every kid who ever grew up on 24th Street knew about Franky Gorky, because he was the little kid who died for no reason because drivers got drunk and people took other people's parking places and he ran out between cars without looking both ways. But those weren't the reasons Franky Gorky reasonlessly died, and every kid on 24th Street with half a brain felt it, deep in their own white bones.

That's what I told the Viz when I got home from work that Christmas morning before dawn when I found him naked on the front porch waiting for Santee Claus. I spotted him from the Falcon, looking a little like a naked Infant of Prague, squatting on Red and Helen's front steps, pointing at a faint, cloud-engulfed gibbous moon. "Dad," said the Viz, pointing to the moon.

I could have corrected him and told him it was the moon, but I was picking up a respect for the power of metaphor.

I told the Viz about Franky Gorky and I told him the truth, or as much of it as I could conjure. I knew more about Franky Gorky everytime I thought about him. I wrapped the Viz up in my coat and sat him in my lap and me and the Viz sat on the porch steps of premorning Christmas under the naked arms of the big maple tree, staring at Red's old Studebaker Rainbow.

"You know," I said to the Viz, "if you remember your mom, she wouldn't want you sitting out here in the middle of the night naked waiting for Santee Claus." That was a strange thing to say, but it was Christmas, I was thinking about Kara Ruzci and how she'd lived her whole life and married me and had the Viz, and now when the Viz grew up he wouldn't even know who the hell she was; sometimes things are that sad and simple. Maybe I needed a long ride to New Jersey to see Kara Ruzci's grave, maybe that's what I needed, a nice long drive, get my own headstone and place it next to Kara Ruzci's with my blank death date. But Louie Ruzci would never let me in there with all those other Ruzcis.

"Do you remember your Mom?" I said to the Viz.

But the Viz was under my coat like a cat. Somewhere near my armpit I felt his faint muffling breath of "Dad."

"You got it right that time," I said. "Come on, let's go eat some ham."

≈ ≈ ≈ ≈ ≈ Bush's Last Christmas, Continued

"N O ONE TELLS YOU anything," said Bush, "No one tells you you're going to spend half your life working and the other half old and still working." She emptied a bottle of beer over her ham and lugged it back into her little gas oven.

Uncle Jon stood next to his pal the refrigerator, his head jettisoning from his shoulders like a silver bullet. He tinkled the Johnny Walker Black that Red gave him every Christmas in his glass. "We shouldn't have Christmas here," said Jon to the refrigerator, "it's too much work."

"What do you know about it?" said Bush. "You don't do any work."

"Which allows me distance and objectivity," said Jon.

"Well," said Bush, "this could be the last one." She looked at Helen.

"You never know," said Helen, "at your age."

"You never know period," said Bush.

In Bush's tiny living room, like every Bush's Last Christmas I could remember, several thousand uncles and aunts and cousins were packed onto the couch and hassocks and chairs drinking Carling Black Label beer or warm Pepsi while the Celtics bounced around on the TV on their parquet floor and Archibald Strong, wealthy and vested husband of Audrey-Mary Pell-Strong undauntedly performed card tricks, card tricks, and more card tricks to the unappreciative masses of cousins, many of whom were now adult-sized and pedigreed, like my uncle Stanley's oldest son, Obo Pell, who had a Ph.D. from Cornell University in cell char broiling and along with his pregnant Ph.D. wife Annabell was experimenting with sheep carcasses in San Antonio, Texas, and Stanley's other son, Squeelie, who had his degree in tax evasion and along with his pregnant wife Wallilia was experimenting with Republicans in Binghamton, New York. Of course Audrey-Mary Pell-Strong was pregnant too. Conspicuously absent from that bunch was Uncle David and Aunt Eleanor who'd packed their brood off to California with the money they got from selling their milkless dairy farm in Mercer which Red and Helen helped subsidize with a thousand dollars that they never saw again. Red and Helen hadn't talked much about that since Red almost drowned Helen in the toilet, though Helen's sister, Aunt Frances and her husband Uncle Harvey Stano were there with all their pinheads and the burgeoning pinhead families of their own; the youngest daughter, Lucinda, was studying to be a doctor and their oldest son, Harvey Jr., was a Michigan state cop in the narcotics division; they had a son named Stanley named after Grandpa Stanley and he was teaching things to the deaf and blind at a special school in Regina, Saskatchewan, and finally they had a son named Robert who called himself Acorn; Acorn had a receding hairline like Andrew and said he was a member of the Rainbow People's Party; he wanted to know how Andrew kept himself so nice and blue; of course everybody but cousin Lucinda had a pregnant wife and everybody sat around trying to adjudicate their individual pregnancy experiences into natural law, from what I could gather you got sick at the beginning or you didn't and then it got better unless it got worse and generally you got bigger though some people got bigger than others; that's as far as any of them got. "After they're born," I told that yawping din, "you have to keep them upside down a lot so they shit less," but no one wanted to be bothered with any real information. I took hold of the Viz and reminded him how he was going to be bigger and older than all his cousins and it was going to be his responsibility to run roughshod over all of them, a bit of advice that he took with his usual monolinguistic deftness.

Now none of this stopped Archibald Strong from performing his card tricks, and though no one was watching, Uncle Stanley did occasionally look up from the Celtics game and say "ayah-yah-yah," at Archibald while Audrey-Mary Pell-Strong got up on a chair and told the story of how one sweltering summer night when she was in the depths of a fever Archibald dragged himself out of bed to get her a drink of water and dampen a washcloth for her forehead, but the bathroom light was mysteriously broken, and there, in the darkness, with Audrey-Mary near death and in swoon, Archibald battled their insidious Korean water faucet that moaned like a rhino when you opened it, and there, in the dark, Archibald cut himself on the wrist, lengthways, actually the correct way if you were trying to kill yourself, many people, even those who attempted suicide, didn't know that, thank the Lord, and he broke his hand, and Audrey-Mary, fever and all, had to rush him to the hospital where they stopped the bleeding and set the fracture but told Archie he'd cut a nerve in his wrist and would probably never have use of his hand again.

There was nothing left for them to do but fly to Berlin.

Where Archibald hired the most famous German nerve surgeon in the world who in a grueling nine hour operation fused Archibald's nerves in such a way that a miracle might save them. What Archibald himself had to do was have a good attitude and learn card tricks, card tricks, card tricks, only card tricks could save him, besides, they were a metaphor for life, and meanwhile Archibald returned home where he sued the Korean faucet company for seventeen million dollars, a court case which set myriad faucet company suing precedents, at the climax of which Archibald took the witness stand and bared his mutilated wrist and struggled through his first couple card tricks; brought the jury to tears, though in fact Archibald knew those card tricks cold by that time and just pretended to be struggling through them and he'd put off his scheduled plastic surgery on his wrist just so he could produce that dramatic affect, all that chicanery being revealed to him during his contemplations on appearance and reality that were generated while he practiced card tricks, card tricks, card tricks. Ironically, he probably should have thanked that Korean faucet company for all they did for him, but instead he rubbed them out.

Most of the teeming masses inside Bush's tiny living room had been ignoring that story for years and efficaciously did so once again, though I went out of my way to help that pregnant Audrey-Mary Pell-Strong down off her chair—Archibald being too busy performing card tricks—and compliment her on how well she'd expanded that story over the years. By filling in all those empty spaces, I told her, she had, in a sense, robbed the listener of essential imaginative leaps while opening up more blatant and traditional moral questions.

"I should probably write it down," said Audrey-Mary. "Archie thinks it would make an excellent movie or TV show."

"Don't write it down," I told her. "If you write it down it dies in its tracks."

"But we could make money," said Audrey-Mary Pell-Strong.

Well it looked like Audrey-Mary Pell-Strong started some kind of trend in there because next thing you knew our cousin Acorn Stano was up on that chair saying that what we all needed to do was realize that post-corporate American consumer democracy was really just another form of totalitarianism which in its apparent toleration of proliferate ideologies merely produced their commoditization and subsequent fetishization, unbeknownst to ourselves our existence was alienated, our consciousness false, our ideas reified into fluffy pancakes; our brains were like food at McDonald's, the French fries and hamburgers looked different but they were all made of the same stuff. What we needed to do, said Acorn Stano, was return to the Tao, work the earth with our hands, share its produce with our hearts, allow our minds to once again become the evolutionary extension of our hands, our tools. We would have a revolution of the soul, America would be green again. We'd all share each other's drugs.

You had to listen real close because there were a lot of new words in there, but I thought the part about sharing drugs was a good idea, as long as everybody else had drugs to share. And since nobody was listening I thought it just as well that I get up on that chair myself. I shook Acorn's hand and helped him down and then got up there and told that unlistening mob that there'd come a time when the traditional hierarchies of power would naturally invert because humanity, the first product of the universe to produce its own useless waste, would unify the dualism of waste and consciousness. As controllers of the waste, garbagemen would be poet kings, they will fly light ships, create worlds, unify galaxies. The waste of generations of stars, the dying universe, will slowly curl itself around the massive cores of intergalactic waste, their cores, heating and exploding in novas, will become the births of new stars, their molecules spreading, traversing space, solidifying and becoming new planets, new moons, new solar systems, new life. The thoughts of garbagemen will control the creation of new multiverses. Garbagemen will rule it all, travel, thought, life. I went on for quite some time and had more to say, too, but not too long into my speech Bush's polynonlingual cousin, Edju, and his wife, Aunt Elizabeth, appeared on the edge of that crowded room, Edju plunging headward and disappearing into the din, only to appear next to me atop that chair.

"Hmmm, Jarvis, so you still so you," said Edju and pushed me off.

"He thought you were done," said my Aunt Elizabeth.

Edju peered down over that madding crowd, hat brim dipped, lips pursed like a lotus eater. "So so very, so very so so long ago," said Edju. "So hmmm, so hmmm," said Edju, "so very very so."

"We're so glad you threw this party for us," translated Aunt Elizabeth, "but we can't stay."

Neda emerged from the throbbing mob and got Edju down from the chair. She gave him a kiss and called him Uncle Ed.

"Hmmm, Neda, beauty, hmmm no?" said Edju and gave her fifty bucks.

Across the way, our cousin Stanley Stano who worked with the blind and deaf in Saskatchewan was trying to talk to Joseph, but every time Stanley Stano spoke to him Joseph shut down and every time

Stanley Stano started communicating with his river of fingers Joseph jumped and woke up. He didn't trust Stanley Stano, there was just no good reason to be that anxious to teach anybody anything.

Just then that Celtics game ended on TV and some major network news announcer came on and showed pictures of our boys having Christmas in Vietnam. It was a long way to go to have Christmas but it was requisite for soldiers to have Christmases in exotic and hostile places. They showed U.S. Marines eating turkey and waving letters from home and then they showed a row of Vietcong body parts and then some more soldiers loading American body bags onto helicopters. Then they gave some number counts; we'd rubbed out some 6000 Communist Vietnamese for Christmas and lost about fifty-seven of our own, not that much in comparison to them, but one American life was always too much, unless of course we considered that those lives were given for freedom. That was certainly something to consider, those Dialecticians were probably up in Willie's attic right at that very moment, gambling their lives away and considering that very question. But even that announcer pointed out that it looked like we were losing a lot of American lives over there considering we weren't even at war.

"Looks like war to me," said Helen.

"It's not a war," said Uncle Stanley, "We're just helping out the French."

"We helped them out so good they're all the way out," said Acorn Stano.

"Now we're helping the Vietnamese," said Uncle Stanley.

"Looked like we were killing them to me," said Helen.

"We're just killing the Communist ones," said Uncle Stanley. "It's like killing the weeds in your lawn."

"It is the eternal war between good and evil," said Uncle Jon, coming into the room. "Between Christianity and atheism, freedom and Communism."

"If we let Vietnam go Communist," said Uncle Stanley, "then Cambodia will go Communist, then Laos, then Thailand, Burma, the Philippines, they'll all go Communist. The Russians will own them all."

"If it's so lousy," said Red, "How come everybody wants to go Communist?"

"They want to stand in line for toilet paper," yelled Bush from the kitchen. "They work on their farms all day, it's the only chance they get to see each other."

"Oooh, so oooh ow oooh," said Edju who knew because he'd surrendered to nations all over the world during World War I.

"In Russia the toilet paper is like sand paper," said Aunt Elizabeth.

"So very oooh," said Edju.

"But it's free," said cousin Acorn.

"They pay dearly for that free toilet paper," said Uncle Jon.

"They give up their freedom for that free toilet paper," said Uncle Stanley.

"Where would your family be if Red wouldn't have been able to sell toilet paper all those years?" asked Aunt Frances.

It was a good thing Bush had her ham and Polish sausage and duck's blood soup done in the kitchen or that conversation might have started to make sense. Uncle Stanley carted his extended family into the kitchen, card tricks, fetuses, and all and left us Loops and Stanos in there with Edju and Aunt Elizabeth. Jon split for the kitchen to man his rocking chair at the head of the table.

Off in the corner of that room, Helen sat so quiet as to be conspicuous. She had her eyes on her two babies, Joseph and Andrew, and I knew what she was thinking. She'd sent her husband to war once and almost twice, she'd put in her time waiting for death. And for Red, he saw enough Japanese radios and German automobiles to know what he fought for. He'd send his kids to defeat Communists and the next thing you know he'd be wiping his ass with Russian toilet paper.

"So, hmmm, war, hmmm so big new," said Edju.

"You wouldn't like Vietnam," Aunt Elizabeth told him, "and you couldn't surrender to them without going over there."

"Well," said Aunt Frances who still looked like a wiry version of Helen, except unlike Helen her hair hadn't gone gray, "my boys would go, but they're all married and their wives are expecting."

"That's right," said the cousins.

"That's wrong," said Acorn.

"Somebody has to protect the future of all these babies," said Aunt Frances.

"Let General Motors protect them," said Acorn.

"GM did all right by you," said Uncle Harvey who was a bigwig in Detroit for Pontiac.

"What are we protecting, from whom, for whom?" said Neda, who up to that point had spent a pretty quiet Bush's last Christmas.

"We're protecting the American Way for the Vietnamese from the Russians," said Uncle Harvey.

It was nice to get that straight before the Uncle Stanley crew got done eating and left and those Stanos went into the kitchen for Bush's Last Christmas fest. Us Loops and Edju and Aunt Elizabeth just kind of sat there contemplating the war effort and watching some scientist on the TV who said the Star of the Magi was caused by the confluence of Mars, Saturn, and Jupiter.

"Does this mean it wasn't a miracle?" I asked Helen.

"It was a miracle they could follow it from China and end up in Bethlehem and not on Mars," said Neda.

"It was a miracle of coincidence," said Helen.

"One of them was supposed to be black," said Joseph. "I never heard of a black Chinese."

"He was Cantonese," said Helen. "They're darker."

"Bethlehem didn't exist at that time," said Neda. "And the Romans didn't make everybody go back to the place of their ancestors to take a census. It would be ridiculous and inefficient and besides there are no records of it and the Romans kept meticulous records of everything."

"There were prophesies," said Helen. "Everybody had to follow them, even if it meant breaking from their habits or inconveniencing themselves."

"I think it's baloney," said Joseph.

"It's an important myth system," said Andrew.

"Rumor elevated to myth, myth elevated to dogma," Joseph said.

"That's right!" said Andrew.

"According to some," said Neda, "myth mediates ineffable truths by means of powerful signification, the semiotics of which reach into consciousness through naturalized imagery and deep into the cultural and racial unconscious so central to human essence, a system of symbols and layers of symbols without which we would not be human, let alone spiritual."

"Boy is that right!" said Andrew.

"Baloney," said Joseph.

"It just happened," said Helen. "Thinking about it won't help you."

"Do you want to eat?" said Bush from the door. One nice thing about always being the last family to get in there, we usually got Uncle Jon all to ourselves, though this year we got packed in there around Bush's little kitchen table with Edju and Aunt Elizabeth, Uncle Jon who never got up from his rocking chair at the head of the table unless he needed more scotch, and Bush herself who always waited till every last one of us was served before she sat down to eat. That kitchen table was built to accommodate about four people and there were ten of us. And one new addition. Hanging above Uncle Jon from a pole was a little cage with a canary. Up till then I hadn't noticed that canary.

"You got a bird, Bush," I said.

"So if the air gets too thin, he'll die before I do and I can get the hell out," said Bush.

"Does he sing?" said Helen.

"Only to himself," said Bush.

"He keeps the men and me awake all night," said John.

"I'd like a bird," said Helen. "And a piano."

"You don't know how to play the piano," said Red.

"Red would just bust it up and throw it in the basement," said Neda. "It'd be in the basement forever like everything else."

"I wouldn't," said Red. "I'd fix it or get her a new one."

That marked some kind of change in Red, but it was hard to tell just what kind of change it was.

"I'll take lessons," said Helen. "Then I'd teach my baby."

"That Infant does a lot of things for you," Bush said to Helen, dishing out the duck's blood soup, "but I don't think he'll play the piano."

"I'm pregnant," said Helen.

"That's wonderful," said Jon, "I think you should leave Red and raise this child without his influence." He sipped his scotch. "No offense to the rest of you."

"Could I have a leg with my soup?" Helen asked Bush.

"You can't be pregnant," Bush told Helen, "You had an operation."

Well there it was, somebody'd finally said it. You'd have thought that with all Red's bigness and stubbornness he might have said something to Helen in all this time, but he didn't. No, it had to be Bush. Not that it stopped Helen for an instant.

"I haven't had a period," said Helen.

"You can't have a period," said Bush.

"Because I'm pregnant," said Helen.

"You're not showing," said Bush.

"Not yet," said Helen.

"It's a miracle," said Jon.

"That's right," said Helen. She got up and put her fingers in the bird cage. "You should get that bird a mate so it will lay an a egg," Helen said to Bush.

"He's a male," said Bush.

"He's a nice bird," said Helen, "but he needs an egg."

In many ways Christmas was not a pleasure because everybody was so busy doing unpleasurable things they didn't want to do and then shoving them down other people's throats because it was our duty; that was the important reason we always ended up over at Aunt Jelly and Uncle Bif's; Red spent the year avoiding his family, most of whom he purported to like, and spent his time helping Bush and Jon who he felt a lot of ambivalence about because Jon hated him and was nuts and always accused Red of trying to kill him, which was barely true, Red could have killed him anytime he wanted but hardly ever tried. But on Christmas he felt it was his duty to go over to Bush's, he felt it deep within his giant not-wanting-to heart. And if there was anyplace else he had that much ambivalence about it was Bif and Jelly's, who had a great and mysterious and convoluted past involving Red and Helen, so of course they were the only relatives on his side we ever went to see. So that's where we always went after we left Bush's Last Christmas.

Uncle Bif always had the biggest Christmas tree in the world in his house, it took up most the living room, and Red's sister Aunt Jelly limped around the room on her one little tiny leg she got from polio and her one normal one and served everybody 7UP mixed with the liquor of their choice and told everybody not to go underneath that tree because they might not come out alive.

But this year, underneath that tree, was the legendary train set of Uncle Lefty Limburg, the train set he kept up in his attic all for himself for decades. The only evidence there'd ever been for the thing, aside from testimony, was a key Uncle Lefty carried on his belt that he always called the key to heaven. He always said he was going to set it up under his tree for his kids, Sweety and Sweaty, but he never did and now they were too old to give a shit. So Lefty's wife, Red's sister, Tilly, convinced Lefty to bring it to Jelly and Bif's.

"You finally brought it to earth," Helen said to him.

"More like earth to it, ha!" said Bif.

"It's just a story you can make yourself happy with," said Lefty. He looked as leathery as beef jerky. "It's a story."

"He's trying to explain something to himself," said Helen.

"What's to explain?" said Jelly, limping by with a tray of drinks. "It's a train set."

"Plenty," said Helen.

"That's right," said Lefty. "Nothing to explain. Just set it up, turn it on, let it run. Runs itself."

"Unless you want to change something," said Red.

"Revise the story, ha!" said Bif.

"It's not a story, it's an argument," said Helen. "Stories don't make you happy."

"Arguments make you happy?" said Lefty.

"Catholics, ha!" said Bif.

"Are we arguing?" said Jelly.

Well you knew what Helen was thinking, that you just couldn't use subtle reasoning around protestants.

But that train set was so big that there were two separate cities on either side of the tree. I looked for garbage trucks, for an incinerator where yellow dump trucks rolled in and out of the dark with their loads of garbage. I open the pit for them by pulling an old, thick chain that hangs against a brick wall and the black metal door swings open like a wing, the pit spewing orange fire. I guide the garbage from the back of the truck with my coal shovel, watching a million tons of waste burn at my feet, a hundred thousand things from a hundred thousand beings come to me to be burned in my city of light. I put them to the flames as if they were the buildings in which lives were lived. I narrate the victims into the fire.

"Things got a will of its own," said Lefty. "You change something, it just goes right on." He moved to his huge, black transformer and started the trains. In the cities were streets and houses and grocery stores and train stations and little downtowns with multistoried buildings on the roofs of which parked tiny helicopters waiting for business executives who obviously didn't want to take one of the two passenger trains that left every couple minutes or so for the next town, or maybe they were taking the helicopters to the airport that sat on the edge of the train set, you had to go through the ritzy suburbs to get to it and it looked like the bus lines only ran downtown. There were several Piper Cubs, a couple small jets, and even one of those new passenger prop-jets, props spinning. There were cars on the streets, people on the sidewalks; in front of their homes, folks watered their lawns or sat on their porches drinking lemonade. I guess it wasn't Christmas down there, or maybe it was Florida or California, though up in the mountains, where each of those two passenger trains and four freight trains with cars that said Reading Railroad and Pennsylvania Railroad and New York Central and Chesapeake and B&O, passed through tunnels, disappearing underneath the earth for minutes at a time, sometimes longer, sometimes an hour, there was snow; people skiing and sled riding and cutting wood, packing it on the backs of their sleighs for the cold nights, to warm their brown cabins behind the hills.

On the other side of those hills, in the other town, daylight had yet to break. Lights dimmed yellow from the windows of the houses, webs of columnated light spreading into the shadows of labor and false dawn. Men held lights in the train yard, working the lines with the beams of lantern's guide, trains like dark dragons following the light. In the factories stretching along the river, clangs and fire rose from the smokestacks. A train stopped, leaving coal for the furnaces; men in cranes loaded steel beams onto its flatcars. If the first city was one of warmth, leisure, and light, then the second was one of darkness and labor. The trains took the oil barrels and steel beams and cleaned logs from the city of darkness and left them in the city of light, where now, looking closely, you could see the whitened churches and towers of glass. In the City of Darkness a light snow dusted the ground. There was a cemetery.

A man knelt in front of a grave. His hair was like the feathers of a fine bird, his hands marked like the crossroads of stories. He sat back on his feet, rocking slowly, waiting for daylight. Did he know what was on the other side of that grave? An old man, wings folded under his coat like a beetle. Polished nails. Clean black shoes. He crouched. His breath an animal in the air; he made things with his thoughts.

He made the trains that made the city go. He made the houses and the shops, the darkness, and the light from the windows that spread like spider webs into the streets. He made the factories and the labor. Worlds shifted with the adjustment of his wings.

There were times when he walked the streets like an old man among other women and men, and times when he flew in the air above the cities, a black insect of decision. There were nights when his animal breath ran in the minds of the populace like rats beneath the floorboards. Yet other nights he thought his thoughts behind the gravestones, feeding and eating the dialectic of mourning. His breath the mist.

And tonight he was rich. Drunk with the mourning of this man before his mother's tomb. He had planted the thought of her death years and years ago, placing it in a spot just behind her right ear, slipping it into a crevice of her brain as gently as he might lay a seed under her breast. Then, slowly, he brought it upon her. Developed it. Permitted it to blossom. He gave her insanity, paralysis, a long slow death. It was one of his best.

There had been a time when the woman was as strong as light, as deep as darkness. She'd raised four children, this one, before her grave, the last. And when her husband was surprised by the thought of his death, thinking it suddenly in his heart as he checked the couplings between train cars, the woman returned to the work she did before she had a husband and four children. She cleaned the train stations. She polished their wooden benches, kept the marble floors like glass, the ticket booths like varnished confessionals. And this one, her youngest, she sneaked to work beneath her coat, hiding him in the supply closet where she could return to feed him, touch him, bring him lost keys she found on the floor of the station; keys from Brownsville and Toledo, Boston and Istanbul, Los Angeles, Rome, heaven; keys from the City of Light; she strung them above him, just out of his reach, so they glistened and clinked in the heat of the ventilator that she lay him near to keep him warm.

He was the youngest of four sons, and the old man with wings had found it ironic. The woman prayed because the old man thought "God," and when she asked for a daughter the old man thought "sons." He had a special place for her. He'd picked her out. It is what happens, he told himself, sometimes. There are balances of leisure and labor, dark and light, fortune and misfortune. They must play themselves out in small and large ways. Even he could not an escape that. His heart was motivated by joy. He only thought their lives, their illusions. He did not think their thoughts.

And that is how he took her through her life. He took her husband. He took one son in his youth, allowed another to grow and die, a third he permitted to marry before he took both husband and wife. It was not that difficult. And this one, the one before the grave, the last, he let her keep. He simply laid the seed of her death in the lobe of her brain and did not let it blossom until she was ready to let her last son go. He married, and as his daughter grew in the womb of his love, his mother died.

First she went insane, stringing her house with keys and clutter until she couldn't walk in it and had to build herself a lean-to on the roof where she talked to the birds and mimicked their flight. She flapped her arms, chattered and whistled and crowed until her neighbors pleaded with the son to have her removed. Which he could not do. She clung vice-like to the rafters of her home, eventually learning to hoot and murmur more softly under the stars and pale moon and dustings of the first snows. But slowly her left shoulder began to sag, the side of her face dipped. Her mouth slouched, her eye closed, her leg lay like a club. Then he took her from the roof to his home where he made a bed for her in his front room near the window. There, she rotted, flapping her single wing and muttering profanities and invectives until she could not speak at all and her eyes became dull gray things that killed light.

He turned her to prevent bed sores, washed her, cleaned her excrement, cooked her meals until she no longer ate solids and he fed her through a straw. Soon she no longer ate at all, sinking into little but her own rattling breath.

But on the morning that his wife gave birth, just before they left for the hospital, she awoke and called to him. Her eyes, dark blue circles of concentration, she motioned to him with her good hand. But when he bent to her lips with his ear she had nothing to say. He stood. She placed her hand on her stomach. When he returned in the afternoon, she had returned to her coma, and on the morning they brought her the child, her granddaughter, she was dead.

This is how the old man, black wings packed beneath his jacket like obsidian shells, brought the son to him. He himself, submitting to the balance of his own thoughts, had grown old, and before he passed his world to other thinkers, or let it fall apart under the annihilation that a world suffers without illusion, he would reveal himself. He would, for a moment, open a crack in the world he enclosed within his mind. He would write upon the page of his world like a mother writing with her own milk, dying in a metaphor which folded upon itself until it disappeared within its own subtlety. And this was the man on whom he would write it. He was thinking this behind the grave, certain that he would do it, but now, listening to the beat of his own heart, watching his creaturely breath crawl into the air, he wondered about time. He was thinking time. He watched himself permit time.

Shall I reveal myself? he asked. Should I reveal?

He must have given his world a moment alone, because it was then that he was discovered. The younger man stood above him, as quiet as a crane, holding his coat closed against the cold.

The young man had seen the mist rising from behind his mother's grave. He rose and walked over to the stone, and found the old man crouching behind his mother's tomb like an egg, his bald head arched forward like a snail shell, clean black shoes, fists against his chest like carved rocks. His eyes were jewels set in stone. It was a strange sight, but he'd seen stranger things, like the lizards from Africa that made balloons in their throats and floated away from predators, and fish from Polynesia that if left to dry in the sun became the skeletons of tiny men; he thought of his neighbor's child who went to sleep one night two years ago and since had only awakened twice, at night, to scream of a nightmare that she'd been buried alive, that a tomb had been placed in her and grown into a life. It was a cold night and the cemetery was a good place to sleep.

The old man gazed into the eyes of the younger one who stood with the single-mindedness of a mourning bird. Now he knew that he could, at any time, change everything. He could stand and lower his coat, expand his black wings until they covered the graveyard, encircled the night. He would reveal himself. Slowly, he stood.

"Do you need a place to stay?" said the young man.

And the old man with wings like shells thought, yes, a place to stay, a place for one night in which to be warm, to walk inside the caverns of one's thoughts, to live in a place like an insect covering itself with silk and waiting.

"Yes," said the old man. "That would be a fine thing."

And the old man went with the younger one to his dark house and took a small room and for the first time in years beyond memory lay down in a bed and spun from the deepest part of himself a world of night and a cocoon of dreams.

An indulgence. A night's sleep. Then, in the morning, he would reveal himself. He would begin the beginning of the end of the world.

But in the morning he did not reveal himself. The oldest daughter, Martha, a teenage girl of light hair and white skin, brought him breakfast: a soft-boiled egg, coffee, and a piece of toast. He imagined himself eating as slowly as wind eats, delicate, passive, strong. He imagined the family downstairs preparing for school and work; three more daughters, Ruth, Judith, and Beth, the woman, Evelyn, who worked as a ticket clerk at the train station, and the man, Paul, to whom he'd come so close to revealing himself, who like his father was a brakeman in the yards. The old man with wings let them have their breakfasts, had them prepare their lunches. He got them on their busses and in their car and put them at work. Then he emerged from his bed and unfolded his wings slowly in front of his mirror, allowing them to fall toward the floor like the hair of a woman. These wings were no gift. He'd spent his life in the streets, the air, the night, waiting behind graves, crouched beneath floorboards, perched in attics, planting the charade of life and the time of death. He was old. He might stay another day.

He dressed and went downstairs, running his fingers along the tables and chairs, touching his lips to cups, his tongue to china plates. He marked the furniture with his urine, wiped his perspiration on the cheese and meat, drooled in the milk and juices, He laid his excrement in the sun, crumbled it and fouled the flour and cereals and bread. This will bring him to me, he thought. This will bring him to me and then I will reveal myself.

When they returned he was back in his room, but when the girl brought him supper he could barely eat it, it smelled so like himself.

This is the way his life with them progressed. In the morning someone would bring him his breakfast; either Martha, the oldest, who was fair and white; or the next oldest, Ruth, who had red hair and rosy cheeks; or the sallow one, Judith, with olive skin and green eyes; or Beth, the youngest, with skin like evening, eyes and hair blacker than his own wings. On the fifth day, the woman came, dark and powerful, stoically kind to his needs, the red of her cheeks hinting at her skin like dawn, the blue of her eyes suggesting night, and on the sixth day, the man, as bland and impermeable as daylight. The old man wondered what he'd ever seen in him; he wondered whether he'd spent so much time creating his life and destiny that he'd forgotten totally about character, forgotten to give a line to his face, a tint to his eyes, an edge to lips. He had worked for generations on the misery of this lineage to the point where he himself was now old, and the pinnacle of his work now came to him like water sitting in the sun.

That is why, the old man told himself, that I must stay, that I must wait to reveal myself and stay. And each day, after the family left for work and school, he did his server his mischief. He entered her room and smelled her underwear, mixed his secretions with her ointments, his excrement with her make-up. He spent the day in her clothes, leaving his scent. He planted in her diary and cabinets the scales from his wings. And on the sixth day he did the same to the man, fouling with his body more than he could have ever dreamed in his thoughts. But at the end of each day his victim returned to him, the women more beautiful, the man more banal and good.

On Sundays, when he was left alone, he sat by his window and did his work, stretching his thoughts to the train yards and factories, the hospitals and graves. He was less attached to this work now, content to put it in motion like a clock and less anxious to sit within its gears. He imagined himself spreading the cloak of his wings at night and pulling them back in the day. He contemplated his winged flight in the insect sky, picking the dead. But his life was now in this room, in this house. This is where he prepared for his emergence, nurturing the egg of the end. That is how the days passed, and the weeks and the months, until he had been there a year.

And after a year he finally chose to speak.

When white skinned Martha brought his breakfast he pushed himself up in his bed and caught her with his eyes. For the first time, he thanked her. "Why do think I'm here?" he asked her.

The girl did not seem to have much trouble with that. She sipped from his coffee and took a bite of his toast. "Because you're old," she said.

He took the toast and coffee from her, smelling the pungency of his own acids in the butter, in the steam of the coffee.

"This is the reason I stay?" he said.

"Is it a reason to leave?" said the girl.

That day after she had gone, when he placed himself in her life, he lay the thought of age in her shoes where it would begin in her toes and curl her feet into knots, spreading through her calves and thighs and finally her spine until she was crippled with bones like bars, her heart and mind young in a cage of pain.

On the second day he spoke to red-haired Ruth. "Where did I come from?" he asked the girl.

"From behind my grandmother's grave," she said.

"Doesn't that frighten you?" he said.

"You were cold and we felt sorry for you," she said.

So that day he filled her blouses with fear, so that slowly she would begin to feel as if the world were seeking her with its hands, that there was nothing and no one, not her mother, not a spoon, not even her own clothes, that was not trying to strangle her.

When he asked Judith where she supposed he would go when he left their house, she teased him and said he would go to his grave if he didn't eat breakfast. To her he gave the thought of nausea whenever she saw food.

He asked Beth, the youngest and darkest, "Who am I?" and when she told him he was an old man who was afraid of death he gave her an obsession with suicide. To the mother, Evelyn, he gave pregnancy and miscarriage, and to Paul a slow cancer in his groin. This is the stuff of life, he thought, and began to enjoy himself again.

He spent the year laying cracks in their walls, dismantling machines, stuffing heat vents and water pipes with dead rodents. He was working very hard, and on Sundays found himself sleeping so late that when he got to his window the City of Darkness had gone on without him. Ice floes melted in the rivers and shadows crept out from beneath the trees. In the train yards, long freights sat dormant while the inhabitants of the city, left to their own illusions, abolished laws and spent their mornings and early afternoons lolling in cafes or drinking in bars. It took the old man the rest of the day and deep into the night to think the people back into their homes, the shadows beneath their objects.

Running the world was a challenge again, he had his family to thank for that, but now more than ever he needed them to stir with complaint, to come to him, to acknowledge him, so that he could answer them with the underside of his wings. But they continued, through the havoc and misfortune he brought them, to bring him his meals.

On the eve of the third year, on a night as black as any night he had ever created, the old man spread his wings till they filled his room, his body a cave within him, his thoughts like lead, silent and thick with night. He would speak to them again, he thought. He would speak to them, and this time, when he spoke to the man, he would reveal himself. He would not have to die himself to end this world. There were other places for old men with wings like black jewels. He would place a crack in the thought of the world and allow it to widen like a wound. He would reveal.

But as he spoke to them in turn, none of the women gave him satisfaction. They made no complaint of the stench of rodents in their heat and pipes. They took their afflictions like unwanted gifts, as if we had given them a toaster when they had one already. They saw no connection between his presence and their misery. Until, when he spoke to the man, Paul, he said, "You are sick. If your cancer continues you will die soon."

Paul took a chair next to the bed of the old man. "What do you know of the City of Light?" he said.

"Your family needs you," said the old man.

"No one here speaks of the other city," said the younger man.

"When you die," said the old man with wings. "Do you think your family will put me out?"

"Before my mother died," said Paul, "she awoke from her coma and I bent my ear to her lips. Though she said nothing, she spoke to me. She said there was no labor in the City of Light, no winter, no cold, no illness, no death. That the darkness there was like the gray before dawn, the light like the wing of eternity."

The old man's wings rolled under his bed shirt. His shoulders arched. "In the City of Light," he said to the younger man, "everything is hollow. Everything is made of plastic and tin, the buildings, even the trees. The people are plaster statues, sentinels of nothing, seeing nothing, thinking nothing. The trains from here empty their goods below the mountains. They return empty from the City of Light because they enter there with nothing aboard. No one leaves the City of Light because no one is there. No one goes there because it is nothing and emptiness is unthinkable. It is a lifeless mask and that is precisely the purpose of it. Where nothing is lifelike, nothing speaks of death."

"The trains," said Paul.

"Nothing drives the trains but illusion."

Paul stood. He pushed away his chair, "But I am thinking of the City of Light," he said.

"Your life has been nothing but labor and goodness," said the old man, "but you and your family have known nothing but misery. Since you brought me here, things have only gotten worse." He got up from his bed and stood before the younger man. His black wings itched at his back.

"You are an old man," said Paul, going to the door. "You can stay as long as you like."

"Wait," said the old man. He knew now that misery would not bring the young man to him. "Across the alley is a child who sleeps and sleeps. She ages in her sleep and wakes only with the moon. She dreams she is buried alive and yet within her a tomb grows like a mushroom. This is all she can say when she awakes. Sometimes you bring her family food. Your wife brings flowers for her bedside. Go there now and then come and tell me what you see."

Paul found no good reason not to go and visit the child. The night was quiet. There was no moon in the sky. Her parents seemed to appreciate his visits. Downstairs he found Evelyn and told her, "The old man wants us to visit our neighbors."

"Well," said Evelyn, "it's the first thing he ever wanted," not knowing that the old man lived a life of desire, and everything that the world became was his want, and having all that he wanted he changed what he wanted, and now he wanted to reveal himself to them, he wanted them to come to him questioning their misery, which he would answer with the odiferous rise of his wings, the end of everything. But she couldn't know that.

So Evelyn and Paul went across the alley to the house of the girl who dreamed that death was around her and in her though she herself was not dead, but when they got there the child was awake and crying in her mother's arms. She'd been sleeping so long that she was no longer a child, now as large as her mother, though she wept on her lap. Her waist, though emaciated, widened to womanly hips. On her chest were well developed breasts. They stayed through the night with the parents and the girl, but in the morning, with the girl still weeping, they left.

The old man with wings waited out the night in his room, and then, with the dawn, prepared himself. He bathed himself with a sponge and preened his wings. He put on his suit and black shoes. He sat in the chair beside his bed and faced the door and waited. He waited a long time.

Downstairs he heard the bustle of activity, the clomping of feet, the voices of the daughters, the movement of boxes and furniture, until, as the sun came through his window, low and gray in the afternoon, as bright as the City of Darkness ever received, he heard silence. He waited longer, but hearing nothing he rose and went downstairs.

The house was bare, stripped of its tables and chairs, its carpets rolled up and removed. The clothes were taken from the closets, the dishes from the cabinets. There was no food. Pictures had been lifted from the walls, mementos packed. The old man with wings was left alone in the barren house that smelled only of him.

He left the house and crossed the alleyway where he found the dream child, now a young woman, weeping in the yard.

"Why do you cry like this?" the old man with wings of death said to her.

"Because I do not want to be awake," she said to him.

The old man approached the young woman and stood in front of her. He dropped his coat. "Do you know who I am?" he said.

"Yes," she said. "You are my baby, my child."

With that the old man took off his shirt. His wings dropped to the ground like a blanket, then, slowly, rose with his breath. They rose above his shoulders like slate in the gray eve, then encircled him, turning him into an obsidian egg, etched like a tombstone. The light on his wings. Then he opened them again, spreading them around the young woman, and then, in a thrust, around the yard. The wings of the old man, their undersides raising the stench of a million corpses, grew like the night, grew like the darkest night of the world until they encompassed all of the City of Darkness in the last dark explosion of night.

The young woman found only a pile of dry bones which she gathered in the wings and buried in the yard.

Uncle Lefty moved to his transformer. It had caps of colored bulbs, huge calibrated power dials for every train. He hit a button and a switch track shifted a train into the dark train yard where he stopped in front of a warehouse. He opened a boxcar door. "Christmas," said Uncle Lefty. "Free rides."

"You got garbagemen in those towns?" I said to Uncle Lefty.

"Train set garbagemen, ha!" said Uncle Bif.

"Garbagemen, heh, heh," said Grandpa Whitey Loop. He blew smoke at me.

"There's some dump trucks," said Uncle Lefty Limburg.

"You should get them compactors," I said to him. "It's too hard to work with dump trucks."

"I don't think they make toy garbage trucks.," said Uncle Lefty.

"Toy garbage trucks, heh, heh," said Grandpa Whitey, blowing smoke at Lefty.

"What's all this about garbage trucks?" said Grandma Emma Loop. "We don't care about garbage trucks."

That was the first time in my life that Grandma Emma Loop ever said a word to me. She tended to sit around like a mountain with a pie for a head and make disparaging remarks into the air. Though she wasn't looking at me, maybe she just made that one into the air too.

"It's his livelihood," said Helen, putting her arm around my waist, which was even stranger. Helen wasn't that affectionate with me. I'm sure she fed me when I was a baby. But Helen was deep and abstract. She had both hot and cold water running in there, but most the time she preferred it dry.

Grandma Emma Loop offered a grunt to the living room.

"Dad!" said the Viz to nobody in particular.

"Dad, heh, heh," said Grandpa Whitey and blew smoke in the Viz's face.

But it wasn't too long before things settled down and Uncle Lefty started telling his annual stories like the time he and Red put on white sheets and chased their drunken neighbor, Arnie Zuttefeffel, all around the neighborhood, and the day Lefty was supposed to marry Aunt Tillie when Lefty woke up still drunk and with a hangover from his bachelor's party at the Kronenburger Club and Red convinced him that it was still the same day and his wedding wasn't until tomorrow, took him to the nearest bar to clear up his hangover and didn't tell him he was late for his wedding until he was an hour late and half back in the bag.

"Nah, I never did that," said Red.

"You did too," said Aunt Tillie, who had two wandering eyes like a chameleon; they moved around like they were suspended on the ends of rubbery wieners. "I waited at the church in my wedding dress for two hours. The only reason I didn't leave was Red was missing too and I knew they were up to no good. The two of them showed up drunk as canaries."

"Canaries, heh, heh," a said Grandpa Whitey.

Then Uncle Lefty told the baseball story about when Red was too young to play on the St. John's Lutheran Christian League adult baseball team, only being sixteen, so had to be the bat boy, but in the championship game in the bottom of the ninth when they were down 1-0 with two on and Cowley Caldwell who was 0 for 22 in the playoffs due up, their manager, Blacky Burns, who Lefty said was an old son-of-a-bitch who farted in church, Blacky Burns grabbed Red and said, "shit, anybody can strike out, you go do it," and Red went up and put the first pitch to him off the left field wall, got to third standing up, won the championship for St. John's Lutheran and spent the next ten years catching for Lefty; they won the title nine out of those ten.

"The count went 3 and 0," said Red. "He served up the last pitch on a platter."

"You looked at the first two pitches for strikes," said Aunt Tillie, her eyes on the lookout for predators. "I was there. The third one was neck high and you shouldn't have swung."

"Went right off the wall," said Lefty.

"There was no wall," said Red. "Just that hill in front of the school."

"There was a cyclone fence," said Aunt Tillie. "You two don't know what you're talking about."

Then Lefty told the other story he told every year about the time he and Red snuck a giant pumpkin into Whitey's pumpkin patch that had only tiny cooking pumpkins and Grandpa Whitey didn't even blink, just got a wheelbarrow and put the giant pumpkin in his Model A and drove to the County Fair. Even back then Grandpa Whitey didn't give much of a shit so the joke was on everybody else.

"Heh, heh," said Grandpa Whitey. "I grew that pumpkin." He didn't look at all like Red, he was little and dapper and wry.

After a wile I went up to my cousin Nancy's bedroom with Neda and Joseph and Andrew and Bifboy, Nancy's older brother, and Sweety and Sweaty Limburg, and shared very powerful marijuana just like Acorn Stano's Taoist Communists. We listened to all those stories through the smoke, repeating these exact stories to each other, including the disagreements. Without those stories, said Neda between puffs, we lived in the fragments of unspoken poems, our lives metonymically vacuous, our bodies metaphors of nothingness. Well, if you needed a reason, there, you had one. I went to the window and lifted the curtain. In the sky, the planets spun like leaves turning in the wind.

⁔   ⁔   ⁔

Over in the corner of the room my cousin, Bifboy, who just not too long ago got out of the Air Force, sat with a bottle of beer on his belly like a lily. I was about to ask him what he knew about Vietnam when suddenly, downstairs, there was a big commotion. So cousin Nancy sprayed us all up and down with Alberto V05 hairspray and the bunch of us lumbered down the stairs.

There in the doorway was a little man, not so little as he'd fit in the train set, but short, shorter than any of the women in the room, in fact about the size of Grandpa Whitey. There was a woman next to him smoking a cigarette and wearing a fur and he himself had on some kind of expensive long coat, the two of them looking like a picture that Aunt Jelly dragged out every other Christmas or so that was taken not too long after the wedding of Grandma Emma and Grandpa Whitey. He took off his hat and gave a wry little smile. He had blond hair, too, just like Grandpa Whitey. Then he said, "heh, heh," just like Grandpa Whitey.

"Shorty," said Emma.

I don't think I'd seen her standing more than six times in my life, but there she was standing with tears in her eyes.

"Shorty," screamed Tillie and Jelly, and ran and limped respectively over to the man and the three of them hugged.

That little man came over to Grandpa Whitey Loop and shook his hand, looked like a mirror shaking hands with a pond, and Grandpa Whitey said, "Shorty, heh, heh," and blew smoke in his face.

Then Grandma Emma smothered that little guy in her breasts. She cried, "Shorty, Shorty, Shorty," then held him by the shoulders at arms length and said now everything was okay, she was ready to die.

Shorty said, "heh, heh," and looked down and away.

Then Shorty looked at Red who was standing in the kitchen doorway, arms at his side but fists hanging like mallets. You could see that what he needed was his bowling ball, but there wasn't a bowling ball anywhere around. There was seismic activity in Red's forearms, brooding volcanoes under his biceps. Under that strawberry red hair, that was now somewhat thinner at the crown and grayer on the sides, was a face brewing history. Whoever the hell Shorty was it meant some kind of deep something to Red.

"Hello, Red," said Shorty.

But Red didn't say anything.

Well I might have smelled like I just came out of a hashish and hair salon, but I'd been around Red long enough to recognize the edge of an abyss. I got out of that stairwell and pushed my way out the front door, went down the driveway to the garage and found a sledge hammer, put the thing over my shoulder and brought it in there where predictably nobody'd moved an inch, except now you could see the muscles in Red's stomach and chest rippling like a lake in front of a thunder storm. Then I did the only thing there was to do. I gave Red that sledge hammer.

Shorty took a step back and everybody else did the only logical thing, they ducked behind chairs and couches and crawled under rugs. Even Grandpa Whitey lifted his butt and grabbed the cushion from his chair and covered his chest and head. That pretty much just left me and Red and Shorty.

Red held that sledge hammer all the way down at the end of the handle. He rested the hammer head on the floor. He looked at me for a minute, then he looked at Shorty. Red raised that sledge hammer straight out on his extended arm and held it there, then, slowly, he raised it with his wrist until it stood straight in the air. He looked around the room, then, just as slowly, without bending his arm, lowered the head of that hammer until it touched his nose. He held it there a minute, then reversed it all until the head of that hammer was back on the floor. Red took that hammer in his left hand and did the same thing with his left arm until the head of the sledge hammer was back on the floor again. The whole business must have taken about ten minutes. Then he offered the hammer to Shorty.

"I got to pee," said Red, and went into the kitchen and out the back door to the shed where Bif let Grandma Emma and Grandpa Whitey stay after they gave him the house. Red always used the bathroom back there because it was his bucks that paid off the mortgage of that house during the Depression and since Whitey and Emma gave the place to Bif and Jelly, Red wouldn't pee anywhere but back in their room; you had to figure it was just something deep in his mammal brain.

Of course Red never said anything about it, but you knew he held Bif and Jelly responsible for the whole business, whatever it was, not that Emma and Whitey didn't have a hand in signing away their own goddamn house. It was a mystery as enigmatic as the infamous Celebration Five & Dime that Red and Helen owned with Bif and Jelly sometime between the Second World and Korean Wars and that somehow, I suppose because of something Bif did, went up in smoke. Red and Helen never said anything about it except that they lost the store and a ton of money. Now there was this Shorty, whoever the hell he was.

"I don't think anybody else in the world could do that with a sledge hammer," said Uncle Lefty coming out from behind a chair.

"Not without breaking their face, ha!" said Uncle Bif.

"Oh it's not that hard," said Aunt Tillie, her eyes moving in on her nose. "You just have to be strong."

"He's just a big baby," said Aunt Jelly, limping out from behind the Christmas tree.

"Baby, heh, heh," said Grandpa Whitey.

"Shorty," said Grandma Emma Loop. "Shorty, Shorty, Shorty."

"Dad!" said the Viz to Shorty.

"That's not your dad," I told him.

"I'm his dad, heh, heh," said Shorty.

The Viz looked at me like I was Don Quixote. Maybe if everybody kept confirming what he believed he'd stop believing it.

The woman who came in with Shorty now crossed the room and put her arm around his waist. She looked like something out of a gangster movie.

"This is Babs," said Shorty.

"Shorty, Shorty," said Grandma Emma.

That's when Shorty noticed Helen sitting in a corner of the couch. He walked over to her and they looked at each other like a couple Canadians waiting for the summer.

"Hello, Helen," said Shorty.

"Hello, Shorty," said Helen.

Then Shorty turned back to Babs and said he couldn't stay. He just stopped in because his train was delayed on the way to Buffalo where he had some business, so he'd just thought he'd take a cab in and see if everybody was still alive. He said, "heh, heh," after he said that. But now the train was leaving soon so he had to get back. He said he was writing teleplays in Hollywood for "The Twilight Zone."

"That true, Shorty?" said Lefty.

"Nah," said Shorty, "I made it up."

After Shorty left, Grandma Emma Loop sat back down and cried for a little bit, then Red came back in the room.

"Hey Red, you missed Shorty leaving," said Lefty.

"I had to pee," said Red.

"Ha!" said Bif. "Let's all the men go in the kitchen and drink whiskey and talk about the women!"

So Red and Lefty and Bif, and Bifboy and Sweaty and Joseph and Andrew, and me and even the Viz, and finally Grandpa Whitey Loop, all got up and went into the kitchen where we stood in a circle and Uncle Bif poured shots of whiskey. Grandma Emma Loop and Helen and Jelly and Tillie and Neda and Sweety and cousin Nancy stayed in the living room with the Christmas tree. It was an important segregational event that occurred every year which usually resulted in some apocryphal phenomenon like Karl's cannon ball landing in the yard or Funly hijacking Neda's rocket, and though often beforehand we made various toasts, none of them were ever apocalyptic and we never did ever talk about the women.

Grandpa Whitey lit a cigar, Lefty lit his pipe, and Bif and Bifboy lit up Chesterfield cigarettes. I took the Viz and hung him upside down in the far doorway between the shed where Whitey and Emma lived and the kitchen.

"He like that?" said Lefty.

"He loves it," I told him.

"Dad!" said the Viz to Lefty.

"He thinks I'm you," said Lefty. "Must be because he's upside down."

"He's just saying it backwards," I said.

"Hey," said Lefty puffing on his pipe. He looked at Bifboy. "What do you know about Vietnam?"

Bifboy blew out cigarette smoke. He looked more like Jelly than Bif, with a round face that looked like it needed a motorist cap. "I was in Sacramento," said Bifboy.

"He flew a C-150 Transport, ha!" said Bif.

"I saw some people who were there," said Bifboy.

"He flew round trip, Sacramento to Saigon," said Bif.

"You talk to any of them boys?" said Lefty.

"Nope," said Bifboy. "They were all dead."

"Flew cargo," said Bif. He adjusted his green hat with the red 7UP logo on it.

"Flew live cargo in, flew dead cargo out," said Bifboy.

"That must have been an unusual feeling," I said to him.

"Yes, it was an unusual feeling," said Bifboy.

Suddenly I had an uncommon urge, an urge I seldom had at these family gatherings, mostly because Willie'd controlled my experiments so well in the past, but also because I enjoyed liquor; I needed a fix. I bummed a cigarette from Bifboy.

"I don't want you smoking," Red said to me, downing a shot.

"Okay, I won't."

"You'll stink up my house."

"Okay," I said as Bifboy lit me up.

"I'd go to Vietnam," said Sweaty Limburg, "but I'm getting married and going to college."

"I'd go," said Andrew, "but I'm joining the Infant of Prague Institute in Quebec."

"I think I'll go," said Joseph. He had that euphoric look like there were a dozen angels having a party in his soul.

"You can't go," said Andrew, "you're deaf in one ear, blind in one eye, and you can't smell." Drinking whiskey took some of the blue out of him.

"I think I'll go," said Joseph.

"Why would those gooks want to go communist," said Uncle Bif. "We could give them Zeniths and Buicks and 7UP, ha!"

"They make good transistor radios," said Uncle Lefty.

"Because they're very patient and have tiny yellow hands, ha!" said Bif.

"They're inscrutable," said Lefty.

"Tiny yellow hands, heh, heh," said Grandpa Whitey. He blew smoke in Bif's face. Granpa Whitey didn't give a shit.

"They ain't yellow, they're brown," said Red. "And the dead ones smell like flowers."

Inside the Christmas tree room Grandma Emma Loop had stopped crying about Shorty.

"What do you think they talk about in there every Christmas?" said Tillie, one eye addressing the other women and the other looking to the kitchen doorway.

"Who cares," said Aunt Jelly as she limped around offering everybody a bowl with mixed up pretzels, peanuts, and Rice Chex.

"They don't talk about us," said Helen.

"You're goddamn right they don't," said Grandma Emma to Helen. That might have been the first time Helen and Grandma Emma Loop ever agreed about anything.

"It's simply a ploy to get us talking about them," said Neda.

"It's working," said Helen.

"Old as Moses," said Neda.

"Eden's more like it," said Aunt Jelly.

"Let's go up to my room and listen to records," said cousin Nancy. Nice as she was, she still looked a little bit like an off-road vehicle with glasses. She looked like a homecoming queen runner-up who was going to have a million kids and a pet dog.

"It's starting to snow," said Aunt Tillie. "Let's take a walk."

"That's a good idea," said Helen, getting up to check behind the window shade. I guess nobody could guarantee that there wasn't something malevolent out there in that snow.

"It sure as," said Aunt Jelly, limping to the closet and throwing everybody their coats.

"What's going on in there?" yelled Uncle Lefty from the kitchen.

"We're going for a walk in the snow," said Aunt Tillie. Her eyes roved jovially.

Those women all put on their coats and headed for the front door.

"A walk in the snow, ha!" said Uncle Bif.

"I don't think I've taken a walk in the snow in my damn life," said Grandma Emma Loop heading out the door.

That left all us men standing in the kitchen drinking shots and sweating and talking about how those women could all go off and walk in the snow without us; we wondered what got into them; that's when Lefty said to the rest of us, "What the hell?" It was the Bush's Last Christmas of Unanswered Questions. I blew some cigarette smoke into the air. "So who the hell is Shorty?" I said.

But just then the room filled up with an amazing light, pushing at the curtains with an orange blaze. Following Red, we pushed out the back door and through the shed where Emma and Whitey slept, out into the yard where the women had already gathered, pointing to the stars. A white-orange streak hissed across the sky, splitting it as if it were a curtain, obliterating the clouds, the stars, and even the moon.

"It's one of them meteors," said Aunt Jelly, because usually when she saw anything she couldn't explain she guessed it was a meteor.

"It ain't no meteor," said Red.

"It's another one of those cannon balls, ha!" said Bif.

Grandpa Whitey blew smoke at him and said, "Cannon ball, heh, heh."

But Red said it wasn't a cannon ball.

"Shooting star," said Lefty.

"Nope," said Neda.

"It's the Russians," said Aunt Tillie, her eyes saluting the expanse of the sky. "It's the End of the World."

"No," said Neda, "it's just a comet."

"There are no comets scheduled to pass," said Helen, one hand holding the top of her coat and the other pressed on her stomach.

"Well," said Neda, "they can't predict everything."

"It's a sign," said Andrew, regaining his purple color in the cold. "It's the dead opening the letter of the sky, the blank page beneath the traces of the stars. The zipper of myth, the suckle milk of phenomena; without this we'd be dust."

"Baloney!" said Joseph.

"Well it's gone now," I told them.

"It's damn cold out here," said Grandma Emma Loop.

The next morning it was in the papers. Bobby Hansen was dead.

♒♒♒♒♒Domination of Black

I T WAS A NICE funeral. It reminded me of Kara Ruzci's. It wasn't as sad as Kara Ruzci's, but just like Kara Ruzci's, at the end, they made you throw holy water on the casket instead of dirt. And they didn't let you stay to see the coffin lowered into the ground, or the grave diggers cover it with dirt, even if you wanted, though I'm sure it wasn't that beautifully ritualistic, I'm sure they just plowed the dirt in with a bulldozer. That's what garbagemen would do, use a bulldozer. I know this because we're akin to grave diggers. We deal in the same thing. Besides, when they buried Kara Ruzci I spent most the ceremony back in the work shed. They had a tractor back there with a back hoe and a plow, and a big pulley with chains and hooks. All the cement casings and lids in there had eyelets on them so you could hook them with that little crane and get everything in place.

All that cement. You don't even get to get buried in the earth. I wanted to take Kara Ruzci out of her white casket, before they lowered her into her cement encasement and bulldozed her with dirt, and steal her away. Somewhere in the woods I'd dig my own grave for her and lay her there and join her in her grave. I'd hold her to my chest with my knee between her thighs and bring the earth around us like wings. I could sleep like that. That's the only way I could sleep.

Instead, after they gave the holy water to Louie and Barbie Ruzci, who sprinkled little dabs of light across the top of the coffin, I went to the ground beside the grave. I took armfuls of brown earth and spread it over me, over my wedding suit, into my eyes and ears and nose.

Then I hefted mounds of dirt and spread it over the casket with my arms and chest. I spread mud with my body till I lay on top the coffin like pounds of dust. That's all I remember, though there are people who tell me I wasn't even there. Then neither was Kara Ruzci.

Bobby Hansen looked nice in his coffin. He looked better than he had in years. He wasn't hooked up to any bottles and he wore an interesting shade of artificial pink under his suit. He was very quiet. His eyes didn't follow me. I was no longer his garbageman.

Bobby Hansen's funeral was more stoic than Kara Ruzci's. I guess because he'd been ill longer and he was a hero; he was a man; he didn't leave any children. When his family went up to see him for the last time in the funeral home, they quietly put things in his coffin: his letter sweater, a football trophy, a rosary, looked like the one I got at First Holy Communion, and his medal, the one he got for fending off the Cuban invasion of Lake Erie. Then they shut him up in there with all that stuff and put him in the hearse. I missed the Mass. I'd heard just about everything there was to say about Bobby Hansen in several years of high school assemblies.

I dropped in a soda fountain across the street from Bobby Hansen's church, The Sacred Heart of Jesus, bought some cigarettes and drank a bottle of orangeade. I found cigarettes to be a wonderful habit. Every time I finished one I felt sick. I sat on the steps of that place and waited for the church doors to open, watched everybody pour out, then got in the Falcon and followed the procession out to the new Catholic cemetery south of town where all the suburban Catholics were now getting buried. They had a giant stone crucifix in the center of that place, mounted on a big marble stone; beneath the crucifix were life-size cement statues of the Virgin Mary, Mary Magdalene, Mary of Cleophas, and the apostle John, frozen eternally in that moment when Jesus said to his mother, "Woman, behold, thy son," then he said to the disciple, "Behold, thy mother." Then John went off and wrote the Apocalypse. It was a big moment in Christianity that I never understood. All those Marys.

In the old Catholic cemetery downtown they were overcrowded with corpses and you couldn't just buy all the space you wanted or throw up giant monuments to your dead anymore; they regulated everything, and in the new sections you even had to have a flat stone so the grave diggers could mow the lawn on a big sit-down mower; didn't have to be dodging around all those little graves, a big pain in the ass. It was a good idea. I liked the egalitarianism of it. It was nice to see some catering to the workers. There was even some talk of starting to bury people straight up and down in there, to save room, but of course that raised some theological issues.

But in this new cemetery, they didn't have those problems. They had a lot of room, being situated out in the country south of town near the St. Nicholas Grove; I guess the area used to be a farm owned by somebody named Stolinski and the old man wanted to be buried on his property when he died, which he certainly did, but then Mrs. Stolinski found out you couldn't be buried on your own land anymore, too difficult to control the contingencies; people'd be burying themselves without the proper cement casings etc., then there'd be bodies touching earth, worms escaping with dangerous microbes, that stuff might leak into the air, next thing you know we'd be breathing dead people; anyway she couldn't bury him on the farm so she turned the farm into a cemetery, turned a nice profit, gave the whole thing to the diocese when she died, a happy tale, and now, if you had the bucks and were Catholic and died within the graces of the Church, you could bury yourself in there with as much at distinction as you pleased.

Bobby Hansen's headstone was a winged football player, football tucked, left knee raised, left arm out in a straight-arm; he was delicately balanced on his right toe, you could see he was inches from the end zone; on his shoulders they'd engraved "B. Hansen" on his uniform, just like the pros; if anything it made you want to run over there and tackle him, but with those wings he'd probably just slip out of your grasp and spring to his heavenly touchdown. Those were nice wings. And those Hansens must have been thinking about Bobby's death for quite some time because you didn't get a headstone, particularly one like that, made overnight.

There must have been several thousand people there for that burial, Bobby Hansen being so famous; the Mayor, Dean Hadrian Sullivan of Marycrest, our senators and congresspeople, even several contingents of the Pennsylvania National Guard and the Erie, Pennsylvania Coast Guard Reserve, as well as Bobby Hansen's extended family, all our old classmates from South High, sportswriters, editors, and they were all circled around the face of that grave. I couldn't even get close and I thought there were some preeminent ironies that should have placed me near the front.

So I took a little walk around the perimeter, ventured aways into the graveyard, then came back upon the ceremony from behind; found a seat right behind Bobby Hansen's winged football player headstone, there was even a piece of canvas there to keep my butt from getting too wet. It wasn't really that nice of a day, low purple sky, a thin crust of snow over the ground, just enough to let the tips of the brown grass through, like the head of a balding man. I sat behind that headstone watching my breath. I smoked a cigarette. I was trying to avoid inferential thinking, but it had a way of imposing itself on me. This whole Bobby Hansen business, taken in the wrong light, really made me look bad.

It got me thinking about the difference between what goes on and what you think about it. Even if you are what you do, what you do requires interpretation. That usually requires a brain. But you put the brain on something and it's gone. Slips away. Who murdered Bobby Hansen? Me?

Up front, they finished talking about Bobby Hansen; they rested his soul, they gave him unto the Father, they passed him on to a better world, they got the hell out of there. I heard the mumbling and the engines, listened to the hydraulic jack that placed Bobby Hansen in his subterranean cement, felt the bulldozer move across the frozen earth and push and backhoe the dirt over his coffin, a sound like a hammer on walnuts; the laying of the wreaths over that fresh grave hissing like the wind.

I waited there, I waited as the day turned brown and then blue. I sat behind that grave into the night, waiting. I thought someone might return. Someone might come and kneel in front of Bobby Hansen's grave and pray. Someone should come and stick this out with him, his first cold night in the earth. If they did, I would reveal myself to them, I would step from behind his headstone and tell them, "I am his murderer. I killed Bobby Hansen."

There was a time I waited in the night and the cold for Kara Ruzci. Impaled to the earth by a silver rod, my blood in constellations on the snow. Then an angel flying before the dawn brought Kara out of the sky. I shot him, like I did Bobby Hansen, in self-defense.

But there at Bobby Hansen's grave, no one came.

At the first hint of gray in the east I rose from behind the headstone and walked to the gravediggers' shed where I climbed the cyclone fence and snapped the door lock. I found a sledge hammer and took it back to the grave. Just a little tap at the shoulders and those wings broke off clean.

Angela Corona really liked those wings.

"I didn't bring them for you," I said. "I thought maybe we could sit around and stare at Cuba."

"Had my mother died when she was just a little girl, she would have had wings like that on her grave," she said.

"Now you're her wings," I said.

"This brother of yours," Angela said to Neda, who sat on the nearby couch and shared a cigarette with Crow.

"He's one metaphoric son-of-a-bitch," said Neda.

"My mother is dead," said Angela Corona. "But in the future I will die and there will be no wings on my grave."

"Not while Jarvis is around," said Neda.

"Can I have a cigarette?" I said to Neda. "I'm feeling a bit exhilarated."

"You have walked too far with your wings," said Angela Corona.

I put those wings on the floor and took a seat across from her, on the other side of her unlit globe. It sure was beautiful in there amidst all those plants and animals. Angela Corona broke open pistachio nuts and fed them to a waiting Iguana.

Crow alighted on her shoulder. "Cough up," he said.

"Your brothers would not like this bird back?" she said to me.

I figured I didn't have to answer that.

Crow pecked at that Iguana till it got the message and split. "Bombs away," said Crow.

"The burden of language," said Angela.

"Proof enough," said Neda, "that signs cannot only precede ideation, they can function without it."

"Cough up," said Crow.

"He only says what he's already heard," Neda said.

"Me, too," I said.

"And he says it pretty good," said Angela.

"So what you going to do with those wings?" Neda said to me, lighting my cigarette.

"I think I'll wear them," I said.

Angela Corona broke out the Amaretto. She turned on her globe. "Wings or no," she said to me, "for you I still see Cuba."

〰〰〰〰Evening Without Angels

"**I** DON'T QUITE KNOW how to say this to you, Loop," said Zippy Freeburg, "but you got some cement wings on your back."

I was on the back of the truck, doing my stomp. Contrary to what you might think about wings, these made me more effective at garbage crushing; weight beyond my dreams.

"He thinks he's some kind of smart ass," said Fatty Schlosky from the cab, "but he ain't so smart."

"You know, Loop," said Zippy, "people are going to notice. You go around with cement wings on your back like that, people notice."

"He thinks that's going to get him laid," said Fatty. "Something special, a garbageman with cement wings."

"He ain't going to get laid, he's just a crazy kid," said Zippy.

"The last guy who tried that didn't get laid," said Fatty. "He got fired."

"You're going to get tired of that," said Zippy. "And don't think people don't watch us. We're public servants."

"Slaves," said Fatty.

"Wage slaves," said Zippy.

"People should appreciate us more," said Fatty. "They should bring us their daughters."

"Not everybody down at the plant is illiterate," said Zippy. "A few of us read the papers. You go stealing wings off graves and go around wearing them, people notice. I'm telling you this for your own good, Loop. You're a nice kid, but you got no common sense."

"Garbage is garbage," I told Zippy.

"We get all the nuts," said Fatty.

"The planets," I said to Fatty, crawling onto the roof and peering upside down into the cab, "are the waste of the stars. We are their sons and daughters, garbage, elliptical and intelligent. Garbagemen will control the land masses of dung upon which the icons of culture will be built, sports complexes and marinas, cities of leisure and light. Instead of working in darkness, we'll fly lightships."

"You better leave him alone," Fatty said to Zippy. "He gets worse if you talk to him."

"He's not a bad kid," said Zippy. "He's just mixed up."

It was true, I was a bit mixed up. But I had my actions to believe in and I needed sleep. Around me, the wind spoke like floating, rife tongues, like embryonic, furious seasons.

"He's a nut," said Fatty.

"They catch him with those wings, it's going to look bad for the Union," said Zippy.

"What Union?" I said.

"Just forget it," said Zippy.

My friend from Glenwood Castle had returned from Tahiti or Zaire, I'd forgotten where; the intricacies of the surf world had eluded me. In her yard, the state of garbage had returned to normal, the garbage unsorted, no children back there doing my work. I spent a lot of time that night with the Merlots, thinking of the movement of sun and water, oxygen and earth within the deep juices, contemplating the sedimented lips of the bottles, how the contents mixed with roasted red meats. I saw the bottle neck as some kind of tunnel that I could pass through into other lives like an insect emerging from larva. I saw the earth shaking with ideas, fissures opening and spilling them into the air with glittering vacancy.

I separated the garbage and moved it out to the curb, put the dolly back behind the garage. My friend came out in a night dress, the wind pressing it against the goose of her flesh. In her kitchen, a cavern of wood and tile, metal pots big enough to boil large mammals hug from the ceiling. We went to her living room and drank Irish coffee which I'd never had before and didn't like; seemed like the stuff in it shouldn't have been mixed together; the world had gone through so much trouble to refine the differences.

My friend slipped from her clothes and got in the hot tub.

"Something's different about you," she said. She had a way of moving and talking as if everything she did was her very last resort, that it had a kind of inevitability that precluded response, otherwise I might never have answered her.

"I might not be coming here anymore," I said.

She placed her Irish coffee on the edge of the tub and spoke to the air. "Well, I might not be living here anymore."

"I think there's going to be a garbage strike. It's against the law, but I think they're going to do it anyways."

"There are a lot of strikes in South America," she said. "Italy, too. I like them. The leisurely unrest."

"I'm not in the Union, but I won't collect garbage if they go on strike."

"Your umbilical cord to the *Gemeinschaft*."

I never knew whether this woman was trying to insult me or impress me.

"Listen," I said, taking off my clothes. "If there's any gemeinschafting going on around here, it ain't on my part. You think you're somebody special. You're on that end of things. You think you got things I need. That's what the devil thinks. That's what God thinks. That we need them. It's sophisticated, but it's simply dualistic." I made sure I kept those wings on when I got into that hot tub.

"This is the moment you succumb," she said to me. "You have been so pure. Your denial like snow, your body a blade in the Absolute. The common man in a whirl of ideas he despises. Of course, we deny our addictions. Poverty seeks wealth," she whispered, "wealth, death. There are no cracks in between. You fill yourself. You fill yourself so completely that your soul oozes. The world is the festering and dripping of that. Everything is full or seeks to be full. Even death fills itself until it bursts. There is no hunger as great."

This woman had a real sense of humor, that's what I was thinking. She came over to me and maneuvered my butt in front of an air jet, placed herself on top of me, filled my mouth with her tongue, my anus with her fingers, her soft insides with as much of me as would go in. I guess Fatty would say I was getting laid, but that's not what it felt like. That's not what it felt like at all.

"Would you like to go to Nassau?" she asked me. We were upstairs in one of the bedrooms in one of the beds; thing didn't have a regular mattress, it was more like sleeping on a whale, if I slept; reminded me that was one thing I hadn't moved out of that place at one time or another, the beds.

"You want me to move these beds out of here?" I said, "This one looks like it would make good garbage."

"I have some business in Nassau if you want to come."

"That south of New York?" I said.

"It's a little south of New York."

"I got a busy schedule, "I said. "I got to be back by dawn."

"Dawn can be arranged."

I suppose should have been more specific about the day I had to be back because she drove us out to the airport, put us on a plane to New York, my first commercial flight; pretty much felt like being a sardine while somebody played catch with your can; then we caught a jet to Nassau, which seemed a little silly at first, seeing as I figured that we could have just caught a cab, but the Nassau we went to was in the Caribbean, palm trees, swimming pools, movie stars, a dream green ocean so clear you could see the garbage on the bottom. It was comforting to know there was work in paradise if you wanted it.

We checked into a hotel that had its own private beach, the British Colonial Sheraton, though there weren't too many British around there, just a lot of guys with very black-blue skin the color of Chicago Bears' helmets; they took to calling me "Moan." Looked like blue skin and white clothes was very fashionable down there among the service classes, even the police had that get-up. My friend and I went up to our room and had sexual union.

Very muggy. We lay around sweating after each other for quite a while before she told me she had to meet somebody and would see me back in the room later that night.

I was a free man in Nassau. Went down to the outdoor arcade just across from the private beach and bought myself a pair of madras Bermuda shorts and a black T-shirt that said "ganja" on the front, a pair of water buffalo sandals and a straw hat much like my denim garbage hat only straw, carried my garbage clothes in a plastic bag they gave me for my new clothes; fond as I was of my tourist wear I could see that two blocks from Main Street, away from the ocean, I'd be better off in my work clothes because the social strata of that island came clear real fast; a lot of white people by the beach surrounded by black people trying to figure out legal ways to take their money, inland, just a lot of black people, housing very much resembling the Pile System, and you had to figure they were figuring out ways to take your money too, and who the fuck could blame them.

One of the things about Nassau was that I could smell it; white people like sweet oil, black like walnut soap, the ocean like a scrub brush in your nose. Across from Main Street, in the urban pile system, a smell that reminded me of work, though I'd never smelled my work, and in the streets, wafting from the bars and into the white sunshine streets, the sweet dirt-roasted smell of marijuana and hashish. I tooled down Main Street as men in vests and ties, jewelry in their ears, stepped from shadowy doorways and asked if they could help me and I told them how much I appreciated their offers. Near the docks I found a bazaar where there were a lot of booths, mostly run by women, where they tried to sell you conch shells and sea shells, carved wooden statues, beads, rugs, hats, and hot dogs; I didn't really see a lot of the natives shopping there, but nearby there was an old, white, wooden building with an outdoor stairway leading up to the second floor and up on its balcony there were various slovenly looking characters, black as well as white, a policeman passed out with his white hat over his blue face, his hands and feet sticking out like dark water balloons; there was a young woman wearing his gloves and his shoes were down at the bottom of the stairs.

I went in there and drank scotch on the rocks. A hashish pipe cir-culated around the bar. A breeze came through the windows as cold as a ghost on Sunday and the smoke in that place danced like a ballet company from Buffalo. It tempted me to believe I could live just like this, that I could pass my days in dark bars, forgetting the heart. The sun outside like the bright blind eye of God.

I wasn't used to drinking scotch and smoking hashish, so my head swam. Maybe I should go out and sit in the sun. Maybe I should go drink a clean British ale and eat a racket or a wicket. I was never one much to question the randomness of my *wanderjahr*, nor the linearity of my dream life, in fact, looking back, there wasn't much to distinguish one from the other, especially since I no longer slept, but there was something distinctly unreal about the last several hours, and I said that to myself in full knowledge that that's the way people usually described things that were all too real, in fact I was muddling on the dialectic of that, having moved on to how in a dream sometimes you get commenting to yourself about how too real it all is, maybe implying that unconsciously you always know, given dreams are a kind of consciousness, and thinking how you could live your life stretched on the rack of that dualism, when Kara Ruzci sat down next to me at the bar.

"Well, elephant," she said to me. "I see you made it."

Well I guess you could say I'd made it, depending on what the hell you meant, but Kara Ruzci was never one much to put her fly in the bottle; nonetheless, it sure was good to see her, regardless of the circumstances and ambiguities. Her hair looked blacker and her skin whiter, her eyes a deeper blue. She wore a white blouse and skirt like some of the natives did, made out of something soft and translucent. That blouse had a crescent moon neck that let her hair touch her skin at the nape.

"I miss you," said Kara Ruzci, hugging my neck.

And I couldn't help it, I started crying. It wasn't really something I'd thought through. But now that Kara Ruzci was here next to me, I just kept thinking already about how I couldn't bear to let her go again, how I might prefer just to not see her at all.

"Don't cry," said Kara Ruzci. "I have a plan. We'll go over to Paradise Island and win a lot of money."

"Okay," I said. "That seems like a pretty ridiculous plan."

"It's been thought out," said Kara Ruzci, "which as you know is the important thing about plans."

"Yes," I said through my tears, "and specificity."

"Especially specificity," said Kara Ruzci, "or you could hardly have disruption."

"You haven't seen Tony Blanion, have you?" I said to Kara Ruzci.

"Maybe on Haiti or St. Croix. Someplace he could practice his French."

"How do you know abut his French?"

"His French is notorious," said Kara Ruzci.

Given the circumstances, I was willing to give some of that to Kara Ruzci. So we stepped outside into the Caribbean sun and caught a taxi to Paradise Island, a place that pretty much looked like a sand bar with casinos, crossed the causeway that separated that dirt pile from the main island, and stepped into one of those little palaces with its felt bumpers and clank of coin and perpetual neoninity and proceeded to lose all my money in a quarter slot machine; you needed all oranges or all lemons or all bars or all something to win, though if you got a cherry or two in the right place it gave you your coin back, but then you stuck it back in and pulled the handle and didn't get dick.

"This is a good start," said Kara enigmatically.

"Seems to me," I said, "could buy wieners with this money, at least you'd have wieners."

"You can't double your money with a wiener," said Kara Ruzci. "That's something you can live by. Give me some more money and we'll move on to silver dollars."

Her logic was irrefutable. I gave Kara Ruzci some more money and she came back with a stack of silver dollars. A woman dressed in a sheet and high heels came by and gave us free drinks and then me and Kara Ruzci began putting my money in the dollar slots. We got lots of fruits and nuts and bars and sevens, but never in the right places and soon we were out of money.

"Want to try a different game?" said Kara Ruzci.

"Can we get a motel room?" I said.

Kara Ruzci looked at me like I was the last bus to the ball game. "There are no motels on tiny islands," said Kara Ruzci. "It's probably time to risk the rest of your money."

So I gave Kara Ruzci the rest of my money and she came back with another stack of silver dollars and the woman wearing that little sheet and high heels came by and gave us more drinks.

"Why don't we just pretend we're playing the machines and get drunk," I said to Kara Ruzci.

"Now," said Kara Ruzci, "this machine has cherries and lemons and oranges and, especially, blue fruits lying on their sides. It is hard to guess the origin of these blue fruits, but also you will notice that you can get bars, one bar or two bars or three bars. All of these are fine things, but what we want are bars with big 7s going through them, three in a row, one, two, three, and then, sweet, we win a thousand dollars."

As much as I loved Kara Ruzci, and as much as I missed her and ached for her, she was reminding me what a frustrating person she could be. All this time since her death I'd recalled the gentle communication and the depth of our love and intimacy and forgotten her penchant for irrelevancy in crucial situations which, in the past, when time was a rope of the heart, was as simple as a mating dance, but the present circumstance, contradictory as it might seem, did not seem so eternal.

"I don't want to lose all my money," I told Kara Ruzci.

"Do not worry about losing all your money," she said. "You can't gamble if you're worried about losing all your money."

"That's the point," I said to her.

"Yes," said Kara Ruzci, "that's the point." And Kara Ruzci began pouring my money into that slot machine. When she put the money in I pulled the arm, and when I put the money in she pulled the arm, but any way we did it we didn't get anything back.

"We're warming it up," said Kara Ruzci, and pretty soon we were down to our last dollar.

Well that was an important dollar in a lot of ways, though by this point most of those ways were symbolic, something Kara Ruzci was quick to point out.

"Now," said Kara, taking the bottom of that last silver dollar between her thumb and index finger and raising it in the air between us. "*Dominus vobiscum.*"

"Fine," I said to her. "Let's get it over with."

"It is everything and nothing, my love," said Kara Ruzci. "Meaningless and totally meaningful. It is all that is left and what is left? A loop between life and death, samsara and nirvana. They are one, they are here, they are gone, they are back. Yes or no?"

"It's our last dollar," I said to her.

"It is the last thing that can come between us, sweets," said Kara. "Not even death separates us."

"It hasn't done a bad job up to now," I said.

"Till now," she said. "But you are my love and I am your love. When I place this dollar in the machine we will have a thousand more, and then more and more, until the money becomes a veil. It will be as if we had come that close, but the veil will become a wall and the wall a world. It's a sad thing."

"Then give it away," I said.

"No one wants it but us," said Kara Ruzci. "Besides, my sweet elephant, it is just a metaphor."

With that Kara Ruzci put our last silver dollar in the slot machine. I placed my hand on the lever and she placed her hand on mine as I pulled down. The machine whirled. There was an eternity of whirling in there. Slowly, slowly the first column swung down its 7 & bar as slow as the sunset, and the second left us there a day, taking a full turn of the earth, the 7 & bar settling down in the row with the solidity of Brazil; the third whirled as slowly as the center a of the galaxy, and within that eternal frantic whirling, huge, imperceptible, I found Kara Ruzci, a scrawny cry, a part of the colossal sun, her coral wings like new knowledge, something real; I held her within me; I held her and held her as deeply as the deepest grave in the womb of the earth, as fully as the sky holds the tunnel of night.

≈ ≈ ≈ ≈ ≈Sky Pirates

"WHERE YOU BEEN?" said Fatty from the cab of the truck. I vaguely recalled moving recliner chairs out of bedrooms, out of living rooms, dining rooms, attic garrets, garage hutches, pool houses; it was hard to believe how many recliner chairs she had around there, or even out front, now that they were out there, and even harder to believe I moved them all, but I must have, how else would they have got out?

"It's hard to say," I said to Fatty, moving the handle at the side of the chair so I could sit up and get a good look at him.

"Is it a big word?" said Zippy. "You're pretty good with big words."

"You been gone a long time," said Fatty.

"How long?" I said.

"Hard to say," said Zippy.

"Is it a big word?" I said.

"You could have just been missing and not gone so long really," said Zippy.

"I think you're right about that, Zippy," I said. "I think I was just missing."

"You're just fuckin nuts," said Fatty. "Now you believe he's been gettin' laid?" he said to Zippy.

"Just missing what?" said Zippy.

"I think you could have been a different kind of garbage man, Zippy," I said.

"One of them star captains," said Zippy.

"That's right," I said to Zippy. "In a different age. Garbagemen will be the poets and captains of the stars."

"Smart people like me will get the good jobs," said Zippy.

"Like now," said Fatty. "Who the hell thinks they're stupid?"

"Don't capitulate to that kind of solipsism, Zippy," I said.

"Shit, it don't matter," said, Zippy.

"That's right, it don't matter about Saul's lips or his lips or anything else," said Fatty, "because we're on strike."

"You can't go on strike, it's against the law," I said.

"So was the American Revolution," said Fatty.

"And the Revolution of 1848," said Zippy.

"So you're out of work unless you're going to be a garbage scab," said Fatty.

"You should have gone Union, Loop," said Zippy. "Now you don't belong to anybody."

"You should've went Union," said Fatty, "instead of getting laid."

That plane of Karl's looked more like a flying squirrel, a little bigger, not quite as furry; I wasn't that crazy about getting in the damn thing, but sometimes there are things you just have to do. It had one big wing strutted on top, no roof, and just a tiny windshield so you could reach over it and maneuver the cannon.

"Pretty primitive structure," I said to Karl.

"It's got an engine, wings, flaps, fuel; it's better equipped than most birds."

"You flown it yet?"

"Think I'm nuts?" said Karl.

I took that as rhetorical on any number of levels. "Why don't we just buy ourselves an airplane," I said to Karl. "Get a credit card or something and just buy one."

"You buy an airplane on credit, you'll be on every computer in the universe," said Karl.

Besides that cannon there was a gun rack on either side of the fuselage, a shot gun and M-16 on each.

"You going to wear those wings up there?" Karl said to me, rubbing his beard.

"You got parachutes?"

"Just going up over the lake, where it's safe," he said. "Little test flight."

Karl got in the back seat of that thing, turned on the ignition and had me give the propeller a spin. The engine kicked right in. He sure did know his primitive technologies. He pulled some lever and down went the ailerons; you knew what they were because he had the names of all the parts written right on them so you couldn't get mixed up. Then he dropped his arm and pulled me into the front seat.

"You're up there because you can't smell," said Karl.

"Only in Nassau," I yelled.

"Anything you say," said Karl.

"There's nothing up here to play with," I said.

"I don't want you thinking about anything but the cannon, besides, there's nothing back here either."

He let go of another lever and there was a clunk. "Brakes," said Karl, and then that thing started to move.

We bumped along across that old vineyard as Karl made a big loop until we were pointed toward the cliff. I guess he figured that way we couldn't crash into anything but air. We picked up speed and even though we had a good day going for us, nice winter thaw, clean wet air that felt like a cold day in summer, enough blue sky to remind you of daylight, once we started really moving I was freezing my ass off, though being a imminently airborne helped keep me slightly distracted. Something told me it wasn't going to be like that jet ride to Nassau, which, as much as I tried to suppress it, kept oozing into my consciousness. It was as if my life was disappearing under the whirr of actualities. I couldn't reconcile my generalness with my specificness. In fact I couldn't reconcile anything. I'd been de-reconciled before I'd even attempted conciliation. Events speak for themselves, I told myself, and they don't need me to explain them to me. My life was the burnt end of a match, a mode without production, a flight in a bad machine with no controls.

Beyond that cliff the sky opened like a maw. I heard another clunk behind me and the plane leapt, hit the ground, leapt again. Then we were over the cliff. We caught a gust of wind, lifted, dipped, then lifted again. Then the head of the plane pitched forward and we began to dive.

"Oh-oh," said Karl.

Probably should have brought oars instead of guns. I was going to mention that to Karl, but the quick approach of the lake robbed me of my sense of humor. It was an interesting sound I was making. Something behind my throat was going click-click.

"Hold on!" yelled Karl.

I heard a lot of clunking and flapping behind me, then the left wing of the plane dipped a bit, and pretty soon it straightened again. The plane lifted, jumped, and then we were headed straight down, at least that's how it looked from the hood of the engine where I'd been thrown and was now clinging to the neck of that cannon. I was trying to figure out whether I should hold on or let go and it struck me like one of those falling elevator propositions, like whether or not you should try to jump just before the elevator hit bottom; I was thinking about that truck load of canaries and whether it weighed less when somebody scared them when they all started flying around; I was thinking I should know this stuff, as I hung there on that cannon looking back at Karl's grizzly face, my cement wings spread airward and earthward; what a grand moment for meditation! I was as factless as an asp.

"Dump the wings!" yelled Karl.

"Dump the guns!" I yelled.

"The wings!"

"Never! Do everything the opposite!"

"Why?"

"Maybe we'll go up instead of down!!"

You never know when belief will create the fact.

Maybe Karl'd been thinking about that elevator proposition too, because he threw all the controls in the opposite direction. Our flaps flipped, our ailerons ailed, our engine sputtered. Then it went dead. The plane flipped upside down. The bottom of the nose, now facing the sky, edged upward. A gust caught the propeller, the engine sputtered again, and then kicked in. Soon we were headed straight up, and a moment later we were right side up again. I crawled back into the front seat. I looked back and Karl put up his thumb, shook his head and grunted.

"I guess we'll get this figured out eventually," he said. "Hell, people have been doing it for years."

Then the nose of the plane dipped back down and we crashed in the lake.

The only good thing about it was we were close enough to shore to walk in, wings, guns, and fuselage. Then we went back out and dragged in the wings. It sure was cold.

"We have to get wet suits," I said.

""Maybe we should make the fuselage like a canoe," Karl said.

"I know somebody who knows somebody who might have surf boards," I told Karl.

"I hate to say this," said Karl, "but maybe we should talk to Neda."

"I doubt she'll be interested," Stinky told me as we pulled that tuba, Funly Funster, into the visitors' room of the County Jail to see Grandpa Funster. "Dad should be back on the truck soon and we're gearing up for Europe."

"You and Big Dick?"

"Neda and I," said Stinky. "We have the AAU Northeast Regional in the spring, then Salt Lake for the Nationals. I really have no idea what to wear in Salt Lake City, some kind of pioneer avant, I suppose."

"Ice skating," I said.

"It's been awfully quiet in that tuba lately," said Stinky. "Oh Funly!" said Stinky. He knocked on the tuba, but he was right, no response. "See?" said Stinky.

"My feast of joy is but a duck of pain," said Grandpa Funster as he struggled to the interview window. Dead as he was, he usually looked better. His skin was like gray tissue paper, his eyes in a different land.

"I think that's 'dish' not 'duck,'" said Stinky.

"He's no common criminal," I told Stinky.

"I sought my death and found it in my womb," said Grandpa Funster. "I trod the earth and knew it was my tomb."

"Don't worry, Grandpa," I said to Grandpa Funster. "We'll get you out. Funly has a plan."

"Not at the rate he's eating," said Stinky. "I pour soup in there, it drains right through!"

"Both foot and hand grow cold," mumbled Grandpa Funster.

"When's your trial, Grandpa?" I said.

"Skreak and skitter, the moon and moon," he said.

"Autumn," said Stinky.

"Measureless measures," said Grandpa Funster. "A yellow moon of words. They also kill who wait."

ဢ   ဢ   ဢ

Grandpa Funster might have been making more and more sense, but it didn't take a Dialectician to figure out where Funly was. I dragged Stinky right over to the Funsters' and went down and checked the basement. No submarine.

"When did you notice this missing?" I asked Jimbo.

"Christmas d-d-day," said Jimbo Funster. He looked more and more like the Michelin Man, though not so happy. "I th-thought may be N-Neda took it."

"Do I get my tuba back now?" said Mosha Funster.

It pretty much meant she got her tuba back. When me and Stinky found Neda over at Angela Corona's, Neda didn't know anything about the submarine.

"You can probably reach him on the short wave," said Neda.

"What a marvelous place!" said Stinky to Angela Corona.

"Today," said Angela Corona to her unlit globe, "I will water the plants."

"Neda," I said, "you aren't going to wear one of those silly little costumes."

"I'll design it!" said Stinky. "He's certainly become a prude," he said to Neda.

"In a moment," said Angela Corona, examining her Tarot cards, "I will break out the sherry."

"Can you have sherry in training?" said Stinky.

"Funly can't hurt anybody, can he?" I said to Neda.

"Just himself," said Neda.

"He can't get that thing to Moscow," I said.

"We could be skating in Moscow next year," Stinky said. "We could all link up!"

"All he's got are conventional tactical weapons," said Neda. "A few small torpedoes, a surface cannon, anything else he dragged on board."

Angela Corona broke out the sherry.

"Jarvis," said Neda, lighting a Pal Mal, "you're becoming so," she furrowed her brow, "so earthbound."

Stinky snatched the cigarette from Neda's mouth. "She's so hard to work with," he said.

"I was ever ethereal?" I said to Neda.

"You see," said Neda, lighting up again. "You wouldn't have answered that before."

"You should have told me that before I answered you," I said to Neda, hitting her up for a cigarette.

"Do not be so defensive," said Angela Corona, dipping a spouted pitcher into a nearby stream. "You are wearing wings." She began to water her plants.

"I was trying not to notice!" said Stinky.

"It's a bit like peeing in public," said Neda.

"Neda," said Stinky, "may I have a cigarette?"

Angela Corona poured sherry for everyone.

In Willie's attic the Dialecticians were still playing poker. To them, life had become just like a card game. I brought bourbon.

I put my wings and my empty lunch bucket on the floor and Willie dealt me in.

"What are we playing?" I said.

"Whatever you want," said Raymon.

"Yes," said Revis, "it does not matter."

Revco just raised his eyebrows enough to get them over his cards.

"Each Dialectician chooses his own game," said Raymon.

"But it does not matter," said Revis.

"Because Willie always wins," I said.

"Maybe," Willie said to me, giving me a lopsided grin, "fis will be your lucky day."

Needless to say, it was a strange card game and not my lucky day. Raymon, always the most abstract of those Dialecticians, laid down Bridge meld, Revis played Black Jack, Revco five card stud, while I, myself, decided on Crazy Eights, even made up my own rules, jokers wild, twos made everybody else pick up, fours reversed directions, and jacks made Willie skip a turn. Nonetheless, Willie beat everybody. Every time your turn came around, Willie had the right cards and the right play. If you thought about it you might think it contradictory, but you had the reality in front of you to subvert yourself. One minute Willie had meld, the next he held an ace and a one-eyed jack; he'd turn to Revco with a royal flush and by the time he got to me he'd be out of cards and I'd be stuck with eighteen million points in my hand, all of this as continuous as the Great Wall of China. It got me thinking about how life just didn't make any sense.

"Eternal chaotic inflation," Willie said to me. "But do not extrapolate. It is just a card game."

Just then I realized, as you often do with someone you've known almost all your life so know better than you know yourself, that I hardly knew Willie at all. I didn't know what he did with his free time or where his parents were born, in fact, in all this time I'd never even seen them; I couldn't tell you if he brushed his teeth, if he trusted insurance salesmen, or if he was ever afraid of the dark when he was little; I couldn't even tell you whether he preferred chocolate or vanilla. We'd spent our lives experimenting with deaf and splitting dualisms, but it was like all this time we'd really been sitting at a table playing different games.

"You are finkin' we are not in the same game when I, myself, am only in fis bigger game," said Willie.

And it wasn't like we weren't in that attic with the other Dialecticians, but once again, just like the last time I was up there, it was like me and Willie were sitting in a bottle of time.

"So why all fis falling into the deep end?" said Willie.

"I got a question for you."

Willie lifted one eyebrow. "And I can keep fis question for my own."

"If you'd like," I told him. "But I'd rather you answer it for me."

"I would prefer not to," he said.

"Deaf is your specialty."

"You see," said Willie, "maybe you know more about me than you fink."

Well maybe he was right. Maybe I knew more about Willie than anyone in the world, more than anyone should know, but it was like pocketing essentials without copping form, substance without qualities, metaphorically speaking, because in general I preferred qualities without substance; but I was starting to think that there were people in the world, unlike myself, people like Willie, who controlled things; not just themselves or even themselves, it wasn't an issue of will, though you could construe it as such, I guess enough people did; no, there were just some power nexus around who or which didn't conform to the normal exigencies; maybe the rest of us needed dualisms.

Willie opened up his hand of cards and turned it to me.

"Don't show me card tricks," I told him. "I got a cousin-in-law who's great at card tricks. Card tricks are a lousy metaphor."

Well that seemed to please him pretty much. He folded up his hand, produced a new deck, shuffled and dealt. Those other Dialecticians came to life.

"Let us postulate that I can know only what is in my own mind," said Raymon. "But how can I ever be wrong about anyting I think?"

"In fact," said Revis, "how could you ever be wrong about anything?"

"If the mind is an aviary," said Revco, talking without looking up from his cards.

"And I go to my aviary looking for the twelve bird," said Raymon.

"How do I ever come out with the thirteen bird?" said Revis.

"So," said Revco.

"The possibility of error," said Revis.

"Implies the existence of multiverses," said Raymon.

"Or," said Revco.

"It is a perfect universe," said Revis.

"And none of us are ever wrong," said Raymon.

"Fis is why we can play so many games all at the same time," said Willie.

"You got any *threes*?" I said to Willie, examining my hand. I hadn't told him, but I'd changed my game to gin rummy or hearts.

"No," said Willie. "Fish."

I stayed and played cards for a few days and nights, losing to Willie every time before heading home to the Pile System whether it existed or not. It looked like those Dialecticians could be up in Willie's attic a long time trying to decide what to do about the draft, though if it took the draft board as long to find them as it did the high school they could all be in their forties before they had to go anywhere. I'm sure they wouldn't have to worry about missing out on a war, as Red said, we'd just change enemies, though I'm sure he didn't think that up himself, well, maybe he did.

≈≈≈≈≈The Infinite Winter

S PEAKING OF THE devil, there he was sitting on the porch.
It must have been evening or Saturday—it was still pretty
light out, so I guessed Saturday—because those were still porch
sitting times for Red after he got the groceries and took the car down
to one of those new do-it-yourself car washes with the stalls and long
metal sprayers—he liked the way you could put that hot power spray
up under the wheel wells, he believed that was the way to prevent rust
up there, defrosting all that muddy ice—then he'd come home and
instead of watching sports on TV or taking a nap, he liked to sit on the
porch and watch everybody go by, friendly as pie, his ball bat stored
behind the porch railing, his bowling ball being pretty much saved
now for special occasions; though as I thought about it, he really didn't
sit out on the porch that much in the winter, human furnace though
he was, the summer was more apropos. Something else about him, he
didn't look so good. He had on a red-plaid wool jacket and hunting
cap, of course he never hunted, hadn't touched a gun since the Marines, and sat in his metal chair with his hands perched on the arms,
elbows out, as if he was frozen between sitting down and getting up.
When I got out of that Falcon his eyes shifted and that was it.

"I'm not trying to tell you how to run your life or nothin," said
Red when I got to the steps, "but your car's real dirty."

"I know," I said, "but you know what happens when I clean it."

"It gets dirty again," said Red. "Don't tell me."

Well you don't have to be subtle to be ineffable.

Red moved his hands down to his hips. On cold days like this he had a face like the bottom of a thermometer. Now the purple of the day started to glisten a bit and soon small snowflakes sparkled in the air.

"I don't want to tell you somethin you know already," said Red.

"You don't," I told him.

"But you got a son. A little kid."

He handed me an envelope and I opened it. It was a letter from the new City Garbage Workers' Union. "I lost my job," I told him. "The garbagemen are on strike."

"Tell me about it," said Red. "I got garbage up my ass I got so much garbage."

By now the air glutted with thick white flakes, the sidewalks already filmed with white, the lawn like white foam.

"I couldn't come around because I had to be miserable for a while," I said.

"You know what the garbagemen would do for me if I went on strike?" said Red.

"What could they do?"

"That's right," said Red. "You work your ass off all your life. Nobody gives a shit."

Well I guess he'd been out there thinking about something. I guess he'd been thinking and thinking. The snow came down now in walls and columns of huge wet flakes, swirling over the steps and onto the porch, collecting on Red's pants and piling at his feet.

"You smell like decay," said Red.

"If you remember," I told him, "I can't smell anymore."

"You should get that fixed," said Red. "Somebody could fix that."

"A doctor?"

"Somebody."

You had to figure if he could smell through ten feet of snowstorm he could say what he wanted, but now that snow was coming down like rockets and I was ready to get inside.

"I lost my goddamn job," said Red.

That snow was thick enough now to rub its belly on its back. I spread my arms straight out and let the snow collect over me like a snowman Jesus.

"I sold too good. My territory was saturated, they hired some kid."

"Helen know?"

Red turned his head a little to look right at me. His lower jaw tightened, then loosened again. "You got some kind of wings on your back," said Red.

Our house wasn't warm inside but it was better than a snowstorm. Helen'd finally got the last of that statue rubble cleaned up in there and had it collected in aluminum garbage cans at the foot of the dish cabinet arabesque, right under the Infant who, since that rite of passage with Red's ball bat, looked more or less like the Teenager of Prague, kind of an abstract, cynical look on his face, his left brow a little low, his passive smile skewed. From the backyard I heard Honky passing through the waves of snow like a ship. The walls of that holy room looked as if a tiger'd been working on them. It took me a minute, because it was dim in there, the only light that of the votive candle flickering under the Infant, but I found Helen clinging to the far wall.

"Did I ever tell you the story," said Helen, "about the man who brought a Sacred Host home from church and nailed it to his wall?"

"The nuns told us all the time," I said. "It bled."

"It bled until the blood filled up the room," said Helen. "But it wasn't blood enough. God didn't know how much blood it would take. That's the one thing He didn't know."

"They didn't tell us that."

"You were just a boy," said Helen, scraping her fingernails across the wallpaper. "When they took the girls into the other room, they told them. They told them there would never be enough blood."

"It's snowing pretty bad out," I said.

"Do you think Christ was a man?" said Helen.

"Red looks like he's going to sit out the storm on the porch."

"The blood of Christ was female blood," said Helen. "You want to find a woman in the Trinity, look for the blood." Helen moved across the wall like a spider. She inched toward the ceiling, hesitated, then came back down.

"I didn't see you at Bobby Hansen's funeral," I said to her.

"You represented me," said Helen, coming to the ground, allowing her eyes to rest on my wings.

I opened my empty silver lunch bucket. "The garbagemen are on strike."

"I quit my job," she said. She straightened herself. She ran her hands down her skirt, aligned her shoulders with her fingertips.

"Quit?"

"Jarvis," she said. "I don't know how we protect ourselves from madness. We are sponges for it."

Well I hadn't had a talk with Helen in a long time, but it didn't seem like we could find a place to start that wasn't in the middle somewhere. Helen was almost always right about everything, I was the first person to give her that, it was just hard to figure out what it was she was right about at any given moment. It was Helen's universe and she was absolutely right about it.

"Do you know how close death is?" said Helen.

"Do you want to pray, Helen?" I said to her. "If you'd like, I'll pray with you."

"A fortress of words," said Helen. "But the storm is inside and the storm is outside. A shell protects the self from the same." Nonetheless, she got her rosary from the top drawer of her bureau, thinking she wouldn't let me out-think her, thinking that now that she'd shown me prayer as shell and symptom, I would indulge her and she could choose, if she desired, to refuse me, though she had little interest in whether I prayed or not, and though she herself no longer needed prayer; knowing all this she would have us both pray, because it would sooth me about her sanity. So Helen and me knelt beneath the Infant, at the foot of the dish cabinet arabesque, between the garbage cans of broken saints, breathing the powder of their wounded dust, and prayed for each other, equally and Godlessly and absolutely, we prayed the rosary—Our Father, Who art in heaven, glory, glory, glory—we prayed—forgive us sinners now, now, now—and at the hour, at our hour, of our deaths—we prayed—and while our heads were bowed we did not see the Infant lift his cloak and spread his black and featherless wings.

Outside those walls the storm raged in its white blankets, such powerful whiteness, such quiet, filling the windows with its white absence. Helen fell asleep. And I found the Viz upstairs, thick in the Pile System and naked, sleeping with Polly Doggerel. Underneath what might have been another pile, and might have been a tent, I spied a light, and in there I found Joseph, Andrew and Neda huddled over a flashlight discussing, of all things, the Pile System.

"The Pile System," whispered Andrew, the light shining into his nostrils, "gives form to space, supplies definition."

"He's trying to say it's a semiotic that defines potentialities," said Neda. "To say a pile exists is to say that it would he a pile, essentially, even if there were no piles anywhere. But its potential configuration, which separates it from the plenum, exists whether it is ever observed or even actualized, because it is categorically defined by the nature of signification as it simultaneously defines signification; neither exists without the logical, not ontological, but logical necessity of pre-conceptual feeling and sensation which in themselves have no form, no substance, no *reality* until the moment of the co-arising and infinitely interpretable symbol. That's why you know what I mean when I say 'pile' whether you believe in them or not."

"What do you mean?" I said.

"Don't be silly," said Andrew.

"Pardon my saying so," said Joseph, "and I'm sure you'll find what I'm about to say quite idiosyncratic, subjective at best, maybe even nihilistic, but I really think what you're saying is just so much, oh, how shall I say this? *Baloney!*"

"Are you saying it's true, but trivial?" asked Andrew.

"I'm saying it's baloney," said Joseph.

"We're not talking about the individual piles here," whispered Andrew, a bit insistently. "Not this pile or that pile, or this pile of something or that pile of something."

"He's talking about Law," said Neda. "And not positive law, not the laws that say not to park here on Tuesdays because the street will be cleaned or the garbage picked up."

"The garbage won't be picked up," I told them. "We're on strike."

"I'm talking about the processes which, signified as within the universe, undoubtedly, tautologically, exist within it. What governs what happens across the street at the Funsters' also governs what happens here."

"I wouldn't use the Funsters as an example," I said.

"And what happens in Cleveland and Japan and on Mars!" said Andrew. "It's common sense!"

"After the strike," I told them, because I felt the Mars thing had brought them into my intellectual territory, "garbagemen will seize control of the mode of production of waste disposal. It will happen at the Funsters' and in Cleveland, Pittsburgh, Buffalo, Japan, Mars. The false dualism of Capitalist and Socialist states disputing the nature and ownership of the mode of disposal will be subverted by the poetry of waste. Waste, the foundation of all energy-matter and space-time, waste *ex nihilo*, will come into the hands of those who dispose of it. We will return to our birthplace in the stars. We will return to the womb of the moment we arose from nothingness. Mars will be a poem yawning on the fingertips of garbage space captains."

"I don't think you fellows are quite ready to pull that off yet," Joseph said to me.

"Andrew is trying to say that consciousness arose coterminously with reality," said Neda. "Its preconditions, quality and existence are implied by the cognitive, so reality defers its preconditions. Reality can't create its own preconditions, yet they're necessary, and they're nothing without an intermediary through which both consciousness and reality take their form *and* substance simultaneously, if I can use those words loosely. So the Pile System might not be a thing, but then there are no things, only relations.

"I would like to add, if I may," said Joseph, "that this is quite a lot of baloney."

"This wouldn't be a semantic dispute, would it?" I ventured.

"Semantics is a symptom of signification!" yelled Andrew. "Are there piles out there or not? Is there baloney out there or not?"

"You're being rather literal," said Joseph.

"It's hardly an either or issue," I said to them. I guess despite myself I'd been drawn in.

All that must have up woke the Viz because he came inside the tent with Polly Doggerel. "Dad!" said the Viz.

"Viz'," I said, holding out my arms.

"Dad!" said the Viz, spreading his arms to Joseph.

"That's right," said Joseph, "I'm your dad."

"You're not his dad," I said.

"Not for long," said Joseph, "because I'm enlisting in the Marines."

"Dad!" said the Viz, running into Andrew's arms.

I took the Viz from Andrew and went back out into that Pile System, for lack of a better term, and found him some clothes worthy of a trek into the snowstorm, then went downstairs and got a broom and went out on the porch. I poked the broom handle into the snow pile where Red used to be and sure enough, he was still in there.

"Ouch, goddamnit," said Red.

"Dad!" said the Viz to that snowpile, Red. I brushed Red off with the bristle end of the broom.

"You coming inside?" I said to Red.

"I ain't never coming in," said Red. "I'm done coming in."

An inch of snow had already accumulated on him and I had to brush him off again.

"Pretty big snowstorm," I said to Red.

"I could give a shit."

"It's going to get pretty cold."

I had to brush him off again and he didn't budge a finger.

"You can't stay out here forever," I said.

"You don't think so."

"No, I don't."

The snow was getting pretty deep around us so I brushed Red off again and then cleared an area out around the chair. That left us walled in there on the porch behind two or three feet of snow.

"Well when's the last time you slept?" said Red.

"That's hard to say."

"So don't tell me," he said.

The Viz extricated himself from a snow pile, threw a few "Dads!" stormward, then waded down the porch steps into chest deep snow. The maple tree, limbs laden with snow, bent over us like a nave, the street now a long white tunnel. When I left the porch to gather in the Viz the world looked like a great white bed.

That's the way it was, and that's the way it stayed for a long, long time. We pulled that cold sheet of snow over ourselves and underneath the cold and wet we decayed and birthed; we waited for a new world without lust or bitterness; a world filled with intelligence as nourishing as warm milk; the snow came down and down, our legs and arms rising, etching beneath the surface, writing invisibly beneath, our elbows and arms spreading like snow angels that never broke air; that is how we lived, waiting for the sleep the cold brings on its wingless back; that is how we lived that winter and that is how we live. We are buried before our lives ever surface.

From underneath those floors of white deaf soft walls there was only one thing you could hear, the slow *oompah-oompah* of Mosha Funster's tuba. Across the way, where once Grandpa Funster, now in jail for murder and plagiarism, once mumbled his ineffables, Jimbo Funster removed the sandbags from his porch roof and barricaded himself into his stuffed animal room, connected to the kitchen by a single vacuum tube communicator through which Betty Funster sent him factory wrapped cellophane packages of brunswager, ham salad, pimento spread, and cheese spread. Umbilicaled to the outside world by a simple short wave radio, he hoped that if conditions were right, he might catch Funly who, according to himself, would submarine from Lake Erie into the Niagara River, over or under or around the Great Falls, on past Lake Ontario and out the St. Lawrence Seaway.

A dim light flickered in the windows of Karl Marxman's basement. On his porch roof bevies of generations of nameless dogs curled into warm piles under the snow, while the rest of his animals and children, Beemas and Maggies and Karl Junior, innumerable cats as well as his new baby born at the wedding of me and Kara Ruzci, huddled beneath the warm tent of Sophie Marxman's dress, everybody dragging in their own home made transistor radio and ear phones, sending up their antennas through the back of Sophie's shirt where they spread behind her head like a peacock or a turkey or a Madonna. The pig stayed in the basement with Karl who had his own short wave radio and his own reasons. In the faint, orange cellar glow, Karl diverted heating ducts from the kitchen and bedrooms, driving the wings of model planes.

At the Jinxes', Big Dick Jinx lay in Stinky's divested trophy room, Stinky's trophied legacy now a metal shell protecting a bubble of air around that notorious hijacker Funly Funster. Big Dick's own Buckhorn Potato chip truck now a shell, too, sitting in the garage protecting stale potato chips, pretzels, stale corn curls and pork rinds. Pat and Becca brought him sandwiches made from factory wrapped cellophane packages of brunswager and ham salad, pimento spread and cheese food spread on white fluffy Sunbeam bread but it hardly mattered, the ham salad wasn't even made out of ham. Big Dick mumbled, "You have to buy it local."

Neda abandoned her defense of Andrew's Pile System and in an aluminum building not so far away, or a spot on the Erie Bay cleared with a shovel in the sunset, or on a pond south of town in the twilight of dawn, Stinky Jinx, sequined and spangled like a million eyes shining, a sculptor of dance, scarf afurl, twirled my genius sister Neda, lifted her from the ice, her silver form dim and whirling in the gray mirror, the air sucking behind them in the caves of their absence, the light kaleidoscopic, huge flakes of snow melting around them in the heat of their fury, exploding like sparklers in the carved space: Stinky and Neda igniting passion and talent, genius and destiny, prepared to become the greatest ice skating pair in the history of Erie, Pennsylvania, if not the world.

And there in my own front yard, buried at the foot of a cathedral of snow, I tucked the Viz to my chest and thought, Helen, Helen, are we sponges or shells, you can't have both.

But it didn't stop Angela Corona, her windows painted with snow, from predicting that she would have a candle light dinner with her husband, Rafael. She set the timer in those rooms of life and gave it all an hour more light. She gathered oysters and abalone from her salt water pools and served the oysters alive with Tabasco and home grown fresh ground horseradish; she pounded the abalone until it was flat and tender, dredged it with flour, drenched it with egg, breaded it and fried it quickly light brown, its juices waiting like an explosion; she steamed watercress from her stream, gathered wild rice, shucked it, and cooked it perfectly by leaving it alone. When Rafael Corona came home that night, he fed the parrots, and then Angela Corona served him a candle light dinner. Afterwards they sipped Benedictine and brandy. They let it grow dark. And then, moving over her like an insect, Rafael Corona undressed her and they made love. She had not predicted it, but it was not unexpected.

And there were the lives of the dead, too. Vast lives in death. A universe of death above the snow. A single death is all we are given, and then we empty ourselves like a horn.

The snow reached the windowsills of the attic of the Dialecticians, flying down like cards and lying like lead. Willie looked up from his hand, sipped bourbon, and looked at his cards again. He made some choices. The Dialecticians changed their games and played their cards, and then Willie picked them off, one by one.

And above me on the second floor at the front of Red and Helen's house, underneath that Pile System, whether it existed or not, my brothers heatedly debated the world inside the signs of the world; once saints and mystics, they'd made the irrational leap to the rational, from God to systems of God, from systems to denial, from denial to God and back, that endless fragmenting and figuring as fragile as neon.

Helen awoke from underneath the Infant and went to the back window, peeking under the shade into her backyard where her white dog, a white shark in the snow, surfaced and opened his maw, a momentary blood yawn in the white field, dipping and exploding. She saw it as somehow more than a great white dog, more than a red yawn, more than a yard of snow; she saw the red flower to the tunnel of his intestines against the white field of purity. She pulled the shade and, leaving the Infant, descended into the basement, into her labyrinth of the unusable and destroyed.

And Red sat on the porch under the snow.

But in the front yard, the Viz, my son, huddled against my chest, as my hands and feet grew numb, my head heavenly. The snow shifted beneath my feet and something opened below. I floated, then tucked around the Visitor in the darkness until the cold lifted from a gust of pushed warm air, reminding me of the cold winter nights when Kara and me gathered up Polly Doggerel and the Viz and pulled a sleeping bag over us in front of one of the wall heaters, spending the night with red wine and a flashlight in that bag of warm.

"Do you want to go to the zoo?" said Kara Ruzci?
"It's too cold for the zoo," I told her.

"It's never too cold for the zoo," said Kara Ruzci.

"It's night," I said. "The zoo is closed."

"I've never been to the zoo when it's closed," said Kara, holding out her arms to a sleepy-eyed Viz.

"Dad!" said the Viz.

"That's right," said Kara Ruzci. "I'm your dad."

"You're not his dad," I told her, but as she clutched him to her breast, and he clung to her, she began to cry; the Viz's back heaved with sobs.

"Okay," I said, "we can go to the zoo."

"We don't have to go to the zoo," said Kara, crying into the Viz's hair.

"I don't go to the zoo much anymore," I told her. "I tend to go to graveyards."

"Do you go to my grave?" said Kara.

"It's in New Jersey."

"I know where my grave is," said Kara Ruzci.

"I thought you lived in Nassau," I told her.

"You should go to the graves of the dead," whispered Kara. "It is all we have."

"You don't have Nassau."

"I only went to Nassau to see you, my sweets." She held the Viz at arm length, under his arm pits. "My baby," said Kara Ruzci, crying a little again, but the Viz fought the separation, struggling until he was back in her lap, huddled and purring.

"Now my sweet elephant," Kara Ruzci said to me, touching my cheek, "you must never make love to anyone else. You are my love," she said. "My love."

And with that I began to cry too. It felt so miserable and good to get the pain and heat out. I felt Kara Ruzci's cheek against mine and suddenly I'd covered the three of us with my hot tears, tears streaming over us like the sweat of passion on a close summer day, a blinding hot cement as primal as the sun's core; we were transfigured, three in one. And it would have been the end of all of us, the end of all of this, this whole sweet story if I told the eternal truth here, if I lay down the infinity of that water and time, then it would have been the end. But it was not the very end. I thought of how much I loved Kara Ruzci and suddenly she was so very very far away, though holding her with all my strength, I could barely feel her, barely see her, barely hear her voice when I whispered to her, "but you are dead, Kara, I am alive and you are dead," and she responded, "yes, yes, my love, yes." Though there was a moment, as she drifted away, that I saw her clearly once again, lit at the end of a tunnel, a dark virgin, my son in her arms, a point at the end of time.

Kara Ruzci was certainly possessive, even unto death, and when she was around and when she wasn't, I often forgot how possessive and controlling she'd been. Maybe it would have all ended in divorce, or dissolution, like everything else. But that's the gift of death, isn't it, our imaginations left fertile with possibility, even our memory shrouded with future and infinite fortune.

It was a long time ago. Not endlessly long ago, but long ago enough so that the winters were longer and colder and more grave, when my grandmother, Grandma Emma Loop, had her second son. She shouldn't even have had him. She was over forty and it was the Depression. Her husband, my Grandpa Whitey, had lost his job at the National Forge and Emma spent her days and nights over her ovens, one in the kitchen and another in the back shed, baking breads and kuchens with her oldest daughter, Tillie, when Tillie got home from school. Then Whitey left at dawn with Red, their oldest son, and sold the baked goods door to door, on foot, returning for new loads until they were all sold sometime late in the night. So who knows when they had time to conceive a child.

Because Emma was all business in the kitchen and Whitey out all day and night. Then one morning the youngest of the three children, Jelly, collapsed in the living room not too many months after she'd learned to walk, and after a few days of that Whitey and Emma counted up what little money they had and took her to the doctor at the edge of Germantown who sent them downtown to talk to a specialist. His place was discouraging. Everybody in that waiting room was on crutches or in wheelchairs. Red remembered that day because on the way Whitey and Emma stopped at a cigar store and Whitey bought himself a cigar and the kids and Emma suckers, one of those things you do for yourself when all your money's already going out the window and bad news is coming, and of course Red chewed his sucker up in a couple seconds, but later, in the specialist's waiting room, Jelly threw her half sucker on the floor and Red snatched it up and polished that one off too.

A half a day later the specialist, Dr. Hanke, collected $15 from Whitey and Emma and diagnosed Jelly as s having Infantile Paralysis. That sucker Red snatched off the floor got him in quarantine for a month.

That night Emma cried. She was a large, athletic woman, bigger than Whitey, who believed in work. She believed we were born for work and that if faith had any manifestation it was work. And if it was faith that brought us to God, then it was work that brought us faith and brought God to us. Situations could be worked in, problems worked out, hardship worked through. You couldn't stop a human being who was willing to walk on his feet or work with her hands. But that night Emma Loop felt worse than stopped.

This was years before Grandpa Whitey Loop didn't give a shit about anything anymore, though even then he was small boned and dapper, blond and well manicured; even while he worked at the forge he was always cleaning himself up between jobs; he liked to be clean and he liked to laugh and he liked to stay out of trouble, which kept him pretty noncommittal. He had a big heart but he seldom had anything to give. He had a theory about trouble finding you no matter what. Now he'd lost his job and in the foreseeable future, after much pain and debt, two of his three kids would be dead.

That's when I figure they had the time.

It was a moment of union and despair. A bet on, and a bet against, the future. It's what I'd do.

And it had to happen. Like the dogwood trees that twist into the sky and bleed in autumn, payment and balance for the death of Christ. If not them, then something else. Even if there was no Christ. There must be those bleeding dogwoods.

Tillie was a large girl, broad shouldered, her head filled with common sense and a wandering eye. Not a metaphoric one, a real one. But she had Whitey's disposition. She spent her childhood keeping Red out of trouble and her adolescence reeling in Lefty Limburg, the lanky dark kid from up the street who was the second best athlete in the city, after Lank Ward. She was as sane as daylight.

And Red was a big one too, a giant, an Emma Loop inside a boy. He set his mind on one thing at a time and if you stepped between him and it or made him think two things about it he'd kill you.

Jelly was that way too, but she was tiny like Whitey, and after recovering from polio, an ordeal that ended in an operation where Dr. Hanke removed her Achilles tendon and sewed it into her foot to straighten out her foot which had folded into a fist, an operation that worked but left Jelly with a tiny leg and a flat foot that flopped like a lever, after that Jelly wasn't the most optimistic of people; an experience like that might make some people appreciate life all the more and some people it doesn't; it makes some people kind of nasty and in the end you can't blame them; that's the way it was with Aunt Jelly.

Of course, Red didn't get polio at all.

But he did get a little brother. A very little, little brother. With small bones and apple cheeks, fine hair as blond as snow. He looked more like Whitey than Whitey did, except he might have been built a little smaller, though it was hard to tell until he grew up and made it true. One thing for sure, Emma Loop loved that kid more than anything in her life. She breast fed him till he was two, though she said she did it because they were so poor and couldn't afford milk.

Her and Whitey's bread business became so popular that Whitey could afford to put gas in his car and expand their area of delivery. You had to double clutch that Model A to shift it and use the emergency brake to stop it, but it ran as long as you knew how to finagle the choke when you were starting or stopping or stopped. It didn't have heat, so Red and Whitey kept moving, and they delivered bread from before dawn till after dark until it was all gone and if they got hungry, well, they could always eat bread. They used all the extra money they made to pay for Jelly's check-ups at Dr. Hanke's which were still fifteen bucks a crack and to pay off her operation.

But, as Whitey reasoned, often accurately, there being nothing like success to instigate disaster, soon their expansion began affecting the business of some of the town's larger bakeries and those guys, exercising acute business sense, threatened to take their business away from the flour and yeast distributors if they continued to sell Whitey supplies. In a couple months Whitey and Emma's bread business was dead. Whitey started bootlegging whiskey out of the basement. Red picked up two paper routes and a job nights sticking bowling pins at the Kronenburger Club. Tillie married Lefty Limburg. Jelly learned to get around with that floppy foot and little leg but she had a temper. Emma and Whitey re-mortgaged the house. And Emma breast fed the baby till he was two to keep from spending that much more on real food.

Even when that baby was two he wasn't much bigger than Emma's forearm; it was a large forearm and he was a very small baby. Once he learned to hang on she could cook a whole supper with him on her arm like a chimp. He got a lot of attention. But amidst all that commotion of staying alive, Emma and Whitey never bothered to name him.

Naming a baby is harder than it seems and it seemed like all the names were too big for this baby. He was too small for anything biblical, too delicate for John or Peter; two syllables or less seemed too harsh, three or more like an explanation. They tried calling him "the baby" or "the little baby" or "the baby baby" until he got big enough to stand up and they could see how really little he was. That's when they started calling him Shorty. One thing for certain, Shorty was Emma's boy.

Unlike Red, Shorty never had to wear his older sister's boots be-cause Jelly had one regular foot and one tiny foot and Shorty's feet only fit in the tiny one. He had to have new boots and new shoes. He couldn't wear hand-me-down clothes because Emma obviously couldn't put him in girl's clothes, he was already diminutive enough, and Red's clothes were all too big unless you wanted to wait for Shorty to grow into Red's baby clothes, though he'd look pretty silly wearing baby clothes when he was seven. So he had to have new clothes too. Emma walked Shorty to school so he wouldn't get picked on, gave him money for hot lunches on the outside chance it might help him grow. She picked him up after school and fed him hot soup, chocolate chip cookies, fresh milk. She let Shorty do anything he wanted.

Shorty took piano lessons. Shorty had birthday parties. The family changed their tradition of opening Christmas presents on Christmas morning so Shorty could get his presents on Christmas Eve and play himself to sleep instead of lying awake all night worrying about what he was going to get. Not that it made Shorty a bad kid. Once he developed a personality beyond short and cute he was pretty easygoing, though at times a bit indolent.

And none of this affected the rest of the family very much because everybody was too busy to know it was going on. Tilly married Lefty Limburg and was busy starting a family. Sometimes, when she visited, she saw Emma give Shorty money or make him a snack, but all she ever said was, "Mom, you spoil that boy," and Emma said, "Well I have to spoil somebody, there's nobody left after him," afterall, the Depression was over, Whitey was back to work at the forge; and now Red was out of high school and had a job at the forge too, at least for a little while, at least until he threw off every ounce of tradition and common sense he had to marry that Polack he was running around with, either that or ended up in the war or both; Red was trouble from day one and she'd been lucky enough to keep the reins on him for eighteen years; she knew she'd lost him; but for now they had a little money for the first time in a decade and what didn't go to pay off Jelly's doctor visits and operation, well, why not give it to Shorty, why deny Shorty just because he was healthy, he needed things too, besides, he'd grow to be a man, and the Depression taught Emma that you could lose everything you had, you could have nothing and then go into debt, you could have nothing and go into debt and then it could get even worse, and meanwhile you got older, you got older and closer to death and less able to help yourself, less able to work your way back to where you started before you'd been knocked down.

And it turned out she was right about Red. One day he came home and said he was marrying the Catholic Polack and Emma got so mad she threw her meat knife at him. Stuck in the wall next to his head. She was sorry she missed. Before the summer was over Red was married and before the next started he was headed to the Pacific to fight Japs. He wrote her once from Midway and said, "I've been working for the family since I started school. I helped out. I got you the mortgage back on the house. The only difference now is that I'm working for my country and when I get back I'll be working for myself and my family. Sometimes some of us get some beer and go out and watch the Goonies come in from sea after they've been out there for years. They forget how to land." (He wanted to tell her they were just like him, but he couldn't put the feeling into words). Instead he sent her some pictures of Goonies. He didn't know they were albatross and neither did she.

Well what did he think, it wasn't her house? That food was free? That he hadn't spent a year on her breast crying for food every two hours even in the middle of the night? People forget what they don't even know, then they get reminded too late. It was that way with Jelly too. Life wasn't a good enough gift. You couldn't explain to her that there was a doctor who lived in Glenwood who drove a Cadillac, who bought a Cadillac for his wife, who had a garage he kept them in that was bigger than a house, that half of everything Red and Whitey and Emma made went to a man paid to save Jelly's life and it bought a tire for his Cadillac, an hour or so on the golf course, a day in Miami Beach.

Maybe if she had it to do over, maybe they'd all have piano lessons. Maybe they could all have eaten a lot less but learned to play the piano. But now Tillie was gone and Red was gone and Jelly wanted everything and accepted nothing because she was a living scar. A man could limp and make a living. A man could have something underneath. But a woman was a pond of ice. That's where Emma stopped, she froze with the ice. Jelly couldn't be normal, she couldn't be beautiful, she couldn't solve her problems with dance lessons or a satin dress. Anyway, Shorty quit the piano.

Red never minded Shorty. Shorty was his little brother and little brothers got things, even things you never got. Shorty was the baby. Besides, Shorty was really little. You couldn't expect much from him. And he wasn't one of those feisty little kids that tried to make up with his mouth what he didn't have in size. Red never had to beat anybody up because Shorty mouthed off. Shorty was the kind of kid who had every bully in the vicinity protecting him already. They fought each other for rights.

Girls liked Shorty too, because he dressed nice and talked nice; he had deep blue eyes and white blond hair, delicate hands like some kind of artist or poet; he wore cologne and smoked British cigarettes that made him smell exotic, foreign. And Shorty was clever. He could even do a few things, though he didn't like to do them.

Somewhere he picked up a little bit of tap dance and soft shoe; he could break out in one or the other to accentuate a point, but he didn't like to do either one, there was something onerous, he said, about a short man dancing by himself. He could act. He could entertain you at a party doing his Gene Autry or Errol Flynn, but he never let himself get dragged into a school play to do Hamlet or Napoleon or some King Henry or Richard because there was something both a bit too irrepressible and precious at the same time about a little man standing on a box and shouting, besides, his head was too small, only small men with very large heads could do those things.

Shorty could do a number of things he seldom did, but the one thing he did do that he had no business doing was go out for football. That's what he was doing when Red got back from the war and that was the one thing that Red always wanted to do but Emma never let him do, the thing that Red could have done, because on Sunday afternoons he'd sneak off to the Baker's Field with some old clothes and an old pair of shoes and play with the players of the South High varsity, guys like Lank Ward and Lefty Limburg who had their names in the paper every week for blasting everybody in the city as well as teams from Youngstown and Pittsburgh, Canton and Niles, off the map, and he could run right through those guys, he could bowl them down like duck pins, but Emma never let him do it, he had to work, he had to peddle bread and papers, he had to stick pins at the Kronenburger Club, and instead of going to college on an art scholarship, he went to work at the Erie Forge; he helped pay off that second mortgage on the house; everything he made went to Emma and Whitey until he met Helen and then he got married and then he went to war. But when he got back he went home to see Emma and Whitey, he went home bursting out of his dress blues trimmed in red and gold with his three bold sergeant stripes on the shoulder, and there was Shorty, flopping inside a South High football uniform, tan-gold pants with pads at the thighs, blue jersey with gold numerals, yellow helmet, black leather cleats. They were all headed for the stadium and Emma invited Red along too, as long as he didn't bring Helen.

"Don't bother," said Whitey. "Shorty doesn't even get in." There were enough contradictions in that situation to drive Red mad. He'd figured he'd be taking Whitey and Emma by the arm and walking door to door around the neighborhood, from one Ebhart and Sugart and Limburg to another, doffing his cap and shaking hands, having a drink or two and shrugging off the awe and pomp of his bravery in face of the yellow hordes; he'd tell them they weren't yellow, they were brown, and how the dead ones smelled like autumn flowers a day after they began to wilt, but now it looked like that's not what was going to happen, looked like they had another agenda all together which forgot about all the work he'd done and all the things he'd sacrificed, like football, to help get the family through the Depression, and it looked like they weren't thinking about how his getting all those Japs off those Pacific Islands kept Whitey and Emma and Shorty too, among others, from having to eat raw fish and seaweed with chopsticks. That's when Red decided he was never going to talk about the war with anybody.

Shorty reached up and belted Red on the bicep. He had to reach up to do it.

"I never thanked you for those bird pictures," said Emma Loop.

"I got a picture of me in a hula dress," said Red.

"Hula, heh, heh," said Whitey, and out the door they went.

Well you couldn't really blame Shorty, that's what Red told Helen, you couldn't really take it out on Shorty.

"Well," said Helen, "you *could* take it out on Shorty." Helen was wondering who else he might take it out on and he might take it out on her, or even his son, Jarvis, who Red didn't want named Jarvis but when he got back from the Pacific that's what he had, a three year old son named Jarvis who decided the best way to deal with that problem was call *everything* Jarvis, something that wasn't going over so terribly well, or he might take it out on her mother, Bush, and her brother, Jon, who'd just been kicked out of their apartment building because Jon burnt it down to get the Communists out, and who now needed a place to stay. Red found that out a few hours later when Bush and Jon came to visit.

"Frances is in Detroit," said Bush. "David has a farm. We can't stay on a farm. Edju lives in Cleveland and white people can no longer live in Cleveland, besides, Edju is a cheapskate. Jon lives with me."

"That leaves Stanley," said Red.

"You want us to live with Stanley?" said Bush.

"We choose you," said Jon, his silver widow's peak shining like an arrow.

"And we have all the furniture you need," said Bush.

"I thought you burned down the house?" said Helen.

"And leave the furniture inside?" said Jon. "Think about it, Helen."

"We got our own goddamn furniture," said Red.

"Ours is much better," said Bush. "And it's free."

Those were unusual times for me too. Not only was I calling everything in the world Jarvis, I'd spent the first three years of my life with Helen, and Bush who came over every afternoon and gathered up two neighbors to play pinochle. They sent me out to the sand box. I buried a lot of insects named Jarvis and did my share of shifty eyed defecation. I kept pretty quiet. But other than those women, the only person I really ever had any contact with was Uncle Jon who carried the Atlantic Ocean around in his head and fought naval battles in it, commanded a fleet of LSTs, took soldiers ashore on Italy, Normandy, North Africa; often he replaced one of the neighbor women in that card game and also, in times of excitement, he had a tendency to float; I vaguely recall Helen and Bush standing on chairs and tying a rope to his ankles and dragging him down to his seat; it used to worry Helen but Bush said it happened in Poland all the time, it happened to a lot of Polish men if they didn't marry young enough and, as anyone could see, it happened to Jon. Nonetheless, enough of that kind of stuff happens in your childhood and it affects you, in terms of rationale if not perception. The worst thing about it for me was I knew that Jon taught kindergarten somewhere in the mornings. I felt something wordlessly disconcerting about sending children into his care. It made me afraid of the wrong people: the Pied Piper, the Good Witch of the North, Walt Disney, Marlin Perkins, Little Lulu.

Jon was my male model until Red came home.

Then Red came home. A nut of a different kind. When Red got mad it was miraculous. In a normal though seldom achieved repose he was simply enormous, inches over six foot and something over two hundred and fifty pounds, and that was when he left boot camp, in the best shape of his life, the last time he got weighed. Arms like legs, legs like diesels. But when angry he expanded, he reddened, he doubled, and he did so unpredictably. The funny thing was that he was capable of such simple joy, like a baby, and that was the scariest thing of all. There was something so deeply primitive in him that you could see him in there not understanding himself and then giving up, then he could tear down a house and sometimes he almost did, like that night, after he got back from Emma and Whitey's when they were on their way out to watch Shorty not play football and told Red that Helen couldn't come, and then came home to find Bush and Jon who hated him for being protestant sitting in his living room and telling him to sell all his furniture and move all theirs in and give them a place to stay, and there was his kid who he'd never seen and was scared as shit of him and called everything, everything in Erie, Pennsylvania, if not the world, Jarvis, the name he'd abandoned and the name he didn't want his son to have, and his wife who he loved more deeply than anything he'd ever loved, well she tended to side with her family, in fact it was scary the way Bush and Jon already seemed to be taking over, made him mad enough to break chairs, which he did, they were going to be replaced for free anyways, but it made his kid afraid of him and his wife afraid of him, just because he broke a few chairs, he didn't hurt anybody, and it drew that bunch of Polacks even closer together, sometimes huddled into a corner, which was a good place to keep an eye on them, goddamnit, but he loved Helen, he was an adult now, he had duties, and his kid, what did his kid know, his kid didn't know him from shit, so as he stood there in the dining room above his huddled family, a half of the dining room table in each hand, he already started to calm down; Bush and Jon could stay for a while, what could it hurt.

"Okay," said Red.

"Okay what," said Helen.

"He's not going to kill us," said Bush.

"Not just yet," said Jon.

"I don't like this change in you," Helen said to Red.

"What change?" said Red.

"Don't worry," said Bush. "In Europe they do this all the time. They get the war in them."

"They've had more practice in Europe," said Jon. "There's something to be said for having your culture blown to bits every few decades. It sophisticates the citizenry."

"It gets them out of the house," said Bush. "They hit some tanks with swords, they come home, they feel better."

Helen got up and put her arms around Red's waist, or as much around it as she could get. "Go bowling," she said to Red. "You'll feel better."

Well, she understood him, he had to give her that. And Bush could cook. He'd deal with Jon. He'd kill him if he had to. And he'd get to know his kid. He'd teach him sports. Kids loved sports. So Red got out his black sixteen-pounder, pumped it a few times, and headed down to the Kronenburger Club where he used to stick pins when he was in high school, after he got done peddling papers, and spent an hour knocking the shit out of pins. There was a kid in the back working three alleys. Red remembered that when he worked there two kids worked the whole joint, and Red tipped this kid ten cents a game, pretty good considering the games only cost him a quarter and he brought his own shoes. There were lots of places now that already had machines doing the cleaning and setting, sent the ball back on an automatic belt between the alleys, had little air blowers to dry the sweat off your hands instead of towels, but that took the work away from these kids, and the machines broke down, then the bowling machine mechanic would come out and put an OUT OF ORDER sign on the machine and wait for the Brunswick man to come out and scratch his head and send for somebody from the main office in Akron or somewhere and have him look around underneath for a half-hour before sending out for a whole new machine. He knew. He saw it in the Marines.

A tank wasn't worth the metal it was built out of, you just blew it up with a bazooka or another tank. He wondered if Shorty needed a job. People around there knew him still. He could pull a few strings for Shorty.

Red tipped his setter and headed to the bar for a couple beers and sandwiches, Koehler Beer, local beer, liverwurst and ketchup, limburger and onion on rye. He didn't know what kind of schedule Shorty had, but Emma and Whitey were probably making a pretty big sacrifice letting Shorty sit on the bench for the football team. Emma always told Red he couldn't play because she couldn't afford to have him get hurt, but by being too little to play Shorty was assured of never getting hurt; now he'd probably be thinking of ways to repay them, put some money in on the remortgaging, feel like he contributed; after football ended he'd probably have plenty of time.

Those limburger and onion sandwiches came on small slices of thick rye bread, cut down the middle, so Red could down a half-sandwich in one bite, though he always took two, one, two, that was the way he liked to eat a sandwich, first the limburger so he could get that rich aftertaste rising from the back of his throat and into his nostrils from behind, meeting the aroma that came through the front, then the hops in the beer just helped it linger, and then the liverwurst, sweet and creamy. By the time Red finished his second beer he was ready to go home and have a late night lunch. That's when he saw Shorty come into the Kronenburger Club, a long wool coat over his striped double-breasted suit, white polka dots on his dark blue tie, a girl on his arm as blond as Shorty himself and in her high heels not quite as short; they looked like they belonged on the top of a wedding cake.

"Hey," said Shorty when he saw Red, reaching up to poke his biceps.

"What the hell," said Red.

"Let me buy you a beer," said Shorty.

"You're too young to get in here and drink," said Red.

"Right," said Shorty, flagging down a waitress. He ordered a vodka gimlet and a sloe gin fizz. "You want something?" he said to Red.

"You work here?" said Red.

"Shorty got in the game tonight," said the girl.

"I play deep, deep safety," said Shorty, winking at Red.

"He was the last one in and everybody clapped."

"It was a running down. I got to stand in the end zone. What a feeling," said Shorty. He was laughing so you could see he wasn't going to tell you what kind of feeling that was.

"We waved," said the girl.

"This is Anna," said Shorty, introducing her to Red. "And this is my brother."

"You guys aren't brothers," said Anna.

That winter Red went back to ice skating. When he was a kid he did a lot of ice skating and roller skating, he could roller skate across the short part of the city, from Germantown to the Public Dock and back, and in the winter, after peddling papers, on the nights he didn't work at the Kronenburger Club, he walked up to the Mill Pond south of town, his thick hockey skates that he bought from the New-Used Store strapped over his shoulder, and helped shovel the snow to clear the ice. On weekends he hitched rides out to the Peninsula, packing both skates and shovel, and walked in deep from the neck of the land where families anxious to get on the ice after a long ride from the city shoveled out their little spaces; Red walked down the flooded Peninsula roadway, past the flooded docks and frozen lagoons, and there, where only a few of the heartiest ice fishers dotted the Bay with their tents and fires, in that landscape frozen and silent, he shoveled out an area as large as an ice rink, and against that silver mirror in the ice cold dead of day, the only sounds the hissing of his skates against the ice and the rhythm of his own breath, he learned to skate: backwards figure eights, splits, jackknives, twirls in the January sun, in the mind of winter, solitary.

When he first met Helen he borrowed Whitey's Model A and brought her here. He saved his money and bought her white figure skates. He shoveled the ice, he whirled for her, he taught her to skate. Afterwards they gathered wood for a fire and unpacked blankets and pots, cups and cocoa from the car, they boiled ice and drank hot chocolate made from the ice of the Bay. They held each other, their faces warm, their backs to the cold, and didn't think of any misery in the sound of the wind, in the sound of a few dead leaves.

But that winter, after the war, when Red decided to skate again, he didn't clearly yet remember those days, he thought only that he needed to get out of the house, away from Bush and Jon, away from his kid who didn't know him from Adam and named everything Jarvis, and he didn't want to bowl at the Kronenburger Club anymore because he didn't want to run into Shorty. But he had to go back to Emma to get his skates.

He picked a Saturday afternoon when Whitey would be out shopping, Jelly out with her new boyfriend, Bif, Shorty out doing whatever he did. Red was supposed to be shopping himself, and he was supposed to take Bush with him because she studied the papers and knew where the bargains were, but he'd snuck out, left at a moment when everybody was in the kitchen, anyway, the '42 Chevy was his car, he'd found it and bought it, he held a job, he was the one in debt for it.

He found Emma in the basement picking up canned peaches and green beans and tomatoes from the shelves to transfer them from the fruit cellar to the kitchen. To see her there, concentrating, her thick hands trembling slightly on the jars as she put them down, made him feel sad. As large as she was, he was gigantic next to her. He tried to remember her holding him. He tried to remember being her child.

Emma Loop looked at that giant child and knew he was there for something more than what he came for, but there was something about a child asking you for more than everything you'd already given, after you'd given him everything, something about what she had left, about power and denial, all of it unnamable, that kept her from addressing this giant male baby on his terms; his life had been fine, hard but fine, good even, considering the times, until someone came along and seemingly got more.

"I'm looking for my skates," said Red.

Emma finished filling the box with jars and handed the box to Red. "Where'd you last leave them?"

She pushed by him and he followed her up the stairs with the box of jars.

"They're too big for Shorty," he said to her.

"He doesn't skate," said Emma.

At the top of the stairs she took the box of canned fruit and vege-tables from him and went into the kitchen. It was a wooden box. Red thought about that, how boxes were cardboard now. This wooden box had lasted years.

"I left them with the tools," said Red.

"They're probably rusted down there," said Emma.

"Whitey didn't move them, did he?"

"Did you look?" Emma said to him. She put the jars in the cup-board. She didn't turn to him to speak. "When did Whitey ever do anything?"

"I thought you might know," said Red.

And then Emma turned to him thinking, this is what happens, a son rejects you, leaves his family, his nationality, his religion, takes in a woman and her family, then comes back for his skates. And Red was thinking that all it would take was that she go get them. Red was that simple. Emma wondered what she'd done to make things that simple for him.

"I was thinking of skating again," said Red.

"If you want to skate, skate," said Emma Loop. "No one ever stopped you."

But that wasn't true. Like everything, it was true, but it wasn't really true.

Red came home with a new pair of skates. Helen and Bush and Jon were in front of the Zenith. Bobo Brazil gave Gorgeous George a Cocoa Butt. I was on Bush's lap. Red stood there in the doorway with his new skate box under his arm. It was a red and white box made out of cardboard, the skates folded over each other inside, toe to heel.

"I see that's not a ham under your arm," said Bush. Back then she wasn't nearly as old, her hair was still a little blond and she seldom wore her glasses. Back then she had a different view of things because she hadn't yet started to outlive everybody.

"It's skates," said Red.

"You only think of yourself," said Jon, his right leg over the left, foot bouncing.

"I need them," said Red.

"You haven't skated in a long time," said Helen.

"That's why," said Red.

"Jarvis," I said to him, spreading my arms.

"Don't call me that," said Red to him, and Bush tucked me in a little closer.

"You know," Red said to Bush, "that's my kid, not your kid."

"Easy for you to say," said Jon. "But in his formative years you were not around."

"You were around," said Red.

"That's right," said Jon.

"And I fought," said Red.

"We all fought in our own way," said Jon.

"What the hell way did you fight?" said Red.

That's when Helen got up and went to Red. There were ways in which she felt that the guy she got back from the war wasn't the guy she sent. One night in San Diego, in the rain, she found out her husband had left to kill other men somewhere in the Pacific and when he came back, that's what he had in him, he couldn't turn it off, it wasn't like the movies where the lovers kissed gently and then the man went out and killed and then came back again, the killing killed out of him, the loving intact; whatever evil they found in them or put in them to make them do that stayed in there and looked for things to kill, outside, inside, it kept killing things; she wasn't sure she wanted to turn her kid over to that, she wasn't sure Jon wasn't right, that the war at home was the real war and the men who left it were cowards too afraid not to kill.

"You want to go skating with me?" Red said to Helen.

"We have shopping to do," said Helen.

"And furniture to move," said Bush.

"You'll have to think of something to do with all your things," said Jon. "I'm speaking to Helen, Red. I don't expect you to think of anything."

That's when Red thought of something. It was a big thought because it started a trend that lasted years and years. His chest expanded and a flush went to his cheeks and biceps; he doubled like one of those fighting birds, except there weren't any feathers on him, just muscle. He left the room and yelled back in. "Dining room table. Need it?"

"I have one," said Bush who followed him. She was the only one who wasn't afraid.

Red picked up the dining room table and cracked it like a cracker, stacked it in pieces, took it out the front door and threw it off the porch. Then he went back in and handled the chairs. After that Bush just pointed and Red expulsed, though when he struggled getting the couch out the door, he had to tear the doors off and he didn't bother with the hinges; he put the couch on its side, grabbed the door in one hand and ripped it off. The next door, the bigger one, he kicked out with the couch on his back and the screen door he took out with the simple jab. Helen had hold of me now, tucked like a football, and moved through that carnage like a halfback on the fast track. She'd been athletic in high school. I think she was mostly concerned about our safety till the doors went down and it got cold. As for me, these were important years, harbingers of habits, the light of my inclinations, the kelson of what I'd become.

Red demolished some beds, some lamps, a toilet seat. He looked around.

"Red," said Helen. I felt her trembling as she wielded me like a flashlight. "Red."

Red pointed to Uncle Jon. "How about that?"

"Just the chair," said Bush.

Jon tried to unfold and get out of it, but he wasn't quick enough. Red was like a storm and the lightening inside. He picked up the easy chair, Jon and all, and threw them out the front window. This was one of the reasons Jon didn't like Red. But Red didn't like Jon either and he had his reasons, too, besides, all that activity seemed to relax him a bit; his breath steamed the now icy air but at least the fire was out.

Bush got her coat. "You get things done, I'll give you that," she told him. "Now let's get a ham."

So not too long after that Red went back to ice skating. In his own subtle way, he often got what he wanted. Though if you asked him he'd have told you that's not what he wanted. He wanted Bush and Jon to stop raising his kid and he wanted them out of his house. He wanted his kid to stop calling everything Jarvis. He wanted to be alone with Helen again, like before the war. He wanted his mother, Emma, to give him some indication that she loved him as much as she loved Shorty. He even wanted to go bowling at the Kronenburger Club and tip the pin setters and eat liverwurst sandwiches and limburger and onion on rye, wash them down with Koehler Beer. He didn't feel at home in his home anymore. He didn't even have his own lousy furniture. So he went ice skating. On Saturdays after he finished taking

Bush shopping, after the garbage was taken out and the trash burned, he stood before Helen with his nose flexing and his great frown, or on Sundays now, he let Bush and Jon accompany Helen and me to church, he stopped going himself, and drove out to the Peninsula, striding out onto the Bay with his shovel and skates, clearing an area the size of a football field, and there, in the morning or the sunset of the January sun, Red sliced the air with his silver skating; he listened to the sizzle of his skates on the ice, to the dry wind, to his windy breath like the sound of the land full of the same wind blowing in the same bare place; he listened in the snow, waiting like a moment between moments for something to come to him, something other than the wind and the sizzle of his skates, other than his breath, the cold, the ice, the sun. There should have been someone there to tell him. There should have been something to make him other than he was. To want so little is too much.

"I got an idea," Red said to Helen. He went to the pantry in the cellar way and got out the Guckenheimer. He poured them both shots.

And Helen drank a shot with him. Jarvis was in bed, Bush and Jon in front of the Zenith, and ideas were hard to come by.

"Let's me and you go ice skating," said Red. "You got your old skates. Bush and Jon can watch the kid. We'll pack a lunch. We can be alone for a change."

And Helen thought about it. It was a positive thing, she had to give him that. It beat divorce, and that was something she had to think about all the time, but then she could never marry again, though Jon said she could get the marriage annulled because Red was protestant; even Bush thought that Helen should think about leaving Red, that it might knock some sense into him, but where would she go? She couldn't go to her mother's, so maybe Red was right after all, maybe men were right about that, that you just had to get away from everything sometimes, except that she didn't want to, she liked having everything right there, having everything close.

"I don't know where my skates are," she said.

"I already found them," said Red.

"My ankles," said Helen.

"You don't have to skate that much," said Red. "Just come with me."

He had his eyes big and blue underneath his red hair. He had his broad pleading face. He kissed her forehead. Despite that body, like an engine in rocks, his lips were so soft, softer than a baby's.

"I don't think you've changed one thing about your life since you met me," Helen said to him. "You give something here, do something there, but you have your own life. You just go around, you go off, nothing changes."

Red couldn't think of anything that hadn't changed, not one thing. "That's right," he said to her softly. "I got everything I want."

But that's not what she meant. She meant that you want to see some kind of change in a man. He can change his job, go to war, take in your family. He can do those things without changing. He can just go about his life and keep something inside the same, some identity, something, when what you want is that he give it up, that he put things aside, put himself aside, that he keep you inside him, not himself, you; that's what she had done, and that's what even the best men didn't do. That's why he could move mountains for her, think he had done it for her, and yet it could mean almost nothing, certainly less than a moment alone waiting for him, waiting for him to return from somewhere.

"We'll shop Saturday?" said Helen, knowing what she'd done in asking him that, asking him to behave, like his mother would, letting him do that for her and not wanting that from him.

"Yes," said Red.

"You'll go to church with us." Because you had to ask them for what they had to give.

"I love you," said Red. He came to her. "And then we'll go skating." He knelt in front of her there at the kitchen table and put his head on her lap. What else was there to do?

It was one of those days when you thought God had blue eyes; a light snow from the night trimming the trees, the lawns white, the cement wet black under the melting sun. Red and Helen came back from church and packed the Chevy with blankets, filled the thermos with hot chocolate, wrapped sandwiches and hard boiled eggs in wax paper and put them in the big square brown basket that they used every Easter for Red's candy, then they took bottles of Guckenheimer whiskey and Mogen-David wine; they got all that stuff in the car and then got their ice skates; Red got Helen's sharpened and cleaned that week, white leather and silver runners shining like the feet of a princess, and then they dressed in thick socks and double pairs of pants, sweat shirts under heavy coats, scarves, wool hats. It was a big project and it made them happy just to get ready. They left me with Bush and Jon and headed out into the day. The car blew white smoke from the rear as Red scraped ice from the windows and Helen threw snow. Then the two of them got in and waved and left.

Red took the scenic way to the Peninsula. He drove all the way down Celebration Avenue to Sixth Street, then headed west, though when he got to Perry Square, where on the northwest corner of Sixth and State he and Helen began their courtship at the Arthur Murray Dance Studio above the Rexall Drug Store, he took a right and drove down to the Public Dock to look at the Bay from the city side. As they expected, the light snow and heavy sun had left the Bay like glass, a cold mirror reflecting sky and stretching a mile to the Peninsula on the other side. It was a beautiful day. They rolled down the windows of the Chevy and the cold air blew a soft, sweet edge into the car, as if somewhere something might come to life.

They rolled up the windows again and headed back to Sixth Street, driving through all the old Yankee neighborhoods, the large red brick mansions, the street canopied with snow-laden trees. At the Frontier Park Red headed down to the Bayfront Drive so they could catch glimpses of the Bay through the gaps between the Tudor homes built to overlook the water. At the neck of the Peninsula, near the "Welcome to Presque Isle" sign, they watched some families ice skate.

"Do you know what Presque Isle means?" said Helen.

"It's the name of the Peninsula," said Red. He watched a man and woman strapping skates on their kids, kneeling in front of the open doors of their woody station wagon, the kid's feet twisting.

"It means almost an island," said Helen.

She knew those things. She'd studied Latin in high school, and again while Red was in the Marines, when she spent her days pregnant and alone in the war housing on the East Side. She looked at some French then, too, and Spanish and German. She thought the world was on the verge of becoming international.

"We should bring the kid here," said Red. "We should get him some skates."

"We can't keep him in shoes," said Helen, thinking that they would not come out here again, that it was a long drive, that families on the East Side did not own station wagons with wood paneling.

It was a peninsula, thought Red, a piece of land that went out into the water, that made a bay. There was always talk about the sand shifting here at the neck of the Peninsula, of it washing away, of how it might get separated from the land someday or get pushed northeast up the lake to Buffalo, then Buffalo would get all the tourists or they'd have to build a bridge to get to it, then the city could fight over where to build the bridge, on the West Side, near the neck, or where the neck of the Peninsula would have used to have been, or on the East Side, at the channel, where the tip almost touched the land. The West Side would get the bridge. He knew that. That's where the money was. It was like the French, two hundred years ago. They were already thinking like that.

"Those French," said Red.

"They think differently," said Helen.

"Half of Quebec is French," said Red, remembering, remembering ahead to something. He wished when he married her he'd had more time, that they could have gone from Niagara Falls and into Quebec, up to Montreal and Quebec City. He bet they had some great places to ice skate in Quebec.

Red pulled the Chevy out of the parking lot and headed into the narrow part of the Peninsula, past the boat docks and the little inlet where they were going to put the new marina, past the ranger's station at the Lily Pond. On the left, signs pointed to parking for beaches; Shell Beach, the Stone Jetty, Waterworks. Someone with power in the state government had suggested getting rid of the names and just numbering the beaches consecutively, one through eleven, replace Lighthouse Beach with Beach 8, Pine Tree with nine, Sunset with ten, Coast Guard with eleven, that it would make it easier for tourists to figure out where they were going. They'd probably do it. They probably would. And in a generation kids would grow up without ever knowing the names.

God how he wanted to take his time today. The car warm, Helen snuggled next to him under his arm thinking, *one day all of this will only be a memory*, we will walk out together among the ten thousand things, each scratched too late with such knowledge, *the wages of dying is love*; but Red couldn't think those kinds of thoughts, or imagine she could think them; he drove past the Perry Monument and Misery Bay where Dobbins built the ships for Perry, only to die of the 1812 Plague with half the rest of the men, where Perry himself, on the eve of the battle, the British frigates lying in wait, found out that the channel to the Erie Bay was too shallow, that the fleet was trapped in a spoon; there, feet from this road, hundreds of men had died to build futile ships, to fight the British for a lake, back when the British were evil like the Japanese; to think that it happened there.

They followed the road toward the tip of the Peninsula, through the Lagoons, now a frozen marsh, rain drops frozen on branches like a thousand million moons, and then to the last view of the Bay, the city lying across the icy mirror like smoke and stars. There they stopped. They opened the picnic basket, drank wine and ate sandwiches. And Red said to Helen, No matter what, no matter what, I love you; one of the truest moments, one of the moments which kept them together till the end, a moment that stuck in them both so deeply that they saw the bones beneath each other's faces, and guessed. Then they put on their ice skates.

He laced them for her, tight enough to hold her ankles, loose enough to keep the blood in her feet. He told her to remember to wriggle her toes, then he finished his own, took her hand, and they walked on the water of the Bay.

What a day it was. The sun strolling in the sky, streaking their feet with lightning, the ice clear enough to reflect stars, but being daylight, was like the blue of the veil of the Mother of God. They could see themselves in the ice. And it came back to her. She moved close to him, lifted a leg; he held her ankle like you'd hold the tongue of a young child, he lifted her as she jumped; they spun.

This was enchantment, the opening of some greater eye. They had never skated like this before. Across the Bay the city rose like crystal, the woods behind them like a cathedral of snow, underneath it the buried bones of things still warm, waiting to return.

After an hour or so they skated to the shore of the Bay. They drank hot chocolate from a red thermos, warming their faces with the steam that rose from their cups. Red put his arm around Helen and they kissed. They poured more hot cocoa and laced it with Guckenheimer. Red had been right. They needed this. It had been so long since they'd been alone together. They didn't talk about Bush or Jon, or that their son, Jarvis, called everything Jarvis, that Red was Lutheran, she Catholic and their families hated each other, even the very family he took under his roof did not like him, and that his own mother rejected him for that kindness. They were in love. They had each other and together they had that. They would wade through these things.

Red stared out across the Bay. He remembered coming here as a kid, how on days like this he thought he could skate all the way across the Bay to the Public Dock, all the way there and back; he wondered if anyone had ever done it. He'd like to do it. The way he felt, he could do it now. How far was it? A mile or so? How long could it take?

"I could do it," he said to Helen. "I'd like to."

"You don't need to do it," Helen said to him. "Who cares?"

"I could do it," said Red.

"Then why don't you do it?" said Shorty. He'd been driving the Peninsula, doing some thinking, and recognized Red and Helen's car. He parked behind them in his new car, a black Ford, and got out and watched them watching the Bay. Or maybe it wasn't an accident at all, maybe he'd known they were going to be there. He'd left the house that day to find them, to tell them something, something important, but found they weren't home; Bush and Jon told him they were skating at the Peninsula and he went looking for them.

"You don't know what the ice is like in the middle of the Bay," said Helen.

"It's been frozen for months," said Red.

"One break and you go under, you'll never get out," said Helen.

"Sure he could," said Shorty, "You use the points of your skates. You have to take them off in the water."

"The ice keeps breaking," said Helen.

"You keep pulling till you hit a solid part," Shorty said.

"Till you freeze," said Helen. Though she realized then that this is what it came to, that she gave him everything and then he asked her for one more thing, and then when she gave it, when she bound herself to him inextricably, he would step away. She wondered if she would ever come to hate him, what the signs would be to tell her. She loved him because he was a giant, capable of gigantic things, and yet had something in him so gentle. She thought their children would be magnificent. But already she'd begun to reconcile the gulf between expectation and acceptance. She thought of the death of her father, of Bush's hard-edged fatalism, struggling with the polarity of inevitable end and survival.

"We're having such a good time," said Helen.

"We'll drive and wait for you at the dock, then if you don't want to quit we'll drive back and meet you here," said Shorty.

"You drive," said Helen. "I'll wait here." That was how you said no to a man, with your body, as little as it meant, the words meant less.

"Finish the cocoa," said Red, handing her the thermos, the wine, the Guckenheimer. "I won't be long."

"Red," said Helen.

"I won't be long," said Red. He rose and stretched. The winter sun poured on him; he sucked it in. He sucked it in so much you couldn't see his reflection on the gray ice. He looked at her, but Helen looked away from him. "I'll be right back," he said.

He squatted, rose, gazed to the dock, barely a speck across the Bay. He pushed off, spun, skated backwards, lifted and came down, his back to them, pushing out, arms swinging, in minutes beyond the ice fisherman, in minutes a speck, and gone.

"I better get going," Shorty said to Helen, "or he'll beat me over there." He went to his black Ford, removed and inspected the inside of his brimmed hat.

"He wouldn't have done it if you hadn't shown up," said Helen to him. She watched Shorty in his long wool overcoat, his shiny black shoes, cuffed pants, neatly cut blond hair. He was barely as big as her. Maybe this was not such a great price to pay if this was all Red needed to do, that in his own mind he could tell himself that he could do things that Shorty could not do, that he could leave Bush and Jon and even she herself behind him if he chose; this was the kind of masquerade he needed now to stay close.

Shorty got in his car. "Well then, lucky I showed up," he said. And in a moment he was gone, too.

Red on the ice. He writes his self on the pale slate, his red jacket, his tan khaki pants that he wore in the Marines, his swinging arms and the engine of his breath, shining in the ice, each new self a flicker, shady, momentary, vanishing under the white slice traces of his skates, letting the body say itself, letting the body alone to seek and find what it likes, and then everything is right and nothing is wasted, the waste is covered over and then all is swept away in the torrent; the sound of the city is so near, so close, he can hear it brushing against the lip of the Bay, he can hear it under his skates; he is alone now, the ice trembles and he flies over it lightly, as if it were Helen's skin, as if the body of water below were the soul of Helen beneath him; alone on the ice Bay he thinks of the frozen lake beyond the Peninsula, stretching to London, Canada, he thinks of the Indians crossing the Bay here to camp on the Peninsula, to trap, to watch the red sun sit on the Lake; he remembers their name, something he learned in grammar school, the Eriez, how they were rubbed out by the Iroquois, the men and boys scalped and castrated, the women and girls taken as slaves; he can see the smokestacks of the city now, etching into the sky, their smoke like clouds, billowing, he thinks he can hear the men on the docks; can they spot him as he moves across the mirror of the Bay? They point, what is that? a man? a man crossing the Bay? doesn't he know how dangerous that is? how unevenly the ice freezes? what the chances would be against an exhausted man if the ice broke and he fell through? The ice slithers beneath him now, it slithers and sweats, it is soft like a woman's underthing; his skates are gone now, he can no longer hear them, he feels nothing at his feet, finds no solace in his breath; before him the city disappears and leaves only a mouth, white and yawning; he pushes into it; he spins, he leaps from the ice.

Helen, do you remember that night? I remember. I remember how he came to you. I remember how you feared for everything then, how the world stopped, how his heart opened, caught in death, caught in evil and death, love and evil and war ahead, how that filled you with something so unexplainable, how you thought then that if he died, if the vacuum took him in, leaving nothing, you would have something inside you that was him, something that would be the both of you and yet outlast you both; we do so poorly with our love, our leisure, with our lives on the line, we think of our destinies as if we played a part, creation springing from our minds, our wombs, using us for passage, becoming passages of their own; you are thinking of the water beneath the ice, how it is trapped, how it buoys the world, how it is filled with life, how beneath his feet sentient things twist in the muted sunlight, fish swim sluggishly, amphibians wait in the mud; inside the glass of the wine bottle, blood that you mix with your blood, oh Helen, my mother, I see you there, I would blow the flame out of your silver cup, I would scrape the rust off your ivory bones, I would let nothing of you go, ever; reach deeper into the sorrows to come, hear the wind crying across the black stones, see him in his undanced cadence of vanishing, it is winter, and love the wages of dying.

The sun is broadening the sky behind you now, there is yet a colder chill, the wine is gone and in the east, over the city, a pale moon resurrects in the pale blue sky; how could something born in the heat of the universe become so cold? why should a rock so large fly so beautifully and so slow? as it rises you can see it in the ice, mixing in the red of the sun's descent.

You open the whiskey and drink until your head is dark and your stomach climbs into your throat; you bring it all back out of you and onto the Bay; you are crying now and sleepy.

You didn't want me to ever see you like this. You hid it from me all your life. You never let me know. But I have been inside of you, I have stolen from you, I have taken so much of you in me, and for what little I am you have sacrificed your life. We children, when we discover this, our mothers are gone, and our children, they can't be told.

So it is dusk now and you go back to the car to wait for Red. In the back seat, wrapped in blankets, you fall asleep. And that's when Shorty returns. He is not a man who has ever been tested, he wouldn't recognize a test. He sees you asleep, his brother's wife, and tomorrow, though he has told no one, he is leaving and plans never to return. This is what he came to tell you. This is what he came to tell Red. But he saw you there, huddled together on the edge of the frozen Bay, he saw that small thing and thought how precious it was, and how easy to take. Shorty is a small man, but a man, strong enough and quick, and you are ill, drunk in loneliness and fear, and when he reveals himself to you, you are not even awake, you are dreaming and you dream that his touch is one of your children; "my baby," you mumble, "my child," and he spreads himself over you, as dark as infinity; had it not been for the way he left you, cold and exposed to the light of the moon, you might not have ever known he was there.

How long can any winter last?

Outside the window of the house that me and Kara Ruzci once shared in the country, the snow fell in layers. The wind swept in over that first long hill that broke the plain off the lake, the first hill, once the ancient shore, before the lake most recently receded some hundreds of thousands of years ago; the wet wind hit that first long hill and opened its belly, laying down layer upon layer of snow until the drifts curved and clung to the roof gutters and the windows went black. Nothing anywhere moved.

Back in the neighborhood, on 24th Street, on the porch, Red sat in the snow. He watched it cover his knees, his hands, his chest. He looked out as the snow filled the street, covering the cars, moving up the sides of the houses, blanketing the windows. He raised a hand once to brush the snow from his eyes. The wind came down the street in white devils, sucking at the trees, moving up the steps of homes and onto the porches, leaping at the black eyed second-story windows. Red wiped the snow from his eyes again. The wind came down the street in a wave, it crested, it covered, and this time he allowed it to bury him.

Beneath him, in the cellar, Helen sat at the bottom of her labyrinth, her thoughts rising like opium smoke into the rusted metals of the broken machines with which she'd spent her life; there are refrigerators here, ovens, toasters, blenders, waffle irons, Electra-Perk coffee makers; and whatever made her think they were immutable, that they would not at some moment blossom, grow fruit, reproduce, why wouldn't they become small animals, or elephants, or children; how she'd sacrificed herself; she thought of the spring and how the birds spent their time building nests, tugging worms, returning to the trees with their bits of string and twigs, winding them, how they sat on their eggs, hatched them, found food for their young, ate it and gave it back, taught them to fly; she'd seen the sparrows and swallows dive bombing the cats and dogs who wandered too near the grounded chicks, she remembered the wild canaries who used to come in the late summer to eat the bitter cherries from the huge wild cherry tree that blew down one night in a storm, and how the birds still came to those dying limbs, yellow breasted, black winged, she remembered throwing bread out for the sparrows and starlings and robins and cardinals and blue jays; she loved those female cardinals, muted red against the lawn, not bright like the males, and then she remembered the summer that the tiny hawk roosted in the pear tree, how Red loved that hawk, dragging her out every dusk to watch it dive for invisible insects, how it arched its wings as it neared the ground, pulling up, it made the same sound, said Red, that the Zeros made when they dove, the sound of wind against an arched wing, a low, rumbling, vibrating sound; she thought of how the birds scratched out their living through winter and then in the spring started again, how many short seasons were given to that cycle, and now, she, with something waiting to kill her, too, wondered how long these broken machines, these things built to kill her, could protect her.

Willie held those Dialecticians in his attic for winter upon winter, his hands of cards like a fan; the snow came over the windows as they poured and drank whiskey as slow and brown as love; the smoke of their cigars filled them until they could breathe fire as easily as dragons, and then, when finally there came some spring, he wrote their winning hands across the faces of their cards and they won cruel things.

My brothers, Joseph and Andrew, became adults in this time. They let their virgin beards grow on their faces. They never shaved.

Angela Corona, beneath a comforter filled with the feathers of her own birds, held Raphael to her breasts and predicted she would never love snow.

Big Dick Jinx recovered from his heart attack and waited to get back to work. Jimbo Funster waited by his short-wave for Funly's call. In jail, Grandpa Funster cut and counted the unspun threads of time like fallen fruit. And in a metal building on the edge of town, Stinky Jinx and my genius sister, Neda, spun on the ice like the center of a cold star; he lifted her above his head, her pelvis resting on his palm, her arms spread like a jet, and Stinky himself lifting now, leaving the ice, his legs split in the air, parallel to the surface, they hung there like a delicate bird or moon; they were becoming the best ice skating pair in Erie, Pennsylvania, if not the world.

And I, alone that winter in the arch of time, found that place where souls go when they rise from the soft blanket of mind and touch the fingers of the dead, the dead who crouch above us in their holy way, with their frowns, their memories, the dead whose voices you hear when you rise in the middle of the night, calling you back to that place without thought, that clean black space you thought was sleep; I didn't know it, but I'd heard them moaning in my water tap when I drew water for my midnight thirst, in the engine of the refrigerator, behind the voices of the voices on the radio I flicked on to remind me there were other living beings; the dead, they talk to those thoughts you feel thinking behind your thoughts; they are everywhere but it is so hard to keep them company; this is where I found Kara Ruzci, waiting at the cusp of her tunnel.

We did simple things. We made breakfasts of poached eggs, pota-to pancakes, fresh muffins; got fresh milk from a farmer up the road. We lunched on baked bread and fresh butter, wiled away the after-noons with tequila and sunlight. In the evenings we sipped wine, we made love, we played with the Viz and taught him to speak. When he slept, we held each other and whispered, love and love, love, and love. We spent our days in these ordinary things, the thrill of these common things, the repetition of simple acts; to make and eat food, to name objects, to watch the light change behind the snow-covered windows, the pleasure of a word coming from our lips.

There was never a moment we didn't touch each other. But as the nights shortened, my love, Kara Ruzci, began to fade in the lengthening light; at times the sun from the windows refracted through her, beam-ing through the wound in her womb; at times, though I was in her so deeply, though I held her so closely to me that her flesh fell through my own, I could barely feel her, as if she were insubstantial. Soon, through most the day, she was completely invisible.

"Don't leave us, Kara," I cried in her arms, "Don't leave us again."

"You must never make love to another," said Kara Ruzci. "I am your love and you are my love."

"Just don't leave," I whispered.

"There are things you must realize, my love," said Kara.

"Don't leave me," I said.

"But I have never been with you at all," Kara said, holding my face. "No more than I have ever been away."

"You're going to leave."

"Yes," she said.

"Will I see you again?"

"My love," said Kara Ruzci, rocking me gently, endlessly rocking, "that which is only living can only die. I will be your cradle."

〰〰〰〰〰Spring And All

AND THOUGH THAT MIGHT be reason enough to believe none of this happened, in the spring, when the snow melted in cataracts of brilliant light, the streets, during the days of the thaw, becoming black water avenues, my only son, Visitor Loop, could speak. I suppose it could have happened naturally, behind my back, or while I was sleeping, though I never slept, or, of course, during one of my insane delusions, but once you give in to that kind of thinking it becomes easy to find excuses, harder to draw lines, find beginnings and endings; things that happen, as well as things that do not, have lives of their own. Stories are just things inside other stories, like multiplying the world by itself over and over until you get satisfied with an explanation. Some of us never get satisfied

And on one of those spring days when the sky cleared and the streets dried, when things gripped down and began to awaken and the wetness of the earth filled the air with a moist gray film, we got a call from Uncle Bif who told me that Grandma Emma Loop was dead.

Red got up from his chair on the porch, his clothes still damp from the mud of melted snow, and went upstairs and drew himself a hot bath. I followed him up there. I watched him strip off his clothes and throw them behind the bathroom door, a kind of hamper, a Pile System for people who didn't have the pile system, whether it existed or not. Red got in the tub and I sat on the toilet, not that uncommon a thing around there, seeing as it was so crowded and we only had one bathroom, no lock on the door. He lay back in the tub. He wasn't circumcised and that huge untrimmed dick of his floated right up. It took me a long time to figure out what was wrong with him, not having a mushroom top on his dick, looked like something on a big animal, and people'd told me that when penises were uncircumcised they looked smaller. Anyway, it got me thinking about Helen; everytime she made a baby she had to deal with that heathen penis. I wondered if she knew that before she married him. That was something Grandma Emma Loop always had on her, though maybe I was thinking too patriarchally, it sure didn't stop Helen from having kids.

Red soaped himself there, he always did that first, then he washed his face and worked down his body, armpits, chest, legs, He knelt to wash his butt. He did his hair last, I could see he was balding a bit at the crown when he bent under the spigot to rinse. Then he dried off and combed his hair. He shaved naked, he always did, and creamed his face using a brush and a jar of Noxzema, blue jar, white cream, Gillette razor, the kind that you opened up and dropped in the blade.

He went into his and Helen's room and put on a T-shirt and boxer shorts, a white shirt, blue pants, dark socks, black shoes, his blue suit coat. He chose a tie, went to the mirror at Helen's dressing table. He had to stoop to see himself.

"Get your mother," he said to me then. "Tell her."

I went down the stairs, across the living room and holy room, through the kitchen and pantry and down the stairs into the cellar where a maw in the labyrinth opened up at the bottom of the stairs. I went in and wandered around for a good while, but I couldn't find Helen, in fact I started to worry I might not find my way the hell out of there; I got to a crossroads in that dead machine cave and gave a yell. "Helen!" I yelled. "Grandma Emma's dead!"

I waited for the echo to die away and then, from the back of one of the corridors, it was hard to tell which one, I heard something that sounded like rushing water. I waited there as the sound mounted, a noise like you'd imagine a locomotive making as it ran through liquid. I felt the humidity for a moment in my nostrils before I heard the sound directly behind me. In a second it was flowing over my feet, warm and red. Then I heard a roar and saw a wall of fire and blood. Helen stepped out from behind it with the Infant. The wall disappeared.

"Where's your father?" said Helen.

"He took a bath and got all dressed up."

"A good German," she said. "All business." She peered at me. "You're sweating," she said.

"I thought I saw something," I told her.

"You never know," said Helen.

"You don't," I said.

"No," said Helen, "you never do."

I followed her and the Infant upstairs where she met Red in the living room. He was waiting there by the vestibule door, I guess he couldn't quite figure out what to do after getting all dressed up because he held his bowling ball there at the center of his stomach, hands on either side of it, contemplating his reflection in the black, a look on his face I hoped I'd never see again, his cheeks both set and soft, his eyes watery and mean. Helen faced him with the Infant tucked under her arm. The bowling ball and the Infant, I'd never put it together before.

"You coming?" said Red.

"Of course," said Helen. Those two loved each other, afterall, after everything. I wondered if I would've ended up living with Kara like that, separated by such disparate symbols. Maybe I'd been duped by telephones and television, icons of communication, into forgetting that I lived my life alone.

These were strange thoughts, but it was a strange circumstance, and I teetered for a moment on the verge of trying to explain something to myself. There, in front of me, my mother and father. His mother had just died. She bore him, sustained him, denied him. She never accepted his wife, another woman whom he loved and did not understand in the least. And now his mother had died with all of it unreconciled. Is any of that true? These words slither, they dry and crack open and there is nothing inside them.

"Let me get ready," said Helen.

"I used up all the hot water," said Red.

"That's all right," said Helen. "I'll just be a minute."

"I'm coming too," I said. "I'll get the Viz."

They hadn't done a thing yet with Grandma Emma Loop by the time we got there; she was lying on her back on the bed, just right of center, eyes closed, jaw dropped just a little, so still, so huge and deep in her solidity. Grandpa Whitey hadn't moved either; he was still in bed, curled up, his back to her; I'd seen it before when a kitten died in a litter, the rest of them just moved away. Bif and Jelly were in there, cousin Nancy, Bifboy, and now me and Red and Helen and the Viz. There'd been some talk on the way over there in the Rainbow, mostly on Helen's part, about keeping the Viz from seeing this, but he told her he wasn't afraid.

"Because you don't know what you're not afraid of yet," said Helen.

We were in the back and she had to turn around to talk to us.

"Deaf," said the Viz.

"Death," said Helen.

"Mommy's dead," said the Viz.

"You don't see your Mommy," said Helen.

The Viz looked at me and I looked at him, but that's as far as that went.

"He saw her buried," I said.

By then we were already at Bif and Jelly's.

"What do you think, Red?" said Helen.

"I think he's talking pretty good," said Red.

I guess Red was concentrating so hard on the present he wasn't quite in it, that's why when we got in Emma and Whitey's room he could go to the bed and touch Emma's forehead, then he opened her nightgown slightly and felt her chest. "Still warm," he said softly. He kissed Grandma Emma, closed her nightgown. I'd never seen him move so delicately. Then he went over to the other side of the bed, took Whitey by the shoulders and sat him up. "Come on," said Red.

"Come on, heh, heh," said Grandpa Whitey.

"Ma's dead," said Red.

"Dead, heh, heh," said Whitey. He started to cry.

"Call the doctor," said Red to Jelly. "And the funeral home."

"Funeral, heh, heh," weeped Grandpa Whitey, his round face falling down and down in a thousand lines.

Red and me got to be pallbearers, along with Uncle Bif and Uncle Lefty, Bifboy, and Sweaty Limburg. Grandpa Whitey sat across the aisle with Helen and Jelly and Tillie, Joseph and Andrew in their scrawny new beards, cousin Nancy and cousin Sweety Limburg. Neda was out of town with Stinky for the AAU East Regional figure skating finals in Pittsburgh, and who else wasn't there was Shorty, old Shorty, Shorty, Shorty; Shorty wasn't there.

Those protestants didn't really know how to run a funeral, big on dignity, brevity, and discretion, a lot of bland optimistic commentary, flowers, gay colors, some cool old hymns like "Old Rugged Cross" and "He Walks with Me," but I couldn't help but think they'd lost something there in the Reformation, and it was something I felt I had business thinking about since I'd spent a lot of time with funerals in the last few years. The Catholics did a lot more screaming and wailing, more processions, more kneeling, more praying, candles, smoke, black colors, they made a big deal out of it. If you'd asked me a couple years ago I'd have said I thought all that was ridiculous, but now I thought those were important things, I thought it was a big deal, I thought you should be sad and scream your bloody fucking head off, it was your last chance. Of course, probably everybody in that funeral parlor had an opinion about funerals, that they should or shouldn't have them, what they should or shouldn't do, all to keep from thinking about the funeral in front of their faces. I was sitting next to Bifboy and he said, "They should just bury them at sundown, get them the hell off the planet. Life's for the living."

"And death for the dead," I told him. "But death's for the living too, if you think about it."

"I try not to think about it," said Bifboy.

"You might want to. We organize our lives in reciprocity quadrants," I said to Bifboy. "One of the corners doesn't reciprocate and it becomes a mystery. The only part of the quadrant that doesn't have apparent reciprocity is that living is not for the dead." I knew I was in Neda's territory, or maybe even Andrew's but sometimes you're the only one there to do the job.

Bifboy had fine features, like Bif, a small nose, chin and cheeks like golf balls. He had thin lips and wavy blond hair that he kept wet and combed back. He lowered his brows a little bit and tweaked my nearest cement wing.

"You learn that on the garbage truck?" he said.

"I learned that shooting heroin."

Bifboy's upper lip curled a little bit on one side, a kind of smile. He was deciding maybe I had a sense of humor.

"I'll tell you something about garbagemen," I said to him. "This garbage strike is misdirected, but it's just the beginning. Someday garbagemen will control the tunnels that arc between death and eternity."

I told him all of it. I guess I was depressed. The minister was handing out the "dust to dust" and I was searching my dusty corners, as one should at a funeral, though I felt like somebody was inside me entertaining himself with what I vaguely appropriated as my consciousness.

They closed that mountain of Grandma Emma Loop into her coffin for the last time then. We said the "Our Father," the protestant version with the glory stuff at the end, then we put Grandma Emma's coffin on the dolly and pushed her to the hearse, got in our line of cars with little flags on the antennae and drove out to the protestant cemetery near the Peninsula. Then we put Grandma Emma down. Whitey looked so little I thought when he put his hat on he was going to disappear under it. He didn't want to leave that grave either. Red had to grab him by the elbows and drag him out of there. He didn't make it too long after that. By Easter he was dead and we had to bury him too.

≋ ≋ ≋ ≋ ≋An Interlude

T HEY FINALLY TOOK Grandpa Funster to trial, railroaded him on plagiarism even though he'd never written a word of poetry, just spoke it, and they couldn't prove he'd even read those guys whose stuff he'd lifted, but the junior prosecutor had an English degree from Yale or Harvard or someplace where they made her memorize Homer in Greek or Chaucer, and she quoted from a list of poets who Grandpa Funster'd stolen from with impunity just since he'd been in jail: William Carlos Williams, Stanley Kunitz, Chidiock Tichborne, Wallace Stevens, an absurd list of people you'd never heard of.

"And the nameless ones," whispered Grandpa Funster from the witness stand, "and the unborn, and the words of poets who have yet to write."

She figured he stole that one too, but she didn't know from whom.

"A skunk searches the moonlight for a bite to eat," said Grandpa Funster.

So they nailed Grandpa Funster on plagiarism, arguing that the absence of stolen texts was compensated for by the sheer quantity of unfootnoted verbiage. The defense attorney told Jimbo and Betty that the verdict would never hold up in an appeals court, once they got the trial out of Erie.

The argument for murder was a little more sound; the police report, pack of lies though it was, came off pretty convincing. Liverwurst certainly was dead and it was hard to argue self-defense because he was a cop and got shot in the back; of course he pulled his gun out first even if he did point it in the other direction, he might have shot somebody in front of him if somebody else hadn't shot him in the back first, but that kind of argument never goes over with authority figures, especially when you've done in one of their own kind; if the situation were reversed I'm sure old Liverwurst would have a been exonerated. The defense made its last ditch effort when it tried to prove that Grandpa Funster was dead already, but, as the judge said, this was a court of law, there wasn't any precedent for that.

"The people who dig up corpses and rape them I understand are not reported," said Grandpa Funster. "You put too easy questions on lonely roads."

It was an ironic event to say the least, so of course they didn't give Grandpa Funster the death sentence after they convicted him, no, they gave him life. And after that murder trial was over he was up for plagiarism again, Empson, Lowell, Auden. Ridiculous. The judge, a Princeton man himself, scolded Grandpa Funster for mouthing words above his station in life, for aspiring for too much without being willing to put in the work. People went to college to learn those kinds of things. They got jobs and earned large incomes. They earned the leisure time to think about death in big ways, ways that Grandpa Funster could never understand. The crime, said the judge, was not even so much that Grandpa Funster stole these things, but that he hadn't earned the right to say them. If he had to, he'd try Grandpa Funster for plagiarism every time he opened his mouth. He'd drag him out of jail and into court till the day he died.

Well it was a sad thing, because anybody with half a fried egg for a brain knew it was an indictment of our whole neighborhood. Too many of us used big words and we hadn't even been to college; we'd crossed into the vocabulary Twilight Zone, lived in a place that couldn't exist, or worse, was socially unacceptable. We were misfits. We mixed diction. It was only a matter of time before they hunted us all down.

"The poem of the mind in the act of finding what will suffice," said Grandpa Funster in his final statement. "It has not always had to find: the scene was set; it repeated what was in the script. Then the theater was changed to something else. Its past was a souvenir."

"You'll be twanging your instrument in the dark a long time," said the judge. And he got away with it.

Red went back on the porch after Whitey's death, stoic and immobile. Helen went back into her labyrinth of dead machines in the cellar. Neda and Stinky won the AAU Regional Pairs Figure Skating Title held in Pittsburgh. Joseph and Andrew grew long wispy beards and inhabited the Pile System. Garbage piled up in the city streets. Myself, I took the Viz and collected all the unemployment checks and picked up the welfare food. I stood in long lines for days at a time to get cards to verify that the cards I held verified who I was, who, of course, often, I wasn't. When I was passing as Helen or Red I always sifted right through. Proving I was me was harder; I looked so much like myself it was suspicious. They didn't think the Viz looked like me and didn't want to give me dependency credit. They didn't like my attitude. They didn't like his attitude or his fur. They didn't like my wings.

Not working was getting to be such hard work I went back to Karl.

"Okay," I said to him and Pig. "I give up, I'll fly in anything."

"Good," said Karl, "that's just the attitude we need."

One thing about the new reconstructed version of the *Flying Armada*, if we went down it was going to float; thing looked more like a catamaran than it did an airplane; wings like a bat, pontoons everywhere, and it looked like Karl lifted the fuselage from the body of a bug-eyed Sprite; folding canvas top, Plexiglas windows you could slide open for conversation with your prey, two cute little headlight eyes like a talking car, foldable windshield like a Jeep so I could get to the cannon; the only thing it might have lacked was air worthiness.

So just to be safe we hoisted it down the cliff and onto the beach, pushed into the water and started it up in there; in seconds we were skimming like a water bug, hopping across the water like a flying fish, into the air like a sultry gull; I have to admit, it was exhilarating.

Karl turned that plane toward the airport and that's where we hovered, near the flight path that took the small planes over the lake; no sense pushing our luck and flying over anything solid. We flew around up there a long time and were just about to turn back and call it a day when I spotted some kind of little aircraft head out from the airport and doddle over the lake, beautiful little thing, white as nines. We flew up near them and dipped our wing and they dipped their wing back. We smiled and waved, they smiled and waved. From where I was sitting they looked like a small bunch of wealthy Arabians, probably smuggling oil or hashish into Toronto; two young fellows and two young women, white polo clothes that matched the exterior of the plane and contrasted nicely with its red upholstery, looked like martinis in their hands there, I thought I saw olives. Karl motioned for them to open a window; we had a radio but we weren't about to have our conversation monitored. They slid a window open and Karl yelled, "I don't want you Arabs to take this racially, but stick 'em up!" Karl had entered the era of ethnic sensitivity.

Well they got funny looks on their faces and started yelling to us that they weren't Arabs, they were Iranians, but then I think they recognized us as certain as we recognized them, our old friends, those Cuban sympathizers who we'd held up on our very first commercial enterprise on the floating *Armada* not so many years ago.

"It's too bad," said Karl, pointing his M-16 over the abyss, "but give us all you got." He pulled out a weighted bag on the end of a long cord and motioned that he was going to throw it, but they indicated that they weren't going to catch it. One of the women picked up the radio microphone.

Karl fired. "Now don't do that!" he yelled, and that seemed to have some influence on them because she put the thing down.

Well there we all were, suspended in the blue sky like kissing fish, negotiating with our Iranian acquaintances, of all people, above Lake Erie about whether or not we were really having a hold up. You just couldn't have predicted it, but it felt like old times. Though the longer that discussion proceeded the more it became apparent to those Persians, that was something that we learned up there, that those guys were Persians like Xerxes and Zoroaster, and though many Persians were Muslims like the Arabs, they themselves weren't Arabs, that is, Semites, and, in fact, they themselves weren't even Muslim, they were Christian, or at least raised Christian, now they tended toward materialist atheism, a return to pre-Zoroastrianism if I heard them right. That was pretty sophomoric, that's what I told them; because their wealth, I said, yelling over the wind and airplane drone, entitled them, in fact obligated them, to think about life and death in bigger and more innovative ways.

Well they took that poorly and, calling our airplane a vinegarroon, they hit their throttle.

It's amazing what you can learn from the right people in the right context.

We took off after them in our first burst and Karl caught up to them as I readied the cannon, because we knew we couldn't keep up with them for long.

"What's a vinegarroon?" I yelled.

Their wing tilted and they began to peel away, so I fired.

I don't know what happened to them, but the recoil of that cannon blast flipped us over a few times, upside down right side up, upside down right side up, upside down, then we went into a spin and crashed in the lake. We should have had pontoons on the roof.

You can do all the thinking you like and it won't move a spoon. There just comes a time when you have to make some choices about feeding yourself, and the people you love, even if they're refusing that choice. Red and Helen would straighten out, just like the Viz; they were cocooning; they just needed someone to get them through a hard time.

So I crossed the picket lines and became a garbage scab. Needless to say, there was a lot of resentment. That garbage compound was surrounded by a wire fence topped with a "V" a of barbed wire, always was an indication, to my mind, that somebody on the top already knew how valuable all that waste was. Inside the gate a small parking lot sat on the left where you could park your car, and to the right a large dirt area in front of the garage where all those big yellow garbage trucks sat like moths. In the days when everybody was working we'd sit there waiting for the shift to begin, because you couldn't leave the compound, couldn't even get in your truck till the whistle went off and your garbage shift started, made absolutely no sense, but it was a rule, so most of us hung around on the truck bumpers or riding boards, drinking coffee or sleeping, or sometimes you'd wander over to some-body else's truck, play a hand of cards, look at the sky and say something ominous about the coming weather, the night, the loads; you had to complain a lot no matter what; we were like bomb squads, we took off together, it was romantic. Between those two lots was the long runway up to the furnace, now empty, but when we were all working there'd be a line of trucks bursting with waste edging up to the inferno; that building glowed in the night, the fires spit and roared; we'd enter that ignited maw full and leave empty; from the roof the smoke poured black out three long, dark smokestacks.

It was at the foot of that long drive, at the front gate, that you had to cross the picket line, and that's where I ran into Fatty and Zippy.

"You come to visit?" said Fatty, "You miss us?"

"You get all dressed up just for us?" said Zippy, "You didn't have to."

"Can't get laid without a garbage truck?" said Fatty. "That it?"

"You know my family ain't eating steak either," said Zippy. "There are things as important as food."

"Like getting laid," said Fatty.

"Like loyalty, commitment, principles," said Zippy.

"That chick's probably fucking the trash man," said Fatty. "She's rich, paying somebody else to move her garbage."

"What about the stars?" said Zippy. "Kings of the furnaces of creation."

"He's a fucking nutty kid," said Fatty. "He don't give a shit about us."

"You're not going to spend the rest of your life doing this, Loop, are you?" Zippy said to me as I crossed the line. "You're going to grow up someday and do something else. Well everybody thinks that, Loop. Everybody thinks they're going to end up being something else."

"Everybody thinks they're going to get hard-ons all their life," said Fatty.

"Why not a little heaven right here, Loop?" said Zippy. "A little of the stars right now, for the workers?"

"He don't care," said Fatty.

"He cares about something," said Zippy.

"He's just going to that castle in Glenwood," said Fatty, "to try and get laid."

Well there was garbage all over the town and you picked it up wherever you wanted whenever you wanted, work as long or short as you liked; thing was, there wasn't any reason not to go up to Glenwood, they had garbage up there as well as anywhere else; the choice had gone beyond the existential; I was already a scab and it didn't make sense not to go up there just to prove Fatty wrong. Besides, I had my own truck now, a compactor, yellow and domed, a huge hump like a space ship, and I ran it myself, automatic everything, hydraulics everywhere, power levers at my fingertips; I'd park the thing, get out and get the garbage, load it into the back, get back in the truck and crush it up; left a note on the porch as I left that said if they wanted to continue having their garbage picked up, the next week it better be waiting for me on the curb. In a week I wouldn't be dragging my own can around into back yards and crushing garbage into it, carting it back out, I'd just be stopping and loading, stopping and loading, a cakewalk.

Of course there was one place I was willing to keep going back into the yard, but Fatty was right about that, too, there wasn't any garbage back there. She had somebody else, some private trash people collecting her garbage. Got me thinking about how transient everything was, the flimsiness of contractual obligations, society slowly peeling away without cores of loyalty, tradition, even retribution, a pile system coming apart, nothing under the piles.

"You understand, of course," I heard her say from behind me as I stared at those empty cans. "I couldn't wait."

I wondered if that's what she told her surfer, if she told him anything, if he existed. She'd grown her hair out, shoulder length, where it rested on the shoulders of her white silk blouse, open at the neck to show the tops of her breasts, the lace of her bra. She had a belted short skirt, heels, and tan nylons so sheer they shined in the dawn light. It was the first time I'd ever been attracted to someone who wore tan nylons.

"Want to go for a ride in my truck?" I said.

"Does it have a cocktail lounge?"

"Please don't get rhetorical," I said to her. "In the end I'm a garbageman. Even when we conquer the stars we will not be rhetorical, nor have cocktail lounges in our trucks. We will live on dialectic. Our words will be like diamonds."

"You have some time," she said. "You're not punching a clock."

"I would if I had to. I've punched cakes."

She tilted an eyebrow, her left, downward. This woman could tilt an eyebrow and make you think she had you in her mind all night.

"So you want to go for a ride in my truck?"

"No," she said, "Come on in."

I didn't know who was picking up her trash now, but that place was completely refurnished once, new carpets, new paint job, looked like a set from *Forbidden Planet*, rather modern. We took the elevator upstairs, got a couple Pernods at the wet bar, and went into a cavernous white bedroom, thing looked like a pillow, had a bed bigger than the whole Pile System put together whether it existed or not. Then she kissed me. She put her hand under my shirt and caressed my nipple. And though it goes against my grain to say so, she aroused the biggest passion in me I'd ever felt in my life; there wasn't a part of her I didn't want to touch, kiss, caress, grip powerfully and gently, to hold her beneath me and push myself into her, my life reduced to strip and fuck. I couldn't take my lips from her lips, my hands from her breasts, I bucked against her as she locked me with her thighs. I came in my pants.

She got a good laugh out of that. "Men," she said. "Who'd want to be a man?" And that's when she undressed me, slowly, kissing me. It took her a long time. And by the time I started on her, unbuttoning her silk blouse, peeling those nylons as sheer as light, stripping her of her slip, her bra, her panties, I was back.

"Oh my sweets, my sweets," said Kara Ruzci. "Is this what my death has done to you? Driven you to the other side of death?"

"I can't sleep," I told her. "Kara, I can't sleep."

"I will sing you a lullaby, my elephant," said Kara Ruzci. "I'll sing you such a sweet lullaby that you will sleep and you will love me again. You will remember the day we married and think I am the most beautiful woman in the world. You will love me, and you will not be unfaithful to me. You will visit me and cry yourself to sleep at my grave. And when you have reached the bottom of darkness, I will come to you, and you will lie your head on my silver breast. I will grow wings and we will fly to the light." And then she sang to me in that old way. She repeated what she said, over and over, in that beautiful voice, rising and trilling like a flute, like the song of a pond. "Lie down," she sang. "Lie your head on my silver breast, and sleep."

"You're really something," the woman said to me, "once you get those cement wings off."

"They have their own life," I told her.

"They go well with the room," she said.

Though I think it was more the way I laid them down, spread out, spaced with an invisible body between them.

"Do you always sing?" she asked me then, but I really didn't know how to answer her, I didn't know what she meant. "When you're inside a woman," she said, "do you always sing?"

≈≈≈≈≈ Gifts

IT WAS NOT THE WINTER of my discontent. It was a year of change. Revis Danger was drafted and sent a letter to the draft board thanking them for their offer, he thought their organization sounded interesting, but for now he had some other things to take care of; he went to work at the Forge. Raymon held up a gas station, got in a scuffle with the attendant, wounded him and escaped with thirty-two bucks. They found him in a bar a block away. Revco joined Joseph and enlisted in the Marines. Andrew crossed the border at Niagara Falls and was hiding out in Toronto for awhile with Leonard Cohen; he found Cohen in the phone book, called him and introduced himself; the two of them hit it off and were heading up to Quebec City where there was going to be a vigil to the Infant of Prague. After sweeping the Eastern Regional Pairs Ice Skating Championships, Neda and Stinky went on to Salt Lake City and took the Nationals by storm. They were heading for Europe soon, and then Russia where they planned to study ice dancing; maybe they could link up with Funly there when he found the water route into Moscow; Jimbo'd lost touch with Funly somewhere under the North Pole; he came over and shared our front porch with Red to escape Mosha's perpetual *ooompah-pah, ooompah-pah*; they talked about fishing, bowling, how beautiful it was in northern Ontario, Algonquin Park, tons of fish and game, you could hide out there forever; "Th-that's where Andrew should g-go," said Jimbo. "He shouldn't b-be with L-Leonard Cohen."

Red had read some Leonard Cohen during *The Year of Two Hundred Books*. It was sad stuff, like everything else, sex and sadness, a little death, too poetic; Leonard Cohen couldn't even tell a good story.

Across the street, Angela and Rafael Corona moved out of the flat on top of Dean and Tina Danger's. A giant van came and moved the birds and fish, the hundred cats and exotic woofling dogs, the palm and avocado trees, the ponds and streams. I went over there near the end of the move, while Angela was moving her fortune-telling paraphernalia, just as she was carrying out her globe.

"Soon," said Angela Corona, waving, "I will not live here anymore."

"Neda will be sad to see you gone," I told her.

"Neda can see me anytime," said Angela Corona. "She found Europe, she can find me."

"Where will you be?"

"I am predicting Akron," said Angela. "Rafael has a job there, the signs are good."

"Crow?" I said, peering into the van.

"The bird left last night," said Angela. "He does not like good-byes. This you should already know."

Well maybe I did, or should have, but some people are better at predicting stuff than others.

"Did you see the street last night?" said Angela to me.

"I saw a lot of streets, but I didn't see this one till this morning," I said.

"They were filled with blood and fire."

"Where I was," I said to her, "they were filled with garbage."

"With that thinking you will not be a poet captain of a starship," said Angela Corona.

"Is that a prediction?"

"That is advice," she said. She spun her globe on its axis, raising it up and down for an occasional eclipse of her head. She closed her eyes and put out her finger and of course it landed on Cuba.

"I know," I said.

Angela held out the globe and put Cuba in my face.

"You sure you don't mean Nassau?"

"Nassau is an island of ghosts," said Angela. "One moment it is there, the next it is not. The lives there are like the heartbeat of the air." She jumped into the back of the truck, large as she was, and nestled that globe between a couple of ferns. Rafael came around the side of the truck.

"Close it up," Angela told him. "I am riding back here."

"It is illegal," said Rafael.

Angela lifted her eyes toward heaven, or maybe just toward the roof of the truck. Then Rafael closed her in there and they took off.

"Is it the end of the Dialecticians?" I said to Willie.

Willie was back in his pillows, his ebony skin covered with a residue of gray, pallid. He smoked a cigarette, a short Camel straight and I bummed one from him. Willie exhaled, the smoke dancing in the air suggesting figures. It was the most beautiful smoke, dark gray and curling, infinitely dimensional. A beam of sunlight came through the attic window and sliced the smoke, lighting a square on the pale wall, an eyelet into fire.

"There were once two madmen," said Willie, "who escaped from an asylum on the beam of a flashlight."

"Who held the light?" I said.

"I, myself, would not get on that beam," said Willie.

"And you think I would."

Willie took a long puff, exhaling phantasmagoria. He propped himself up. "This is what I like." He paused. "What I love. You, yourself, are not so very faultless."

"You're pronouncing 'th'," I said.

"Death," said Willie, "does not listen, but it has the eyes for everything. Deaf was a pun, but I am tired of no one getting it."

Now I noticed that his tool box was gone, and the hammer, too. "No more experiments," I said.

"You do not need a fix," he said.

"No." He was right. I made the stuff in my brain now. I didn't need it, never thought about it anymore.

"Most of us do not escape anyway," said Willie, lifting the corner of his lip, "and most of those who do, return. There is nowhere else to go."

I guess that's what he did with those other Dialecticians, returned them.

"It was not up to me," he said.

"Who was it up to?"

Willie got himself another cigarette. Lit it. "We are haggling with the words."

"That's all we got, Willie, right? Words?"

"Is this what you believe?"

"What's belief got to do with it?" I stood over him now, looking down on him.

He leaned back again. "Something," he said. He shook his pack of Camels and a pyramid of cigarettes jutted out the opening like steps. "Have another cigarette," he said.

So I took it. I sat down next to him and he lit me up.

"Do you remember?" he said. "You found me hanging from a tree by the neck. Our friend Mr. Tony Blanion opened my stomach with a knife and your daddy taught me to fight."

"Yes," I said. "It didn't work."

"It did very much work, but now our friend Mr. Blanion is not around so very much either."

"He's dead," I said. "You hit him on the head with the hammer."

Willie shrugged at this. "Maybe I have given up the 'f' for the 'th', but I have not become so silly as to accept logic packed in the suitcase, besides, you have seen him since."

"Once," I said.

"I would be thinking that once is enough."

"The circumstances were ambiguous."

"And you do not think he is making love to your wife."

"In the Afterlife?" You'd think after what I'd been through I'd have been beyond incredulity, but in actual fact, if I can be so dualistic as to say so, the affect was the opposite.

"Shall I hold the beam for you?" said Willie. He got up from the pillows and limped over to the window, standing in front of it, not blocking the light but diffusing it; he glowed, transfigured, and then the orange glow worked itself into a beam again, slipping under me like a hand holding a small bird; it scooped, and it opened, and I slid in light.

"My sweets," said Kara Ruzci, standing in a field of light. "My sweets, are you asleep?"

"It's hard to say," I said.

She came to me, putting her hands in my hair, her fingers lighter than rain. She pressed herself into me, her tears now hot on my neck. "Never leave me again my love, never again."

"The man who haunted you," I said to her. "Your brother, is he here? Is Blanion here?"

"Everything is here," sobbed Kara Ruzci. "Everything is here and nothing is not here."

"Do you make love to them?"

"If it were true," said Kara, drying her tears now, looking up into my eyes, "would I tell you? Would you be a happier man with knowledge, my love?" She pushed herself gently away and spun slowly, her dress moving around her like woven starlight. "Now that you see me again, have you solved death? Do you believe anything new? Do you think I know any better now who I am, what I should do next, whether I exist in my mind or yours, what are my thoughts, what keeps me from this moment to that?" She came back to me, her hands on my chest. She kissed me. "Do you think it matters who God is? Do you pray now, my sweet love? Do you pray yet?"

So, my reader, you have been with me a long time, maybe you can help me decide, do I pray? Is now the time? You didn't know this was my prayer, that I have whispered it over and over in my sleep for years; that ontology has collapsed here; narrative distance collapsed; no, of course I am a feint. How long can you suspend disbelief? Myself, I have suspended it from the start. As I speak to you now I fade behind myself, this voice, this I. I disappear infinitely into the universe of discourse like the regress of Buddhas into the Void. God disappears into the world. He could only disappoint us by changing his diction.

I am trying to show you my hand, but it disappears in front of me. Everything explicit explodes. What is the will of God who has disappeared into the world? All stories start in heaven and end in heaven.

This all really happened. One night, long ago, Willie placed a hypo in my vein and we took a bus ride downtown. There, in a bar, sat a man with dark wings under his coat, the man who haunted my lover in the night. When he left the bar I took a cab to Kara Ruzci's and found him wailing behind her house, and then Kara Ruzci came through the wall of her bedroom and the two of them shimmered like crystal under the stars. His wings expanded like blackness and they flew into the night. I was impaled by a silver rod and my blood flowed into the earth.

I waited there in a snowstorm till dawn, till they returned, till my lover re-entered her home, and I rose from where I was impaled in the earth and shot the man in the back. His wings folded over his wound and he became a black egg in the snow. I married Kara Ruzci and now she is dead from a wound which pierced her chest and exited her groin. It's that simple.

First you get on a bus.

Or someone holds a light for you.

You can ride down a lightbeam, but you can't ride back up.

So let me tell you my last funny story. That spring I got to know my cousin Bifboy pretty well. Along with Willie we hung out on street corners smoking cigarettes and drinking sixteen ounce cans of Colt 45 or quarts of Old English 800 wrapped in brown paper bags. We got drunk in the sunshine in cemeteries, visited Raymon or Grandpa Funster in jail, sat on the shores of the Peninsula and watched the lake lick at the sand, the sun dip, the blue of the water deeping at Canada. We took a weekend and drove to Hoboken where we sat at Kara Ruzci's grave like Buddhists or Indians, sucking smoke, stinking of cheap booze, breathing. We spent an uneventful night, drank Ripple for breakfast in the dawn, and as the sun climbed high enough to warm us a long white Cadillac appeared on the small, curved road of the cemetery and behind it, a police car. A short man with a toupee got out of the Cadillac and put his elbows on the roof. He looked very familiar, like someone from a past life. He smoked a cigar, or rather took it from his mouth and threw it in the road. The police, large, red-faced men, came over with their clubs and put their shadows on us. They said something about the War.

"We are here for all the dead people," said Willie. "It is okay with us if this includes the War."

Bifboy displayed his discharge papers.

"That's my wife," I told them, pointing at Kara's grave. I brought my marriage license and I showed it to them. They only hit us a few times before they cuffed us, threw us in the back of the car and kept us a couple of days in jail.

We were a quiet bunch. We didn't talk much, even to each other. In the a evenings sometimes, after Bif's work at American Sterilizer, and before mine, we met Karl Marxman at a corner bar and sat quietly around a small table smirking at our beer, sometimes looking up with a grin. It was funny. We were a funny bunch.

Then I'd go to work, sometimes taking Willie with me on the truck. On the nights he didn't come I stopped in Glenwood for a spa and a B&B. My friend would slip out of her dress or skirt, unbutton her blouse, stand in front of me in her nylons and white lingerie, still in her heels like Liz Taylor, her voice like silk and the sound of her softness inside those things like silver in the air, like having your blood turn soft and silver. On those nights, inside her, feeling a passion so great that I became the woman beneath me, that I breathed her breath, that I wore her clothes, that I moved in her softness, another part of me wailed balefully, and Kara Ruzci held my face and cried tears so deep that the trails etched in her skin.

On one of those leaden nights when I came out of there, the light not yet quite alive in the air but playing with the wind in the trees, myself still adrift somewhere loosely under my own skin, I felt a presence hovering near me like a dark spoon, the cement wings on my back, though I seldom felt them, suddenly lightened and I felt as if my ears would bleed; near the truck I tested the wind, which had the first aura of summer on its fingertips; I heard whispering.

"Wearing ruins wasteman?" it said. "Got anything in the back of the truck for me? Some moon or stars?"

I threw back the lock on the compressor, then got in the truck, pushing the transmission to lock the wheels, releasing the hydraulics and opening the maw at the back of the truck; a huge steel panel swung open and swept down on the trash back there, crushed it, brought into the bowels of the machine.

"Come on," whispered that familiar voice. "Open up your heart, your truck, your mind. Want some help tonight maybe?"

I wasn't in the habit of talking to disembodied voices, there was too much of that in my family history already. You didn't have any choice about listening to them, like the old joke, you didn't have to talk back; anyway, you couldn't trust them, they could turn the flashlight beam off on you halfway down. But there's a first time for everything.

"I get paid by the hour and I don't have a quota," I said. "I do what I want. It's my truck. It's my trash. A whole city of it."

"Listen to me, hell-hole," said that voice. "You're forgetting some important things, like the aftermath, the Afterlife, the waste after death, the palpable nonexistence all around you, what you were before and what you'll always be, a blink, a bird in a church. Are you listening?

"I can't help but listen to you. I'm not even sure you're not me."

"I'm not you, believe me."

Well that begged the question. It didn't take a Dialectician to recognize that, not that there were many of us Dialecticians around to recognize it anymore.

"What do you think would happen if the dead went on strike?" said that voice.

"I'd be a death scab," I told him. I started the truck and headed down toward the West Side where there was an Italian bar on the corner of 18th and Liberty. They used to give me and Fatty and Zippy free leftovers, mostly cold pizza, and all we wanted to drink, as long as we picked up their trash, which was illegal, seeing as they were a private business; private businesses had to have private trash collectors, so we always saved them a lot of money. Of course being an Italian bar they supported the strikers as well as the mayor so now I collected the trash, business as usual. Besides, the mayor found most of the Italians jobs in the interim anyways, it was only the Polacks wasting away on the picket line. Nonetheless, if my voice wanted to keep talking to me it was going to have to do it over breakfast and beer with Willie, Bifboy, and Karl. If the dead went on strike I'm sure some things would change and some things would stay the same.

"Yeah, but *what* would change, and *what* would stay the same, Socrates?" said that voice as I pulled up to the bar.

"It strikes me as moot," I said. I went into the bar.

"Some of my favorite issues have this mootness," said Willie from his bar stool. Bifboy and Karl were there waiting with him and we all moved to a table, taking the chairs off it so we could sit down. "Why did you bring our friend Mr. Tony Blanion?"

"I should have known," I said.

"I thought I was incognito," Blanion said.

"Your voice," said Willie.

"You're a lot less metaphoric than you were in life," I told Blanion.

"It was that blow on the head," said Blanion. "It cracked something."

"It soldered his signifiers," said Willie.

"You're not the one who hit me on the head, are you?" said Blanion to Willie.

"I liked it better when we didn't talk," said Bifboy, putting his hands in his blond hair. "We got drunk, we kept our mouths shut."

"They're not talking to anybody so I suppose it amounts to the same thing," said Karl.

"Let's get some breakfast," I said.

"I didn't come here to eat pizza with garbage scabs," said Blanion, almost poetically. "In the sea of the afterlife, I'm a message in a bottle."

"This is what happens when one begins making sense," said Willie. "The beauty is sacrificed to the truth."

We went into the kitchen behind the dinning room and sliced up some leftover pizza, nice thick square stuff, light on the sauce, crusty ends, especially on the corners, as warm as the room it sat in over night. Bartone, the bar owner, came into the kitchen and dragged out some pepperoni, mozzarella, and Italian bread and put it on the long wooden counter in the center of the kitchen, then we dragged it all back out to the barroom.

"Everybody here's still over twenty-one, right?" said Bartone.

"Same as ever," said Bifboy.

"Okay," said Bartone. "I just want everything legal here in case one of those state boys comes in."

"I'm not twenty-one," said our friend Mr. Tony Blanion.

"You're dead or you would be," I said. "Besides, you're not drinking," I said.

"I'll tell you something, Loop," said Blanion. "You have become really banal."

"It is the more subtle side of his capacity for evil," said Willie.

"None of you are interesting anymore," said Blanion, "There are a lot of us forced to watch you and you aren't interesting anymore. You don't have any commitment to your audience."

"Is this the message in the bottle?" said Willie.

"Why not end your life, Loop? Why not have ended things earlier? Why not end everything? You just collect trash, eat, drink beer, fuck some rich chick on Tuesdays and make your poor dead wife cry."

"From where I'm sitting I don't see that as a problem," I told Blanion. "By the way, you aren't seeing Kara Ruzci, are you?"

"As if that would matter to you."

I finished off a piece of pizza, a nice corner piece with thick crust, and looked around the table.

"You know," said Bifboy to me, "you should talk to yourself on your own time. I come around for a little company, some silence and inebriation." He had his beer on the table and both his hands around it. "Bif and Jelly told me your mother's side of the family had some strangeness," said Bifboy.

"There's a reason why we're all here," I said to Bifboy.

"Now you're talking, star teeth," said Blanion.

I watched Bartone taking the stools down from the bar, setting up for that 7 A.M. crowd, the good customers, the regulars, the people who gave him his living. Maybe Blanion was right. Maybe I wasn't cut out for the day to day. Maybe I had an obligation, if only to myself, to get on with the bizarre.

"Now listen," said Blanion. "The next Fourth of July—We Love Erie Day won't be at the Public Dock. It's going to be at the airport. There's going to be a big air show and they're flying in a Galaxy C-500, a big troop and equipment mover, biggest airplane in the world, and they're going to bring in every serviceman in Pennsylvania and put them on that plane and fly them all to Vietnam. It's going to be a big patriotic deal."

"I, myself, was thinking the Spruce Goose was the biggest airplane in the world," said Willie.

"Don't talk to me about airplanes," said Karl.

"Don't get drawn in," Bifboy told him.

"The Spruce Goose don't fly," said Blanion.

"I know all that already," I told that voice, Tony Blanion. "In fact, I'm probably the source of your information."

"Don't mince pie with me, star garbage. Your brother and Revco will be on that plane. You want to see them jumpin' in pits and shootin' gooks?"

"They volunteered," I said. And I refilled my beer glass from the pitcher.

"And we don't watch the television," said Willie.

"Listen bird poop," said Blanion, "you already made your decision. Fate is character. Do I got to spell it out?"

Well no, he didn't have to spell it out. I just thought, well, I'd got this far, why do the inevitable?

"It'll be funny," said Blanion.

"It won't be funny," I said. "It's too late for that kind of funny. Everything just comes apart in pathos. That's what's left. Pathos and misunderstanding. Do you know what I think?" I told him. "I think you're too idiosyncratic, Mr. Tony Blanion. You might be an audience for all this, but you're a lousy audience and maybe the only audience and we don't do it for you anyways. What the hell do I owe you?"

"You'd be nothin without me. You wouldn't even exist."

"I've heard it before," I said.

"I, myself," said Willie, "prefer to see existence as mutually co-arising. You are stuck with each other."

"All of this has already happened," I said, not to Willie, not even to Blanion. "Most everything is crossed out of our lives before it's ever done, and what does get done crosses out everything else. Or somebody else sees it and changes it or forgets it. It floats up like mist and burns away."

"It rises perfectly formed and eternally fills the universe," said Blanion. "Don't fuckin kid yourself."

"You are both taking yourselves too seriously," said Willie.

"This is serious stuff," said Blanion.

"Like most things, it does not bear thinking about it," Willie said.

"Bifboy," I said. He was slouched back in his chair, eyes closed. Karl slumped forward over a whiskey and beer. Willie ate a piece of pizza. "Bifboy."

He stirred.

"Can you fly a Galaxy C-500?"

"Right out into the eternal fucking universe," said Bifboy.

ഌ   ഌ   ഌ

Bifboy dragged us down to the Army-Navy Surplus and got us some green uniforms; baggy pants, black boots, some nice canvas hats with patches on the front, silver wings coming out of a circular medallion with a shark in the center of it, flight jackets, under which, of course, I had to wear my cement wings; people gave me a lot of leeway with those wings, but they weren't exactly Army Air Corps regulation. Then Bifboy dragged out his old pilot's manuals for the C-150 and the C-141, which he figured would be close enough, the issue was size, not technology, and from the way Bifboy described it, that Galaxy C-500 was like a giant moth, you just spread its wings and let the air pick it up.

Still, there was plenty to learn. Bifboy might know that plane, but he couldn't fly it by himself. He needed somebody to co-pilot and somebody to keep track of where we were going. At the time we were thinking Nassau would be nice, seeing as none of us had been anywhere except Bifboy to Hawaii and Vietnam and me to Nassau, maybe. There were some strong arguments for Hawaii, one being that Bifboy had been there and another that it was in the same general direction as Vietnam; once we took off in that thing somebody might figure out that the wrong crew was flying it, but if we were doing the same thing as the original crew it might buy us a few minutes with its ambiguity, besides, the weather was pretty good in Hawaii. But Hawaii was American, so there'd probably be Americans waiting there, and it would mean more time in the air. We thought about Canada, but Canada was too friendly and too cold, besides, Karl said Canadians were hicks. I suppose that had implications for Andrew and Leonard Cohen, but Leonard Cohen probably liked hicks, he looked Greek and his use of symbols was heavy-handed. Also, if we were lucky, we'd make the flight without Blanion.

YOU DON'T TAKE OFF on something like this without saying good-bye to significant people. Rash acts require rational preparation, suicide is a good example. In this case, there was also the issue of triumphant return. You have to have people waiting, though most everybody I knew was dead or in jail or waiting for something or somebody already, the rest were out of town or involved in the caper. But I decided not to regard any of that as deterrent to my destiny, so first I headed up to Glenwood to say farewell to my generous friend.

As usual, she looked beautiful; black leather skirt that fit like a glove, black shoes, a silk blouse the color of the sky. She gave me a kiss. "Daytime?" she said.

"It's a special occasion."

"Well I'm glad, because this will be the last time. Arturo is coming home."

"I'm not worried about Arturo," I told her. "I'm not even convinced he exists."

"Well you should worry," she said, unbuttoning my shirt and putting her nose in my hairless chest. "If he finds you, he'll kill you."

"He knows about me?"

"Of course. How else would I get him back?"

"I'm disappointed," I told her.

"I'd think you'd be suicidal," she said.

"Somehow I imagined that you lived above context," I told her.

"I'm going to place you inside me for the last time," she said. "Contextualize that."

"I thought maybe you were evil, or above evil. That you didn't touch things the way other people touched them, taking them in. That you transformed them. That you were a link to the dead."

"I am," she whispered.

"Is Arturo really his name?"

"Yes."

"Does he really surf?"

"Yes."

"Do you love him?"

"Yes, I do," she said.

It was a very good afternoon. We made love with the passion of asps, like snakes eating each other, the blackness of orgasm as pure as ether in the blackest space. And Kara Ruzci didn't come. Afterwards we drank gin and tonics in the yard, smoked marijuana, the sun pouring on us in sweatless rings, the air beating like a heart. I tried to make love to her again, but she refused. "Didn't you come here to tell me something?" she asked.

"That I loved you," I told her. "I came to tell you that I love you."

She tilted her head slightly, squinting at me with one eye, her mouth wry. "So I made a sinner of you afterall." She got up from her lounge, her legs disappearing under her robe, her hands folded under her arms. She hunched her shoulders and let the collar of her robe cover her neck and the back of her head.

"Arturo will be here soon," she said. "You'd better go."

And before she disappeared completely, I'd like to say I did.

Grandpa Funster, given his milieu, was feeling ambiguous, complex, ironic. "The jungle humped in silence, then spoke the thunder. Da," said Grandpa Funster from behind the Plexiglas. He knew he was coming up for trial again and they were recording every sentence.

"I'm going to be gone for a little while," I told him. "But I'll be back."

"The surrender is not to be found in our obituaries," said Grandpa Funster. "Our memories are draped at nightfall like ethereal rumors."

"You going to be okay by yourself for a while?" I asked him. "Can I get you anything?"

"Prison and palace," said Grandpa Funster. "He who was living is now dead. We who were living are now dying. With a little patience."

Now that I was with him by myself I could see that he was not an easy man to talk to. "We'll get you out of here," I told him. "We won't let you die in here. I just have to take care of a few things."

"London Bridge is falling down falling down falling down," said Grandpa Funster.

Well you had to wonder if Grandpa Funster was worth saving, if he wasn't better off where he was. I guess you had to wonder that about all of us. But those Funsters were now a pretty incapacitated bunch and retirement homes were expensive. Grandpa Funster was an old man in a dry month if you ever saw one, and there was no boy to read to him and wait for rain.

"The lighting of the lamps," whispered Grandpa Funster. "Your wings are merely vans to beat the air."

"My wings," I said. But the guard told me I had to leave and I told Grandpa Funster I understood.

            ಠ   ಠ   ಠ

Back home the Viz was pretty well supervised as long as he was on the porch or in the basement. Red didn't say anything to me as I went in and I didn't say anything to him either because I figured I'd start in the basement and work my way out. But I found the Viz in the kitchen eating peanut butter so I ended up starting in the middle. He had a Peter Pan jar open and he wielded a butter knife.

"How you doing?" I said to the Viz. "You miss me?"

"No," said the Viz.

"I've been pretty busy," I told him. "I have to work to support everybody."

"So what?" said the Viz. He took some peanut butter off the knife with his thumb, ate it, pointed the knife at my forehead. "Get chunky next time," he said.

"You know something," I said to my only son. "Speech has made you pretty fucking ordinary."

"My farts smell like diamonds," said the Viz, dipping that knife back into the jar. "How's that?"

"That's nice."

"Nice?" said the Viz, eating off the knife this time, "What kind of word is nice?"

"Do your friends tell you it's not a good word?"

"My friends are invisible, of course," said the Viz. "They hide and they're very quiet. They practice being invisible and speechless."

"I take it all back," I said. "You old enough for kindergarten yet? Maybe kindergarten would be a nice place to meet some new friends."

"A nice place?" said the Viz. "What kind of a place is a nice place?"

"Can I have some peanut butter?" I asked him.

He put the knife in the jar and shoved it across the table. I didn't remember being this difficult, myself. Of course before I started talking I called everything "Jarvis," not "Dad," and after that Red took the time to introduce me to sports and death. I guess I should have introduced the Viz to sports or death. Maybe I'd neglected him. Even if Red was trying to kill me, it was a form of attention. I ate a knife-full of smooth Peter Pan and gave him back the peanut butter jar.

"I have to go on a little trip," I said, "but I figure I'll be back."

"You figure," said the Viz.

"Yes," I said.

"And then what?"

"And then I'll be back and I'll change."

"You're already changed," said the Viz. "Good-bye." And he got down from his chair and left.

In all honesty I'd never really thought about changing, but maybe it was something you had to say to find out what it meant. Maybe the Viz was right, I was already ready to change and maybe that was the change. I was supporting them all, I'd settled down. And pretty soon I was about to give up crime, if I hadn't given it up already; our borrowing the Galaxy C-500 wouldn't be criminal, but heroic, if in a countercultural kind of way. Though I suppose I never saw robbing from the wealthy as criminal either. That was just too conventional a way of looking at things.

So I suppose I shouldn't have tried to explain anything to the Viz. Change was an issue probably worked out somewhere in the Vedas and the rest of us should have learned to keep our minds off of it. Maybe that's why I'm writing all of this down, it's a treatise against reasons, and not a treatise against Reason either; reasons are a perfectly fine idea, in fact so fine as to be invisible, so delicate you can walk right through them, so nice as to be dangerous; Locke it up; but there's more complexity in a single breath and you'd have to put a gun to your head to keep yourself from breathing. I suppose there've been the worst kind of murderers, with the worst kinds of intentions, who've done somebody some good. And you turn on the lights or eat a donut and it kills somebody in Ceylon. We are held together, driven on, by that nonexistent opposite of nihilism. That's in your soul and you don't have to be smart or articulate or wealthy or educated or intellectual or write for the newspapers to know it; but those who decide and those who judge, they don't know it. I don't think Jesus knew it either. Nobody's going to save the world. That's the good news. And that's the bad news, too. It's not news.

That's what I was thinking when I went down into the labyrinth of dead household machines to see Helen. You have a talk with your kid and you get real serious about things. Big words roll through your consciousness like helicopter accidents. You turn yourself into some kind of hero and think you have something to protect. It made me appreciate Helen all the more.

If you wanted Helen you had to go down and stand at the mouth of those machine caves and call her. You ventured too far inside there and you might not come out. One of her dreams might sneak up behind you and drown you in fire and blood, or eat you up and spit you out like the devil did to St. Theresa. You come out unharmed, but you can't help but be affected.

I stood there quite awhile listening to my echo before Helen finally emerged, cuddling that Infant of Prague. You might think that with all the time she spent down there she'd have shown some wear and tear, but she looked more beautiful than ever, her hair silver and her eyes bright and clear. She held up the Infant.

"Kiss him," she said.

"I have to go for a while," I told her.

Helen turned the Infant to face her and they gave each other a good long stare, then she faced him out again.

"I'm going to try to keep Joseph from getting sent to Vietnam."

"He enlisted, didn't he?" said Helen.

Well I didn't really have an answer for that one.

"You don't want to be bothered with the facts," said Helen.

"I thought you were against war," I said to her. "You never wanted Red to go."

"I never stopped him," she said. From somewhere behind her, inside the labyrinth, there came a roar, like something you'd hear at the zoo during feeding.

"I thought maybe I'd take Joseph to Nassau, let him hang out there till things cooled down overseas. He'd still be gone but he'd be safer there."

"That's in the Bahamas," she said.

"That's right," I said.

"Pretty arbitrary."

"It's warm. It's close," I told her. "It's not Vietnam and it's not American."

"British," said Helen.

"It might be," I said. "I don't really know."

"Have you told Joseph he's going to Nassau instead of Vietnam?"

"It's going to be a surprise," I told her.

Helen put the Infant down, then sat down next to him on the floor. "Does it bother you that I stay down here all the time?" she asked.

"You're my mother," I said to her, "you can do whatever you want."

"Can I have a cigarette?"

I got a pack of Chesterfields from my pocket and offered her one. "You don't smoke," I said.

"No," she said, turning down the cigarette, "I don't."

Well I had one out so I lit it up.

"I wish you wouldn't smoke down here," said Helen.

"I left some money up on the dish cabinet, where the Infant used to be," I said to her, putting out the cigarette on the side of a broken refrigerator. But that information didn't seem to affect her.

"Did you speak to your son?" she said.

"I told him."

"Tell Red?"

"I will, on the way out."

"I worry for the future," said Helen.

"Well that's pretty much what there is to worry about," I said.

"I didn't say, 'about'," said Helen.

No, I guess she did say "for" and I guess that's what she meant. Helen was a human sacrifice.

"Things will be different when you get back," she said. "Do you believe that?"

"Maybe."

"Well," said Helen, "maybe you should."

Red hadn't moved from his chair on the porch, which wasn't that surprising because he never moved from that chair anymore.

"Everytime I move, somebody dies," said Red.

"I don't think that's what happened," I said to him. "I think somebody died and then you moved."

"What's the difference?"

"The second way is better," I said.

"Look at your kid," Red said to me. "You bring a kind into the world and think, there, that's who's going to bury me. You look at a little baby. My parents were little babies once. Somebody who's dead now loved them, changed them, gave them a bath, thought about protecting them from everything."

"I've been thinking about Joseph going to Vietnam," I said to Red.

"I told him not to do that," said Red. "He told me I did it, he can do it. I told him that's why he shouldn't do it, so he says that's why he has to do it."

"You and Helen going to see him off on We Love Erie Day?"

"I don't think we should go to war anymore," said Red. "We go over there and twenty years from now we're going to be driving their goddamn cars."

"We don't drive Korean cars," I told him.

"Give them another decade."

"I'm thinking of hi-jacking that plane they're going to send him off on. Take them all to Nassau."

"Don't he run Egypt?" said Red.

"It's an island in the Bahamas."

"Who's helping you?" said Red.

"Karl and Willie. Bifboy, he can fly."

"That's sounds like a good idea," said Red, "but it's crazy."

"I suppose we could get in a lot of trouble," I said.

"You going to wear those wings?" said Red.

"Probably."

"Leave them here. I'll keep them for you under the chair. Nobody'll take them, I'm sitting right here."

I couldn't remember the last time Red ever offered to do anything for me. He sat in that old metal chair, hands folded over his stomach, staring straight out into that neighborhood, most everybody who lived there when he and Helen moved in now dead or long gone. Around us now, in some of the other neighborhoods, especially to the north, people had already started burning down their places for the insurance. There'd been some rioting, too. A block went down in flames down at 18th and Holland, less than a half-mile away, and there'd been race riots at South High; school closed down for a week, even got a little picture in *Time Magazine*.

"Leave the wings," said Red. "You don't need them. You don't owe that Hansen kid anything."

"What do you know about Hansen."

"You don't owe him anything, that's all," said Red. "Don't think like your mother."

Well Red didn't talk much so you always thought there wasn't much going on, I guess it was just a behavioral bias on my part; product of Sixties education, if it didn't get done it didn't exist. You just never knew what people knew and chose not to know, or at least not talk about, it was just a fuzzy area and you had to figure Red's fuzzy area covered everything or nothing, but then he'd surprise you.

Anyway, since I'd become the main provider around that household, Red and Helen gave me a lot of leeway.

"Does it bother you that I'm a garbageman?" I said to Red.

"There something wrong with it?" said Red.

"Does it bother you that I'm scabbing?"

"You think the garbagemen stopped taking baths in porcelain-enamel tubs when I got fired from selling the stuff?"

"Is that the same?" I said to him.

"Is it?" said Red.

"Okay, I'll be back when this airplane stuff is over," I said.

Red didn't budge. "You should sleep," he said to me. "The body's like a machine. It needs regularity. You don't sleep, you don't dream. You don't get any release. You lose touch."

"I'm losing touch."

"I worry about you," he said. "Things are falling apart everywhere. There's no place to hide. You can't sleep all the time. You can't stay awake all the time. You can't hide in the basement. Sometimes I think Whitey and Emma were lucky. They got to die in the old way, get buried together." He raised his head a little. He was looking out at something. He wasn't looking at me. He was looking out, his blue eyes with worlds in them.

"You remember when we used to take Bush to Stanley's grave?"

"Some."

"It was before Joseph and Andrew. We'd get her and Jon, take you and Neda, and drive out Peninsula Drive to the Cemetery. Bush had her grave there next to Stanley's with her birth date and just the nineteen on the other side for her death. And Jon had a grave there. And there were those two babies of hers that died. Bush planted flowers in the spring. You used to fill the water bucket with me, the one with the spout that let the water out like rain. Then everybody'd pray there in front of those graves. Everybody'd kneel in front of the graves and pray."

I remembered. I remembered the wet ground soaking through my pants at the knees. "You didn't pray," I said to him.

"I didn't kneel," said Red. "Protestants don't have to kneel." He'd been looking at me for a second there, but now he looked away again. "After that we'd go get ice cream," he said. "You'd think it was a warm day, but after that ice cream you'd start to shiver. You kids would get cold and want to go home and your mother would tell you about how when you ate something cold your body got colder, and Neda, even back then when she was little, had something figured out and said it didn't make sense, that if you got colder then the air should feel warmer, and your mother always said, 'You're cold, aren't you? That's because you're cold. It's got nothing to do with the air. Your mother," said Red, "is very practical."

There was a cold side of Helen, I knew that. And Red was right, you could get her practice mixed up with what she practiced and miss that cold logic that drove her around.

"I'm amazed," said Red, "by what becomes memory."

I left Red there on the porch, and after that I did an unusual thing. Way over on the southeast side of the city, on the edge of a suburb called Wesleyville, there was a deep gorge with a stream running through it, the Wintergreen Gorge. There was a soft ice cream place out in that direction, out Pine Avenue where it became Wattsburg Road, Pennsylvania Route 8, and after going to that ice cream place, after we were all cold, for whatever reason, after eating that ice cream, Red drove us to a cemetery at the top of one of the highest cliffs over the gorge. At the front there were giant black wrought iron gates towering over a stretch of low white brick wall; a small white house to the left of the gate, and to the right, a huge pond with four great white swans. We used to stop there and watch the swans. Helen thought they were beautiful.

Then we'd drive through the gates, up a long, long tree-lined drive until we reached that cemetery, a small one, its graves encircled in two loops of the road, all the headstones discrete and gray beneath firs and maples, and we'd get out and walk among the graves. There wasn't anybody there we knew, but from every grave in the place you could stand and peer through the woods toward the edge of the cliff that surrounded the place, peer into the light that came through the trees and out into that broadening, expanding space beyond, through the woods and into the sky.

Red really loved it there. He always talked about getting buried there, everytime, and Helen always said it was impossible, it wasn't a Catholic cemetery, the ground wasn't sacred. Then Red said, "The ground takes everybody," and Helen told him she'd be buried in the Catholic cemetery, near Bush and Stanley, and of course Red couldn't get in there, couldn't get buried next to her unless he converted. I didn't understand it at the time, but I guess that was her wild card. She'd bet on eternity. She'd give him her whole life and bet on eternity.

But before they'd really get fighting, usually about Helen's family, because that's who Red had to consider spending, or not spending, eternity with, we'd all get back in the car and follow the looping road out of the graveyard and into the woods, stopping where the trees opened to a view of the gorge, so full of green that you couldn't see the stream hundreds of feet below; though you could hear it, you could hear it rushing over the rocks, its sound rising and mixing in the swirl of wind.

Across the gorge stood another cliff and from it jutted a narrow wedge of rock connecting yet another cliff. That wedge of sandstone ran about seventy-five feet with a two hundred foot drop on either side. That was the Devil's Backbone. You couldn't climb it, the rock was too frail, and there were a thousand stories of people dropping into the gorge when the edge of the cliff crumbled underneath their feet. I didn't know it then, but it was a good place for suicide, more certain than the Bay, cleaner than a gun. Lovers went there and stood on that tiny three foot sliver of unsteady stone, halfway between the cliffs, holding each other with space expanding infinitely around them, hundreds of feet of death dropping on either side.

Red always showed us the path that lead down from the clearing where we stood; it sloped steeply, then ran thinly along the edge of the cliff before disappearing around the other side. He said that path took you to the Devil's Backbone. Red had a cousin, a distant one, who fell off it, just like Helen had a cousin who drowned in the Bay. We got those stories depending where we were, the stories about death that kept us alive when we were young. Gorges within us. Deeper than the soul, or at least the Bay.

It is a night in late August. There is a war in Europe, and in a few months the Japanese will bomb Pearl Harbor. In a few days Red and Helen will marry. In a few weeks I will be conceived. Within the year Helen will be alone and pregnant and living in war housing. Bush will visit her in the afternoons and bring Jon who is home now from the University of Pennsylvania. He'll flunk the bars twice. He'll become unstable and be refused when he enlists in the Navy. They will play pinochle with a woman from Alabama whose husband is also a Marine, a woman, like Helen, who is alone and pregnant and who will lose her child in childbirth, lose her husband in a battle on Midway, and will take her own life by throwing herself in the Bay on the night that I am born. Red should die in that battle on Midway, too. He's there, surrounded by the Japanese, the flow of his blood louder than the drone of Zeros in the skies. They'll take him down, the last surviving Marine. They'll cut out his heart and raise it to the sky because he killed so many of them so well, because he did it without hate. They'll raise his heart to the sky and from it the blood will pour like the sweat of lightning, covering them in sunlight and death. And Red will emerge, because it is not his time to die.

But it's a Saturday night in August and Red and Helen don't know any of this yet. They've driven to the Gorge, but not to the cemetery, parked near a bridge over the stream at the mouth of the Gorge, a place where you can follow the stream down into the depths, where sometimes, on the small ledges above the creek, people camp above a waterfall or swimming hole, picnic in the fading light, breakfast over a fire, douse themselves in the cold water before heading home for church. From here you can also follow the path beside the stream that leads up the cliff opposite the cemetery, gaze at the cemetery from across the Gorge, then follow the path down from that ledge to the other side of Devil's Backbone.

Red and Helen get out of the car and follow the path. On the way, below them, they spot the fires of campers on the edge of the creek. In the dark, they reach the cliff opposite the cemetery. It's a moonless night and they can barely see across the Gorge, but the sky is lit so full with stars that light trembles from them, the Milkyway flowers across the stomach of the night.

The Devil's Backbone stretches darkly, like the back of a sleeping dragon between the cliffs. It's near midnight and Red takes Helen's hand. They descend the path that follows the cliff edge and suddenly it's upon them, black air gasping on either side, a narrow strip of sandstone and then, around them everywhere, blackness expanding upward to the stars and downward into the deepness of nothing. They hold each other close and feel that they are the only things there, the only hearts beating in that well of infinite space. No one has ever been so complete. No bodies have ever melded so completely, a single hot seed at the center of darkness. That is what they both realize then, and that's what makes Red cling to Helen so desperately; that for the first time in his life he needs something, needs someone so badly, that if a part of her detached herself from him for only a moment he'd disintegrate into the sky. This is the fear he feels, for his own death in hers, how he could live through anything, his beating flesh a miracle against odds, but her death, the death of Helen, would kill him.

So he lifts her, picks her up in his arms to carry her back to the ledge, to take her down from the cliff and back to the foot of the Gorge. He'll never live another moment when he'll look at her and fail to think of the edge of a cliff, when he won't fear for his own life when he watches her walk down a flight of stairs or cross a street, when he won't dream of her with death at her ear whispering when she births his children. This is why he holds her so tightly, and this is also why she struggles, and that why, despite the massiveness of his arms she slips from his grasp, eludes him. She spreads her arms in that instant of freedom. She wings from him. She leaps from the cliff, her arms like fans of light she rides in the blackness.

I drove the Falcon to the bridge at the mouth of the Gorge and walked the path that followed the stream. It ascended until even at the edge of the cliff I couldn't see the water, though if I stopped to listen I could hear the sound of it rushing over the rocks. Humidity hung in the trees and it was hot and windless.

At the top of the path there was a cliff where rock protruded from the forest floor and the woods opened up. I could see the stream again from there, hundreds of feet below, winding between the steep cliffs of the Gorge which were layered and red like wafers, the stream silver with tufts of white where it surrounded and flowed over boulders in the creek bed. Farther down, the cliffs diminished and the sides of the shores spread into rounded hills of green forest. I looked across to the other cliff to spot the cemetery, but it was midsummer and the woods had covered it over. Below it, I spotted the brown line that lead to the Devil's Backbone from the cemetery side.

I took off all my clothes except for those wings of mine, white and concrete and borrowed from a grave, as white as my skin that only saw the air of labor in the night. I left my clothes there on the cliff and followed the path down to the Devil's Backbone.

Where naked in the center of that narrow wedge of rock that bridged between the cemetery and the lovers' cliff I raised my arms to the blue expanse, infinite sky, the sun at the center above the gorge, its yellow breath moving over me like hot bees. From the center of the sun a black spot rose and flew toward the earth, circled the globe with a flap of its black wings, twisted in the sky and descended to hover above me; a man in a dark suit, black shoes, a face older than the jagged cliffs. His wings pounded slowly, tucking the air beneath him in hot gushes of wind that pushed against the sides of the cliffs and rose again from the gorge like sulfur or smoke, suspending him; he hung above me in the air. He was a bald old man, completely bald, with a nose like a beak, white delicate hands sculpting the air in front of his chest, but within the world he created in those hands were the voices of choirs, cities imagined by holy men, machines that cured poverty, lives that had yet to be led, thoughts of kindness, and a sensual, palpable love which, if it escaped him, if it left the workings of those delicate hands, the intimations carved in the air by his nails, would make us long for death.

The strangest thing about his face was the way it changed from age to youth, how the lines cleared beneath his eyes, how his teeth filled in, how the hole of his mouth became grim and confident. His head filled with black hair and his eyes darkened and gleamed. And then the joy in his hands faded, the air became cold, blood escaped from a wound in his chest. On his face he had the most quizzical smile before it was blown away, the blood and bits of skull scattering into the sky. Then he became an old man again.

"Sleep," said the old man, his voice merging with the choir and the wind and the stream, inarticulate and inseparable, his voice no voice at all. "Sleep and leave the world to me. I will think the thoughts that are the world and they will be your bed. I will hide myself from you at every instant. I will give you knowledge and ignorance in the same breath, molded from dust and spittle. But you must sleep."

I wasn't necessarily fond of my world, but I'd grown attached to it, and if I was on the edge of learning something, becoming something, I didn't know what giving it up would mean. There was a struggle here between how much of my world was mine, I sensed that, yet had no idea what that might mean. An old man with black wings hovered above me and I scrutinized him the way you might look at a blade of grass or a cup. As I stood there on the Devil's Backbone, arms extended into space, he must have sensed that, that I thought him some part of me that I couldn't take apart, and he thought of me some pregnant and resistant part of himself.

He arched his wings in the heat of his own gusting air and his feathers burned in the sun, leaving him hanging there under a stretch of black leather like a bat, like lizard skin. He folded the wings around him and plummeted, and that's when I found Kara Ruzci.

"I wanted to talk to you before you left," she said.

"Where were you last time?"

"You wanted to arrange a more romantic interlude?" she said.

Whether I was the world's victim or it was mine meant nothing, my search for self a search for sand through sand. How did it matter whether Kara Ruzci was there or not?

"You're silly, love," said Kara. She turned her back to me and faced the expanse, extended her arms and stood on her toes as if to take off. I took her by the waist and pulled her back from the ledge; I couldn't help it, I feared more for her falling than I did my own. "Is it worse to be dead or to want to fly?" said Kara Ruzci, her face now in my chest, wetting my chest now with her tears as she kissed me. "To live only in the thoughts of those who loved you, to watch your image wane, your visage fade in every second behind every ordinary thing. I am sucked from the rot of your fingernails, brushed from your hair in the morning, scraped from your skin when you wash; when you breathe I escape from your ribs. What does it matter that I ever loved you?"

"Let's go back to the winter," I said.

"Can I live on the moisture of your skin, the heat of your breath? Am I only the pain of you missing me? Away from you I fade. Those are the wages of dying. Even in infinity the limits of death and absence tighten. Dying won't bring you to me, it will only bring you peace."

"If I sleep," I said.

"My love," said Kara Ruzci, "I come to you in your sleep."

This is why after I put on my clothes and left the Gorge, I took off my wings and gave them to Red. When I got back I'd tell the Visitor the story about Franky Gorky again, but this time I'd tell him about how Franky Gorky found out that the moon grew and exploded from the side of the earth and became a cold rock deader than anything in the sky, and even that shouldn't have been reason enough to forget what his parents told him and run into the street. I won't worry about whether or not it's a good story. It's a story. He can have it.

Red took the wings and put them under his metal chair.

⋙⋙⋙⋙⋙Fourth of July

YOU TRY TO KEEP your sense of humor, this is how you live. On the Eve of the Fourth it rained so hard that the tree limbs creaked under the strain. The streets flooded. A blanket of clouds covered the Great Lakes from Albany to Duluth, and behind that a cold front was sweeping down through Edmonton and Winnipeg. It would hit Detroit on the Fourth, Erie on the fifth. It could linger for days. There might be snow.

A lot of the exhibition planes were already at the Erie International Airport, but if the weather kept up there wouldn't be an air show, just a ground show in the rain, not much to look forward to, besides, the Galaxy C-500 was supposed to come in that night but didn't because of the weather. The whole thing couldn't be postponed because all those exhibition planes and aerial acts had airshows scheduled in other places. There was going to have to be some kind of weather miracle or the We Love Erie Day—Fourth of July Air Show would be cancelled.

"What kind of war transport plane is it that they can't use in bad weather?" said Karl Marxman.

"Any kind," said Bifboy. "You can't have a war in bad weather, they had to postpone Normandy for days."

It was a rainy Fourth of July Eve and we were sitting in a bar. Soon it would be midnight and then it would be the Fourth of July and it would still be raining.

"It's a kind of cosmic irony," said Bifboy, lighting a Camel. You could hear the rain outside even above the juke box and the other noise of the bar.

Well you wouldn't want to ask Bifboy to explain that, he probably just heard it somewhere, some staff captain on a rainy day on some airforce base outside Sacramento, postponing a shipment of live bodies.

"Makes one think about the weather," said Willie.

"Do something about the weather," I said to him.

Willie gave me a smile with just half of his top lip. "What would you have me do, purchase a bumbershoot?"

"Change it," I said to him. "Make the sun shine."

"You might notice that at present it is dark out," said Karl.

"Put the rain in Pittsburgh," I told Willie.

"You have something against Pittsburgh?"

"It's over," said Bifboy, blowing smoke. "Forget it. It wasn't in the cards."

"Can you change the weather, Willie?" I asked.

"As well as anyone," said Willie. "Let us sit on the doorstep of the bar."

So the four of us went out there with our cigarettes and beer and sat on the stoop watching the rain, watching the rain water cascade down in front of us off the aluminum awning like a waterfall, the sound of the rain on that aluminum like guns. We watched as the water flooded the streets and turned the intersections into ponds, the city coming mirror-deep in its own byways. In the light of streetlights broken gutters spouted streams, the corners of buildings became fountains, flying arcs of white drumming on the tops of parked cars. Just down the street, in the subway under a train bridge, local street kids emerged with inner tubes and leapt from the top of the bridge into the new black lake below. The cops came but couldn't reach them without a raft, so stood in their yellow raincoats next to their cars, their red bubbles flashing, strobing the rain that continued to fall in sheets. We sat there till the bar closed at two and then bought six-packs to go and sat back down again. We smoked cigarettes. The dawn came.

An hour later the bar opened again and we went inside. The morning news came on the TV. The big We Love Erie Day—Fourth of July Air Show was cancelled.

I looked at Willie and Willie looked at me. I don't know what I was looking for, the only thing I'd ever seen in anybody's eyes was myself.

"It's supposed to stop raining," I said to Willie.

"It will," said Willie.

"But it's too late."

"If you were to ask me," said Willie, "I would tell you that you were reducing everything to your own immediate context, and I would also say that you have assumed that to be intelligent and powerful is different from being ignorant and passive, so your desire to effect the world has seduced you into a tenuous duality."

"It seems to me you might have told him that before we sat up all night," said Bifboy. He downed his last beer.

"It was a beautiful night," said Willie, "enhanced by our anticipation."

"If you asked me," said Karl, "I'd say it seems you two spent too much time taking drugs in the attic."

"It seems to have been a risk," said Willie. "Any less and we might have spent too little time."

Well it wouldn't be long before that conversation started coming apart at its seams, so we went our separate ways. And to say the least, I was confused and disappointed. I'd convinced myself that this airplane business was inevitable, destiny, and the next thing I knew it was non-existent. I thought involving Willie was the clincher. I had a project, a purpose. I'd abandoned my meditative state. Now Blanion would find me boring and come after me. Arturo would hear I was in town and I'd be skewered between the here and the hereafter. Revco and Joseph would end up in Vietnam instead of the Caribbean. I felt cold and wet and thought about a hot bath. Maybe after that I'd try to take a nap. I'd probably sleep fine as long as I brought a weapon.

But I wasn't home ten minutes before Karl dragged me out of the house. He'd heard on his short wave that they'd flown that Galaxy C-

500 down to Pittsburgh where it wasn't raining and that's where they were sending all those troops to ship them out.

Karl and I got in the car, picked up Willie, then Bifboy, then headed south of town and got on the new thruway, I-79, and headed for Pittsburgh. Which wasn't easy. That trip had more in common with tobogganing than driving and that thruway didn't go through anywhere, it still stopped and made you drive through most of the little cities, and south of Meadville there was a stretch of swamp where almost all the roads were out and we had to practically drive to Cleveland to get around. That thruway didn't go through any of Pittsburgh either, so we had to meander down that old U.S. Route 19 from Zelianople on in, the only good part about it being that somewhere between Mars, PA and Moon Run it stopped raining.

That long drive gave us a lot of time to plan things out. We'd have to drive around the Pittsburgh International until we spotted that giant camouflaged moth, park at the nearest terminal and put on our military gear in a bathroom. Then we'd walk out of there very authoritatively, get out on the runway, and walk onto the plane. Bif said we'd have to act both very nonchalant and very authoritative or somebody might ask us for our papers. Once on the plane Bif would notify the tower that we were taking off. He wouldn't ask for permission, he'd just tell them it was a military emergency and we were leaving, so clear the sky. Then we'd find Joseph and Revco and fill them in. They were intelligent beings, by the time we got to Nassau they'd realize that fate had intervened.

Of course amidst all that we had a lot of time to reflect on what we were doing, and in that regard things began not to go so well. Karl even suggested that maybe we might have tried to talk those two out of going, maybe just leaving with us and driving off to somewhere like Ashtabula, before we resorted to the extremes of hijacking, afterall, we were committing a crime by conventional standards and we weren't even going to make any money.

"We'll have a big plane," I said.

"And a lot of soldiers," said Bif. "We can back out now."

"It's a little late for that kind of thinking," I told him.

"Only logistically," said Bif. "It might be just the right time for that kind of thinking."

The way I saw it, they were just getting cold feet because it was nuts.

"We could be seen as part of the anti-war movement," said Karl.

"So what?"

"I'm kind of partial to war."

"I am, too," said Bifboy. "There's a Malthusian aspect to it."

"Don't deal in abstractions," I said. "Just get on the plane and fly it to Nassau. Don't think about it." I turned to Willie who was next to Karl in the back seat. "Willie," I said, "explain it to them."

"I would prefer if you noticed that it stopped raining," said Willie.

I was on Route 65 now, following the Beaver River, and we were almost there. To the left of us small towns climbed the hills and looked over the river to factories the color of rust and tar, flames leaping into the sky from tubes like giant torches, from fat smoke stacks puffed dark clouds of smoke. Bridges sprawled over the river after every other mile and beneath the factories, train tracks spread like webs along the river, into the factories, into the maw of industrial barns, out of rain, out of bus ride, earth eating trees, fence posts, gutted cars, earth calling her little ones.

"There's the airport," I told them. I drove into the airport and circled the cloverleaf around the terminals until I spotted the transport behind the abandoned Mohawk Airlines terminal. I entered Long Term Parking, got a ticket, and found a space between a Cadillac and a Ford Galaxy 500 station wagon. I found that portentous.

"The Allegheny terminal is right there, we can dress in one of its bathrooms," I said.

"Tell you what," said Karl. "How about if I wait here with the car."

Well we didn't have time to argue. Karl was just the logistics man anyways. Willie navigated and I was the co-pilot. There wasn't any money in this, I had to give him that, and he was probably still squeamish about our failures in the *Flying Armada*.

Willie, Bifboy and me dashed into the Allegheny terminal and put our fatigues on in the bathroom. We slipped our old clothes and our pistols into black attaché cases that Bifboy said would make us look like pilots. Then we walked very authoritatively and very nonchalantly right out of that bathroom, out of the Allegheny Airlines terminal, and over to the deserted Mohawk terminal where we tore down some cross boards and plywood and went in. Coming out of there, we didn't even have to go by anybody to get out on the runway, though when we did, Bifboy grabbed both me and Willie by the arms.

"Forget it," said Bifboy. "Those engines are running. The thing's loaded. The crew is on."

"We'll just go out and wave," I said. "We'll pretend we're late. We'll get on and hi-jack it."

"I'm not holding a gun on the crew," said Bifboy. "You're nuts. I'm out."

"Of course I'm nuts," I said. "What's that got to do with it?" I don't know what he thought, like he was just going to get on that thing and fly it and never face a gun. Out on the field now, I could hear the roar of that plane's engines and see the air quiver behind them, turning the tail of the plane into something ephemeral.

"I'm beginning to question the level of your commitment," I said to Bifboy.

"Listen," said Bifboy. "You can't get on that plane. It was a long shot to start with. The whole thing was silly, but you got as far as Pittsburgh."

"He is proving anything can be done," said Willie to Bif.

"They won't shoot us down, Bifboy," I said. "We'll have a plane full of *them*. Nobody inside will shoot us because we'll make the pilots get off."

"You won't get on the plane," said Bifboy. "It's taking off."

"We'll go to Nassau!" I yelled at him. "We'll have a good time!"

"I'll be waiting for you in the car," said Bifboy. He looked around, saluted me, very clean, then headed back.

I looked at Willie. I hadn't noticed, but he looked really good in those camouflage baggies, black boots, beret.

"Maybe you are now thinking you were born to command," he said to me.

"We better get out there," I said.

"No," said Willie.

"No?"

"You were thinking you would not go to Nassau," he said. "You would land in Guantanamo Bay because you had Cuba in your future. You would appear trapped, but our friend Mr. Funly Funster would turn up offshore in his submarine. Then you would put Revco and Joseph on board and take them to the Bahamas. You would return home and it would be your happy day."

"What does it matter, Willie?" I said.

"It is too late to be your happy day."

"I don't need my happy day."

"If all of this was so important to you, why did you make it rain in Erie?"

"Who made it rain in Erie?" I screamed at him. "What the hell are you talking about?"

"Maybe I was trying to make a joke," said Willie. "But as you see, it was not funny." He reached over and took my hand, gently. "It is your own fault to let me ruin everything."

"It's not anybody's fault," I told him, and I left him there, standing against the wind, one eyebrow raised, and ran out onto the runway, flagging the plane, that giant dark thing that I knew would take me in, and once inside I'd take its controls, lift its wings into the air, raise its head; I'd rocket the fire in those engines and fly that dragon to paradise.

I ran, waving, and the plane turned. Th engines wound down and its wings trembled. There was a silent moment when all there was on that runway was me and that great dark bird with its bowels full of men, my friend, my brother, a stomach full of things to take to war. There was silence. Then the wind rose. The engines picked up again, roaring. I waved. I waved wildly with my arms. I jumped up and down. But the transport turned its nose to the expanse. It moved. The wind came under its wings and it leapt into the air, into the purple sky. I stood there until the sound of the engines faded. I imagined, above the clouds, the fumes from the engines writing their momentary lines under the sun.

〰〰〰〰〰Dear Jarvis

Dear Jarvis:

If you were the wondering type you might wonder why I'm writing you and not someone else. Well, in fact, I am writing someone else. In fact I think I'm writing my self. You'll notice I did not say, "myself." And I wish to assure you, this is not simply the influence of the French who still use "conscience" to mean both conscience and consciousness, by the way.

Leonard has convinced me that audience exists neither explicitly nor implicitly; it's just a phenomenal prerequisite of the self, a kind of apologia for action and its ghostly kin, morality.

This isn't as solipsistic as it sounds. It doesn't mean I can choose to stand in front of trains. The self is large and we slip inside each other, all of us, in this shrinking world, like syllogisms; and we inhabit this rigid structure of myth, turning our abstractions into obelisks, our obelisks into wars, World Trade Towers, cities, Infant of Prague Festivals.

If you haven't heard, and you probably haven't, I doubt it was on American TV, I was a very big deal here. They re-enacted the Passion of Christ and I got to play the J Himself. Leonard throws a lot of weight around here and was very committed to getting me the part. I got to carry the cross through the streets, get my face wiped by Saint Veronica, and they crucified me right under a giant statue of the Infant. The only drawback occurred during the simulated earthquake after my death. Too much shaking. The globe of the world fell out of the Infant's hand and landed on me. Broke a lot of bones. I'm in the hospital now. This is why I'm writing me.

I've influenced Cohen. He has a real penchant for Catholic symbolism, sex, war. He had some French teenager in his room overlooking the Passion Play and I think he was up to one of his favorite activities when the globe came down. He feels tremendous guilt and it got him thinking about symbolism, sex, and war.

Anyway, I've kind of enjoyed this and I might send it to you. Tell Red and Helen I'm fine.

Yours in Christ,

Andrew

ஐ   ஐ   ஐ

Moscow/Jarvis—You should bother to see Europe while it's still around; everyone here is divided about everything; consider Germany (I shall allow you to consider Germany, I've already considered it and there's far too much to think about, there's no reason to be redundant in print; people get paid to do that, they get tenure for it; I'm too bright and too talented to need a job). Facts are facts. Yes, I believe in them. One of the many things that differentiates me from Andrew.

Moscow is much like Erie, without the lake, and I'm surprised more Erieites haven't come here to find jobs. Once you get one, it's hard to get you out. It leads to some wonderful, excuse me, that's a Stinky word, some beautifully convoluted incompetence, completely rational, in the sense that Weber would use the term. The ice arena is an excellent example. We can't get any heat. I don't know why they didn't just find a pond and put a shed over it, except someone would have had to make a decision to do that. I know for a fact that the Soviet Space Program was bagged when they sent that young couple to the moon in 1958, but the gears were already in motion, they couldn't fire anybody.

I'll tell you one more thing about Moscow and after that you're on your own. Most of it is unfinished freeways. Everything is made out of unfinished freeways. People live on them, under them, break off pieces and build apartments. If you get on one you'll fall off the edge of an unfinished bridge and then if you're lucky your family can move into your car, that way you won't end up in one of the state hospitals where you'll never get out and they'll never let you die because if you do some doctor loses her job if she doesn't go out to the freeways and find new patients (lots of women doctors here because the work is hard and the pay is lousy). None of this will be censored because it's the truth, and if it's the truth, the Russians deny it. The Russians are a people of tremendous depth, negativity, and obscurity. They remind me of you—yours, Neda.

ॐ   ॐ   ॐ

Dungheep Hill, DMZ, Vietnam

Dear Jarvis,

Without acronyms and puns all the Americans would go home. Though our presence here is an anachronism, not an acronym. (Already, I've said too much to get by the censor, fortunately, at Dungheep, I'm the censor; everyone trusts me because I'm so good at turning a deaf ear). I read all the baloney that goes in and out of here. Besides reading letters I don't have to do much, other than go on patrol, which could be dangerous considering what a dangerous place this is. The enemy, Charles, as I like to call him, has a base camp here on Dungheep too, on the other side of the hill. If we didn't pay our rent there might be some bad feelings.

But we're good tenants. I know that we pay our rent because Revco gets flown over there in a chopper the first of every month and leaves off a suitcase full of cash. On the way back they throw some rockets at him and miss every time. On patrol we're told to stick to the main roads and make lots of noise, that way Charles can hear us coming.

Generally, nobody uses the roads around here because that's the best way to get ambushed, and you're certainly not going to sneak up on anybody walking down a road, though because nobody uses the roads anymore (because it's the best place to get ambushed), that used to be the best place for Charles to wait for us because we'd never come. If Charles wanted to find us he'd have to look in the jungle where we're trying to avoid him. You can imagine where that would lead.

We pay our rent for this half of the hill and part of the bargain is that we don't sneak up on them and they don't ambush us.

We get strict orders to make plenty of noise if we patrol the roads because that's exactly where the VC are and we wouldn't want to surprise them while they're waiting to ambush us knowing we'd never come down there because if you surprise somebody, well, you never know, bad feelings could ensue.

Sometimes we attack each other's base camps, but we have an obligation to give each other a one day notice. We usually attack them the day after we pay the rent because it saves Revco a trip over there. Then we take the main road over the hill, making sure we make lots of noise, and when we get there we surround the place and shoot up some empty barrels. When they're coming to visit us we go out and paint a few buildings with red X's.

Nonetheless, we hear of some very nasty stuff. We were ordered to evacuate Khe Sanh near the end. Marines were dropping like flies. We couldn't get the last hundred or so men out of there and every three out of four choppers that went in never got back out. I was monitoring on the radio. We got our orders to go in there but we told them, no, it sounded too dangerous. Why lose fifty of us to save twenty of them? That's the difference between the thinking at the top and the thinking at the bottom. At the top it's numbers and logistics, our bodies for their heroism. At the bottom it's more rational. How do I stay alive?

That's why this arrangement is working out so well here on Dungheep. Our Commander is only a lieutenant, but he's enlightened. We couldn't keep a hill up here this close to the DMZ if we had to fight for it, and even if we could, it would cost us a fortune in equipment and a lot more in lives. Of course, we have to move a lot of heroine to make the rent every month.

From what I can gather Andrew's been writing everyone and telling them not to tell anybody that he was almost crushed to death by a giant cement Infant of Prague globe. Maybe it will knock some of the baloney out of him. Urban North America is not safe.

Your sweet marine,

Joseph

            ಬ   ಬ   ಬ

FROM: Erie County Jail
TO: Jarvis Loop and other Dialecticians
RE: Myself

This jail is all filled up. They want to make me leave because I have no previous record, which could take me years to build. Your momma, Jarvis, has agreed to supervise my probation against my wishes, not understanding why I got in jail in the first place. She seemed to agree with me about that, but she did not seem to understand the nature of my commitment. She said she could get me a job with the Diocese as a janitor, and that would be stereotypically black enough without living in jail. I told her that jail is what I want, why did she think I went there? But your momma is rather unshakable.

I suppose I shall have to shoot to kill the next time. Hop probation, purchase a long coat, get some jewelry; rings on every finger.

I have seen Grandpa Funster, and I told him that I, like him, was searching for my real state in life. He said there was something filling me. Something like the twilight sound of the crickets. Immense. Filling the woods at the foot of the slope behind my mortgaged house. Of course, this is possible.

Equivocally,

Raymon

Saigon

Dear Jarvis:

I would be wishing to assure you that my concerns here are dialectical. I will give you the phenomena only and with it you will do as you please.

I am thinking that your brother, Joseph, is playing with too many cards in the deck. He does not seem to think that there is anyone here who wishes to harm him, which one might say would amount to a dangerous assumption in this war but for the fact that he remains unharmed. This is true also for anyone else who participates in his patrols and, of course, this has made him very popular. It has also made him a patrol leader, though he is only a private. As of now, he is the only patrol leader at Dungheep Hill, where he is stationed. He takes the patrols out, they walk down the main roads and major paths, then they return. Even when he has lead attacks on the enemy base camp everyone has come back safe.

Some of the soldiers say that when they are with him they become phantoms. It is like they cannot be seen, or if seen, and fired upon, as if they cannot be touched. When they fire their own guns, they hit nothing.

I do not know if you read about the evacuation of Khe Sanh, but several platoons from DH were ordered in to help evacuate and everyone refused but your brother. It did not seem to make much sense to go in there. The last men were surrounded. We heard on the radio. Everything going in, stayed in. But your brother organized enough men to fill a transport chopper and got about twenty-five of the last troops out. He went back with only the pilot for the rest, but his ship went down. They got back a week later in only their dogtags and their underwear. Also, there is a mystery abut the pilot, a southern white kid named Derk Delco, Jr. who was short and built like a rhinoceros. He disappeared after getting back. No one knows where he came from and now there is no record of him.

Myself, I do not see much combat because I am the armed escort on the payroll chopper. We fly from Saigon to the major base camps with a suit case full of money. This is why I sometimes get to see your brother at the Dungheep, and how I hear the stories at the bars. Maybe they are only stories, but we are Dialecticians and know that the story is a metaphor for yet another story. If there is a lie in every line, it yet moves us forward, would you not agree?

Well, if I am the silent Dialectician, I am also the wordy one in my own way.

Especially,

Revco

ප   ප   ප

Moscow!

Dear, dear Jarvis:

The freeways here are wonderful! They really are free. Anyone can have a piece of one! And they don't go anywhere! It's really delightful. Funly sure is wrong about the Russians, I don't think they want to blow us up at all. They really are quite involved with this freeway thing and I just don't think they're going to give it up to sponsor the end of the world.

But that's not why I'm writing you. I'm sure Neda forgot to tell you, but we're pregnant! And I bet it's mine. Neda would call that patriarchal, but I really do bet it's mine. Of course she's not saying, she wants it to be a surprise. She really does have a sense of humor once you understand her.

Well, our skating is kaput! I bet you just can't wait to be an uncle!

Always,

Stinky

❧   ❧   ❧

Québec

Dear Jarvis Loop:

I won't tell you what I went through, the War was old, the child was new, we thought we'd found a symbol for our shelter. But in the manufactured quake I touched my virgin in her lake and everyone was running helter-skelter. Yes, everyone was running helter-skelter. He was just some Andrew looking for a manger. He was looking for a card so high and wild he'd never have to deal another. So we've put him in the hospital where none are sick and none are well. He's just some Andrew looking for a manger. And I said, "Okay, the bridge or someplace later." I left him with the Sisters at the shelter.

When I left they were sleeping, but I hope you run into him soon. You won't need any light, you can read his address by the moon. And it won't make me jealous to hear that he's sweetened your night. We weren't friends quite like that and besides it would still be all right.

Sincerely,

Leonard Cohen

～～～～～Crossing the Water

W HEN THE GARBAGE strike ended I couldn't get rehired through the Union. I got a job as a bowling machine mechanic at the Kronenburger Club. When a machine broke down I went out and hung an OUT OF ORDER sign on it and called Brunswick. In a week or so they'd send somebody in to fix it and he didn't. He'd order a new machine. I got free beer and sandwiches and put on some weight. Sometimes I thought about what it would take to turn automatic pinsetters into spaceships, but it was no good, they ran on electricity. And the Brunswick repairmen were unreliable.

Red got off the porch and found work selling bricks for a new company, Rosswelter Bricks. Up till then there'd only been one brick company in Erie, Puchini Bricks, and of course they had that Italian connection, got a lot of local tax breaks, etc. Red's new boss, G. Rosswelter III, inherited a fry pan manufacturing dynasty from his old man, G. Rosswelter Jr., who made millions manufacturing the famous Rosswelter Iron Skillet which you could find in places all over the world, including Cuba. After Red got that job he used to go around picking up iron skillets wherever he was, friends, relatives, garage sales, and sure enough he found ROSSWELTER printed on the bottom of every one. It was the closest link we'd had to money since Audrey-Mary Pell married Archibald Strong.

Anyway, G. Rosswelter III made all his bucks when he sold his dad's iron skillet company. And he'd been living as well as he could in his cliff mansion west of town overlooking Lake Erie, with his sailing yacht and his motor yacht, his Lear Jet, and his vacations around the world; he was doing pretty okay but he was now middle-aged and wondering what to do with his life and, following in his father's footsteps, he thought a company might be nice, besides it would be a tax write-off.

He didn't want a large staff and he remembered that a few years back there was a big red-headed guy who sold him a decade's supply of toilet paper for his mansion and his yachts and his jet and that same guy drove up in a truck and unloaded it all himself. That was the kind of guy he wanted working for him, somebody who could do everything, sell, manage, and lift, somebody who would be the employee, and so he got hold of Red. Called him at home. Of course Helen was in the basement and Red on the porch so the Viz was the only one answering the phone, good thing he was speaking English at the time. Red ended up with a job.

So G. Rosswelter III started a brick company called G. Rosswelter Bricks, the only competition Puchini Bricks had in town. He had a little warehouse built next to his mansion and he hired Red to maintain the warehouse and order the bricks from the various brick companies in the country and unload the truck and go out and give estimates to prospective buyers and contractors and sell the bricks and deliver the bricks.

G. Rosswelter III was the boss. He had to go to business lunches and play business golf. He didn't want a big business because he didn't want to run head on into the Italians by threatening Puchini's, he just wanted to sell a few bricks to some wealthy associates for their homes and fireplaces. He wanted to join the rotary. He wanted to have things to talk about at the Kakwa Club besides stocks and bonds and the legend about him that he always denied, that he was a Captain in the Marines stationed on the island which Amelia Earhart crashed on after she was shot down by the Japanese for being a spy, even though she wasn't a spy and the Japanese didn't shoot her down. Now that World

War II was long gone and the Japanese our friends who made tiny things very well, G. Rosswelter III's adjutant, Louis Conaitre, gave an exclusive story to *True Story* magazine and claimed he was on Marcus Island with Rosswelter when Earheart crashed and that he and Rosswelter went out and buried her and destroyed the plane so as not to leave any evidence because Amelia Earhart really was a spy.

G. Rosswelter III was always denying that story, though he told Red, unofficially, that he was ordered to go out and bury somebody who died in a plane crash on his island and destroy the plane, but that he didn't know really who it was he buried except that he didn't think it was Amelia Earhart, besides, Louis Conaitre wasn't with him, he didn't know who the hell Louis Conaitre was. Reason enough in itself to start a brick company.

So I had a job and Red had a job. And Helen went back to work, too.

Helen got out of the cellar, and though she put the Infant of Prague back on top the dish cabinet arabesque, she didn't put any other holy stuff in the once holy room, in fact she turned it back into a dining room; put a fake flower centerpiece on the table, brought out her old silver tea set, made Red go out and buy a stereo console, started listening to opera. Then she made an appointment to see the Bishop, which you had to regard as slightly odd, not that the Bishop didn't deserve an audience with Helen, but you had to wonder why she thought he needed to see her, which was answered when she came back with a job as his administrative assistant; up till then, he hadn't known he needed one.

The Viz, now that he could speak, headed out to kindergarten down at Garfield Public School. If language made that kid ordinary, school made him tedious. He spent his time demanding my attention to watch him count things or add things or subtract things, or passing on worthless and incorrect information.

"See what I got here," says the Viz.

"You got a couple oranges."

"That's right. Two oranges. One, two.

"That's really nice."

"Now I'm taking one away," he says. "What do I have now?"

"You have one orange in front of you and one behind your back."

"I have one orange," says the Viz. "Two oranges take away one orange is one orange."

"You find that interesting."

"Do you know where oranges come from?"

"Florida."

"Trees," says the Viz. "Orange trees."

"Not from refrigerators or trucks or stores," says I. "Not from Israel or California or Texas or Mexico."

"No. Orange trees." The Viz put both oranges behind his back. "No other kind of tree."

"Do you have zero oranges now?" I ask him. "Or just zero? Or do you have two oranges behind your back? What does it mean to have nothing?"

"You're no good," says the Viz. "Grandpa Red is better at this."

"He knows an orange when he sees one."

"You're trying to help me flunk like you," the Viz said. "An orange is an orange when you see one."

"There, you finally said something that might be wrong but might be smart," I tell my son. "Flunk like me."

"Flunk like you," the Viz said.

Around this time Red would catch me talking to him and say, "What are you, nuts? He's just a kid." He'd rather I'd hit him with a ball bat or a football than a word, look what that did for me.

"You're an idea dentist," said Helen. "You should be teaching."

"I'd need an education."

"A formal one is all. You're just upside down. Most people go to school and don't learn anything."

"I'm not going back to school," I told Helen. "I like my job."

"Visitor will go to college," said Helen. "You might find him boring, but he'll keep things straight."

"Whether they're straight or not."

"Don't hate your own son, Jarvis. Do you all have to hate your sons?"

Whether I liked it or not, we were having a conversation. "I don't hate him."

"You don't want him to be like you, do you? Then what do you want him to be?"

I had to admit, Helen had dealt with the basic issues. And she'd done it four times from a side of things that I'd never know.

"It doesn't matter what he is," I said. And I think I believed that, that it didn't matter what I was, or what I did; the human race had sanctified itself because it used tools and language, and that our species' self-preservation had become a disease and soon we'd be history like the dinosaurs, if the world got lucky and got us before we got it, so what was another life, mine or the Viz's? Everything. That was the other side of it. Every second counted. Helen was right. There was nothing to do but be holy. Willie was right. Every thought was a blade we cut ourselves with. So in moments like that I just wanted to take the Viz and hug the life out of him, to hold him and hold him and cry with all my love, and I wanted to hold Helen, too, and even Red, but the Viz just beat my ears and screamed when I got that close, and Helen, God bless her, was not a warm person, and Red, well, that would be like hugging death.

Funly came back a week before Stinky and Neda. He radioed Jimbo when he got into Lake Erie and Jimbo went down to the dock and rented him mooring for the submarine, then he brought him back to 24th Street. Funly looked older and more sober. When I saw him he wore a suitcoat and tie, and seeing as he didn't have anybody in the sub to keep up that flat-top for him, he'd shaved his head. He dropped by the Kronenburger Club during one of my frequent breaks and we drank Koehler beer and ate limburger and onion on rye.

"So how'd you get out of that tuba, Funly?" I said.

"How did I get in?"

"You flunked in."

"I'll tell you one thing," said Funly. "The Cubans didn't sneak any fleet down the Saint Lawrence Seaway."

"You figured that out."

Funly sneered. It was good to see that his mature intelligence hadn't rubbed out what was best in him. "I underestimated you," he said.

"Well, Funly," I told him, "sometimes I underestimate you."

After saying that kind of intimate stuff we both had to finish off half a limburger and onion sandwich before we could speak again.

"I waited a week off Guantanamo Bay," said Funly.

So much for oracles. Angela Corona was good at predicting some things and not others, just like everybody else. There wasn't much to say to Funly about it either. Don't explain, that's the first rule. You start saying one thing and end up finding out you said something else.

"Stinky should marry Neda," said Funly. "He should do what's right."

"Neda won't let him."

"What makes her think it's up to her?"

"I don't know, Funly," I said, "some irrational impulse toward selfhood."

"Don't get cerebral on me," said Funly. He finished his beer. "I saw Grandpa. He's getting the chair."

"You're not going to spring him."

"I saw him yesterday. I think he wants it."

"I thought you were going to spring him."

"He wants it! There's nothing to spring."

That's when we got interrupted. A machine went down I had to go hang a sign on it.

All the appeals failed, and then there was a last ditch effort to save Grandpa Funster from the chair on the grounds that he was dead already. That might have worked somewhere else; maybe in a big city with more bureaucracy Grandpa Funster might have had a chance, but not in Erie. The judge saw right through it. They had their man.

"There is a cave in the air behind my body," Grandpa Funster told the judge at his sentencing. "That nobody is going to touch: a cloister, a silence closing around a blossom of fire."

"At midnight when you go to bed, imagine the dead police moving beneath you," said the judge, "luring you downward and downward to share their sleep."

"If I step out of my body I will break into blossom," said Grandpa Funster.

The Ivy League prosecutor stood. "We want you under the lid of the earth that closes over the generations marching to the sun!"

"My bones will turn to dark emeralds," said Grandpa Funster.

"Fry him!" the judge said. And that ended the most literary trial in the history of Erie, Pennsylvania, if not the world.

After that, Funly was right, Grandpa Funster got pretty quiet, through the hearings and appeals, right on up to the end of his last night that he spent with Jimbo and Betty, Funly and Mosha, me and Stinky and Willie.

"Just s-say something," Jimbo pleaded with him. "Even if it doesn't make sense. Even if it's p-poetry."

Grandpa Funster surveyed that gray room, his skin as pale as steel, his complexion so wan there were moments when it looked as if his flesh had faded into the walls, leaving only his clothes standing in the air. "Everything has already been said," he told Jimbo.

That was a difficult moment. Betty Funster cried and Mosha broke into a tune on her tuba, which they'd let her bring in because it had visited before. It might have seemed a bit out of place, but after a while we sang along with it. We sang *ooompa, ooompa, ooompa*, and that's how everybody got through the night.

At dawn they lead us to the small gallery behind Plexiglas that surrounded the electric chair and we waited there while the place filled up with various state dignitaries. Then they led Grandpa Funster in and sat him down. They strapped him in and wired him up, then put the hood over him and gave him his last words.

"Over my head, I see the bronze butterfly, asleep on the black trunk, blowing like a leaf in green shadow," said Grandpa Funster. "Down the ravine behind the empty house, the cowbells follow one another into the distances of the afternoon. To my right, in a field of sunlight between two pines, the droppings of last year's horses blaze up into golden stones. I lean back, as the evening darkens and comes on. A chicken hawk floats over, looking for home."

"Is that all?" said the warden.

"I have wasted my life," said Grandpa Funster.

And then they juiced him.

The Funsters had been in the neighborhood for generations and they were the kind of people who had their funerals in their home. Jimbo set Grandpa Funster up right in his animal room, right over the glass floor that topped the undersea world of dead fish and aquatic animals. The lights from the map of Florida with its helmeted dolphins burned brightly under Grandpa Funster's head. We sat around drinking Koehler beer, Mogen David wine, and Gukenheimer, and ate old fashioned soft German pretzels sliced in half and filled with ham and salami, Swiss cheese, horse radish and yellow mustard.

Jimbo was there, and Betty, and Funly the bald, and Mosha playing her tuba; Red and Helen rejuvenated: Red in his blue suit and white shirt, his stomach beginning to hang slightly over his belt, and Helen in her favorite peach dress, her hair short and professional now, swept back, as silver as the lake after sunset; Karl and Karl Jr., Beema and Maggie, and Sophie with the smallest one, Nedia, named after Neda, tugging at the bottom of the tent Sophie wore as a dress; and the rehabilitated Big Dick Jinx who was back on his Buckhorn potato chip truck and who supplied chips and corn curls; Pat Jinx was there, too, with Becca, now almost an adult, she wore a short shift that stopped halfway to her knees and she hung near Neda who was there with the tuxedoed Stinky who flew around her in a constant ballet of offerings, soda, food, napkins, kissing her face and hands, moving around Neda like a secondary star, and Neda emanating through the room, bending his light, as of yet, she didn't show; and in the breaking of all precedent, Dean and Tina Danger; and Revis, himself newly married and expecting his first child, there with a woman who wasn't his wife, and Willie, himself, by himself, in a dark suit with narrow lapels, sun glasses, and a string tie; black people in the Funster domain.

Angela and Raphael Corona had moved away, Joseph and Revco were in Vietnam, Raymon in jail, and Andrew in a hospital in Quebec City. Grandma Funster, in the past a ghostly presence in the house, when not a nuisance, had, as Kara Ruzci had predicted of herself, faded irrevocably in Grandpa Funster's absence, her presence in the last days like the creaking of doors and soft breathing. Now she was gone. You could feel her nowhere, her movement some rustling in the ears of those already dead. And Kara Ruzci. Kara Ruzci was dead.

But this was the end of death for a while. You could see it in the faces of Jimbo and Betty, Red and Helen, Big Dick and Pat, those Dangers and those Marxmans, you could see the reprieve on their eyelids when they lowered their eyes and measured the lines on their hands, the wrinkles beneath each other's lips; death was a plateau, now only a generation away, and then their generation, their children standing there waiting to bury them. So I looked around and told myself that at every funeral I learned a new thing, that till then I'd seen these rituals as cobwebs, and now I saw myself as living on those webs, as spinning them, as fragile as strings of glass. I wanted to spin them so thick and so deep. To weave eternity so deeply and intricately inside the heart.

I found the Viz explaining two take away one pieces of ham to Revis's girlfriend and I picked him up and held him to me. He hit me on the ears with the ham.

"Down," he said.

"Do you know what happened to Grandpa Funster?" I asked him, putting him back on the floor.

"He's going to sleep all the time now."

"That's pretty close," I said.

"But we can visit him when we sleep, like Momma."

"You see her when you sleep?"

The Viz opened his hands. He looked at them, then at me. "How much ham I got here?" he said.

"You got plenty of ham there," I told him.

"Two," said the Viz. "I got two pieces of ham."

After everybody left I stayed with Funly because it was Funly's job to hold the all-night vigil and he was afraid. That's not what he said. What he said was that he was supposed to stay awake all night but was afraid he'd get too sleepy, and seeing as I had a reputation for never going to sleep, he thought I might help him stay awake.

"What are you going to do if you don't stay here with me?" said Funly.

"I don't know," I said. "Go down to the Kronenburger. Bowl a few."

"You can bowl anytime," he said.

"That's the point," I told him.

But I stayed there with him anyways. I settled down with a bottle of Gukenheimer and some Chesterfields and sat around in that room full of dead stuffed stuff with Grandpa Funster laid out in his coffin in the middle. We sat there a long time. Every once in a while I talked with Funly, but Funly wasn't exactly somebody you could pry open with talk, it was like sitting around trying to hold a conversation with a bald, inarticulate Ayn Rand. Though I did find out that he wasn't going to Vietnam. He'd enrolled in Gannon, the local men's college and got a 2-Y.

"I'll go ROTC and come out an officer," said Funly. "They'll need minds like mine in positions of command." Funly got up and loosened his tie, checked the pistol in his chest holster to make sure the clip was full. "Stinky got off for being a fairy," said Funly, putting his gun back. He shook his head, then swept his hand over its baldness. "He didn't even try to convince them he wasn't."

"The war could be over by the time you're out of college," I said to him.

"There'll be anther one. I got time." Funly sneered and sat on a chair backwards. "When you start smoking?" he said.

"While you were gone."

Funly turned his head so one of his eyes had to look over his nose. We sure had come a long way since those days when me and Georgie Gorky were giving him pink bellies and making him oink out show tunes. I guess maybe he was thinking that. Maybe right then he was thinking about all those years he'd waited to get old enough to have a gun so he could scare me and Georgie out of our minds.

"Do you want to know what's wrong with you, Loop?" Funly Funster said to me. "Do you want to know what I think is wrong?"

Well I had a lot of ambivalence about finding out what Funly Funster thought was wrong with me, but I didn't have a chance to express any of it because we got interrupted by a noise from inside Grandpa Funster's coffin.

It was just a tiny noise, like somebody's fingernails scratching cloth, but you could hear it in there, soft as the sound of something fading.

"Maybe it's a mouse," said Funly.

It was discomforting to think that amidst all this dead stuff there was something alive sharing the room with us. We stayed quiet for a little bit and it stopped.

"You think they put Grandpa in there with a mouse?" said Funly.

"Corpses move," I told him. "You hear about it all the time. Not everything's dead. Nerves, muscles, keep working." I don't know why that should've been shocking, it seemed Grandpa Funster'd been functioning like that for years, only his jaw and tongue worked too and he said funny stuff, at least up till he became a plagiarist and murderer, then he wasn't so funny, in fact kind of obscure. It got me thinking, there in that quiet, waiting for the scratch in Grandpa Funster's coffin, that there Grandpa'd been, dead in our midst for years, and it didn't seem odd until we heard a noise in his coffin.

But the scratching ended. We sat there for hours and nothing happened. By that time we figured we'd probably never heard anything at all. Me and Funly talked about the stories you always heard about corpses sitting up in the funeral parlors, and Funly told that story that everybody always tells in those circumstances about how in our grandfathers' days they used to have wakes in the home, just like the Funsters did for Grandma Funster, and Grandpa Funster the first time he died, and now

Grandpa Funster again, only they'd go all night, and the men would stay up playing cards and getting drunk and watching the corpse till dawn and waiting for it to sit up, and if it did they'd take it out of the coffin and sit it in a chair and deal it its last hand; they'd play cards like that till morning, then put the guy back in the coffin and bury him; Grandpa Funster probably did that himself, or if he didn't, he at least probably told that story a few times, it was the kind of thing that nobody ever really did, but it was an important story because it explained and eased you through a lot of things you couldn't talk about, and it kept Funly from telling me all about what was wrong with me.

After that it was getting pretty close to dawn. Funly finally fell asleep.

Then Grandpa Funster sat up. He turned his head.

"Let's go for a ride," said Grandpa Funster.

"Where do you want to go?" I said. It was a strange situation, but I'd been in stranger ones. I figured he might want to go to the zoo, that's where I'd want to go before my funeral.

"To the cemetery," he said.

"That's awful appropriate," I said to him. "Are you dead? If you're dead you may as well wait a couple hours. We got everything arranged."

Grandpa Funster put his hands on the edges of the coffin. He threw his leg stiffly over the side.

"I'll get the Falcon," I told him.

Grandpa Funster was pretty stiff, but I got him into the Falcon and out to the cemetery, then got him out of the car and walked him to his grave, which hadn't been opened yet. You had to figure what those grave diggers thought. They were told to dig a grave and found out that the person it was for was dead and buried already. They took that problem to the graveyard administration and that's where it would stay until Grandpa Funster's funeral showed up in the morning with no grave.

Grandpa Funster stood at his and Grandma Funster's double headstone in the gray light before sunrise. He placed his hands in his pockets. He stared.

"I dreamed that I was dead," he whispered, "and that wisdom in the ground had no apocalypse or Pentecost." And then he wept. "Woman dead that by my side once lay," said Grandpa Funster. And then, in the slight of the morning, the wind rose. The edge of the orange sun came up and sprayed the eastern sky behind us, and Grandpa Funster raised his arms. "Love," said Grandpa Funster. He lowered his arms again and turned to me. "Shall I at least set my lands in order?" he said. Then he turned to the grave and walked into the ground.

A wind came in from the north, from the shore of the Lake, and the sky grew dark with clouds. In the air I heard the rumble of thunder. And then, for a moment, I thought I saw a figure in the clouds, a dark configuration of black with spread wings. It seemed like the thunder rose from him. It said, "Datta. Dayadhvam. Damyata." But by the time the rain began to fall there was no figure there at all, and I stood listening to the rain fall upon the gravestones, pattering on the stones, pattering shanti, shanti, shanti.

    ಚಿ   ಚಿ   ಚಿ

Anywhere else in the world I might have had a lot of explaining to do, but those Funsters took it pretty well. Of course Funly didn't trust me, and there was a lot of fuss from the authorities, a lot of talk about ending home funerals in Erie, and before the week was out Grandma and Grandpa Funster were exhumed. Of course what they found out was what you knew they'd find out. Grandma and Grandpa Funster had been dead for years.

ᗰᗰᗰThe Best Days of Our Lives

I N THE MEANTIME, and amidst all that, holidays passed. Days settled in like parked cars. Helen reorganized the diocese for the Bishop. She instituted tithing in the parishes, then saved the crumbling parochial school system by using the funds to hire lay school teachers. She redesigned the liturgy so the diocese had a uniform ceremony for the English language Mass, then negotiated the unification of the local Greek and Roman churches. Eventually the Bishop turned over all administrative power to Helen. He made long evangelical missions to Hawaii and the Bahamas. He took up golf.

Red turned G. Rosswelter III's hobby into a business. He gave him too much to talk about at the Kakwa Club. He hardly ever had to deny that he and Louis Conaitre buried Amelia Earhart on Marcus Island because Red was selling and delivering so many bricks. He went out on construction jobs and always beat Puchini's estimates because G. Rosswelter III's overhead was so low because he only had one employee who did everything, Red. Everybody was responsible to Red because everybody was Red. Nobody had to check up on anybody. Estimates were made, orders sent out, the bricks came in and were immediately delivered. Occasional mistakes went right to the top and were corrected on the spot. If Red had any trouble selling to a customer, he'd tell them to go home and check the bottom of his black cast iron frying pan that he'd been frying with for years and see whose name was on the bottom, then the customer would go home and find

ROSSWELTER printed on the bottom of his frying pan and know he'd been living with Rosswelter dependability for decades, maybe generations; well, they could expect the same from the bricks.

Red could really sell bricks. G. Rosswelter III was the talk of the Kakwa Club and the Rotary, which meant trouble with Puchini Bricks. Not that Puchini Bricks could admit it. Up front they said they enjoyed the competition. Then they notified their organizer who represented the combined interests of the bricklayers, teamsters, and truck dockworkers that there was something fishy going on over at G. Rosswelter Bricks and he came over to the warehouse to pay Rosswelter's workers a visit.

He had on a coat and tie and work boots and a yellow hard hat. He wore glasses and had a red nose from drinking too much. He walked around that warehouse a long time before he ran into somebody and as it happened that somebody was Red who'd just come from his locker and changed from his coat and tie to his flannel shirt and khakis.

"You run this place?" said the Union man.

"You looking for a job?" said Red.

"Where's all the workers?" said the Union man.

"You want to buy some bricks?" said Red.

"You don't have unions here," said the Union man.

"You want to go for a ride?" said Red. "I got to deliver some bricks."

"You in the teamsters?" said the Union man.

"You need help finding your way out?" said Red.

"Are you management or a worker?" said the Union man.

"What does it look like?" said Red.

"It looks like this warehouse is out of line with Union guidelines," said the Union man.

"Good thing there's no unions here," said Red.

The Union man pulled out a cigar. Now they were getting somewhere. "Unions can protect you," he said. He and Red had been walking together and now they were at the cab of the flatbed brick truck. He offered Red a cigar.

"You just have a baby or something?" said Red.

"You're working your ass off here," said the Union man. "What do you get paid to do everything?"

"I don't get dick," said Red. "What do you think?"

"I think you're not a young man anymore," said the Union man. "You could use help. And we could unionize."

Well that Union man didn't know he'd played right into Red's hands. "If I get too old I'll get a ball bat," said Red. He got in the truck. "Leave me alone," he told the Union man. "Don't complicate things."

"Things are complicated already," said the Union man. "You're going to be in trouble."

"Either way," said Red.

"You heard of Danny DeVico?" said the Union man.

"Fuck Danny DeVico," said Red. And he started the truck and drove off.

"Who's Danny DeVico?" said Helen. She was having troubles of her own. She was in charge of a coterie of secretaries at the Bishop's office who couldn't run a copy machine, couldn't type, and liked to take two hour lunches. She believed they hated her because she made them work.

"Some tough kid," said Red.

We were having dinner, Helen and Red, me and the Viz, one of Helen's best and Red's favorites, white bread with brown gravy, all you could eat. What Red wasn't telling Helen was that Danny DeVico was the biggest bar fighter in Erie, lifted weights all the time at the Y, worked for the Unions as an enforcer, had a reputation for busting the heads of people who touched the wrong tools at work sites; people said he could lift the front end of a car over his head.

"How many pieces of bread I got here?" said the Viz, holding up two pieces, then eating one.

"One in your stomach, one in your hand," I said.

"One," said the Viz. "Two, eat one, equals one."

"What does he want with you?" said Helen.

"Same old story," said Red. "Somebody's trying to put the crunch on me no matter what."

"Why don't you just back off and let Rosswelter lose money like he wants to?" I said to Red.

"You got no pride," Red said to me.

"I think the women in my office would like to see me dead," said Helen.

That conversation was making it clear to me why we'd always managed to stay so poor. Red and Helen were over-ambitious and undereducated; they knew too much for knowing so little and employed it too well without concern for other people's mediocrity. It got them in positions of responsibility without power. They got frustrated because the world was full of sloth. Then they got fired.

"I got a job," I said to Red.

"So what are you going to do?" Red said to Helen.

"Work it out," Helen said. "Try to make them understand."

"Understand what?" I said.

"The importance of their work," said Helen.

"If I have to, I'll get a ball bat," said Red.

"How much bread I got here?" said the Viz.

It had been a long time since Red carried that bowling ball around. I saw him looking in the closet, but he didn't go get it. He just looked in the closet for a while. Then he went over and sat next to the Zenith. Helen turned it on and sat down on the couch in front of it. She started crocheting that afghan that she was always working on for Bush's next Last Christmas and in few minutes she fell asleep. Red watched her. He stared at Helen as she slept on the couch under the afghan. He folded his hands on his stomach.

I went to the closet and took a look at that bowling ball, dull black and huge on top of a pile of Red's old rubber boots. I never did get him a bowling ball bag for Christmas and now it was too late. He didn't bowl anymore. He never used the ball, not even as a weapon. Though that night at work, during one of my breaks, I picked out a little bowling ball from the rack, about a nine pounder, and did a few curls with it, first the right hand, then the left hand, then the right hand again, then the left. I did that till my arms got sore, then a little later I did it again. In a couple weeks I was up to twelve pounds.

They let Raymon out of jail in Helen's custody. I saw him and Revis on the street corner in front of the Variety Story.

"Congratulate him," Raymon said to me. "He is having some of the babies."

"You having twins, Revis?" I said.

"No," said Revis. "My wife is having some baby and my girl-friends are having some baby."

"And we are going to celebrate," said Raymon, "by having the stick-up."

"I appreciate the information," I said.

"You are the white person here," said Revis.

"That's a pretty dualistic outlook," I said.

"The only way to institute the change is to push what is the same to the limit. Someday then, there may be too much of it," said Raymon.

"You got twenty-ape cents?" Revis said to me. "Twenty-ape more cents I can gep me a sanbwich."

"You want to buy a watch?" said Raymon. He reached in the pocket of his Dialecticians jacket and pulled out a Timex with a Twisto-Flex watchband. "Or the stereo? I got the watch right here."

"You're testing my nihilism," I said.

"You never had the nihilism," said Raymon.

"It may be a test, but you are not in it," said Revis.

Well you couldn't help but wonder what Willie would think about this.

"Willie, himself, is not thinking about it," said Willie.

"So that's it," I said. "There's no more Dialecticians."

"There never were any Dialecticians," said Willie. "There may be some truth to this, but it is also wrong. Do you have your car here? I would like to go fishing."

"You fish now."

"Not now. After you drive me to the Bay. There is no tradition for sitting by the Bay with nothing to do."

So me and Willie got in the Falcon. We drove down to a bait store at the dock where he picked up some worms and minnows and doughballs, then we headed out to the Peninsula and drove till we hit the Lagoons, where Willie had me park. We got out and walked through a lot of weeds until we came to the edge of the swamp. We found a log, sat down. Willie baited his hook with a doughball and dropped the line into the water. We sat there, sweating in the humidity and brushing off mosquitoes and dragonflies. Willie caught a couple small catfish and threw them back. I smoked cigarettes.

Willie changed his bait to worms. "I will not catch a carp if you smoke cigarettes," said Willie. "They do not like the smell of cigarettes."

I put my cigarette out on the log and Willie pulled some Old Crow out of his pocket.

"Bourbon," he said, drinking some, then coating the worm with it. "They like bourbon."

"Cheap bourbon," I said.

"There are those," said Willie, "who think that white people do not like carp, but it is more the case that carp do not like white people."

"I just had this lecture from Revis and Raymon," I said.

A pair of mating dragonflies tried to settle on my knee and Willie plucked one off. He pulled up his hook and re-baited with the bourbon soaked, coitus interrupted dragonfly. He skittered his bait along the surface.

"Are you sleeping?" Willie said to me.

"Not yet," I said.

"And have you seen your wife recently?"

"Not since before the airplane stuff."

"And the Dialecticians are no longer in the attic." He brought that dragonfly in, dangled it, cast it out again. "It is time for a fish to come out of the water and give you three wishes."

As Willie skittered that dragonfly again, a huge fin broke the surface of the water, gliding toward the fly. When it got close, Willie yanked the bait and the giant carp broke water, flinging itself into the air, head, body, and finally even the tail, the whole fish reaching out for that dragonfly, suspended. Then it hung in the air. It turned to me, its head bent forward, its eyes leaning over the curvature of its head to look into mine. Then Willie yanked the fly away and the fish fell into the water again.

"I do not think we will catch a carp today," said Willie. He brought in his line and unbaited the hook. He threw the wounded dragonfly into the water and the carp came up, nudged it with his nose, and abandoned it. "We could have some catfish."

"They like white people okay," I said.

"Poor white people," said Willie.

We didn't fish for catfish. We got back in the Falcon and drove out south of town to the new Catholic cemetery where we walked around looking at baby graves, monuments mounted with cherubs and lambs. "In the old cemeteries," Willie said to me, "the rain and wind steal the detail. This is the future of memory." And then we walked over to Bobby Hansen's grave where that white statue of the football playing Bobby Hansen stood against the blue sky, football tucked, straight-arm pressed against the arid tacklers of eternity, and re-winged. It was clear those wings were the originals, I could see the cracks where they were cemented back on. I'd raised a hammer against the world and all that was left was a little crack on a statue of somebody I didn't even like. When I asked Red why he gave those wings back he didn't even look up from his spaghetti and meatballs.

"It's a dead issue," Helen said to me. "Forget about it."

Viz held up two meatballs. Two wings, take away two wings, you got zero wings.

Then came one day, which contrary to everything I believed about the world, changed everything. One of the complaints Helen always made about Red was that he never wanted to do anything. Helen had a lot of complaints about Red. She thought he was lazy and she thought he was unambitious. She thought he wasn't very bright. She thought he was going to hell. Helen was right about a lot of things, but when it came to Red, despite all those years she spent with him, she was generally wrong. Must have been love getting in the way. Myself, I spent too many years hating Red, for justifiable reasons, and even I could see he wasn't even going to hell, whether it existed or not. But Helen was right about one thing, Red didn't like to do stuff. He didn't like to go out to eat, didn't like to go to the movies or the park, didn't like to go dancing and drinking in clubs, anymore he didn't even golf or bowl or play softball. Mostly Red liked to come home from work and sit next to the Zenith and watch Helen sleep under the afghan she was finishing for Bush's Last Christmas. It was loving, trouble free, uneventful activity. Next to that Zenith Red could relax. But across from him, underneath that afghan, there was Helen, sleeping though she was, who wanted to go to parks and movies and go dancing at clubs. In fact the one thing Helen really loved to do and as far as I remembered hadn't been done since I was young enough to call everything in the world "Jarvis," was go to the beach, the thing, of all the things, that Helen loved to do and Red didn't want to do the most, because Red was fastidious and the beach was the most unfastidious place he could think of, sand everywhere. On top of that, Red had skin whiter than aluminum siding, huge Red freckles on his forearms. Ten minutes in the sun and his head turned into a tomato. And he didn't like the water. He never learned to swim, not even in the Marines when he had to dive off a hundred foot tower into a lake. He just hit that water and skittered to the shore like a cat. Besides, Lake Erie was polluted. And of course Helen loved to swim, she loved to swim ever since she was a little girl and won prizes for high jumping and broad jumping in place and the hundred yard dash.

Helen was a brave, strange, and crazy woman, and sometime in the interval between the basement and the Bishop she'd gone to her confessor to solve the widening chasm between herself and Red, and he'd told her that if she wanted her marriage to work she'd have to acknowledge that Red was the head of the house. She'd have to accept his faults. She'd have to abide by his decisions. Stupid and protestant and lazy as he was, he was her husband, the man, the head of the household; the issue was biblical, she couldn't do a fucking thing about it. She had to accept it. She had to abide in silence. Of course that was absolutely nuts so Helen did it.

And it was absolutely wrong so it worked. Once Red always got his own way, he and Helen started getting along great. They worked all day, had supper with me and the Viz, then hit the Zenith and the afghan till bedtime. Then one day just after I got the Viz to bed and just before I headed off to work at the Kronenburger, and just before Helen went to sleep on the couch under the afghan and Red got tuned in next to the Zenith watching her, Red looked up and said, "Hey, what do you say for Labor Day we all go and have breakfast on the beach?"

Helen woke up. She blinked. She looked at me and smiled, and I knew what she was thinking, me next. Before Red knew it, he'd be buying her dresses and coats instead of mixers and toasters, taking her out to the movies, bringing her flowers home from work. Then he'd convert. Before she was done, she'd have him, and then it'd be time for me to get the hell out of the house before I fell under her hegemony. The Viz, I figured, was already lost. She had him. He'd add and subtract his way into intelligence and responsibility. He'd get educated, get a job where he did real work for real money. We'd reach an eventual kind of compatibility, like me and Red, and Red and Helen could be proud of him.

So that weekend we went to the beach. We got up before dawn and packed an ice cooler with butter and eggs and potatoes and Pepsi Cola. We brought paper plates and paper cups, plastic forks and spoons and knives. We brought a spatula and white bread. We packed blankets and suntan lotion. Red even brought a bathing suit, which meant we might see something that several of us had never seen before, Red in the water, other than a bath tub.

Then I went across the driveway to the Jinxes' and got Stinky and Neda from the flat above the Jinxes' where they were living in ambiguity, moral and otherwise, because Stinky wasn't really supposed to be living up there with Neda. So because everybody knew he was doing it, we could all pretend he wasn't, something we couldn't do if he wasn't actually up there. They piled into the back of the Rainbow with me and the Viz and Polly Doggerel, Red and Helen got in the front, and we all headed out to the Peninsula bright and early so we could get a picnic table in the shade before the whole place filled up with Labor Day revelers and you couldn't find an open space anywhere.

It was a beautiful day, the last day of summer as far as anyone was concerned. After Labor Day nothing really changed that hadn't already changed earlier in August, the nights grew colder and the leaves already turned their undersides up so they rustled dryly in the wind, but everybody said that after Labor Day the currents in the lake changed, the waves got bigger and there was a dangerous undertow; after Labor Day St. Christopher wouldn't save you if you started to drown; Labor Day was an important day for St. Christopher; people stopped going to the beach, the lifeguards stopped lifeguarding and the Lake was deserted. So this was Labor Day, a beautiful day, and the last day of summer.

Red drove down into the Peninsula, around the horn past the first seven beaches, past the Yacht Club Marina, past Misery Bay and the Perry Monument, and past the opening at the tip from where the trees cleared and you could look across the Erie Bay to the city, the Public Dock, the Cathedral, St. Peter's, where Helen worked, the ore piles and grain towers, the few brick buildings downtown that managed to tower over the trees. Red parked the car there and we stopped at the Bay, the water as quiet as glass, the trees on the shore mirrored, the city across the Bay reflected as if another city, another world, inhabited the water, one gentler, deeper, more serene.

Red put his palms on top the wheel and leaned forward, his chin on the backs of his hands.

"Boy, it's been a long time," said Red.

"Yes," said Helen.

"I can't remember how long," said Red.

And Helen turned to him. She put her hand on his shoulder. "If you only knew," said Helen.

And you could see Red guessing, you could tell by how his shoulders rose when she touched them; you could tell he was trying to know.

℘   ℘   ℘

How do I say it, Helen? How can you tell him what happened to you when he was away and you were asleep? But I have been searching for you all of my life and that, too, has raped you like a story rapes the truth. You are sitting now at the edge of the Bay in the front seat of the Studebaker, your generations piled behind you in the back. But now that cold memory is in front of you on the silver ice. Red is far away. He's touched the dock, his breath exploding in the air. And someone hovers over you. Hovers over you in your illness, that illness of waiting, the birthright of your womb; we do not get back the way we came, did you always know this?

Red headed back across the Bay, laden now, his sweat like lead, the sun bleeding across the ice and the moon unblinking. His weight so deep, his skates too sharp for that fragile bay, your skin, cracking behind him, splintering, until at the center, he became too heavy to hold, the ice split in front of him and the black water swallowed him.

He was not a good swimmer, but he remembered from the Marines how to float like a turtle, head down, back afloat, rocking backward to get air. From that position, with his head down, it was easy enough to get his skates off, to struggle to edge of the ice. But something happened in the sunset. The air grew less cold. The ice became a silk skirt slipping away from him. As he gathered it in it slipped away. When he pulled himself up it disappeared.

It took him a long time to realize he wouldn't get back to save you; that he couldn't even save himself. As the ice crept into him he began to feel warm. He began to love you all the more. He began to think the thoughts he'd never thought in all those years of war, that he would never see you again. Now he wanted such simple things, to be near you and to love you. To be near you and to love you. This was all he ever wanted, and what love commits us to lose.

And Helen, as you lay in the back of the Chevrolet, a man over you like darkness, what could you know about this day in the future on the same spot on the Bay; that summer or winter, you would always be waiting near ice.

The sun set over the lake. The moon turned from gold to white. Death placed itself over you, a man named Shorty or Death, an old man, a young man, then a car pulled up behind you and stopped. A red-haired woman with hands like doves and nails painted as red as blood got out of the car with a short, husky man who looked like he'd fought too many fights, and your rapist fled, leaving you with your womb exposed to the moon. The woman sent the man out onto the ice, then came into the backseat of the car. She wiped your face with her scarf and dressed you again. She covered you with a blanket and took you in her arms. "Darlin', we aren't ready for you," she said. "I don't think nobody is ever going to be ready for you."

It didn't take long for the husky little man to find Red on the ice. He took off his coat and lay down, then extended his coat to the water. To Red he looked like a little rhinoceros in sweaters. A man with a horn instead of a nose, small mallets for fists. But he couldn't tell, really, and didn't care. He was out of the water, miraculously, and fainted there, awaking alone an hour later under the frozen stars. Then he walked back to the shore where he found Helen asleep in the back of the car. He took off his wet clothes and wrapped himself in several blankets while he started and heated the automobile. He didn't even wake her to drive her home.

So one thing happens so another thing can happen, because one thing follows another. The Viz points across the water. "Two buildings," he says. "One, two."

"That's right," says Helen.

Stinky nuzzles Neda in the back seat as she stares across the road into the trees. Her pregnancy has changed him. Stinky, the athlete and flower, is now the cuddler. I think about getting him alone on the beach later and asking him why he gave it all up, but what has he given up? "Hooo," whispers Stinky into Neda's ear. "Hooo-hooo." A sound like something coming out of hibernation. Neda turns to him and touches his cheek like a forgiving Christ. Red puts the car in gear. Polly Doggerel nuzzles her nose underneath my hand.

We circle the tip of the Peninsula and come back down the lake side where Red pulls over between Beach 8 and Beach 9, once named Pine Tree Beach and Light House Beach. Red parks and we pile out. Red wants a table in the shade and Helen wants one near the water and they stare at each other a while before Red picks a table up and moves it to the edge of the pine tree grove, the closest shade to the beach. Then he gets another table and makes an L from them. He gets the old grill, a shallow pan that sits on tripod aluminum legs and sets it up inside the L. He pours charcoal in there, douses it with lighter fluid, waits and douses it again. Then he lights the coals and they explode in flame. He turns to the Viz and says, "Don't you ever try this."

"I want a swim before breakfast," says Helen, and heads across to the other side of the road to the bath house, an old wooden shack with MEN and WOMEN carved in wood on opposite sides. On some of the new, popular beaches now, like 6 and 10, they have big cement and aluminum structures, large open air dressing rooms with long, enclosed lavatories, sinks with pedals and sprayers to wash your feet, refreshment stands. Here it is more private.

We follow Helen over and change, then cross back, heading to the beach, leaving Red to mind the fire and stay under the pine trees, out of the sun. It's early and the sun is behind us, over the Bay, stretching the shadows of the trees onto the beach. The water is calm today, blue-green, lapping at the shore in quiet slaps as Helen walks in and wets her wrists. She wears a bathing cap and a green floral one-piece suit. It looks so strange, like the pictures in her old album of her vacations with Bush before she met Red. She glides into the water, stands, and splashes at us. Then she glides off again, out into the lake. It's early, before the life guards have come, and she quickly passes the safety markers, moving out and out, smooth and strong, her head barely turning for breaths. After a while she flips on her back, turns and waves, starts back in. When she gets on shore she tells the Viz, "Don't ever do that," and then takes him into the water. Me and Stinky and Neda join them. We play catch with the Viz, tossing him back and forth between each other and he laughs and laughs. Then we go ashore and back up to the trees where Red is waiting with the hot coals spread and ready and butter melting in an iron Rosswelter pan on the grill.

Helen takes over. She breaks eggs into the pan, lines up bread for toast on the grill around it. We break out the plates and cups and plasticware, drink Pepsi Cola and coffee while we wait. Helen gives Red the first panful of eggs and grill of toast, then starts a new round, giving us each an egg and a piece of toast. She does that several times around before she sits down herself, then Red goes back to the grill and adds a few coals so he can keep the fire going till lunch, a surprise, that he plans to stay for lunch.

So we finish up and go back to the beach, Red staying behind again with the fire and the shade, but in a little while he shows up at the towels near the shore in a huge green boxer short bathing suit. On his head he's got some kind of safari helmet. He looks like an overweight heavyweight, massive, his weight settled, his chest moving slightly downward toward his stomach except when he notices it himself as he approaches the shore and jacks himself up, and then it looks as if he's immediately transferred a hundred pounds to his chest and shoulders. His skin is whiter than the sand.

"I ain't staying out here too long," says Red.

And Helen lathers him in suntan lotion.

"That stuff doesn't work, I'll burn anyways," says Red.

And Neda, who is lounging on the blanket, turns and says, "Put a damn shirt on, Red." Neda, home from Europe, pregnant, miraculously unchanged enough to thwart Red's simplest ambivalent pleasures.

"He doesn't need to put a shirt on," says Helen.

And Red grunts. He gets up and goes to the shoreline where Stinky and the Viz are building a sand wall. The early morning calm of the lake is giving over to the first waves of the day. They beat their foam on the shore and rush the Viz's sand wall, eroding it at the base until it crumbles. The Viz wants to move the castle closer to the water so the waves will destroy it completely. Red wants to move it back.

"We'll make a series of retainer walls," says Stinky. "the first one will get destroyed and Viz can keep rebuilding it, the second one will get eroded, and the third one will be a moat for the castle! Hooo!"

That seems to settle things okay. The Viz works feverishly at the shore, barely building lumps before the waves flatten them, and Red moves back, having Stinky make runs to the water with Viz's bucket so he has moisture to build his edifice. Red constructs an amazing castle with ten inch walls and turrets, inner sanctums and courtyards. I've been sitting with Polly Doggerel who leaves me to join the Viz who's finally given up his battle with Lake Erie. He and Polly Doggerel begin a moat in front of Red's castle.

"We'll need water for the moat," says Stinky.

"You dig it deep enough, you'll hit water," says Red.

And they start digging, but they don't hit water. Red must have built the castle too far back. What they dig up are some old toys. A small metal beach rake. A red plastic car. And a strange thing, an old toy train boxcar. Inside the Viz finds some dolls that look like they belong in a playhouse or a train set, a mother and a father and four little girls, each with different color hair. The Viz adds them and subtracts them for a while before giving them to Red who puts them in his castle. Everybody has their own room. There's even an extra room, a guest room. At the top of the castle Red adds a patio so they can barbecue and get a view of the lake. On good days, clear ones, at sunset, they'll be able to see the silhouette on the horizon, the shore of Canada.

Then Red takes off his hat and goes in the water. Helen joins him. Red doesn't swim well and spends his time bobbing and walking as Helen swims around him. They splash each other. He grabs her and lifts her out of the water. He is so strong that with the water to help him he can put her feet in his palms and catapult her high over his head from where she dives into the lake head first. That just looks too good for the Viz and I have to take him in the water to be catapulted. Red and Helen hug and then we all go ashore. As we dry off Helen looks around. "I love you," she says to us. "I love you all so much."

Stinky takes a walk down the beach and Helen and Red head back to the shade with the Viz. I sit on the blanket with Neda, watching the waves rise. They are almost a foot high now, autumn waves, and they're breaking down the last retainer wall in front of Red's moat.

"You're not going to marry Stinky?" I say to Neda.

Neda gets up on an elbow, then sits up. She laughs. It's almost a giggle. She puts her hand on my shoulder. The waves crash at the base of Red's castle. The sun is rising into the blue sky. It's a beautiful day. "You're going to get a sunburn," says Neda. She gets up and walks back toward the picnic tables. She's still laughing as she walks away.

I stare out over the lake and on the horizon a shiny speck spreads into a line. It floats toward me, and as it gets closer I see that it is a line of gigantic angels, their silver wings spread and touching at the tips. They hover at the waters edge and I turn to see if my family can see them, but the light they emanate whitens the beach. They're shining with joy and powerful delicacy and they fill the air with a sound gentle and deafening. This is the kind of thing I have been waiting for all my life. They land around me in a blinding dome of light. I open my arms. They disappear. Before me stands Kara Ruzci, so pallid as to be invisible. The wind lifts her dress through her body. In her eyes I see the ring of angels like silver fire. I want to tell her that I'm happy to see her. I want to tell her to come and have a hot dog with us. That all the bad things are over. It's a beautiful, warm day and not even death is unbearable.

But when I reached to her my hand passed through her cheek, and when she reached out to me, I was not there for her. "Where are you?" whispered Kara. "I can barely see you."

"I love you," I said to her.

"Yes," said Kara Ruzci.

"And you're leaving."

"Yes," she said.

"And I'll never see you again."

She opened her mouth; she said something but I didn't hear it, and she came to me, passing her hands through my heart. When she placed her lips on mine, I didn't feel them. And then she stepped back and faded away. All I could see of her was the sun glistening through her tears. They fell like rain upon the sand. I knelt to place my hands in their mud, but already the sun had dried them and they were gone.

"You're going to get a sunburn," said Neda. She got up from the blanket and walked back toward the picnic tables. She was still laughing as she walked away.

Back at the pine trees Red had the coals red hot with hot dogs and hamburgers on the grill. He liked to cook hamburgers individually wrapped up inside aluminum foil and he liked to roast the hot dogs until they split and blackened with coal, that's how he could tell they were cooked inside. It made no sense at all. Helen got out the ketchup and mustard and Red spread the buns on the outside of the grill to toast them, then when the hot dogs got good and black, he started filling up buns. Then he got the hamburgers off the grill and opened up the foil. Those hamburgers were dry as farts, but Red had managed to save all their grease.

After that Red dragged out marshmallows and carved sticks for everybody from some green limbs. Helen got out graham crackers and Hershey bars and made sandwiches for those roasted marshmallows out of them. We sat around after that, feeling the breeze come through the trees, watching the sun working its way down to the Lake. Our bellies were full. Soon we'd be cleaning up and heading home. You couldn't think of a thing wrong until the Viz went into a frenzy with Polly Doggerel and ran into the grill. Helen stopped it from falling on him. She reached out and grabbed that scalding grill with her left hand. She didn't feel a thing. She didn't even notice when her skin began to bubble and peel.

The doctors tested Helen for a vitamin deficiency, gave her an overdose of potassium and suggested she eat more bananas. But when the numbness moved up her arm and into her left foot they decided to start taking x-rays of her head. An expert was called in, a lanky guy from Corry, Pennsylvania with thick gray hair and cowboy boots. He had a mustache and didn't wear doctors' clothes and spent most of his time on his farm breeding Arabian horses. He asked Red if Helen had exhibited any unusual behavior recently. When he said that, Red just looked at him.

So Helen had a CAT scan and after that her doctor from Corry, Dr. Sam Sawyer, said she had an obstruction.

"What's an obstruction?" said Red.

"Something in the way," said Sawyer.

"In the way of what?" said Red.

"In the way of what's supposed to happen."

"In her arm?" said Red.

"No," said Sawyer.

"Does she know?" said Red.

"She knows as much as you do," said Sawyer.

"It's in my brain," said Helen.

Sawyer had this habit of keeping everybody separate to give them the same lack of information. He'd have his stuff done on Helen and then he'd call Red in, and then me, to talk, then we'd have to get together to figure out what he didn't tell us.

"He's not telling you I have a brain tumor," said Helen.

"You just got an obstruction," said Red. "It could just be a clot or something. Something they could rinse out. They've got to do more tests."

He was at least right about the tests. The next day they put tubes up Helen and filled her full of blue dye. Then they took pictures. After that Sawyer suggested Helen stay in the hospital because it would be easier to do more tests.

That night, in the hospital parking lot, I waited out by the Studebaker for Red for a long time. I tried to think back to the last time he'd slept alone. The sun went down over the trees. The dusk came in.

Red came out of the hospital squinting. He wasn't crying, but there were tears in the corners of his eyes. He didn't look at me. When he got to the car door he found his keys in his pocket and drove home.

He didn't sleep that night. He spent the night with me, up watching old movies till dawn, except of course he didn't watch them, he sat next to the Zenith in his chair. He watched me smoke cigarettes and drink bourbon. It was after the first late movie, around 2 A.M., when he asked me if that's what I did every night, sit up and drink and smoke.

"Unless I have work. It comforts me," I said to him. "I'm trying to get to sleep."

"You been trying a long time," said Red.

I put out my cigarette. I knew he didn't like smoking and he didn't want me smoking in the house, his house, but I'd been holding back, smoked one for every two I wanted, and this was a special occasion.

"It's going to kill you," said Red.

"I know," I said to him. And that pretty much held him till the end of the next movie. He had his hands on his stomach, looking down at them, in his resting his eyes pose. I capped the bourbon. "You want some coffee?" I said.

Red looked up. "It's behind her right ear," he said. "That's why her left side's numb."

"I figured," I said. I got up and went into the kitchen. I brewed a pot of coffee in there and poured us each a cup, but I added a shot of Guckenheimer. I needed it myself to make the transition figured Red needed it too. When I gave him his coffee he smelled the Guckenheimer but he didn't say anything about it. "You should have a saucer," he said to me.

"You want one?" I said.

"You drink in the living room, you could spill."

Well sometimes Red was the last one to know what was going on, especially inside himself, but I had years of practice with him. Helen was in the hands of the doctors and Red hated doctors. And we all knew what was next. They were going to want to go in there, to saw inside Helen's skull and get that obstruction.

"He said it's accessible," said Red. "I said to him, it's inside her goddamn head, how accessible is that?"

"What did Helen say?"

"She said it's just her head, go in and get it."

But now it was hard to tell what Helen meant when she said what she said. Sawyer had her on Phenobarbital to keep her calm.

The only thing to do in a situation like that one was to call Neda. Neda would probably know enough to perform the operation.

"They're going to draw it out," said Neda. "They're not going to tell us anything they think until they know something for sure. They'll leak the bad news little by little. Then they'll tell us it's fatal but that we shouldn't give up hope."

"You're surmising," I said. "I just want to tell Red something."

"It's a glioma," said Neda. "It's malignant and fast growing. That's based on the symptoms and the rate of their spread. Sawyer knows that, but there's always a chance he could be wrong. When he goes in he'll find out for sure. Helen will be paralyzed on her left side after the operation, because he'll have cut out what he can get to and some of her brain will go with it. With radiation she'll gain a few months, but if they don't go in, Helen could die any minute. Any way we look at it, she's dead in a year."

"You're reconciled to it," I said to her.

"You better get busy yourself," said Neda.

"What she say?" said Red when I went back in the living room. He'd finished that coffee and Guckenheimer and was sitting up now. The dawn was coming, the first push of morning light shining behind the drawn shades.

"She said it's hard to tell," I told Red. "But from the symptoms it sounds like it's benign and easy to get to."

Red got up. He went to the front window and opened the shade, then turned out the lights in the living room. He went around the house doing that. He didn't like to waste light. After that he brought Honky in and fed him. He watched him eat, then he let him back into the yard.

"You work today?" he said to me.

"Tonight," I said.

"Tell your mother I'll see her at lunch." He went to the closet for his coat. "Don't quit your job," said Red.

"I don't plan to."

"Don't work too hard, just keep your job," he said. "The Catholic church has got lousy insurance."

"You got insurance."

"Not anymore. I been fired."

I spent the morning with Helen looking out her hospital window. She slept a lot, but she woke up once just before Red got there and took my hand.

"Are you afraid?" she said to me.

"Yes," I said.

"I'm scared too," said Helen.

"I think Red's afraid," I said.

"Your father's afraid of everything," said Helen.

And that's when Red came in, afraid of everything, maybe that's what made him so capable of destruction. He went up to Helen and took her other hand.

"I can be here every day now," he said.

"You lost your job," said Helen.

"You get back on your feet. I'm going to be here."

"I don't need you here," said Helen.

That's when Sawyer came in, with his cowboy boots and string tie and delicate fingertips. He looked at the three of us there holding hands.

"Day after tomorrow," said Helen.

"You'll be good as new," said Sawyer.

Helen patted Red's hand. "Nothing to it," she said. "Good as new."

That night at the Kronenburger I worked that bowling ball pretty good. I'd got stronger, and sometimes I flipped that thing from one hand to the other, flexing it on the ends of my fingertips without even thinking, because I had other things to think about. It was a big night for machines to break down, too. I was pretty busy hanging signs.

Consequently there was less bowling, but the bar did pretty well. One of those machines I could have fixed. When I went back behind the setters to hang the sign, I saw a wire hanging loose. I connected it and the thing clicked in, swept back the pins, came down, set up the seven-ten split. I pulled the wire and a shock ran through me like a buzz saw. I left that wire unconnected and hung the OUT OF ORDER sign. I was still a Dialectician. I understood my work.

Helen went in for her operation at dawn. They didn't let us spend the night. They didn't let us in there before preparation. Me and Red and Neda got to see her as they wheeled her, out cold, through the hallway to the operating room. They gave us a waiting room to ourselves, told us it would be about six hours, maybe longer.

So we settled in.

Red talked a little bit about losing his job. He said Rosswelter Bricks did too good. Puchini's was losing business to him; he was losing money to taxes because he couldn't re-invest his profits quickly and creatively enough. He made a fortune selling out to Puchini's who kept Rosswelter's name on the company to give the impression there was competition. Red got fired. Puchini's wouldn't touch him. Red wouldn't have to fight DeVico. Helen got a get well card from Rosswelter.

Neda read. I stared out the window at the parking lot. Anybody visiting during these hours had to be special, major operations, babies, deaths. Red kept talking. I'd spent my life waiting for Red to talk and now he was talking up a streak and I could barely listen. He thought he should have recognized something earlier. Maybe Helen's behavior had been a little unusual the past few years. Maybe she slept too much. She was always so tired after work, always sleeping under that afghan. Maybe if he'd have caught this earlier they could have stopped it, they wouldn't have had to cut Helen open.

I turned to him then. Neda looked up. Red put his hands in his pockets and turned away and started talking, about dating Helen, about when he was in the Marines, about the time he left her and ice skated across the Bay; God, how many times had he left her. When she got better he'd never leave her again. When she got better, they'd do things.

Three hours later a priest came. He stopped at the doorway of the the waiting room.

"Are you Mr. Loop?" he said. "The operation's over."

"Early," said Red.

"Yes," said the priest.

"Why a priest," said Red.

"I'm just taking you to the doctor," said the priest.

And we followed that priest down to the hallway outside the operating room. We waited there. We waited there with that priest and he said nothing and we said nothing. That priest just kept rocking back on his heels and looking down at his white folded hands like priests do. We waited there a long time.

Then Sawyer came out of the operating room door with his whites still on. He kept about ten feet away from us and the priest moved in beside him at his right shoulder.

"She's doing fine," said Sawyer. "You can see her in a few minutes." He breathed heavily enough so that his shoulders moved up and down. "But the tumor was cancerous. I couldn't get it all. When she recovers from the surgery we'll begin radiation therapy."

Red bleached. He looked like a white stone, but like something fragile too, like the next word could shatter him.

"The radiation won't get it," I said to Sawyer.

"It will prolong her life," said Sawyer. "Six months to a year. Those are important months."

"Would you like to pray?" said the priest.

"No," said Neda.

"You can go in and see her now," said Sawyer. "She's awake."

"I can't," whispered Red.

"She needs you more than ever," said Sawyer.

"I can't," Red whispered. He had his hands on his face, his fingertips over his closed eyes. If he'd had the strength, I know he would have killed Sawyer right then, and the priest, too. He would have taken them apart. But what was the point. "I have to take a walk," he said. He headed down the hall for the foyer. Neda waited. I went with him.

And that's all we did. We walked. We walked around the hospital in silence, once, twice, again, and again. Red walked slowly, like a baby, his head forward, his knees wobbling. We walked in silence until we were halfway around the block again. Then he stopped. His face broke into pieces and he began to cry. I let him put his head on my shoulder. His weight was like the weight of the world. "I can't live without her," Red wept. "I can't live."

Helen looked gray, and the right side of her head, bandaged, was swollen to twice its size. She was hooked up to bottles. Her eyes were open. A nurse in green pastel fussed around the room, stuffing a pillow in a pillow case and straightening the empty bed on the far side of the room. The nurse smiled and smiled. She had a smile like a high-top sneaker. "She's paralyzed on the left side, but her right side's okay," smiled the nurse.

"I'm left handed," said Helen. She said it real weakly, in the back of her throat.

"You'll learn," said the nurse.

Well I knew Helen, and even in that horrible state you knew she didn't answer because she was calculating how long it would take her to learn against how long she had to live. Red went to her and she tried to smile at him, but she didn't have the strength.

"When's the dance?" whispered Helen.

And Red tried to say something back, but he didn't have anything.

"They didn't get it all," said Helen.

"No," said Red.

Helen reached up and touched her face, then her head. "I look horrible," she said.

"No," said Red.

We stood there silent for a minute and then that priest came in. He had a chalice and he gave Helen communion. She could barely get her tongue out, but what little she did, it made her face look caved in.

The host sat there on her extended tongue until Red reached over and helped her tongue back into her mouth.

Helen didn't try to swallow. She just let it dissolve.

"Is there anything else I can get you?" said the priest.

And Helen waited a moment. Her mouth moved like she was trying to get her tongue out of the way. "Chocolate," she finally said.

"You're breaking your pact with the Lord," said Neda.

And Helen closed her eyes and whispered, "That's right."

Red didn't want to sleep that night either, but Sawyer gave him pills. Sawyer told him the pills wouldn't put him to sleep, so of course they did. Neda went back across the driveway to Stinky's. And then, alone in the living room, that's when I cried.

Helen would die. It was then that I realized that to exist is to disappear. To write is to scribble with white ink on the white void. And that here in that void, in our shared wombs, was the search for my mother. At the beginning of lines, blank spaces, at the beginnings of generations, blank spaces, my mother's life entering that beginning, and here at this juncture of death and death retold I have nothing to offer her, even now, nothing but this. Helen, it is meager, but it has all been for you, and the rest is for you; to never die is the only rebirth. That night, for the first time in years, I slept.

The Cancer Society gave Red a wheelchair, and a bed that he set up in the living room in front of the Zenith, so Helen could look at TV or look out the window, of which she wanted to do neither, and Red could sit in his chair next to the Zenith and watch her. He bought her a wig, which she wore, at first, when she had visitors; Bush and Jon, Uncle Stanley, Aunt Frances, Uncle David who flew in from California, the Dangers, the Jinxes, the Funsters, even Karl and Sophie. Willie came. He went up to the bed and held Helen's hand. He sat down and they held hands for hours.

Helen wore the wig when Red took her for her radiation treatment, too, after which she lost the rest of her hair, and she wore it the one time Red took her for a walk. He put her in the wheelchair and walked her up and down the street, Helen's head lunging forward, the left side of her face drooping. When she got back she told him she wasn't going out again. "Why?" said Red, and Helen told him, "Pride."

That was the first of their fights. Red wanted Helen to go for walks. He wanted her to eat square meals. Helen wanted to eat chocolates and candy and suddenly, after all those years, Red thought she should keep her pact with the Lord. Red wanted Helen to exercise. He tried to get her up in a walker. He wanted her to scoot with one leg in a wheel chair. He bought Helen little boards with wheels and straps that he attached to her left ankle and left wrist. He picked her out of bed and lay her on the floor.

"Make an angel," said Red.

"I can't," said Helen.

"You have to retrain your brain connections," said Red.

"Let me die in peace," said Helen.

"You're not going to die," said Red.

"Watch me," said Helen.

"I watch you plenty," said Red. Then he'd start moving Helen's arm and leg for her and Helen screamed.

"Pain is an encouraging sign," said Red.

"For you," said Helen.

They fought and exercised like that every day and every day when they were done Helen wanted a beer or a soda and Red brought her milk, then they fought about that. It was almost like the old days except that Helen was dying. Red bathed her, dressed her, turned her so she wouldn't get bed sores. He got the bed pan for her, wiped her, held her hand until she slept at night. Every day they fought harder, and every day, for a little while, Helen got a little better. Over the huge scar on her head, a little hair began to grow. She got feeling in her left hand. Made an angel one afternoon on the floor. Then one evening just before I left for work, Helen lurched forward in her bed.

Her left side began to shake uncontrollably. She grabbed herself with her right arm, but she couldn't stop. The bed shook. Helen's eyes filled up like empty bowls. Her face began to twitch. I grabbed her to hold her down, but it was like an earthquake. I felt her tears on my face, her body dancing uncontrollably, the squeals in her chest rising to her throat. I felt the hot wet explosion from her groin as her bowels and urine exploded from her. Red held her legs while I held her arms until she finally began to quiet down, then Red called Sawyer.

Seizures, said Sawyer. We should have expected them. He'd thought he'd told us. Triple the Phenobarbital.

After that, Helen never wore her wig. She stopped exercising. She did what she wanted, and that was nothing. Red fought with her for about a week after that, then another seizure came, and then the fighting stopped, too.

By Thanksgiving, Helen degenerated to a condition worse than after her operation. Her left side was paralyzed completely again. The hair, which had begun to return to her scarred head, grew fitfully. Her left shoulder sagged, the side of her face dipped. Her mouth slouched, her eye closed, her leg lay like a club. There, in her bed near the window in the front room, she rotted, flapping her single wing and muttering until she seldom spoke at all and her dark eyes became thick gray things that killed light.

Red and I made Thanksgiving dinner. Neda came over, her stomach bulging, her breasts enlarged, and stayed with the Viz and Helen while we got everything ready. Then we got Helen from her bed and strapped her into a chair. Red cut Helen's food and she fumbled with it on her plate with her good hand, but she seldom brought it to her mouth. After we cleaned up, Red went up to the attic and came down with an old Yahtzee game. Helen couldn't calculate her numbers, she couldn't collect her dice, she couldn't keep score. She was game, but it was so sad that it made the Viz cry. Red put the dice in the cup for Helen and she lifted the cup and threw it at him.

Nobody said anything for a while.

"I have some requests," said Helen. She held herself up by bracing her right hand against the table. She glowered underneath her dark brows, her scarred head falling forward. She breathed heavily between every word.

"Listen good," said Helen. "These are deathbed requests. Red, I want you to convert. Jarvis, I want you to go back to the Church and bring the Viz up Catholic. Neda, marry Stinky."

"You ain't dying," said Red, "so I'm not taking any deathbed requests."

"You're not in your deathbed," said Neda. "It doesn't count if you're not in bed."

"Four requests," said the Viz. "Four." He held up four fingers.

Helen pushed herself back a little more so she could raise her head enough to look at me.

"You wouldn't want us to change," I said to her. "Would you?"

Helen leaned forward, her head nodding at the table. "Yes," she said. "Yes, I would."

I'd been writing to Joseph and Andrew, but I wrote again soon after that to tell them I didn't know how much longer Helen had and that they should try to come home, which I knew was impossible. Joseph would have to go AWOL. Andrew was wanted in the states. They both wrote back and said they were coming.

And after Thanksgiving, Red became more vigilant with Helen than ever. He stayed with her constantly. He fed her, washed her, cleaned her excrement. Helen slept more and more. She stopped eating solids and Red fed her through a straw. He seldom left the room. Anything that needed to be done, shopping, cleaning, feeding the dog, I did when I wasn't working, which I also continued to do, because it was our only income. I didn't mind it. It let me get away.

The neighborhood quieted around Helen's illness. The Dangers tended their bar & grill. Big Dick got back in his potato chip truck and took Stinky with him while Pat and Becca stayed home with Neda. Karl got work again at Bucyrus Erie. Jimbo Funster took down his sandbags from the roof and Funly started college downtown at Gannon. On the weekends Jimbo and Funly and Mosha and Betty went out to Jimbo's hunting cabin where they ate pork chops for breakfast and Mosha Funster serenaded the forest with her tuba. Revis and Raymon eventually held up the Variety Store and were put in jail, long enough, they hoped, to keep them out of the war. Bifboy got a job as an airline commuter pilot for Keystone Air. Neda got more pregnant every day. She was due in early January. And Willie, Willie sometimes visited me at the Kronenburger.

The sound of those pins crashing at the end of the alleys was like the ocean, a constant wax and wane of sound, the roll and crash. We drank beer. If everything else had changed, Willie had not changed. The machines had changed, but bowling had not changed.

"You are sleeping now," said Willie

"Now that time is valuable," I said.

"It was never so valuable," said Willie. He got up and went to the bar, got us two more beers.

"I'm living through the end of everything," I said. "After Helen dies, I don't see anything going from there."

"Your Momma is the center," said Willie. "Her body is the center. Everything came from your Momma." He sipped his beer. "This is what has been revealed. A price and a revelation."

Well it couldn't be so simple, could it? Life goes on?

"Under the wings of death, there is a world. But who wants it? Myself, my Momma is moving back to Mississippi and I am going with her."

"You won't be here when Helen dies."

"No," said Willie. "I have told her this already. Myself, I will not have this death."

"But I will," I said. And Willie didn't answer. "So I won't see you again," I said to him.

Willie smiled his lopsided grin. "Maybe you will."

A machine went down and I had to leave him to hang a sign on it. When I got back he wasn't there, and I never saw him again.

Who I did see at the doorway was my friend from Glenwood, in a short, tiger striped silk dress, standing next to a man not much taller than her, a dark man, so strikingly handsome, almost dazzling, a man so powerful and confident in his demeanor I felt almost drawn to him. When they came toward me I felt as if I recognized him. His eyes black and wise, his lips sensuous, his brow brooding as if he'd seen everything that ever was and he didn't want to see it again, that it all tired him, that he would die without more. They stopped in front of me, there, in front of the alleys of the Kronenburger Club.

"I'd like you to meet Arturo," said my friend.

I shook his hand, which felt both powerful and ephemeral, like a silk vice. There was something about him, as if he were hiding some horrible news behind him, underneath his long, black hair, under his leather jacket, on his back.

"Do I look familiar to you?" he said.

"Should you?"

He smiled and my friend laughed. I suppose I should have asked him how the surfing was in Chile, but I was afraid to show him I knew much. My friend slid within her dress, within the folds of her coat, movements of joy.

"He's an angel," said my friend, "a brother, the devil in his last re-incarnation."

"I'm her husband," said Arturo.

"I take it you're not here to kill me," I said.

They laughed. "Not today," said Arturo.

"Well would you like to bowl a game?" I said to them. I was be-yond the point of feeling any kind of jealousy, because she was the wife of this man, the wife of death. The more I stood in front of them, the more I realized that it was death that Arturo hid under his jacket, that there were folds of power behind him, like wings, like night, and if he showed it to me I would see Bobby Hansen in there, and Tony Blan-ion, and Kara, and I'd find myself in there, and the Viz, and Red, and Helen, of course Helen. Those were the things I didn't want to see. "I can get you a free game," I said.

I went over and got my bowling ball. I popped it onto my finger-tips, spun it on my right index finger, ran it down my arm and over my shoulders and down my other arm where I popped it in the air and caught it spinning on my left index finger. I offered the ball to Arturo.

"I don't bowl," said Arturo.

"You should," I said. "It's a lot like life."

"We're here on a business speculation," said my friend. "I'm buying the Kronenburger Club."

"That's really great," I said. "That's really a wonderful thing."

"It's completely inefficient. It will go under if someone doesn't take it over, open it to the public, give it some character, Cajun or something."

"Cajun, that would be great," I said. "You could probably get rid of the bowling altogether."

"We'll keep the bowling," said my friend. "Bowling will soon become very chic."

"That's the word I was looking for," I said to her. I had to hand it to her, she was transcendent; a response to cynicism was beneath her, but, of course, I was beneath responding to her transcendence. "You'll probably need a bowling machine mechanic," I said.

She put out her hand to me and I shook it.

"Maybe I won't," she said. She lowered her eyes, then lifted them again and looked into mine. They were pale and blue, like glass, and for a moment I saw myself reflected in them, but the more she caught me in her stare I saw it wasn't me at all, but Arturo, dark and sleek, his black, thick hair cascading behind him like the barrels of guns. "And maybe I will."

~~~~~ Bush's Last Christmas

WHEN I GOT home at dawn I found Red in the small hospital bed in the living room with Helen, his huge body curled by her side under her right arm, his head next to her scarred head, his face next to her drooping face, their lips touching, drawing each other's breath, breathing their last moments together. This is now how I think about love. This is how I remember them.

It didn't look like Helen was going to make it to Bush's for Bush's Last Christmas, so Bush and Jon came to see Helen. Bush sat at Helen's right side, holding her hand, and Jon stole Red's seat next to the Zenith, his right knee over the left, his foot bouncing. Me and the Viz and Red were on the couch on Helen's left.

"It looks like this is going to be my last Christmas," said Helen.

"Tell me about it," said Bush.

"This is a tremendous strain on Mother," said Jon, "to have her youngest child die before she does. "Think about it."

"I'm going to give you something to think about," said Red. "Right between the eyes."

"I want to be buried in the Catholic cemetery," said Helen. "Next to Dad and Bush."

"Red can't be buried there," said Bush.

"Not if he doesn't convert," said Jon.

"Don't worry about me," said Red.

Helen had a rattle in her throat now when she breathed.

"It's always the last Christmas," said Bush.

When they left Red went out and bought a piano. He lugged it in by himself on a small cart, took the couch out of the front room and put the piano in its place.

"You ain't dying," said Red. "You're going to get better and play the piano."

Helen tried to speak, but instead she shook. Tears came to her eyes.

"I love you, too," said Red. "I'll always love you."

"Jarvis," Helen said to me.

"I love you," I said to her.

And Helen said, "Are you going back to the Church?"

"No," I said.

After that Helen went to sleep and Red went into the dining room, Helen's old Holy Room. The Infant still stood atop the dish cabinet arabesque, and the plaques of Jesus and Mary with their sacred burning hearts still hung on the walls. Besides that there was nothing left, except for the picture of Joseph and the boy Jesus that hung above the Zenith in the front room, and the angel babies with wings which now hung above the head of Helen's bed.

"You going to convert?" I said to Red.

"I bought the plot already," said Red. "Got the stone with our birthdays on it. One stone, like Whitey and Emma. It's under a nice fir tree. Looks out over the Gorge."

"That's not Catholic," I said.

"Neither are you," said Red. "Besides, she'll be dead."

Helen went to sleep that afternoon and didn't wake up. She slept all that day and all the next. She slept the next day after that. By the time Andrew got back from Quebec, and Joseph from Vietnam, Helen barely breathed, except for a huge, shuttering breath every twenty minutes or so that shook her whole body. Her eyes hung open, gray and leaden, and her jaw dropped. Outside there was a light sprinkle of snow on the ground. It was Christmas Eve.

"She got a bed sore today," said Red. "I fell asleep and didn't get her turned." He got up and went to her ankle where a huge blister sprung like an eel on Helen's calf. Red got some lotion and gently smoothed it on the blister. "Shit," said Red.

"You can't blame yourself," said Neda. She was tremendously pregnant, her stomach rising in a mound, her huge breasts resting on it like summer fruit. "You've been here every second."

"I can blame myself," said Red.

"When was the last time she was awake?" said Andrew.

"Weeks," said Red. "She don't eat now. She don't drink. Sawyer wants me to bring her in so they can feed her through the veins, put a tube down her throat to keep her breathing. But that can wait till after Christmas."

"She could die," said Andrew.

"Then she'll die here," said Red.

"Don't talk like that," said Joseph, "She can still hear."

"I don't know what she hears," said Red.

I went over to Helen and passed my hand back and forth in front of her eyes, but they ware gray and dead.

"I don't think she hears anything," I said. "I don't think she'll make it through Christmas."

"She'll make it," said Red.

"She hears," said Joseph. "She hears everything."

"I'm in labor," said Neda.

I spent Christmas Eve in the hospital with Neda, while Red and Joseph and Andrew stayed with Helen in deathwatch, the Viz, my son, above them, in the bedroom upstairs, sleeping with the dog of my dead wife. I drove Neda to the hospital in the snowy dead of night, waited with her outside the delivery room as she breathed, as she sucked huge, lifeful breaths. Then the nurses came for her.

"Shouldn't I get Stinky?" I said to Neda.

"Don't worry about Stinky," said Neda.

"He's the father."

"Nobody's the father."

"Do you need me?" I said.

"Are you kidding?" said Neda.

And so I waited.

She had the child on Christmas day, at dawn. I went to her hospital room where they brought the child to her, a girl, with dark eyes and brooding brows, olive skin, and already an expression on her face of deep pondering. Neda took the child to her breast. Then she covered herself.

"Okay," said Neda, "let's go home."

I got Neda her clothes. She dressed, put the baby under her coat, and we left the hospital and drove home in the Falcon.

When we got back to 24th Street Neda told me to go get the Viz, so I woke him up and brought him downstairs. Then Neda took the baby out from under her coat. She showed her to Red, who touched the child's forehead, gently with his finger. He pushed at her hair.

"Like Mother," said Red. "Like Helen."

Neda said nothing. She unwrapped the baby and took it over to Helen.

"I think it's too late," whispered Red.

"Dead," said Andrew.

"Quiet," said Joseph softly. "She can still hear."

The Viz stirred in my lap. Slowly, silently, he spread his arms, as if to hold us all, as if to hold the emptiness of everything.

"Helen," said Neda. "Helen."

She held out the child and lowered it near Helen's face, silence falling like lead. And then the lids of Helen's deadened eyes closed, then opened. Her swollen tongue moved across her lips and then retracted. Her mouth closed. Her eyes were suddenly clear.

Neda put the baby on Helen's breast. Helen raised her right knee, pushed herself up with her right arm and hugged the child.

≋ ≋ ≋ ≋ ≋Epilogue

THE TUMOR WILL SHRINK from Helen's brain. In a day, the fingers in her left hand stretched. A week later she walked. She lived to see her grandsons and granddaughters. She went back to work and learned to play the piano. Red took her in his arms, the arms of the months of her dying, and they loved each other more deeply. They will love each other forever. They will always be in love.

Outside, the snow might fall in an eternal winter. The dead will be silent and dead. But not here, where they live forever. Live forever. Live and live.

About the Author

CHUCK ROSENTHAL is the author of seven novels, *Loop's Progress, Experiments With Life and Deaf, Loop's End, Elena of the Stars, Jack Kerouac's Avatar Angel: His Last Novel, My Mistress, Humanity* and *The Heart of Mars,* as well as the memoir *Never Let Me Go.* His fiction has appeared in many journals including *The Santa Monica Review* and *The Denver Quarterly.* He is a full professor of English and Creative Writing at Loyola Marymount University.

He lives with poet Gail Wronsky in Topanga, California.

Acknowledgements

Parts of this book appeared, in slightly altered form, in the following publications: portions of "The Infinite Winter," *The Chicago Review*, as "the Water Beneath the Ice"; parts of "Pere du Nom," *Hayden's Ferry Review*, as "Pere De Nom"; portions of "Autumn Refrain," *Lip Mechanics*, as "Tuba"; parts of "Bush's Last Christmas," *The Santa Monica Review*, as "The Darkest Night of the World."